SOME
KIND
of
FAIRY
TALE

Graham Joyce

The right of Graham Joyce to be identified as the author
of this work has been asserted by him in accordance with
the Copyright, Designs and Patents Act 1988.

First published in Great Britain in 2012 by
Gollancz
An imprint of the Orion Publishing Group
Orion House, 5 Upper St Martin's Lane,
London WC2H 9EA
An Hachette UK Company

This edition published in Great Britain in 2013
by Gollancz

1 3 5 7 9 10 8 6 4 2

A CIP catalogue record for this book
is available from the British Library

ISBN 978 0 575 11529 3

Typeset by Deltatype Ltd, Birkenhead, Merseyside

Printed and bound by CPI Group (UK) Ltd,
Croydon CRO 4YY

The Orion Publishing Group's policy is to use papers
that are natural, renewable and recyclable products and
made from wood grown in sustainable forests. The logging
and manufacturing processes are expected to conform to
the environmental regulations of the country of origin.

www.grahamjoyce.net
www.orionbooks.co.uk
www.gollancz.co.uk

Praise for Graham Joyce and *The Silent Land*:

'Ravishing . . . his writing is enthralling, agile and effortless'
New York Times

'Beautiful and devastating'
Washington Post

'Near perfect . . . a study in classic supernatural fiction, told with a skill that we enjoy for its own sake'
Independent

'Stark, layered, ominous and yet appealing . . . Mr Joyce delivers relief along with satisfaction and wonder'
New York Times

'You'll laugh, albeit nervously; you'll cry, unless you're completely heartless; you'll give your nearest and dearest hugs without really being able to explain why you're so glad to see them – really, what more do you want from a novel?'
SFX

Also by Graham Joyce from Gollancz:

Leningrad Nights
Smoking Poppy
The Limits of Enchantment
The Facts of Life
The Tooth Fairy
Memoirs of a Master Forger (as William Heaney)
The Silent Land

To my daughter Ella

I

'But we are spirits of another sort.' Oberon, King of
Shadows.

William Shakespeare

In the deepest heart of England there is a place where
everything is at fault. That is to say that the land rests
upon a fault; and there, ancient rocks are sent hurtling
from the deep to the surface of the earth with such
force that they break free like oceanic waves, or like
monstrous sea-creatures coming up for air. Some say
that the land has still to settle and that it continues to
roil and breathe fumes, and that out of these fumes pour
stories. Others are confident that the old volcanoes are
long dead, and that all its tales are told.

Of course, everything depends on who is telling the
story. It always does. I have a story and though there
are considerable parts I've had to imagine, the way I
saw it was as follows.

It was Christmas Day of that year and Dell Martin
hovered at the double-glazed PVC window of his tidy
home, conducting a survey of the bruised clouds and
concluding that it might just snow; and if it did snow
then someone would have to pay out. At the very beginning of the year Dell had laid down two crisp twenty

pound notes on the bookie's Formica counter, just as he had done every year for the past ten. The odds changed slightly each year and this time he'd settled good odds at seven-to-one.

For a White Christmas to be official – that is to force the bookmakers to pay out – a flake of snow must be observed to fall between midnight on 24 December and midnight on 25 December at four designated sites. The sites are the cities of London, Glasgow, Cardiff and Manchester. The snow is not required to lie deep nor crisp nor evenly upon the ground and it doesn't matter if it's mixed with rain. One solitary flake would do it, fallen and melted, observed and recorded.

Living in a place somewhere between all of those great cities, Dell had never collected in all those ten years; nor had he seen a single flake of Christmas Day snow hanging in the air of his home town.

'Are you going to come and carve?' Mary called from the kitchen.

This year they were having goose. After decades of turkey dinners on Christmas Day they were having a change; because a change is as good as a rest, and sometimes you needed a rest even from Christmas. Nevertheless the table had been laid out, just as in previous years. Crisp linen and the best cutlery. Two heavy crystal wineglasses that, year round, were kept in a box and stowed at the back of a kitchen cupboard.

Dell always carved, and he carved well. It was an art. He'd carved well when the kids were small, and he carved well now that there was only Mary and himself to carve for. He rubbed his hands together in a friction of delight, passing through to a kitchen warm and steamy from simmering pans. The cooked goose rested under silver foil on a large serving plate. Dell pulled a blade from the knife block and angled it to the light at the window. 'Gone a bit dark over yonder,' he said. 'Might snow.'

Mary was draining vegetables through a sieve. 'Might snow? You haven't put money on it have you?'

'Hell no.' He whisked the foil cover off the goose and rotated the plate to get a better purchase with his knife. 'Just a thought.'

Mary tapped her sieve on the lip of the sink. ''Taint snowed on Christmas Day in ten year. Plates warming in the oven. Bring it through?'

Each plate boasted a plump goose leg and two neatly carved slices of breast. There were roast potatoes and four types of vegetable, all steaming in serving dishes. The gravy boat was piping and there was stuffing and sausages wrapped in bacon, and cranberry sauce.

'I went in for an I-talian this year,' Dell said, pouring Mary a glass of ruby-red wine and then one for himself. He pronounced the *I* in Italian the way you might pronounce eye-witness. 'I-talian wine. Hope that goes well with the goose.'

'I'm sure it will be lovely.'

'Thought we'd have a change from the French. Though I could easily have had a South African. There was a South African on offer. At the supermarket.'

'Let's see shall we?' Mary said, offering her glass for the clinking. 'Cheers!'

'Cheers!'

And it was the cheers moment, that gentle touching of the crystalware, that Dell hated the most.

Feared it and detested it. Because even though nothing was ever stated and even though the faultless

3

food was served up with wide smiles and the clinking of glasses was conducted with genuine affection from both parties, there was always at this moment of ritual a fleck in his wife's eye. A tiny instant of blade-light, razor-sharp, and he knew he'd better talk over it pretty damn quick.

'What do you think of the I-talian??'

'Lovely. Beautiful. A good choice.'

'Because there was also a bottle from Argentina. Special offer. And I nearly went for that.'

'Argentina? Well, there's one we could try another time.'

'But you like this?'

'Love it. Lovely. Come on let's see what you make o' this goose.'

Wine was one of the fixtures of Christmas dinner that had changed over the years. When the kids were small both he and Mary had been content with a glass of beer, maybe a schooner of lager. But beer had been displaced by wine on the table for Christmas Day. Serving dishes were a recent addition, too. Back in those days everything was heaped on the plates and brought to the table, a ready-assembled island of food floating in a sea of gravy. Cranberry sauce was exotic once. When the children were small.

'Well, what do you think of that goose?'

'Bloody beautiful. And cooked to perfection.'

A tiny flush of pleasure appeared on Mary's cheek. After all these years of marriage, Dell could do this. Just the right words.

'You know what, Mary? All these Christmases we could have been having goose. Hey, look out of the window!'

4

Mary turned. Outside, a few tiny flakes of snow were billowing. It was Christmas Day and it was snowing; here, at least.

'You have had a bet, haven't you?' Mary said.

Dell was about to answer when they both heard a light tapping at the front door. Most people rang the electrical bell, but today someone was knocking.

Dell had his knife in the mustard pot. 'Who the hell is that on Christmas Day?'

'No idea. What a time to call!'

'I'll get it.'

Dell stood and put his napkin on his seat. Then he went down the hall. There was a figure outlined in the frosted glass of the inner door. Dell had to release a small chain and unlock the inner door before opening the porch door.

A young woman, perhaps in her early twenties, gazed back at him from behind dark glasses. Through the dark glass he could make out wide, unblinking eyes. She wore a Peruvian-style woollen hat with earflaps and tassels. The tassels made him think of bells.

'Hello, duckie,' Dell said briskly, not unfriendly. It was Christmas Day after all.

The woman said nothing. She gazed back at him with a timid, almost fearful smile on her lips.

'Happy Christmas love, what can I do for you?'

The woman shuffled from one foot to another, not removing her gaze. Her clothes were odd; she seemed to be some kind of hippy. She blinked behind her dark glasses and he thought she looked familiar. Then it occurred to him that she was maybe collecting for some charitable cause. He put his hand in his pocket.

At last she spoke. 'Hello Dad,' she said.

Mary came bustling from behind, trying to peer around him. 'Who is it?' she said.

The woman switched her gaze from Dell to Mary. Mary stared hard at her, seeing something familiar in the young woman behind the dark lenses. There came a slight gagging sound from Mary's throat; then Mary fainted clean away. Dell stumbled and only half-caught her as she fell. Mary's unconscious body hit the stone tiles at the threshold with a thud and a sigh of wind.

Across the other side of Charnwood Forest at a ramshackle cottage on the road to Quorn, Peter Martin was stacking the dishwasher. Christmas dinner had been trashed a couple of hours ago and he was still wearing an acid-red paper crown from a Christmas cracker but he'd forgotten it was there. His wife Genevieve had her bare feet up on the sofa, exhausted by the responsibility of co-ordinating the domestic crisis of Christmas in a house with a dreamy husband, four kids, two dogs, a mare in the paddock, a rabbit and a guinea pig, plus sundry invading mice and rats that kept finding inventive routes into their kitchen. In many ways it was a house weathering a permanent state of siege.

Peter was a gentle, red-haired bear of a man. Standing at six-four in his socks, he moved everywhere with a slight and nautical sway, but even though he was broad across the chest there was something centred and reassuring about him, like an old ship's mast cut from a single timber. He felt bad that they'd had Christmas dinner without having his mother and father over. Dell and Mary had been invited, of course, but there had been a ridiculous dispute about what time dinner should be served. Genevieve wanted to sit down on the stroke of one so that they could all get their coats on in the afternoon and drive up to Bradgate Park or Beacon Hill for a healthy blast of wind. Mary and Dell liked to eat later, and at leisure, and certainly not before three; they'd done all the walking and blasting they cared for. There wasn't actually a row. What followed was more of an impasse and a sulk, followed by a default decision no party was happy with, that this year they would sit down to separate dinners.

Peter and Genevieve anyway had a daughter who was fifteen, a boy thirteen and two more girls of seven and five. Whenever they went over to Mary and Dell's they garrisoned the place, moving in like a brutal occupying army. It was always easier and more relaxed to stay put in the cottage and this year that's what they did.

Meanwhile Peter had bought thirteen-year-old Jack an air-rifle for Christmas, and Jack was sitting in the yard hoping for mice or rats to turn up. He lounged on an old exploded sofa his dad hadn't got around to taking to the tip. Like a grizzled old-timer from a country cabin he held the butt of the gun on his thigh and pointing skyward.

Peter put his head outside the back kitchen door. 'Don't wave that fucking thing around. If you catch anyone I'll rip your head off for sure,' Peter said.

'Don't worry Dad, I'm not gonna shoot my fuckin' sisters.'

'And don't swear. Right?'

'Right.'

'And don't wave it around.'

Peter went back inside to stack the dishwasher. He went through to the trashed dining room and was dithering what to do with the carcass of the turkey when the phone rang. It was Dell.

'All right Dad? I was just going to call you. When I get the kids lined up to say Happy Christmas and all that.'

'Never mind that, Pete. You'd better get over here.'

'What? We're about to go for a walk.'

'Come over anyway. Your sister's here.'

'What?'

'You heard me. I said your sister's here.'

'What?'

Peter felt dizzy. The room swam. 'Dad, what are you saying?'

'She just showed up.'

'She can't have done.'

'Come over Pete. Your mother's had a bad turn.'

'Dad what the fuck is going on?'

'Please come over son. Please come over.'

There was a note in his father's voice he'd never heard before. Dell was clearly very close to tears. 'Can you just tell me what's happened?'

'I can't tell you anything because I don't know anything. Your mother fainted. She fell badly.'

'Okay. I'm coming.'

Peter put the receiver back on its cradle with a gentle click and crashed down on to a hard chair that lived beside the phone. He stared at the debris of Christmas dinner still littering the table. Pulled-crackers and mottoes and plastic toys and paper crowns were strewn across the room. He suddenly remembered he was still wearing his paper crown. He took it off and held it in his hand, between his knees.

He got up and moved through to the living room,

swaying slightly as he went. The television was broadcasting softly while the three girls were sprawled on the carpeted floor playing with Lego bricks and dolls by the lopsided Christmas tree. A cosy coal fire burned in the grate and two lurchers lay on their backs before the fire, their legs in the air and their teeth bared in grins of pure canine pleasure. Genevieve snoozed on the sofa.

Pete went back into the kitchen and filled the electric kettle. He stood watching it boil and contrary to received wisdom it boiled pretty damn quick. He made a cup of tea for Genevieve and one for himself, gazing at the tea diffusing from a teabag. At last he was roused by the snap of an air-rifle pellet as it struck the outside wall.

Carrying the tea through to the living room, he kneeled before the sofa, then leaned across Genevieve and woke her with a kiss. She blinked at him. Her cheeks were red.

'You're a sweetheart,' she said sleepily, accepting the tea. 'Did I hear the phone go?'

'You did hear the phone go.'

'Who was it?'

'Dad.'

'Are they still speaking to us?'

'Yes. I have to go over there.'

'You do? Anything wrong?'

Peter exhaled a puff of air. 'Tara came back.'

Genevieve looked at Peter for a moment as though she didn't know who Tara was. She'd never met Tara; but she'd heard plenty about her. She shook her head quizzically, knitted her brows.

'Yes,' Peter said. 'Exactly.'

'Who is Tara?' said Zoe, their fifteen-year-old daughter.

'That's impossible,' Genevieve said. 'Isn't it?'

'Who is Tara?' asked Amber, the middle daughter.

'I've got to go over there.'

'Should we all come?'

'There's no point us all going.'

'Who the heck is Tara?' Amber asked again.

'Your Dad's sister.'

'Dad has a sister? I never knew Dad has a sister.'

'No, we don't talk about her,' said Peter.

'Why don't we talk about her?' asked Josie, the youngest. 'I talk about my sisters. All the time.'

'I have to go,' Peter said. 'Is there petrol in the car?'

'Is Dad leaving us on Christmas day?' Amber said.

Genevieve got up off the sofa and winced as she stepped barefoot on to a Lego brick. 'He won't be gone long.' She followed Peter out into hallway and waited while he put on his shoes and his coat. 'Will you?'

'No.'

'Do you want a hug?'

'Yes. No,' said Peter. 'Not right now.'

There was another slap as an airgun pellet hit the wall outside.

2

'Wonder has no opposite; it springs up already doubled in itself, compounded of dread and desire at once, attraction and recoil, producing a thrill, the shudder of pleasure and of fear.'

Marina Warner

Peter drove to Anstey via Breakback Lane. It wasn't the direct route. He had an idea that he should call on Richie Franklin and tell him the news, but he knew he wouldn't. Shouldn't. Couldn't. It didn't stop him driving that way.

The roads were almost deserted, it being Christmas Day. Picked out like lonely ships on an ocean, one or two isolated vehicles passed him along the way, tyres hissing on the wet roads. The sky was laden with snow but it fell only in brief flurries, not settling, instantly melting on impact with his windscreen, barely enough for him to activate his screen wipers.

At the Outwoods he slowed down and turned into the car park. It was empty and lonely. He had some cigarettes hidden in the glove compartment. This was what passed for contraband in his life now: he'd given up because the girls had been counselled that smoking kills and they cried whenever they saw him spark up a ciggie. But he kept a stale packet hidden for moments like these. He got out of the car and surveyed the bare winter trees grouped around the clearing of the car-park. The trees were golden and grey and somehow asleep, off-guard. It was bitterly cold. He tasted a flake of dry tobacco on his tongue and his first drag on the cigarette made him cough. The cigarette smoke hung like a grey rag in the cold air, and so did the sound of his cough.

The Outwoods was one of the last remaining pockets of ancient forest from which Charnwood took its name. It nestled at the spot where the three counties of Leicestershire, Nottinghamshire and Derbyshire almost touched, and seemed neither to belong to nor take its character from any of them. It was an eerie place, swinging between sunlight and damp, flaring light and shadow; a venue of twisted trees, its volcanic slopes of ash and granite ruptured by mysterious outcropping crags of the very oldest rocks in Britain.

He didn't like it.

The last time he'd seen Tara was here in the Outwoods. It had been May of that year and they had walked through the woods, and the bluebells at that time had been astonishing. They had sat on the golden lichen-stained rocks and talked about the future.

Peter flicked his cigarette to the ground half-smoked and stamped it into the earth. Then he climbed back in his car.

Sometime later he parked right outside Richie's house but left the engine running. It was almost a challenge, inviting someone to come out and ask him what he was doing; but no one came. No one even so much as glanced out of the window. Richie's house was a council property in what might once have been a row of houses tied to a local landowner. Squat, badly built and grimy little peasant-hutches. Peter knew them well because he'd been raised in an identical house five doors away. Richie, having inherited the property from his mother, still lived there.

There was a light on in Richie's house, but deep, low and at the back. There was a single living room that ran the depth of the house. The dim light only made the house look cold and uninviting. Just go up to the door, Peter told himself, and when he answers the door just say *Tara's back*, that's all you have to do. *Tara's back*.

But he couldn't. He and Richie hadn't spoken in a long, long time, and two words might as well have been two hundred thousand words. He couldn't do it. He made a curse under his breath and drove away.

'Come in, lad.' Dell spoke in a strange kind of whisper.

'Where is she?'

'Are you going to take your coat off? And your shoes? We've got the new carpet.'

Peter took off his coat and handed it to his father before untying his shoelaces. He felt a wave of frustration with his father, that at a time like this he was concerned with clean carpets, but said nothing. He made to move down the hall but he felt the flat of his father's hand on his breastbone.

'Don't go upsetting anyone. Your Mum's had a fall.'

'I'm not here to upset anyone!' Peter tried to keep the keening note out of his voice. 'Is she through here?'

'Come on.'

Peter took a step into the living room and stopped just inside the doorway. His mother lay on the couch. She was sipping tea and had an ice-pack on the knee she'd cracked when she'd slumped to the floor. But Peter was more interested in the woman nursing Mary from the armchair next to the sofa. Even though she wore dark glasses, it was his sister Tara: of that there was no doubt.

Tara stood up. She seemed an inch or two taller than he remembered. Her soft nut-brown hair was maybe a darker shade, and still fell around her face in a tangle of curls. Behind the shades and around her eyes there might have been one or two lines but she hardly seemed to have aged. She just looked pretty grubby, like she'd been living rough.

'When did you cut your hair?' she said.

'Oh. That would be about fifteen years ago.'

'You had such lovely long hair!'

'Everybody did then. Do I get a hug?'

'Of course you do.'

Peter stepped forward and he held his sister in his arms. She held him tight. He inhaled the smell of her. She didn't smell like he remembered. Now she smelled of something belonging to the outdoors he couldn't identify. Rain, maybe. Leaf. Mushroom. May blossom. The wind.

It was a long time before she broke the clinch. Peter looked over at his mother stretched out with her ice-pack and her leg up on the couch. She gave him a pained smile and dabbed at her eye with a tissue.

'So where you been, Tara? Where you been?'

'She's been travelling,' Dell said.

'Travelling? Twenty years is a lot of travel.'

'Yes it is,' Mary said from the couch. 'And now she's come back home. Our little girl has come back home.'

*

14

Tea being the drug of choice in the Martin household, Dell concocted more of it, thick and brown and sweet. After all, they'd had a bit of a shock; and whenever they had a shock or an upset or experienced a disturbance of any kind they had poured tea on it for as long as any of them could remember. The fact is they poured tea on it even when they hadn't had a shock, and they did that six or seven times a day. But these were extra special circumstances and Peter knew he had to wait until the tea had arrived before he could begin any line of questioning. Even when the tea did arrive, the questioning didn't go well.

Peter had hardly taken his eyes off his sister since his arrival. The same half-smile hadn't escaped the bow of Tara's lips since he'd walked into the room. He recognised it as a disguise of some kind, a mask; he just didn't know quite which emotions it was intended to camouflage.

'So where exactly has all this travelling taken you, Tara?'

'Goodness! All over.'

'Really? All over?'

She nodded solemnly. 'Pretty much, yes.'

'Tara already told us some of it, Peter,' said Dell. 'Rome. Athens. Jerusalem. Tokyo. What was that place in South America?'

'Lima. In Peru.'

'Really? Travelling all this time? Constant travelling?'

'Pretty much, yes.'

'Always moving?'

'Well,' Tara said. 'I might have settled here or there for a few months, but always with a view to moving on.'

Peter nodded, but he was only pretending to understand. He scrutinised his sister's clothes. She wore threadbare jeans with huge bell-bottoms, of a kind that had strayed way out of fashion when he was a young man and had probably come back in again. She wore a grubby dress over the top of them and long strings of beads. A woollen cardigan was a couple of sizes too big for her, the arms of which reached to the tips of her fingers but failed to hide her dirty fingernails.

Peter couldn't help himself. 'You look like you could do with a bath.'

'Steady on,' said Dell.

'But Tara,' Peter said. 'No word? Not even a postcard? No goodbye, no announcement, no—'

'I know,' said Tara. 'It's unforgivable.'

'Do you know what you put these two through? What you put us all through?'

'Before you came, I said to Mum and Dad that I will understand it if you hate me.'

'We don't hate you,' Dell said. 'No one hates you.'

'But—' Peter tried.

Dell cut him short. 'Peter. I know there's a lot to get into. But I won't have you say anything to scare her away again. Okay? I won't have it.'

'I'm not going away again,' Tara said.

Peter ran his hands through his close-cropped hair.

'What about you?' Tara said. 'Tell me about your life.'

'My life?' Peter said. 'My life?'

'Mum says you have children.'

'Get the photos, Dell. Get them,' said Mary, too quickly.

'Tell me yourself,' said Tara. 'I want to hear everything.'

Peter sighed. 'I married a lovely girl I met at university. Genevieve. We've got three girls and a boy.'

'Tell me their names!'

'Well, my eldest is fifteen going on twenty and her name is Zoe and—'

'That's a lovely name.'

'And then came Jack, he's thirteen. Running wild. Then a bit of a gap because we weren't ... well, we did, and we had Amber who is seven and Josie who is five.'

'Amber has webbed-fingers,' Mary said.

'Mum, please.'

'Small thing,' Tara said, smiling. 'A very small thing.' Then her smile dropped for the first time. 'I'm sorry I missed it all. I really am.' Suddenly Tara vented a huge sob. She squeezed her eyes shut and her lip trembled. She wiped her eyes with the back of her sleeve and sniffed. 'I'm sorry I missed it all. They sound so wonderful. Are they like you?'

'God help them if they are.'

'The boy is the spit,' Dell said helpfully. 'The girls take more after their mother.'

There was a silence. Dell had a photograph album that he handed to Tara. 'These are all old. It's all digital now, isn't it? Things change so fast.'

Tara studied the photographs. 'But they do look like you!'

Dell turned to Tara. 'Zoe even looks a bit like you.'

'She's almost the same age as you were when you left,' Peter said. He looked at Mary. She shook her head at him in fierce warning.

'Will I get to meet them?' Tara said.

'Of course. If you want to.'

She held up the photo album. 'Where was this photo taken?'

'Oh that one's in Greece. Before we had the kids. You said you were in Athens didn't you?'

'Not for long. Couldn't get out quick enough.'

'So where were you in Greece?'

'Crete. Some of the islands.'

'Really? Genevieve and I lived for a whole year in Crete. Were you ever in Mytilini while you were on Crete?'

'Yes, one or two nights I think. But I just passed through.'

'Wouldn't that be amazing? If you were there the same time we were there?'

'These things are possible.'

'What year was it?'

'Peter, stop interrogating the girl, will you?' Dell was wringing his hands. 'Look she's hungry and I'm going to rescue what I can of Christmas dinner and we're going to sit down and enjoy it and you can sit down with us too.'

'I've had my Christmas dinner, Dad.'

'Okay, but no more questions.'

'Don't you think this is a day for questions? You realise we are going to have to tell the police?'

Tara looked startled. 'Is that really necessary?'

'You bet it is!' cried Peter.

He explained to her what had happened after Tara had walked out of their lives some twenty years earlier. He explained how everyone had feared the very worst; feared that she'd been abducted or killed. That there had been wide-ranging searches conducted. That neighbours and friends had, along with a huge force of police officers, carried out searches at the Outwoods and at every other place they could think that she might have gone. That her photo had appeared in all of the local newspapers and some national ones; that her face had appeared on national TV; that known sexual offenders had been dragged in for interrogation; that not a clue had turned up, not a hair from her head; that the search was eventually scaled down; that her mother and father went into a state of shock and mourning from which they had never entirely recovered; that he and her boyfriend-of-the-time Richie, who had himself fallen under a cloud of suspicion, had continued to search the countryside and local beauty spots for months and even years afterwards.

'They had frogmen searching the pools and the lakes, Tara. It went on for days. Weeks. Yes, even after all this time I think we have to inform the police, don't you?'

Tara looked ashen at these reports.

Suddenly Mary was on her feet, the ice-pack slithering to the floor. 'Stop it! Stop it! All I know is that Tara has come home for Christmas Day and it's a miracle to have her home and I don't want to hear any more talk of it! I want no more questions today! Peter, you can stay here and be pleasant or you can go straight back to your family. That's an end to it.' And with that she collapsed back on the couch.

'You don't have to go,' Tara said gently. 'I'm the one who should go.'

'No,' Peter said. 'It's just ...' He didn't want to say any more, because he couldn't think of a single thing to say that wouldn't be a direct criticism of his sister's outrageous and hitherto unexplained behaviour. He hauled himself to his feet. 'Look, I should get back. The kids. It's Christmas Day. Maybe you could meet them. Tomorrow. What do you say Dad, do you want to bring Tara over tomorrow?'

'That sounds perfect. All right with that, Mary?'

It was all right with everyone; it was all right because for the moment it got Peter out of the house.

Peter went to the door and Tara followed him. She hugged him again, and with her back to Dell and Mary she narrowed her eyes at him and made a shape of her lips, as if to tell him she had something to say to him, but not in front of Dell and Mary.

He wished his parents a Happy Christmas. Then he regarded his sister sadly. 'Happy Christmas Tara,' he said.

'Oh my. Happy Christmas, Peter.'

3

'A fairy tale ... on the other hand, demands of the reader total surrender; so long as he is in its world, there must for him be no other.'

W. H. Auden

The light was beginning to fade when Peter let himself into the cottage. The door, swollen with damp, was still sticking. He'd have to fix that. Except that he'd repaired the door-hinge recently, which was why the door was now sticking. One job makes another was a common saying in the Martin household.

Whatever was happening with Tara, Peter felt heartened to come back to the cottage, to the mess of kids and dogs, and a cottage permanently falling apart and finding new ways to demand maintenance. He liked to see Jack and the girls sprawled over the carpet absorbed with whatever fad or kiddie toys were the interest or excitement of the moment. He never objected to untidiness in the way that Genevieve did. But Gen was his rescuer. She was the architect of his salvation.

He opened the lounge door and they all looked up from what they were doing. Gen with her large brown eyes and slightly freckled face framed by a tumble of unruly dark curls; the girls who all really did look like her clones; the dogs. Then the dogs laid their heads back down.

'Did you see her?' Gen asked.

'Jack shot a rat,' said Josie.

Peter flicked his head to indicate that Gen should come out to the kitchen. She got up.

'Are you going to talk about your sister?' said Amber.

'Yep,' Peter said.

'Can we listen?'

'Nope.'

'Why not?'

'Well. Now then. Tell them why they can't listen, Gen.'

'It's a touchy subject for Dad,' Genevieve announced. 'He'll tell you all about your Aunt Tara after he's had a chat with me.'

'We'll listen at the door,' Amber said brightly.

'You'll get an ear infection,' Peter said. 'Listening to things you shouldn't.'

'Rubbish,' said Zoe. 'Take no notice of Dad.'

Genevieve closed the door behind her and together they went into the kitchen. They sat down and she held his hand across the table. 'You really do look like you've seen a ghost.'

'Mum and Dad. They're sitting there like it's fucking normal. We all thought she was dead and she walks back into their lives after twenty years and it's like; oh hello, have a cup of tea and a piece of ginger cake.'

'They're probably in shock, Peter. Did she say anything?'

The back door swung open and, along with a blast of wintry air, Jack came in. 'I shot a rat.'

'Good man. Put it in the wheelie bin.'

22

'Do you want to look at it?'

'No, I don't need to look at it.'

Jack looked disappointed. 'It's a big one.'

'Are you in or out?' his mother said. 'Either way, close the door. In or out.'

'I'm in. I'm getting cold.'

'Where's the rat now?' said Genevieve.

'On the grass.'

'Put it in the bin.'

'I was thinking o' hangin' it up outside. You know, like a rogues' gallery.'

'Absolutely bloody not! Get it in the bin.'

'What, pick it up with my bare hands? Not likely.'

'Just pick it up by the tail,' said Peter, 'and chuck it in the bin. You killed it, you dispose of it.'

Jack waited for a few seconds of routine defiance before going outside to confront the dead rat. Peter closed the door after him.

'Well?' Genevieve said.

'She said she'd been travelling.'

'Travelling where?'

'It was cock and bull.'

Jack came back in and went to the sink where he made a great show of soaping his hands and washing them under the hot water tap until they gleamed. They had to wait in silence until he was done. Peter slammed the door shut on the outside cold. 'Were you born in a barn Jack?'

Jack made a noise like a sheep.

Genevieve got tired of waiting. 'How do you know?'

'I caught her out on a couple of details.'

'What's that?' Jack said, drying his hands on a tea-towel.

'Use a proper towel for drying your hands,' said Genevieve.

'Why?'

'You've just been handling a rat. And look at this muck you've trailed in.'

'Jack, give me and your mum a minute would you?'

'Is this about our so-called Aunty Tara?'

'Yes, sod off would you? And take your bloody shoes off before you go in the lounge.'

'Did you get to actually see her?'

'Jack!!!'

After they'd got rid of Jack, Genevieve asked what Tara had said about disappearing without a word.

'Nothing. I wasn't allowed to ask. They're coming over tomorrow. The three of them.'

'Heck.' Genevieve looked round at the kitchen. 'We'll have to tidy the place up before they get here. It's incredible.'

Peter was about to open his mouth when the door opened. It was Zoe. 'The dog's been sick,' she said.

On Boxing Day, what with Dell, Mary and Tara expected around mid-day, it was all hands to the pumps, or all shoulders to the wheel, to try to pull the cottage round to some semblance of order. Which meant that the children pitched in to lift one out-of-place object only to set it down in another out-of-place venue. In the end a lot of Christmas toys got scooped under the sofa or parked behind the curtains, all in the name of tidying. Genevieve supervised while Peter grumbled; Zoe hoovered as Amber hovered; Jack put things in boxes and Josie took things out again.

All because Tara had come home. Peter's confusion

and resentment were growing by the minute.

Genevieve had never met Tara. She and Peter had been together for three years before he even mentioned to her that he had a sister. Tara was two years younger than Peter and she had doted on her older brother. He in turn had always been protective towards her and in childhood they had been as close as the print on a legal contract. Then, at the age of nearly sixteen, one summer Tara had gone out of his life.

When he'd told Genevieve what had happened to his sister – and that they had come to accept that she was dead, perhaps after some sexual predator or psychopath had abducted her and buried her body in a secret place – she had quickly understood what a mighty stone this was in his heart; that the experience had almost been enough, but not quite, to petrify all feeling inside of him. Tara was occasionally mentioned in passing, and Genevieve had always listened calmly whenever he spoke about her, knowing that even his sister's name had been a plug, a bung, a cork to a reservoir of hurt that should be faced but never would be.

Tara's name had occasionally surfaced in conversation with the children's grandparents, perhaps if they opened a family photo album; or referenced if they wanted to locate a particular time in the family's history. But it was always a name that flared for a second or two and was ushered on, a spark from a burning log watched briefly for its danger and allowed to smoke out.

Tara was very smart, pretty, intriguing and she left a lot of people her own age – and older – way behind. She had a cool look about her: an unsettling calm, and nut-brown eyes that blinked with intense appraisal. She had her own effortless style and she was genuinely interested in other people at an age where most teenagers were passionately devoted only to themselves. Boys and girls were drawn to her, but she didn't need them. She was a natural leader, but one who didn't want any followers. Tara came over as someone with an agenda lodged elsewhere: a private agenda, mysterious and esoteric.

It had been Peter who had introduced her to Richie Franklin, her boyfriend at the time of her disappearance. Peter and Richie had put together a rock 'n' roll band, of sorts. Pete kept strict time on drums while Richie, with front-man ambitions on guitar, marshalled various hapless and mostly useless teenagers in and out of the band. Richie was someone who could forgive anyone for playing a wrong note, but not three.

They allowed Tara to come with them to watch their band play in pubs, or to see other bands in clubs, to camp with them at rock festivals, to smoke a joint with them, to let her pretty face and shy smile help them gatecrash parties. She never cramped their style; on the contrary, without even knowing it her simple presence loaned them a radical and chic appeal that neither of the boys had naturally. She plugged them into something. If only she had a voice to go with it, Richie had said more than once.

All of which made the loss of this fey but exciting creature doubly hard to bear at the time. After she'd gone from their lives many people repeated clichés about her being 'too beautiful for this world'. It was said too often and by too many. She was nearly sixteen when she'd been spirited away. Or rather, as it now seemed, spirited herself away.

At last there came the sound of a car horn, a double-toot, Dell's little signature of arrival, something he always did when he came visiting. And this time he would have with him not just Mary, but also Tara; the now semi-legendary Tara, not after all a corpse rotting in some shallow woodland grave but living and breathing, and not after all too beautiful for this world but, in the blink of a lizard's eye, a mere twenty years older without looking it.

Peter sat at the kitchen table with his head in his hands.

'Come on,' Genevieve said. 'Pull yourself together. Answer the door.'

With a great heaviness like that of clanking chains, Peter pushed back his chair and hauled his large frame upright. He took a deep breath and made purposeful strides to the door, seizing the door-handle at the same moment that a finger pressed the doorbell outside. The door stuck in the frame and he had to wrench it open, and there was Mary with bags stuffed full of Christmas gifts for the grandchildren she spoiled, and she was in, kissing his cheek, pushing past him. And there was Tara, again with that shy half-smile and her burgundy lips slightly puckered, that shy kink, an incomplete curlicue at the corner of her mouth; he'd seen it before many time but never noted it, and now it had him mesmerised. But his momentary trance was broken when they were propelled forward by Dell, bringing up the rear, going *chuff chuff chuff*.

'Lovely cottage,' Tara said, kissing Peter.

'It's falling down. Come in and meet everyone.'

'Is that door sticking again?' Dell said.

And then they were all crowded in the tiny hallway,

Dell and Mary taking off their coats, the kids all bug-eyed at the mysterious Tara, the dogs trying to leap up at Mary and Dell.

'Tara,' said Peter, 'this is Genevieve.'

Tara stepped forward. She cupped a hand either side of Genevieve's face and gazed into her eyes. 'I knew it,' she said. 'Beautiful. I knew he would find someone absolutely beautiful.'

Genevieve blushed. Away from Tara, Zoe looked at Jack and pointed a finger down her own throat. Genevieve was still trapped by Tara's fingers resting lightly on her face. At last Tara dropped her hands and leaned in to press her lips to Genevieve's cheek.

'Let me take your coat,' Genevieve said.

'So, this is Zoe,' Peter said. 'And here is Jack, and Amber and Josie.'

'Hi Zoe, hi Jack, hi Amber, hi Josie. I'm Tara.'

'We already know that,' Josie said haughtily.

Tara turned her smile on Josie, who instantly retreated behind the lounge door.

'Why do you wear dark glasses?' Amber said, reasonably.

'I have something wrong with my eyes,' Tara said, and Amber seemed satisfied with that.

Genevieve ushered Tara to the living room and waved Mary and Dell through after her.

'She's tiny!' Gen whispered to Peter. 'And so *young* looking!'

The next hour was taken up with the unwrapping of Mary and Dell's gifts and the merciful small talk that went with it. Tara helped Josie get her package open and congratulated Jack on his ratting, since, she said, she hated rats. She complimented Zoe on her taste in clothes and when Amber struggled to button up the new dressing-gown her grandmother had brought for her she got down on her knees and buttoned it.

Though the kids all seemed to regard Tara as something akin to a unicorn, she easily charmed them. Peter noted how naturally she did that. It was always thus, he remembered. Though no one else but himself and his parents – plus Richie occasionally – saw the moods that sometimes stood in counterpoint to that effortless ability. *Yes but there's a shadow*, he wanted to tell everyone.

She'd scrubbed up well, too. He didn't know how long she'd spent in the bath but she'd come up looking pink as a peeled prawn. All the grime had been washed away. Her hair had recovered its waves and its chestnut sheen was there for all to admire as she tossed her head like a pony. The dirt had been scraped from under her fingernails. She used no cosmetics at all and her complexion was flawless.

She looked very good, and healthy enough, though a little tired. It was just that Peter knew that only someone barking mad would leave home without a word and then wash up at the door two decades later.

'I made a cake,' Genevieve said, jumping out of her chair.

'I'll help you,' Tara said.

Peter saw an opportunity to talk. 'I'll come through, too.'

Tara gently pushed him back into his seat. 'Stay there big brother. I want to bring you cake.'

He didn't know whether to resist. A glance from Genevieve told him to stay put.

*

'He hates me now,' Tara said as Genevieve drew a big knife through her chocolate cake.

'He's confused, hurt, angry, puzzled, baffled and above all he's been told he can't ask you any questions. But I know he still loves you.'

'How do you know that?'

Genevieve sucked a sliver of cake from her thumb. 'If he didn't love you, he wouldn't give a damn about any of it.'

'Not only did I know he'd find someone beautiful; I knew he'd find someone very smart.'

Genevieve took a step towards Tara. 'You seem very nice to me. I think it's a time for honesty, not charm.'

'That's fair. Very fair. I will talk and I will be honest. Right now I'm just trying to find a way to explain what happened. It's not as easy as you think. For one thing, when I tell him the truth he won't believe me and he will hate me even more than he does now. In fact he'll despise me.'

'I know him, and I know he won't despise you, whatever it is.'

'Oh yes he will. And you will, too. Though you may turn out to be my best hope. It's certainly not something I can tell Mum and Dad. I wouldn't even bother telling anyone, not a soul, except that certain people deserve to hear the truth, whether they believe it or not.'

'Tara, I haven't the faintest idea of what you are talking about.'

'Do you know his friend Richie?'

'I've never met him. He told me they had a falling out before we met. They haven't spoken in all these years.'

Tara put her hands to her face. 'That would be my fault that they fell out. They were great friends. Before '

'What happened, Tara? Why don't you just say in simple words what happened?'

The door opened. It was Mary. 'Are you girls baking that cake, or what?'

4

'Are you a witch?
Are you a fairy?
Are you the wife
Of Michael Cleary?'
    Children's rhyme from Southern Tipperary, Ireland

New Year's Day. Tara promised to tell Peter everything on New Year's Day. Why? Peter had asked. Why couldn't she tell him there and then? She said because after she'd told him, he wouldn't want to speak to her again, and that she'd wanted to get through Christmas for the sake of Dell and Mary. But, she promised, she would tell him all of it. Everything.

She asked if they could go for a walk together on New Year's Day through the Outwoods. He could bring Gen and the kids and the dogs. She pointed out that it used to be a great tradition in the Martin household. Dell, Mary, Peter and Tara would always walk in the Outwoods, a couple of times with Richie, too, and always with Peter's terrier Nix.

'Where is Nix by the way?' Tara had asked Peter.

'Hell, Tara, Nix died about twelve years ago. Dad buried her in the garden in the rose bed.'

'Oh; of course.' Then Tara had cried bitterly.

'We had lovely roses come where we buried him.'

'Don't.'

The walks through the Outwoods had stopped after Tara had disappeared. It didn't seem right. There were more walks, but they went instead to Bradgate Park, where the spirit of Lady Jane Grey sighed in the ruins of her Elizabethan mansion or up on Beacon Hill with its Iron Age earthworks and its weird crags. The Outwoods forever carried the stamp of Tara's ghost. Peter had been sure for twenty years that she had haunted the place, and for some reason the sudden unpicking of that belief terrified him more than had Tara's ghost. Now that she was alive he quickly had to review his ideas about hauntings. Perhaps living souls had greater phantom powers than the dead.

'She wants us all to go for a walk with her,' he told Genevieve. 'All of us.'

'What, she thinks we can drag this lot out walking? Doesn't know much about teenagers, does she?'

'Says she's going to tell me everything.'

'You should go alone.'

'You want to come?'

'I'd like to. I'd like to hear what it is she has to say. But I've a feeling it ought to be just you and her.'

'I think I need you to be there. To stop me punching her.'

Genevieve blinked at that. Peter, a strong and powerfully built man, had never talked that way and had never raised his fists to anyone in all the time she'd known him. 'We could leave Zoe in charge. I'll come if you want me to. Have a think.'

Have a think. The problem was that was all he could do: think about it. Last thing at night and first thing in the morning. He considered that maybe he should go back to work early, take his mind off Tara.

Peter was a farrier. He had his own business, mostly shoeing horses but occasionally turning his hand to other bits of ironwork. He hadn't always been a farrier. After completing a degree in social psychology he had looked around for a job related to his studies. A recession-hit Britain didn't seem to have too many vacancies so he took a sales job in confectionery, thrashing up and down the motorway selling bars of chocolate.

He was an affable man and found strangers easy to talk to. He got the orders and didn't find the job too stressful. But it was a kind of sleep to him. You descended into work-mode and hardly noticed that a day of your life had passed. After a few years he became a regional manager; he was efficient, well-liked and he reached his quotas. Then the company he worked for was bought out by a larger corporation and he was made redundant.

With two very young children by Genevieve it wasn't a great moment to be out of work. At the time no one could find a plumber. When he calculated out what plumbers were earning he wondered why the hell he'd bothered studying for a degree in social psychology to become a chocolate salesman; and so he decided to look into retraining as a plumber. Dell and Mary were mortified. Peter had hauled himself out of the working classes only to parachute right back in amongst them.

But then Peter heard that no one could find a farrier, either, and that there was a living to be made shoeing the horses and ponies of leisure riders for anyone who had a strong back. What's more, a local, ancient and crusty farrier had died and his cottage was up for sale, complete with an old forge. That's what the cottage was called: The Old Forge. So Peter, with his redundancy cheque in hand, put in an offer.

'Christ,' Genevieve had said. She had Jack gamely hanging off one tit at the time and Zoe had only just finished breast-feeding.

'I'll retrain.'

'Christ.'

'Are you up for it?'

Genevieve shifted a tumbling curl out of her eye and hitched baby Jack higher on her nipple. 'Do I get to look at the place?'

The property was ramshackle. It needed heating installed and fixing up and decorating from top to bottom. The forge itself was antiquated and hardly in working order, but Peter pointed out that it didn't need to be: most farrier work these days was mobile and done from the back of a van.

Genevieve was not, like her husband, of working class origin. In fact she was very minor aristocracy. Her cousin was thirty-ninth in line for the throne of England. Or something. Her own family were broke, but luckily she was high enough in the social order not to give a damn about social appearances. Had she been a little less upper-class she might have insisted on a showroom-home with a touch of regency style furniture. But she wasn't. She'd married so far 'beneath her' in the social order that it couldn't be interpreted as anything but an escape and a relief.

Peter knew that the decision, ultimately, was hers to make. 'Are we taking it?'

'Christ. Yes.'

So, twelve years on and just two days after Christmas,

he found himself in his workshop, sorting horse-shoes that didn't need sorting, just so that he wouldn't have to feel angry about Tara.

Genevieve had appeared at the workshop door. 'Leave the sodding things, Peter. You promised yourself a week off. Come and play with the kids.'

'Right. Coming.' He clattered some shoes into a wooden box, where they rang like tuning forks.

Two days later he was sitting in his car outside Richie's house again. This time he had taken the step of switching off his engine. It was raining. The windscreen and the side windows of the car had steamed up and he had to wipe the glass to see out. Not that there was a lot to see.

Peter sat there for maybe fifteen minutes. A light burned in Richie's house – the same dim table-lamp he'd seen before, deep at the back of the house. No one seemed to move in front of it anyway, and no one went into or out of the house.

The condensation on the windscreen glass matched Peter's state of mind. He was misted, paralysed between the act of getting up and knocking on the door and sinking further into his seat. He and Richie had been childhood friends up to and until shortly after Tara's disappearance. They shared a lot of history: childish things, stupid things.

One time, when he was eleven, Peter had been foolish enough to walk across a frozen pond. In the middle of the pond he'd dropped straight through the ice. His weight had cut a perfect and circular hole. As he struggled to haul himself back on to the ice it splintered in his hands and gave way again and again, each time sending Peter plunging back down into the freezing water. Richie did everything you are instructed not to do in such a situation: he walked calmly across the ice, reached down an arm and pulled Peter out of the water.

'Stupid,' Peter spat, shivering as they walked home together, he soaked and freezing. 'You could have gone through the ice, too.'

'Yeah.'

'You pulled me out.'

'Yeah.'

'We both could have died.'

'Yeah.'

'Stupid.'

'Yeah.'

Two years after that Peter repaid him. One beautiful summer's evening, with the air smelling of sweet, new-mown grass, they were playing cricket on the recreation ground along with some younger kids. Two older boys appeared, strangers, their faces creased with mischief. One of them had a stick with a rope noose at the end of it. Just for fun, just for meanness, the boy with the stick strolled right up to Richie and hooked the noose tight round Richie's neck. Richie was brought to his knees, his face puce, struggling to breathe.

Peter was holding the cricket bat. Without hesitation he stepped up to the mean youth as casually as if he were moving to the wicket and going into bat. He swung the bat hard and struck the boy across the ear. The boy's head made exactly the same pleasing sound as a cricket ball on a bat, leather on willow. The boy went down as if he'd been shot.

The second aggressor turned pale. 'You're fuckin' mad,' he said. 'You coulda killed 'im!'

'You want some?' said Peter.

Richie, still purple in the face, tore the noose from around his neck and used the attached stick to thrash at his tormentor, who lay on the floor guarding his head. The second boy chose to say no more.

'It's enough. Leave it,' said Peter.

The cricket game was over. They walked home without a word, leaving the assailant lying on the ground.

They shared a lot of history and a lot of hurt.

Peter was startled from his reveries when his passenger door was suddenly snatched open by a man in a grey hoodie. The man had serious need of a shave. He looked at Peter with unblinking bloodshot eyes.

'How long you gonna sit here without coming in?'

'Do you want beer or whisky?' Richie said.

'I'll have a beer.'

Richie seemed not to hear Peter, because he splashed two measures of whisky into glass tumblers and handed one to Peter. 'Quite a surprise. You showing up.'

Peter took a slurp of the whisky. Supermarket special. He settled back on the leather sofa and glanced round the room. There were three electric guitars lying around, and a couple of small amps. One expensive-looking jumbo acoustic guitar. The place was tidy, but dusty. No sign of a woman's touch. Peter had heard over the years that Richie was living with this or that woman; was supposed to have fathered a child by one of them, but there was no sign of children or family.

'Fag?' Richie sparked up a cigarette.

'No. Gave up. No one smokes indoors any more anyway.'

'They do in this house.' He blew a plume of smoke to advertise the point.

Richie wore his hair very close cropped. He once had beautiful long hair, and girls fell in love with its soft waves; some did, anyway, and Tara once said that it was his hair that made her fall in love with him. If the severe crop was to disguise the salt and pepper colour the years had given over, it only drew attention to the bony shape of his head. His pale skin seemed stretched and taut over the skull it covered. The veins on his forehead were a little too prominent and a little too blue.

These days Richie wore round John Lennon old-style glasses. He pushed them up the bridge of his nose. 'I hear you're a blacksmith now.'

'Farrier.'

'What's the diff?'

'Horses. Horseshoes.'

Richie wrinkled his nose and took another sip of whisky. 'Never have been on the back of a horse, me.'

'Sensible. Flighty creatures. You've got to watch they don't kick you in the head.' Peter pointed at the guitars. 'See you've kept the faith.'

Richie grunted.

'Does it earn you a crust?' As far as Peter knew, Richie did the pubs circuit, was in and out of bands, did session work whenever he could get it.

'It is a crust. Half a crust. You're living at The Old Forge, ain't ya? Wife and kids. Four kids.'

'Yeah.'

'You was 'ere on Christmas Day. I saw you. Sat outside. Too scared to come in.'

'Yeah.'

Richie drained his glass and gave himself a top-up.

39

Almost as an afterthought he got up and carried the bottle over to Peter, splashing another measure into Peter's glass. He put his cropped, bony grey head dangerously close to Peter and jabbed an angry finger. 'You're a fucker! A fucker! You hear that? A fucker, not speaking to me in all this time. Fucker.' He went back to his own seat, crashing back into the leather upholstery.

Peter wanted to say that it takes two to make a silence work. Instead he said, 'You feel better now?'

Richie offered him a carnivorous smile. 'Yeah, I do actually. I feel much better. I'm quite relaxed now.'

'Well that's good, 'cos I have something to tell you.'

Richie blinked.

'Tara came back.'

Richie stared hard at his former friend. He said nothing. After a moment he took off his spectacles and polished them on the hem of his shirt, put them back on again and looked at Peter some more.

The two men sat in silence, sipping whisky.

5

'It is strange and weird that I cannot with safety drink ten bottles of champagne; but then the champagne itself is strange and weird, if you come to that. If I have drunk of the fairies' drink it is but just I should drink by the fairies' rules.'

G. K. Chesterton

'We've never been back here since you went away.'

'No,' said Tara. 'Mum and Dad said you stopped coming. But I still love this place.'

Peter shook his head. 'It was too painful to come here.'

The Outwoods is a hundred acres of oak, rowan and birch, of holly and yew, trembling on the lip of an ancient volcanic crater and peering out over the Soar Valley; a timeless pocket of English woodland inside the boundaries of Charnwood Forest. Its rock formations contain the oldest of fossils. In its mineral soil rare plants flourish. The inspirational red-and-white-spotted fly agaric mushrooms spore and fatten around the gleaming silver birches, sucking sugars from the roots and feeding back minerals and water. The trees conduct and transfer energy around the woods. The land is a mysterious freak, where the air is charged with an eerie electrical quality, alternately disturbing and relaxing. The earth echoes underfoot.

It is a place to go, Tara would always say, when there is a fire in your head.

Or, all of this is just fanciful talk and the Outwoods is just an ordinary stretch of ancient woodland. But even the most unimaginative visitor would have to be overwhelmed at one particular season of the year; because thrilling are the bluebell woods in May.

'Did you never come back to see the bluebells?'

'No,' said Peter.

They were walking with the two lurchers, just Tara and Peter. Genevieve had decided for Peter that she wouldn't join them.

Tara wore a long woollen coat that Peter thought familiar, and a ridiculously long multi-coloured scarf that he had never forgotten. He was right: it turned out that Mary had kept all Tara's clothes, wrapped in polythene, in the attic. Untouched, all these years. A polythene shrine in a dark and silent place. Peter would have burned them all.

The Peruvian hat with its ear flaps and tassels, though, was new. 'Do anything special,' she asked him, 'for New Year's Eve?'

'Stayed at home.'

'Really?'

'Quiet night in. Opened the doors at midnight. Brought the coal and a penny inside. Job done.'

'Not like you. Last year you were out whooping it up. You didn't come home for three days. Three days!'

He stopped. 'Last year?'

She stopped in her tracks. Her mouth opened and then she quickly looked away. 'I meant last time.' She picked up a stick and flung it for the dogs to chase. It went spinning through the air and cracked into a birch tree.

'Well,' he said, 'when you have four kids and a menagerie to think about, it changes things.'

'Yes.'

Peter watched her carefully, trying not to make it obvious. He pretended to look away when she glanced at him, noting that she wasn't making a lot of eye contact from behind her dark glasses. She was carrying some guilty secret, he knew it.

But the extraordinary thing about Tara was how her looks seemed to change under different light. Genevieve had remarked how young she looked; and it was true. Under soft lights she could almost pass for his daughter's age, or someone in her late teens. Then again the direct sunlight might reveal care-lines about the mouth, laughter-lines around the eyes. Her complexion seemed unnaturally young, and her delicate and graceful hands seemed never to have done a day's work. At least not when compared to the ruined, scarred hands of a working farrier.

Something in Tara's frame, something in her delicacy, had always made Peter want to protect her. More than once he'd wondered if they had different fathers. He had a large, lumbering physique, a gentle giant, slow-witted according to his own assessment; she by contrast was mercurial, slender-boned and sharp-tongued. He was earthly; she was aerial. He was made of clay and iron; she was made of fire and dreaming.

Richie had fallen for her big time. Peter saw it happening all the way, the way you might see a weather-front moving in: you might not want it, but you couldn't do anything about it. It was Richie in particular who encouraged her along on their jaunts, when Peter might have felt encumbered by having a sister monitoring his moves. But one day Peter saw Richie and Tara laughing together in a certain way. He should have known then and there that they were destined or doomed to become lovers. Peter had a momentary vision of Richie up there in the clouds with her, and on fire. He was more worried for Richie than he was about his sister.

'You're going to have to go and see Richie,' said Peter, 'at some point.'

She said nothing; threw the stick again for the dogs.

'Tara, I went to his house. Day before yesterday.'

'Oh God.'

'You know we had an argument after you left? I let myself be persuaded that he was somehow behind it. Behind your leaving, I mean.'

'That was stupid. Richie wouldn't hurt anyone.'

'He went odd after you disappeared. It all seemed to add up.'

'Everything seems to add up until you subtract.'

'What?'

'How is he?'

'Old. Like me.'

'Old is a state of mind.'

'Cack, is that.'

'You sure about that?'

'I have a weak back, bad knees, fading eyesight and there's a bit of grey in my hair.'

'Shoeing horses gave you the weak back, not your age. Anyway, I know where there is a fountain of youth. God, do you remember when this woods was full of bluebells?'

'That year you left us. They were ...'

'They were inspirational. They swamped the entire woods. It was like the woods were under water.'

'Tara you never went travelling at all. At least not where you said you'd been. Mitilini isn't even in Crete for chrissakes.'

'I saw you were trying to trap me. I knew it.'

'So why not just tell the truth. The bloody truth?'

She turned and grabbed the sleeves of his coat, and almost shouted at him. 'Because when I tell you the truth I will have to go away again. Really. I will have to go away. You won't believe it, not a word of it, and you'll hate me even more and there will be nothing for me to do but leave. That's it. And now I have you back for a short while I don't want to bring it to an end. I love you, Peter, you're my brother. I love Mum and Dad. But once I've told you the truth it will be all over between us. Is that what you want?'

'Of course it's not what I want! What could you have done that was so bad? Did you kill someone?'

'Of course I didn't.'

'Then it can't be so bad that we would hate you!'

'Oh you would hate me. Simply because you wouldn't believe it.'

'Then give us a bloody chance! Just tell it straight up. The plain and simple truth.'

Tara turned away from him. Her acorn-brown eyes dulled as she gazed across the bowl of the old spent volcano. It was as if she were seeing another time, or hearing other words inside her head.

'All right,' she said. 'All right. I'll tell you.'

6

'The iron tongue of midnight hath told twelve;
Lovers, to bed; 'tis almost fairy time.'

William Shakespeare

Oh yes the bluebells were out in May. Do you remember how they were? Their perfume stole the sense right out of your head. It turned you over and shook the juice right out of you. You couldn't walk between them that year they were so dense; you had to swim in them. The madness of it! The scent was so subtle that it got all over you, in your nostrils, in your cavities, and on your fingers like the smell of a sweet sin. Didn't it bind you in blue lace and carry you away?

We walked there together that year, didn't we? There were tiny paths between the bluebells and I went off the path and you told me I'd be punished for going off the trail, for treading bluebells underfoot. You said there was a law against it. But you meant lore.

Yet there were so many of them, troops of them, so scented and ringing out and waving to me that I had to find my own trail between them. At the time I believed – or was tricked into believing – that I hadn't crushed a single flower or green blade or bulb underfoot, that they lifted me a few inches off the ground, bore me up and carried me over. I was wrong. It was a trespass. I know that now.

We all know it now.

Youth fears nothing because it knows nothing.

I lost myself in the bluebells. Heart, mind and soul. I know there was a moment where I was of this world, and then there was an instant when I felt odd, dizzy, estranged. I think that was the moment that the doorway opened. Though I didn't step through it. Not then. Not yet.

We were talking, you and I, and we arrived at that ancient rock covered in thick lichen the exact colour of marmalade, that outcrop poking up like a fist with a finger pointing to heaven. That's what we always said: a marmalade finger pointing to heaven. I was planning to tell you about the argument I'd had with Richie; about how it was all going wrong and what had happened that brought us to the brink of a big decision. I was pretty sure it was going to go only one way, but I hadn't told him yet. I was planning to discuss it with you, to see if there was a way that I could tell him that wouldn't hurt him. But something stopped me from telling you.

It was the rock. There was a cloud of little golden beetles flying around the rock, their sleek backs glittering in the May sunshine like flints striking on a stone. And so the golden light fizzed and crackled with hundreds of tiny sparks of wing-light. You were astonished, too. You, who were never amazed. We both stood and stared. It was like a blessing, it was like a gift.

But I knew something was happening. And I forgot all about Richie, and I forgot all about telling you. I just

47

watched the air fizz with tiny prickles of fire, knowing something was about to happen.

The next day I asked Richie to come with me, here, to the bluebell woods. I was determined to tell him. I don't know why but I thought this was the right place to tell him it was over. I couldn't give him what he wanted. I would never do that again: take someone to a beautiful place to dump them! It's not a good idea. I think if it ever happened again I would take them to some industrial scrapheap to let them down. It's cruel to lay such things over a beautiful landscape. But anyway I knew nothing in those days, and I thought it was poetic and the right thing to do.

He just wouldn't have it. 'This is not going to happen,' is what Richie said to me that day. I told him, 'You can say what you want.'

He was angry and hurt. He cried. I cried. Then I ran away from him, ran through the woods, and I hid. See that outcrop of amber rocks over there? I hid behind one of those rocks. He came shouting for me. Crying and shouting my name. I shrank behind the rock, and when he came round I circled back and sprinted towards the charcoal burners over there. He went off in the other direction calling my name. His voice became more distant and I ran back through the woods, up the slope, higher, crushing bluebells underfoot.

I had no thought at that time of how I would get home. Richie had driven me there in his old Volkswagen Beetle with all those Rock Against Racism stickers on it. He'd parked the car on the grass verge of Breakback Lane, so I was careful to avoid that side of the Outwoods. I found another hanging stone covered in marmalade lichen amongst the bluebells, and I sat there with my back to the stone for an hour or maybe two. When I returned to where Richie had parked the car, he'd gone. I was so relieved.

There was an elderly couple walking back to their own car. They'd been for a stroll. I walked right up to them, looking tearful, and I lied and said my boyfriend had left me stranded there because we'd had an argument. They said what a shocking bad person he must be and that I should find myself a decent chap, one who wouldn't abandon a young girl like that. 'You don't know who is around in a place like this,' the man said. 'A pretty girl like you.' They offered to give me a lift home, which of course I accepted. They took me right to my door and made me promise that I'd have nothing more to do with the lout who had abandoned me in the Outwoods, and I promised.

But something had started. In my head, something had started. It was like the scent from the bluebells that day had ripped me open like a drug. That scent was always just at the edge of my senses, lodged somewhere in my throat, on my fingers, in my nostrils until I tried to smell it or taste it again, and I couldn't. It was there all the time; but when I tried to look for it, to trap it, it was gone.

But it was working a strange effect on me. I felt all the time that I might just float off this planet. And my head was hot. Do you remember that poem:

I went out to the hazel wood
Because a fire was in my head.

I've always loved that because that was how I felt so often and when I did feel like that I would come to these woods until the fire burned out. But this was different.

49

The back of my head felt hot. I knew something was going to happen.

I remember at home, Mum asking me if I was all right and I said I was fine. Richie called but I'd already primed Mum to tell him I'd got back safely from the Outwoods but I wasn't in right now.

'Have you two had words?' she asked me.

Words.

I dreamed of flying golden beetles. But they were like scarabs from an Egyptian tomb. And when they flew around me they would stop dead in the air and the frozen formation of them would spell out words in tiny sparks of fire and light. But I couldn't read the words; they would always break up just before I could make them out.

When I woke in the morning there was a small scorch mark on the headboard of my bed, where my head had touched the pine panel. Do you remember? I showed you. I told you my head was hot and that it had left a burn on the headboard and you snorted and said that was impossible. But I know.

I know, and you don't.

Richie persisted in telephoning. He called every hour. It was driving me crazy and my head was coming apart. Mum said she couldn't keep lying and pretending that I wasn't home, so I went out so that she could tell him the truth. I got my bicycle and cycled up to the Outwoods. I hadn't got a lock for my bike so I hid it behind a tree and covered it with branches, and then I went walking amid the bluebells. This time the scent came up on me in a rush, a cloud, and I was drawn deeper into the woods, following an old bridle path. There were few people around that afternoon, it being a working day.

Someone trotted a pony along the bridle path and that's the only person who passed me.

The scent from the bluebells was overwhelming, but it was also giving me a kind of peace, a serenity. I stopped thinking about Richie. I stopped thinking about what was happening inside me. I walked amongst the bluebells again and I must have known that by treading them underfoot I was releasing more of that strange perfume into the air. After a while I found a rock covered in brilliant green moss and orange lichen. I sat amongst the bluebells and put my head back on the mossy pillow of the rock.

The bluebells made such a pool that the earth had become like water, and all the trees and bushes seemed to have grown out of the water. And the sky above seemed to have fallen down on to the earth floor; and I didn't know if the sky was earth or the earth was water. I had been turned upside down. I had to hold the rock with my fingernails to stop me falling into the sky of the earth or the water of the sky. But I couldn't hold on, and I know I went soaring.

I was wearing a ring that Richie had bought me the day after we first had sex together. My first time. It had been at this very place and at that moment in my life I felt that I wanted Richie to hold me for ever. Now I wasn't so certain. I took off his ring and let it go, and it fell, fell through the blue sky on to the emerald and amber cushion of moss and lichen that sat so soft on the table of ancient rock.

I felt unburdened. Lighter. I sat back with my head against the moss. The twittering of the birds died down and it seemed like all of the woods became silent. I might have fallen asleep. But even if I did, I woke up with a start when I heard someone coming through the woods towards me.

It was a man on a pretty white horse making his achingly slow way along the bridle path. Strung either side of the horse was a large straw pannier, each looking loaded. I thought the man was talking to himself, or to the horse, but anyway he had the laziest seat in the saddle you ever saw, and this horse was hardly moving. The man had a crop and he was twitching it at the horse, but not so the creature would feel it. He'd allowed the reins to fall slack at the horse's withers and I almost thought he was riding this white horse in his sleep.

I decided to keep quiet and lay with my head back on the mossy stone so that he wouldn't see me and he would pass by, but then as he drew near I saw that his eye was fixed on me. He twitched at the horse and turned it off the bridle path and towards me, crushing bluebells under the hooves of the horse.

And they were large hooves. The horse was an elegant creature but its sturdy legs were more like those of a shire, with huge hairy fetlocks. It moved slowly towards me, nodding its head as it came. Then it stopped right before me. The man sat up a little, smiling down, an amused look in his eye.

I should have been a little afraid, but I wasn't.

I said, 'That's the whitest horse I've ever seen.'

'It is,' he said. 'It's the whitest horse you've ever seen; and it's the whitest horse you will ever see.' He had an unusual accent. I don't know what it was, though I liked the sound of it well enough. 'And that's why he's mine.'

He sat there for an uncomfortable moment or two

as we eyed each other. 'What's it called?' I said, just to break the silence.

'Tssk,' he went, and he smirked at me like I was a bit simple. 'You don't give a horse a name. They don't like to have names.'

'I've never heard that,' I said, defiant.

'I expect you haven't heard a lot of things, you being a slip of a gal.'

He was very quick with his answers, but he softened them with a smile on his moist red lips. He wasn't so old himself. Maybe about thirty, so I thought. Too old for me, but not so old.

Then he said, 'That looks like a very comfortable pillow you've found for yourself there. A very comfortable pillow.' And he swung down from his horse.

He dropped the reins of his white horse and I thought he was going to come towards me but he stepped away from me, to the far end of the mossy rock. 'Would you mind if I shared your pillow? Only over here, which is safe, and not too close, because I know what you young girls are like.'

He certainly wasn't close enough for me to be worried, so I said, 'It's a free country.'

'It is and it isn't,' he said and he slumped down and laid his head back on the stone and I do believe he immediately went to sleep.

Or maybe he was just pretending, but anyway his eyes were closed and his breathing changed, and I could see the rise and fall of his chest. It was a hot afternoon and his horse, untethered, plodded away to go and stand under a tree. I waited a while, thinking the man would speak to me at any moment, but he didn't. He lay there amid the bluebells, his eyes closed and his mouth very slightly open.

I sat up and got a good look at him. At first I wondered if he were a gypsy. But he didn't have the manner of a gypsy and they are not so often seen alone. Then I took him for some kind of hippie; one of those crusty guys who get stuck in the fashion of their youth. His hair was down to his collar, a mass of dark curls behind which I saw the glint of a single gold ear-ring, but you and Richie wore your hair longer than that. He wore a white shirt without a collar, and a black waistcoat; and then baggy black trousers gathered at the knee and stuffed into his riding boots.

In repose he looked a little younger than I at first took him. He needed a shave I thought. But he was handsome and he had luscious lips, and they twitched slightly as I watched him; and I watched him maybe for half an hour.

He woke – or pretended to wake with a start. He sat up too quickly. First he looked for his horse, which nodded from the shade beneath the tree. Then he spun round and looked at me, and after that all about him, as if he couldn't make out how he'd ended up where he was. Then just as suddenly he relaxed.

He lay down again, but this time propping up his head with a hand and smiling at me. 'I'm sorry,' he said. 'You must think me awfully rude. I don't know what took me off there.'

'It's okay,' I said.

'I just felt the sleep come over me. And I couldn't do anything. It's like this is an enchanted place.'

'Oh it is,' I said. 'It is enchanted.'

He looked a little worried, though I still think he was pretending. 'Really? Is it?'

'Oh yes,' I said. I do like it when you can get the better of a man. 'I know this place.'

'I think you do,' he said. 'I think you do.'

His horse moved away. 'Aren't you worried?' I said.

'The horse? No, she won't go far from me. She's my best friend in the world.'

'Your best friend is a horse? That must be because you don't get along with people.'

He laughed and when he laughed the skin at the corner of his eyes wrinkled, and I thought he was older, after all. 'You're a girl with a bit o' trunk, aren't you? You're right. I don't get along famously with others. I'd rather my own company, you know?'

'I'm the same,' I said.

Now he squinted at me. 'If I come and sit beside you, you won't jump on me, will you?'

He had this way with him that made me laugh. 'No, I won't jump on you.'

He crawled through the bluebells on his hands and knees and then sat next to me, his back against the mossy rock. His bottom was maybe three or four inches away from mine. I could smell him. He had an odour; fresh, but manly. He folded his hands behind his head and looked up at the blue sky. The birds were twittering in the trees. I know what you're thinking, that I was risking it, there in the woods and all. But I felt quite safe with him.

He had such a gentle air.

7

*'Anno 1670, not far from Cirencester, was an appari-
tion; being demanded whether a good spirit or a bad?
returned no answer, but disappeared with a curious
perfume and a most melodious twang. Mr W. Lilly
believes it was a fairy.'*

John Aubrey

Back at the Old Forge while Peter walked with Tara
in the Outwoods, Zoe paced the living room with
her mobile phone surgically attached to her ear. She
was talking to her boyfriend Michael, a fifteen-year-
old white rapper with heartbreaking acne, a taste for
designer labels and a history of self-harm. Amber tried
to eavesdrop on her sister while watching a DVD her
mother had already described as 'unsuitable' while
Josie had stolen a bottle of Zoe's nail varnish and was
painting both her toes and the carpet. Genevieve was
trying and failing to tidy around them when she heard
the chimes of the doorbell.

She wondered who the hell was calling on New Year's
Day. 'Can someone get that?' she shouted, already on
her way to answer the door since she knew no one else
would.

On her way through the hall she collected a pair of
trainers, a pullover, a T-shirt, a child's pair of pyjamas

and a wet stick one of the dogs had brought in from the garden. She had these things bundled in her arm when she opened the door. Hovering on the threshold was a tall, thin man with a severe crop and round wire-frame spectacles. He had a slight stoop. 'Is Peter in?' His voice was very deep.

'He's gone for a walk up at the Outwoods.'

'I'm Richie.'

'Yes, you are, aren't you? You coming in?'

She dropped the shoes in a tea-chest by the door and led him through to the kitchen. There she dumped the clothes on the worktop. She told Richie to have a seat at the table, opened the back door and slung the stick outside, closing the door quickly before one of the attentive dogs could dash out and bring it back in again. Then she pushed a curl out of her eye before filling the electrical kettle.

She folded her arms, leaning a hip against the roll of the kitchen worktop as she waited by the kettle for it to boil. With her eyes fixed on him, Richie sat down and shuffled uncomfortably under her gaze.

'It's all a bit strange,' she said at last. 'Tara turns up after twenty years—'

'Twenty-one,' Richie corrected.

'—and now here you are.'

A slap hit the wall from the outside. Richie flinched. 'Hell was that?'

'It's our feral son Jack. Peter bought him an air-rifle against my wishes and he's mounting a twenty-four hour rat patrol. He doesn't live indoors any more.'

'When me and Pete was kids we spent hours lying on the garage roof waiting to shoot rats.'

'Some things don't change.'

57

'A lot of things do.'

'Tea all right? I have got fresh coffee somewhere but I can't really be arsed.'

'Tea is good.'

Richie watched her as she flicked teabags into a pair of chipped mugs and poured boiling water from the kettle. When she'd done making the tea she placed the mugs on the table and sat across from him. She offered a hand to shake. 'Pleased to meet you Richie.'

He shook hands without a word.

'You're a luthier aren't you?'

'Fancy word for stringing guitars.'

'Nice work though.'

'Was. Don't any more.'

Genevieve noticed the tremble in his hands as he raised the cup to his lips. 'Why not?'

'Ain't got the patience no more.'

'He'll be sorry he's missed you. Had you said you were coming?'

'No. Just spur o' the moment, thing. Thought I'd drop round. Always been curious, like. Knew this place from when we were kids. Knew the old farrier. Fairy-tale figure; old white-haired boy with great big mutton-chop sideburns. Saw you from a distance once or twice. Knew he had a lovely family and all that. Lovely wife, lovely kids, all that. Felt pleased for him.'

'It's just ridiculous that you haven't spoken in all this time. He said you were best of friends when you were kids.'

'Best mates we were. Best mates.'

'Well, I don't understand it.'

'You weren't there when it happened.'

'I don't even know what happened exactly. Pete doesn't talk about it.'

The door opened and Zoe came in, still talking on her phone. She seemed not to notice Richie. She pressed the mouthpiece into her collarbone. 'Can I go out tonight?'

'Where to?' said Genevieve.

She lifted the phone again. 'Where is it?' She listened and said, 'The White Horse.'

'Drug den, it is,' Richie said.

Zoe flickered a glance at Richie and then looked back at Genevieve.

'You'll have to ask your dad.'

'Should be all right,' Zoe said into the phone and went out of the kitchen.

'Right scruffy hole, The White Horse,' Richie said. 'Used to play gigs there. Wipe your feet as you come out, type of place.'

'I'll see what her dad says.'

'Wouldn't let my daughter go there.'

'Have you got a daughter?'

Richie sighed. 'I have got one. But I'm not allowed to see her.'

'What happened?'

'Long story.'

'You know what, Richie?' Genevieve said. 'Round here, everyone's story is long; but no one's telling it.'

He snorted, and reached for his pack of cigarettes in his breast pocket. Then he had second thoughts and left them where they were. 'I had a daughter with a wrong 'un. She were a witch, there's no other word for it. Now she won't let me see my daughter, and it's a wound every day I don't see her.'

'How old is your daughter?'

'Nearly nine.'

'That's hard for you.'

'Her life has been stolen away from me.'

Richie told Genevieve some of the details of the case. How he hadn't seen his daughter since she was five years old. He talked about his experiences with the courts and how they were stacked in favour of mothers. He was bitter. But he found himself talking at length to Genevieve, as many had before. 'I don't know why I'm telling you all this,' he said more than once.

Then Amber came in and said, 'Tell Josie!'

'Tell Josie what?' said Genevieve.

'She's being a pain!'

Genevieve went to sort out the uproar and discovered the nail varnish spilled across the carpet and Richie took advantage of her absence to go outside and spark up a cigarette. He remembered the lad on the workshop roof, so he took out his white hankie and waved it. 'Don't shoot! For chrissakes.'

Richie stood in the yard, puffing on his cigarette and looking up at Jack. 'Howdoo,' he said.

Jack nodded and then looked back down the sights of his air-rifle.

'They ain't gonna come and play while I'm standing here, are they?' Richie said. 'Who are you then?'

'Jack.'

'What calibre is it?'

'One point seven seven.'

'You wanna ask your dad to get you a two-two. That'll punch a rat's brains out.'

'Are you Richie?'

''Appen.'

'Thought so.'

'Your dad mentioned me, has he?'

'Yeah. Sometimes.'

Richie smoked his cigarette while Jack lay stretched on the roof peering down the sights of his air-rifle as if the enemy might appear at any moment.

Richie finished his ciggie and went back inside. Genevieve hadn't reappeared, so he found his own way into the living room, where she and Zoe were on their hands and knees trying to scrape nail varnish out of the carpet while Josie wailed and Amber, arms folded, sulked on the sofa. His eyes fell upon a guitar in the corner of the room.

'Who plays that?' he asked, above Josie's din.

'Zoe is learning,' Genevieve said.

Richie picked up the guitar, weighed it in his hands and strummed it. He presented it to Zoe. 'Give it a go then, my love.'

Zoe looked at Genevieve. 'I can only play three chords,' she said, and not to Richie but to her mother.

'Then play three chords,' he said. 'Come on, give it a go.'

'I'm not in the mood,' Zoe said.

'I am but,' he said and he held out the guitar for her. Zoe looked up and caught something in his eye that made her a little afraid to say no again. Reluctantly, she took the guitar from his hands, sat down and started to strum. The television set was still running a DVD movie so Richie turned it off. Amber made a gasp of pretended outrage. 'Give it a go, mi'duck.'

Zoe played her three chords, varying the strum pattern, trying to smuggle a little enthusiasm into her playing. Richie listened attentively, and the younger girls watched him listening. When Zoe stopped, Richie held out a hand to relieve her of the instrument. 'Giz.'

He sat down on the sofa next to Amber and he played the guitar, expertly, very fast. Throughout his playing he looked full-on at Zoe. Her cheeks flamed as he gazed at her. She looked away; she looked at her smiling mother; she looked back at Richie.

He stopped playing suddenly.

'Wow,' said Genevieve.

He stood up and handed the guitar back to Zoe. He suddenly seemed in a desperate hurry to leave. 'I'll come back later when he's in.'

Genevieve raised her eyebrows at his sudden haste. Then she got off her knees to follow him, for he was already moving towards the door.

'I'll tell him you called round.'

'Right. Thanks for the tea.'

'Come back anytime.' She opened the door for him. 'Before you go, Richie.'

'Yes.'

'You should know it's been hurting him. All these years of not speaking. He's never told me what happened between you, or what was said. But whatever it was, he's been hurting. Whatever it was.'

'Right,' said Richie. Then he set off down the path. 'Right.'

8

'In the spring of 1895 seamstress Bridget Boland Cleary was living with her husband Michael Cleary and her father Patrick Boland in a small cottage in Ballyvadlea, Tipperary, Ireland. They'd been married about eight years, but were childless; Bridget was twenty-six, and Michael was thirty-five. Bridget, a good-looking woman, owned her own Singer sewing machine and was said to have 'an eye for the fashions of the day'.

Michael Cleary claimed his wife Bridget had been taken away by the fairies, and that they had left a changeling in her place. On the fifteenth of March, Michael Cleary, having spent three days in various rituals intended to force the changeling to leave and bring his wife back, set fire to her.

He and nine others of Bridget Cleary's relatives and neighbours were tried for her death.'

(Summary of court transcripts)

I'll give you a story if it's a story you want. I almost wrote a song about it but it didn't come out right. It was supposed to be a love song and it ended up sounding like a protest song. Though most love songs are protest songs when you think about it.

There was me and Peter and Tara and a couple of other boys in the band and all was well with the world, and then one day everything changed. I wasn't yet eighteen and it was like someone slammed the door shut on my life the way it was then. Everything was right and the world was full of prospect and possibility; and then it was all wrong.

It was always going to be Tara. Always was. She was just Peter's kid sister and I was only fifteen years old and I was round her house on her thirteenth birthday. One day she was a skinny kid and the next day there was this glow about her. And I would catch her looking at me. When me and Peter were talking she would be listening and I could sense her listening like someone stroking you and I could feel her eyes on me. She looked up to me in those days.

And I knew she was a cut above. From that day on I couldn't stop thinking about her though I couldn't tell Peter. For one thing it wasn't cool to go chasing after girls who were younger than we were. The object of lust and fancy was older girls and women, even if they were unobtainable. Girls our own age and younger were treated with disdain.

Except my feelings about Tara were different. One day I was waiting for Peter to get ready and I saw this school photo of her, with the waves of her brown hair all combed and her eyes full of camera catch-light. I stole the photo there and then. I kept it in the bottom of my sock drawer and took it out from time to time. It wasn't the only photo of her I lifted from their house. They must have known where all those photos were going. Must have known.

Like I say, I kept it all secret. But I looked forward to going to school every day because I knew I would see her. School, which before all this was a pile of dung, had become a place of golden light. Though I made out I didn't care. I was too clever to let on. I wasn't about to have Peter or anyone taking the piss.

There were plenty of opportunities to be near her. I watched her blossom every day. No one knew. I don't think she knew. I never let her see me watching.

One day in the playground she asked me to look after her shoulder bag while she went off and did something. When she'd gone I nipped behind the bike-sheds and had a rummage through the bag. I found a comb with a couple of strands of her hair in it. I kept it. A pencil. Kept it. One or two objects like that. I wrote things with that pencil. I wrote *I love you*, just to see how the words would flow out of her pencil. I kept it, that pencil, in a box with a lock on it, like it was the finger-bone of a medieval saint.

I was learning the guitar back then. I wrote some shit songs about Tara. Really shit songs. You wouldn't want them to see the light of day. No.

I noticed that Tara didn't seem to have close friends. Not like most girls of that age. It wasn't that she was unpopular – just the opposite. She held people off. Didn't seem to need them.

But she did want to come with us, wherever we were going. Peter resisted at first, but I talked him round. Peter was always easy to run. I told him that if Tara came along, we'd have more chance with the girls.

"Owz that work?' he'd say.

I told him that if girls see you with another girl they feel less threatened. At the time we had a project to try and get into any girl's pants who came along. But I knew we were coming on too desperate.

"Owd'ya mean?'

It was like he hadn't thought through any of these things. I told him it made us look less like we were on the prowl and they would drop their guard. Plus she might talk to them and that way we would have an in. 'Christ you're slow, Pete,' I told him. 'So bloody slow.'

Anyway he bought it. Tara started to tag along. I was still playing it cool, and the cooler I was with her, the more she got interested in me. But I couldn't stand it. I was dying in love. Dying. I had dreams about marrying her and the two of us flying over the motorway at night. Bright coloured dreams. It was making me ill. After over a year of this I told Peter.

Well, he hit the roof.

'I want to go out wi' your sister.'

'Eh? 'Owd'ya mean?'

'Tara. I want to ask her out.'

''Owz that work?'

'Your sister. I want to ask her. Out. On a date.'

'Hahaha!'

'I'm serious Peter. I want to go out with Tara. I think about her all the time.'

His face reddened. 'Fuck off.'

'I'm serious, mate.'

'Fuck off! You ain't going out with my fucking sister, no way!'

'Why not?'

''Cos I know what you want to do with her, that's why fucking not!'

He wouldn't speak to me for three days. Then I went round there and reasoned with him. If your best mate, who you trust, can't go out with Tara, then who can? And someone will, I said, ''cos she's gorgeous, and it's only a matter of time before some skanky sleazy townie with jelly oil on his hair and a sporty set of wheels comes waving his top gear dick and—'

'Shaddup,' he said quietly. 'Shut up.'

Anyway he came round.

I asked her out. I made out like it was all nothing. A trip to the flicks. Can't remember what was showing. Did she want to go?

'With you and Pete?'

My heart was slapping inside my ribcage. My tongue was sticking to the roof of my mouth. 'Nachuschoonme.'

'What?'

'Just you and me.'

She looked startled. Brown eyes wide, all over me. Raked me. Her eyelashes fluttered once. She smiled and looked to the side, away from mc. 'Yeah.'

So that was it. We were 'courting' as the old folk call it. There is a difference. Difference between courting a girl and just trying to get your leg over. I think there is anyway.

We went to the flicks and I never saw anything of what was on the screen, even though I had my eyes wide open. All I could sense was Tara in the next seat. The smell of her hair. She wasn't my first girlfriend. I knew the ropes. But I was paralysed. Then we held hands and I thought I would float clean out of my seat.

Outside the cinema I kissed her. At that moment if she'd asked me to walk over the edge of a cliff, I swear to you I would have done it. And from that day on it was like she'd put a hex on me. I couldn't look at another girl and I didn't much like other boys looking at her, either. More than a couple of times Pete had to hose me down if I thought some other lad was looking at her a bit strong.

One time I decked a lad who touched her arse. It was in a disco. That's how it is when you're that age isn't it? You have to stand up for your girl. Another time a bloke was getting a bit friendly with her and I stomped him. Pete had to get between us and I caught Pete one on his jaw. The bloke was taken off to hospital by paramedics and his parents wanted to press charges, but nothing came of it. Only Tara said if I didn't stop she'd leave me and I knew she meant it; so I had to sit on my jealousy, which was probably no bad thing.

We started getting gigs and she used to watch me when I was up on stage. She'd stand at the front with her arms folded, looking up at me. She was telling the other girls I was hers. I loved that.

Anyway she fell pregnant, and that was what the problem was all about. Whether to keep it.

Oh, I knew what I wanted. There was no doubt in my mind, none at all. I wanted for us to keep it, to get married, to have half a dozen sprogs all looking just like her. Six little girls if I had my way. The future was all settled in my mind. House, wife, kids, garden, dogs. What else?

That wasn't how Tara saw it. Pete was on the verge of buggering off to university. He was going to complete his studies and he'd been offered a place at Warwick University. That wasn't for me; I'd staked a future on my guitar, but Tara had an idea she might follow him down the college road. She was smart, and she found studies easy. She said she wanted to do what Pete was planning.

'And what then?' I asked her. 'There's two years to go before that, and three years there is five. What then after that?'

'Who knows?' she said. 'I don't like to plan that far ahead.'

'But how you gonna do all that? You've a kid growing inside you. How you going to do that when we've got a kid?'

'That's just it,' she said. 'That's just it.'

She never came right out and said so but she wanted to get rid of it. She didn't want to be tied down at the age of sixteen. I called her a killer and a butcher and all sorts. Stupid ignorant ugly things I wish I'd never said to her. But I was stupid and ignorant and ugly. Remember I was only a kid myself. I wasn't thinking with my head, even though it seemed like I was at the time.

She cried. We had fierce rows about it.

Then I drove her up to the Outwoods one day in my old banger. We often went up there to be alone together. The bluebells were flowering and I thought if we strolled through the woods holding hands it would all work itself out. But it all cracked off again and I must have bellowed bad things at her, and she cried and ran off into the woods.

I spent the rest of the afternoon trying to find her. I thought she'd come out again: I mean how was she going to get home? I scoured the place until dusk and then I started to get worried, so I drove to a phone box and called her home. Her mum answered and said she'd been home a couple of hours and that she'd gone out again. I guessed she was sitting there right next to the phone.

I called the next day. I called lots of times but Tara was never in. I went round there myself but her dad said she was out and he'd tell her to call me. I knew she was just refusing to see me, because Peter told me she was there but that she didn't want to talk to me.

The next thing I knew was that she'd returned to the Outwoods, and she'd disappeared.

So the police come and ask me what I know. And I tell them what I know, and they go away. Then I go round to Peter's house. His mum and dad have always been like second parents to me – they're worried sick, as am I. They want to know what the arguments have been about. I can't tell them the truth about the pregnancy – Tara hasn't told them that. What's more she's not yet sixteen and Dell would probably want to skin me alive anyway when he finds out. So I say it was about another boy she's been seeing.

Peter looks at me. He don't believe that for a second.

So I say okay not someone she's been seeing but someone who has been making eyes at her, and Peter buys that, knowing how jealous I get.

Then after a couple of days a search party is organised by the police, and we go up there to be part of it. Dell is shocking pale and Mary is shaking visibly and Peter is tight-lipped and we all go up there. And the police are out like blackberries in September and they've drafted in dozens more from neighbouring forces: dog-handlers, women PCs the lot; and there are friends and neighbours up there too, with sticks to beat the ground and rake the bushes and I feel this huge weight of a boulder in my guts. And I can tell everyone is looking at me and talking behind their hands, you know, he's the boyfriend, he's her chap. Christ, everyone is there, complete strangers come to help now that her picture has been in the local paper and on the local evening television news. Hundreds of people and we all move forward in a steady line, spread out across the Outwoods, marching between the trees and tramping the dying bluebells.

They find her bike.

I hear a copper telling another copper that it looks like someone has tried to hide her bicycle in the scrub, in some undergrowth, and he looks up and he glances over at me and he wipes his finger under his nose and walks away. And I know; I know at that minute exactly where they're going to take this.

We walk in slow formation through the Outwoods. Every inch, every bush, every depression in the earth, behind every rock. We keep going until the twilight comes and then the police stand us down. They say they'll carry on searching with torches, but they want us to go home. Dell drives. He gives me a lift home. Mary in the front seat, me and Peter in the back. In silence all the way.

I don't sleep a wink that night. I keep snapping awake. My dad is snoring in the next room. There's no one else to talk to. My mother died when I was nine. I sit up all night trying to work out where she might have gone, but it's the same question Dell and Mary keep hitting me with: where might she have gone?

I don't have a single answer.

Next morning I'm sleeping on the sofa when there's a hammering on the door. Dad has gone to work and there's only me to answer. I go to the door in my boxers. Police again. Would I come down to the station?

I get dressed and they drive me to the station. I'm under eighteen so they can't ask me anything, they say, until I have a lawyer with me. Lawyer, I say, I don't need no lawyer. Do I mind getting the fingerprinting out of the way? No I don't mind, here, do it now. I've got nothing to hide.

It's an hour before this lawyer arrives. Woman. I don't like her much. She's got this long jaw and her teeth are like too big for her mouth. Face like a fucking race-horse. Shergar. All she does is nod at me, no kiss your arse nor nothing. Just sets out a notepad and pen on the table. She sees from the ink on my fingertips that they've already started. There's this copper sitting beside me, bloke with a big wart just beside his nose. He's been all right, told me not to worry, brought me cups of tea.

She looks at the copper. 'You shouldn't have begun this before I arrived,' she says sourly.

Copper smiles at me and scratches an eyebrow, as if it's all a joke between him and me.

'He's a minor,' says the lawyer.

'Giz a break,' says the copper. 'We just got a few things out of the way.'

'Has he said anything?'

'No.'

'Excuse me,' I puts in fiercely. 'I'm here.'

She turns to me and through the narrow gap between her two rows of teeth she says, 'Have you told the police anything?'

'Only what they asked me,' I says. 'I haven't got nothing to hide.'

She looks at the copper again and he just folds his arms.

Two new coppers come into the room, plain clothes. They don't even look at me. They introduce themselves to my lawyer as West Midlands CID. I'm trying to think where I've heard stuff about West Midlands CID. Something to do with corruption charges.

'I'm Julia Langley,' my lawyer says through her over-crowded mouth. I think it's funny how some people's names ring against their own teeth.

The two newcomers settle into the plastic chairs around the table. One of the CID men is so big he can only just squeeze into the chair. He sits back from the table, the seams of his trousers almost bursting round his fat thighs. He rocks back in the chair with his legs apart and the fat fingers of this huge paw digging in under his collar, as if it's too tight for him. He still hasn't looked me in the eye.

The other one is most definitely looking me in the eye. He's way over-focussed on me. And he looks sad. I mean sad, like he might at any moment burst into tears. Is he faking it? I don't know. He's kind of scruffy. An old raincoat with a shabby cardigan underneath. He's wearing a tie but the knot is tiny, pulled way too tight, and the collar of his shirt even I can see is dirty. His face is wreathed in lines. I've never seen a bloke with so many lines on his face: brow corrugated, wrinkles wreathing his eyes, lines around his mouth like ripples from a pond, a big cleft in his chin. His face is a ruin. He takes his eyes off me very briefly to nod at the uniformed copper who's been with me for the past hour. The uniformed copper leans forward and switches on a tape machine and says my name aloud and what time it is.

'Hello, Richie,' says the man with the lined face. His voice is very gentle. It's so gentle it scares the fucking liver right out of me. A gentle copper. Really, I want to shit. 'I'm Dave Williams. Are you all right?'

I look at my lawyer. She just clamps her teeth together like a horse and stares back at me. 'Yeah,' I say. 'Yeah.'

'They treating you okay?'

'Yeah.'

'That's good because I don't want anyone to give you a hard time. We just want to get to the bottom of things.'

'Right.'

'Richie,' he says, and the lines corrugate deeper on his brow, 'we're pretty much sure we know how it happened.'

'How what happened?'

'Look. I'm going to be dead straight. It really is better if it comes from you.'

'If what comes from me?'

The big fat fucker suddenly coughs and leans forward, fingering his collar again like he might want to rip it off his neck. He says nothing.

'Richie, I want to help you.'

'Who are you?' I say.

'I told you Richie. I'm Dave and I'm from CID. You know what CID is don't you?'

'You think I've done something to her, don't you?'

'We have her bike, Richie. It has your fingerprints all over it.'

I look at my lawyer, like, is this a joke? She just makes a little nod of her head, encouraging me to answer. I go cold and then I feel a wave of heat roll over me. 'Well that would be because I ride it with her all the time.'

'You have a car,' says the fat copper, looking at me for the first time. He has an incredible, high reedy voice for such a fat bloke. He sounds like he's nine years old, except there's menace in his voice. 'Why would you need a bike?'

'For cycling,' I says. 'And by the way, I gave her the bike. It was my bike and I fixed it up for her and gave it to her. The chain was always coming off. It would have my fingerprints on, wouldn't it?'

The other one, Dave, the sad one, leans in. 'We know she was pregnant.'

'What?' I say. 'What? How could you know that?'

'Was it your child she was having, Richie?'

'Is having,' I say. 'Is having. How do you know that?'

'Her pregnancy was confirmed by her GP.'

'Thought that was confidential,' I say to my lawyer. 'Wasn't it?'

'How old was Tara?' says the fat one. He can't say his Rs. He says *Tawa*.

'Have you found her?' I ask.

'Can I have a word?' my lawyer says to the policemen.

Dave, friendly Dave, dead straight Dave, sad Dave, my mate Dave, steps outside with my lawyer, leaving me with the uniformed bobbie and the incredible hulk still fingering his collar. Only now he's looking at me with dead-fish eyes. He sniffs. Then he does it again. Sniffs. Like he's telling me he can smell something.

After a moment they come back in. Sit down again.

Dave says, 'Richie, you must have known that Tara was under the age of sexual consent, which is sixteen in this country. But for the moment, for the moment, I'm quite prepared to let that go. I want to make things easy on you and I can guess how hard things have been for you.'

'What things?'

'Were you the father, Richie?'

'I thought doctors weren't supposed to reveal confidential information,' I say.

'In situations like this, it's different.'

'What is this situation?'

'For God's sakes!' says the fat one with his squeaky voice. Then he actually wipes his own spittle off his own black trousers

'Richie, we know you had a lot of very angry rows with Tara. We also know that you have a pretty hot temper.'

'Violent temper,' says the fat one.

'No.'

'We've got information about your violent temper. We found some records about a case in which you badly beat up a young man in a disco pub.'

I turn to my lawyer. She's busy scribbling. She's not behaving like the lawyers you see on TV. 'Why are you here?' I shout. 'You're saying nothing!'

The lines crease even further around the copper's face. He looks incredibly depressed. 'Richie, I'm going to say something now in front of these other people and it shames me to have to say it. Things happen. Some years back, Richie, I used to take a drink. Not any more, but I did then. One night I went home drunk. I'd been married for twelve years and I had three lovely children. My wife and I got into an argument.'

My solicitor stops scribbling and she looks up at him.

'That's all I remember, I swear to you,' says Dave. His blue eyes are burning into me. 'Then, in the morning, I woke up and I found my wife sitting at the kitchen table. Her face was a terrible mess, Richie. Puffed and swollen. Split lip. Two black eyes. I don't remember anything about it, Richie, I swear to you now as God is my judge.'

I look at him. He's leaning forward and gazing deep into my eyes, like he wants to look right into my soul and back again. His eyebrows are raised. I look at my lawyer. I glance at the fat cop, and at the uniformed cop. They are all looking at me, and their eyes, all of them, are like water swirling down a drain.

And for the first time I think: did I do it? Did I?

9

'*The unrealistic nature of these tales (which narrow-minded rationalists object to) is an important device, because it makes obvious that the fairy tales' concern is not useful information about the external world, but the inner process taking place in an individual.*'

Bruno Bettelheim

'Is there something wrong with our Aunt Tara?' said Amber.

'What do you mean by "wrong"?' said Genevieve.

Genevieve, Amber and Josie were baking a chocolate cake in the kitchen of The Old Forge. Zoe was out with her white-rapper. Jack had got bored shooting rats and was now trying, from a distance of twenty yards, to ignite matches suspended by string on an outhouse door.

'She squints and pulls faces.'

'No she doesn't.'

'And her skin hangs off her like there's too much of it. And she wears dark glasses indoors.'

'She's certainly very slim. Wish I was.'

'And Zoe says she only looks fifteen and there must be something wrong with her.'

'You're spilling that. Pay attention.'

'And she does this,' Josie said, half-closing her eyes

78

and moving her head from side to side while affecting a smile.

'Stop being mean, you two. I thought she was very kind and sweet to all of you.'

'And she smells funny,' said Amber.

'Oh that's patchouli oil. I used to wear that. Now stir.'

Outside Jack was still trying and failing to ignite matches from a distance. When he inspected the damage he found that the pellets were embedding themselves in the soft old wood of the outhouse door. It all looked a bit of a mess. He thought he might have to reckon with his father about that. Then he thought he could maybe get his penknife and dig the pellets out of the wood before his dad got back from walking in the Outwoods.

Jack was no great fan of shank's pony. His parents had taken him walking in Charnwood Forest many times over the years, dragging him up Beacon Hill or pushing him through Bradgate deer park, mostly in freezing weather. Before Jack could walk Peter or Genevieve would carry him in a papoose-style back-pack. He could never understand the appeal of walking without having a place to get to. He'd once argued with his dad that it was a bit like jumping with no fence or obstacle in front of you, or running when there was no pressing need to get anywhere fast.

What's more the strange unresolved landscape of Charnwood Forest spread too many shadows. He had an early memory; or rather the memory was so early he wasn't sure if it was only an infant dream. Or a memory of a dream. Anyway, in the memory or the dream, he was strapped in the papoose, facing backwards as

Genevieve strode through the woods. The rocks around were formed of gleaming dark blue slate, sliced and cracked into fine layers so he assumed the scene was Swithland Woods, a place he'd been force-marched through many times later in his life.

His father had been slightly ahead, carrying sister Zoe. There were creatures looking at him from behind the blue slate rocks; they pointed their fingers and smiled cruel smiles. He felt safe in his mother's papoose but still afraid of the creatures. He was only just old enough to talk. He'd tried to make a sound but he was almost mesmerised by the creatures stirring in the wake of the family's passage. He knew intuitively that if he had been able to alert his mother or his father, the creatures would be able to disappear.

He'd recounted this experience to his mother many years later. It was Genevieve who had put the idea in his head that it must have been a dream. She'd suggested that no one could remember something that had happened when they were only two years old. But Jack knew that if it was a dream, it was a full-colour dream. And it had stayed with him: an uneasiness, a low breathing that seemed to exude from the soil and the volcanic rock of Charnwood.

He didn't hate the place; but he never felt at ease there either.

Jack decided to take a few more pot-shots at the match-sticks before giving up for the day. Anything was preferable to staying in a house full of sisters. He took up a position closer to the door, and sighted the rifle. He knew that to ignite the match he had to graze it, not hit it centre-punch. Not that his shot was good enough to accomplish the latter. But he sighted the air-rifle on the match and tried to hold it perfectly still before squeezing the trigger.

Before he fired, something moved at the periphery of his vision. It was a blur of red-rust at the bottom of the garden, a furry thing, half hidden behind a shrub. He knew instantly it was a fox. Foxes visited the garden every evening, eyeing the chicken coop. Sometimes you could see a fox calmly scrutinising the coop and its occupants like it was a mathematical problem that could be solved by patient application and attention to detail.

The thing moved again, creeping through the bushes. Jack swung his rifle, quickly sighting it, and fired.

The tiny slug hit its target. There was a brief flurry of earth and fur as the thing made a leap. There was a moment of writhing, and then stillness. His dad had told him that his 1.77 slugs weren't big enough to kill a fox, but Jack slipped down from the garage roof and ran after his target in hope.

At first he couldn't find anything. Then he spotted his kill. A dilapidated wooden fence surrounded the property, and he saw a ball of ginger fur brushed up against the base of the fence. It wore a little red collar.

'Bugger bugger bugger fuck.'

He squatted beside his kill. It was a pretty ginger cat. Its eyes were wide open and it lay still. Jack tried to poke it.

'Fuck bugger fuck bugger.'

It was a neighbour's cat that he'd seen in the yard once or twice; a sweet thing owned by the elderly lady who lived a few doors away across the street. Jack felt his stomach squeeze. He could see where the pellet had gone in the head. There was also a tiny clot of blood in the cat's ear. Why did he have to suddenly be such a good shot?

He stared back at the house. He didn't think anyone could have seen what had happened. He held his head in his hands, trying to ward off a deep thrill of shame. Then he recovered, got up and walked back to the out-house to open the pellet-studded door. Inside he found a garden spade.

Returning to his kill, he dug a hole in the earth as deep as he could, but after just a couple of feet he hit clay that made the spade ring, as if it was iron. He put the cat in the shallow grave. He thought about taking off its red collar but decided against. Then he covered the dead cat with loose soil. He scattered a pile of dead leaves over the grave to disguise his handiwork.

He returned to the outhouse, put the spade away and went back inside the house.

Genevieve watched the boy kick off his boots at the door and hang his jacket on the banister post of the stairs.

'You okay, Jack?' she shouted, still busy with the girls and the cake.

'Yep,' he said, swinging upstairs.

She hadn't meant *are you okay*. She had meant: *gosh I've hardly seen you for three days*. But his answer had told her that he wasn't okay. She gazed at the spot on the stairs where he'd been, as if his imprint or a ghost of him was still there.

'Are you sure it is Aunt Tara?' Amber said.

'Why on earth do you say that?'

'Well I heard you saying to Daddy that she should be

nearly your age. And she's not. So it can't be her can it? She's not old enough, is she?'

'Don't be so silly. Of course it's your Aunt Tara.'

And Genevieve picked up the cake in its baking tin and put it in the oven, which had been warming.

10

'Come away, O human child: To the waters and the wild with a faery, hand in hand,

For the world's more full of weeping than you can understand.'

W. B. Yeats

He also had a great way of listening. It was as if everything I said to him was important. Counted for something. And it was like that with everything he said, too. Nothing lost, or loose. We rested there amid the bluebells with our heads leaning against the moss-covered stone and with the lark twittering in the infinite sky, and it was as if time didn't shift.

No one came or went. Usually on a lovely day such as that there would be several people strolling in the Outwoods but today none passed by. I didn't even think it strange.

'A lovely girl like you,' he said, 'you must surely have a boyfriend.'

'I do. But he doesn't make me happy.'

'Why's that?'

'He thinks more of his music than he does of me.'

'But I love music and music-makers. You could have a worse fellow than that, you know: one who makes music.'

'I don't know about that. I think they just like to have the girls look at them. That's what it's all about.'

'Is that such a bad thing?'

'It is for me. I want to be somebody's special person. I don't want to be with a man who looks at other women.'

'You'll have your work cut out for you to find a chap like that,' he said.

That sort of remark would normally make me prickle. He was mocking me for being naïve but he had a way of softening it with a smile and with these lovely wrinkles around his eyes, so that I didn't take the least offence. Plus his experience was an attractive thing. He was so relaxed in his manner with me. Richie was always so intense, so full-on. Richie, or any younger man for that matter, would be so focused on getting his hand down your pants that he would drain all the fun out of things. Whereas even though I knew this man had a fancy for me he was so enjoying the moment, and making me enjoy the moment, that he seemed to have no care or interest in what might happen next.

'What about you?' I said.

'What about me?' He knew exactly what I meant, and that I was trying to discover if he were married or had a girlfriend of his own somewhere. But he was teasing me.

'Are you spoken for?'

'Spoken for. What a lovely turn of phrase you do have.'

'It's what we say round here.'

'And I'm not from round here.'

'Where are you from then?'

85

'Well if I'm not from *round here* I must be from *round there*.'

I pulled up a straw of grass and threw it at him. 'Cagey, ain't ya?'

'I am.'

'So are you married?'

'Hahaha!'

'Is that a no?'

'Never found the right one. Been looking. I'll know her when I find her.'

'Do you believe in love at first sight, then?'

'No I don't. You have to have a bit of agitation first.'

'Agitation?'

And then he started banging on about physics, which I must say is not the most romantic thing to set a girl's heart racing. It's not a subject that much interested me before. I mean I did do some physics at school but it didn't exactly stir my blood. He started talking about molecules colliding and how only certain collisions have the energy to connect effectively and this is because only some of the molecules have enough energy at the moment of impact to break any existing bonds and form new ones. And then he looked at my face and he must have seen me with my mouth open because he laughed out loud and rolled around in the bluebells, laughing his head off and hugging his ribs as if they were cracking.

'I'm sorry I'm sorry I'm sorry,' he said and then he laughed some more.

I folded my hands in my lap and looked at the sky until his laughter burned itself out.

'Dear dear dear,' he said, recovering his breath. 'Oh dear! What I mean is this: you meet someone, you think

86

about them. You're already changing because of the way you think about them. You meet them again, you think about them some more, you're changing again. And on it goes. You are changing right now. Before my eyes.'

'I am, am I?'

'Yes. Through meeting me.'

'Think a lot of yourself, don't you?'

'Maybe I do. But you know it's true.'

And he looked into my eyes, and I looked back into his, and I knew what he was saying was true, and I thought *I want to know more about you*.

'It was called courtship once upon a time.' I thought he sounded a bit melancholy. 'Nowadays, sad to say, there's none of that. You're supposed to meet on the dance floor, rub up naked against each other for five minutes and then on to the next person. Now, that's just a knock; whereas what I'm after is an almighty collision.'

'So where is it you live?' I asked again.

He pointed vaguely to the west and told me he lived exactly on the county border, and I assumed he meant on the county border between Leicestershire and Derbyshire or Nottinghamshire. He said where he lived there was a stream and you could stand astride the stream with one foot in one land and one foot in the other. He told me he had a house by a pool and that it had no electricity or television because he didn't like those things. He said he preferred to live by the sun and the moon and by the light on the water.

'That's beautiful,' I said. 'Like poetry.'

'Perhaps one day you'll come and see my house, Tara?' he said, smiling.

'I never told you my name,' I said.

'Yes, you did.'

'No, I didn't.'

'Yes, you did.'

'No, I didn't.'

He got up and walked away from me. I thought he was perhaps offended but he'd gone to fetch his white horse. After a moment he led the animal back through the bluebells towards me. There he stood, holding the reins, just looking at me.

'Well, do you or don't you?' he said.

'Do I or don't I what?'

'Do you or don't you want to see the light on the water?'

I was able to answer in a beat. 'I do.'

I know I should have refused his offer. Then things would have been different. Then there would have been no trouble. But there are times in life when a door opens and you are offered a glimpse of the light on the water, and you know that if you don't take it, that door slams shut and maybe for ever. Maybe you fool yourself into thinking that you had a choice at all; maybe you were always going to say yes. Maybe refusing was no more a choice than is holding your breath. You were always going to breathe. You were always going to say yes.

'Then up you get,' he said.

There was no saddle on the horse. There was just a dusty red blanket. He blinked at me, and smiled, and I got up and went over to the horse and he dropped the reins and locked his fingers together for me to step into the palms of his hands. Then I was up on the horse's back, the big straw panniers swinging at either knee.

He led the horse through the bluebells and on to the

bridle track. There he walked me through the woods without a word. After a while the track became a bit wider and there he stopped the horse and leapt up behind me. He reached for the reins and I could smell his manly smell again, and the smell of the horse.

He reached a hand in front and placed it on my belly and I felt a terrible excitement.

'Is that comfortable for you?' he asked.

'Yes,' I said, 'that's comfortable.'

'Then we do go.'

II

'Witness asked for admittance, but Michael Cleary said they would not open the door. While they remained outside they stood at the window. They heard someone inside saying: "Take it, you bitch" or "witch." When the door was opened, witness went in and saw Dunne and three of the Kennedys holding Mrs. Cleary down on her bed by her hands and feet, and her husband was giving her herbs and milk in a spoon out of a saucepan. They forced her to take the herbs, and Cleary asked her: "Are you Bridget Boland, the wife of Michael Cleary, in the name of God?" She answered it once or twice, and her father asked a similar question. Michael Cleary [witness thought] then threw a certain liquid on his wife.'

Trial transcript, recorded in Folklore vol. 6 no 4 (1895)

It's like a door opens in my mind. A big, creaking black door. Behind the black door is the possibility that my friend Dave of the West Midlands CID is right.

Maybe I lost it. Maybe I did something to Tara after all. There's a horrible sound coming from behind the black door. It's a low and distant wailing, but it starts off like a feeling deep in the gut and on its way up it turns into a sound.

Maybe I did it. I was angry enough. And I've been

out of my head before. Me and Pete drank a bottle of vodka each one night, speed-drinking, like we were trying to kill ourselves with it. We lost several hours that night. When we woke up we'd both got neither our shoes nor our shirts and we had vicious scratches on our bodies and bits of hedgerow in our hair. Neither of us could remember a damned thing about what we did. So where did that time go? The things we did must still be there, in a corner of the mind somewhere, waiting to be remembered.

And I look up and I see that they are all leaning in towards me, the coppers and my solicitor, waiting for me to speak.

'Get it off your chest, Richie,' says my friend Dave in a fatherly whisper. He sounds more like a priest than a copper. Loving. I can only just hear his words over the wailing. 'I think you want to. I think you want to tell us. You'll feel better if you do. Get it off your chest.'

And the wailing from behind this big black door stops suddenly. And I realise that this is the door to prison. The door bangs shut.

'What?' I say. 'Get what off my chest?'

They all lean back. All four of them lean back, like it's all a dance show.

I turn to my so-called lawyer. 'What is he talking about? What does he want me to say?'

She bites her teeth together before turning to the policemen. 'I think you've had your answer,' she says. 'But could you put it straight. For the record.'

The sadness and compassion drains out of my friend Dave's face. He sighs and looks like he's really, really tired.

'Richie. Look at me please. Come on, boy. Look me in the eye. Did you kill Tara?'

'You have got to be joking.'

'Just answer the questions *yes* or *no*, Richie,' says my lawyer. 'It's better for you.'

'Right. The answer is no. Now can I go home?'

'Not yet,' says Dave. 'Not yet.'

'Am I under arrest?' I ask. I've got this idea they can't keep me unless they arrest me.'

'Is he?' asks my lawyer.

'Right-o,' says Dave. 'Richie Franklin, I am arresting you on suspicion of the murder of Tara Martin.' And the rest of it. Anything you say. Held against you. And all that.

'Ridiculous,' says my lawyer. It's the first time she's spoken up for me. 'You don't even have a body. You've no idea where that girl is. She might have gone off with another boyfriend for all you know.' She turns to me. 'Don't panic, Richie, they can't keep you here for long.'

'Well, we haven't finished,' says Dave standing up. 'Do you want a cup of tea Richie? I think we could all do with one.'

I say yes I wouldn't mind a cup of tea.

'And I desperately need a pee,' says my lawyer.

'Come and show me where the tea-room is,' Dave says to the uniformed copper taking notes.

The uniformed copper looks up, puzzled. Then something dawns across his features. He says, 'Oh, right. Sure.' And out they all trot, leaving me with the fat bastard. He of the squeaky voice

When we've got the interview room to ourselves, fat bastard sniffs and then he fingers his collar again. 'We know you done it.'

'No, you don't.'

'See, what you don't know, son, is that, never mind what you've seen on telly, *nearwy* all murders is done by the husband or the *boyfwiend*. It always comes back to that. Always. You should *wisten* to Dave. He's on your side.' Then he stands up. 'I ain't, though.'

And he walks slowly round the table.

I don't even see the punch coming. His huge knuckles connect with my chin, lips and nose all at the same time, and I think I black out because I'm on the floor when I come to my senses and I can hear him hissing at me: 'Get up you *wittle shite-hawk*, get on your feet.'

It's all very well him telling me to get up but there's a ringing in my ears and I can't balance.

'Don't think that *wying* on the floor is going to help you. That's just a taster for what's coming your way. You think I'm a cunt?'

'No.'

'You do. You think I'm a cunt.'

'No.'

'It ain't me who is the cunt, Wichie. See, what I am is the *stoowy-teller*. I know how all the *stoowies* work. 'Cos I've heard 'em many times over. You get so you know which ones to believe. Here's one I know. Are you sittin' comfortably? You get *Tawa* up the duff. She don't want to keep it. You do want to keep it. Sometimes it's the other way *wound*, but as often as not it's the bloke as wants to keep it, 'cos that way he can keep his girl, see, *Wichie*? So we has a peek into her *medical wecords*. And she's *got wid of it*. And she tells you. And you ain't happy.'

'Liar!' I shout. 'You're a liar.'

'She tells you she's *got wid of the baby* and you lose

the plot, eh, *Wichie*? You lose it. You completely lose it.'

'You're lying! She wouldn't do that!'

'It's in the *wecords*! Don't make out you didn't know!'

'You're a fucking liar!'

He smiles at me. 'No, son. I'm not a liar. I'm the truth. I'm the fucking *stoowy-teller* here. What am I?'

'Fuck off!'

Next thing he gathers me up by my lapels and stands me on my feet. My knees buckle, but he easily holds me up with one hand. He places this huge polished black boot on my toes and presses down. That in itself doesn't hurt; but then he punches me again, hard, and I go backwards and I feel the tendons in my ankle tearing with my foot still trapped under his boot.

This time I scream.

No one comes.

He gathers me up a second time and sits me back on my seat. I'm hyperventilating and the pain in my foot is almost making me black out again. 'Let's do that again. What am I?'

'Sto-reh,' I gasp.

'Can't hear you, *Wichie*.'

'Story-teller.'

He dusts me down and rearranges my collar and he chucks my cheek like I'm a crying five-year-old. 'Calm down, *Wichie*,' he says, in his reedy voice. 'Pull yourself together. Look at the state you're in.'

He sits back in his chair and smiles at me. After a few minutes the uniformed copper comes in with a tray of tea in plastic cups. He looks at me and then glances at the Hulk and there's just enough of a pause to make

94

me realise he's clocked what's happened. But he's not going to say a word, I know that. We all know that. He lays the tray on the interview table, sets one of the plastic cups of tea in front of me and reaches for his notepad.

I pick up the tea but my hands are trembling and it spills all over the place. I manage a sip. My lip is already fattening.

I hear laughter in the corridor. It's DC Dave and my lawyer sharing a joke as they come back to the interview room and it hasn't occurred to me before that she's actually been on their side all along. But then she takes one look at my condition and my rapidly swelling lip. 'For God's sake!' she says.

Then Dave leans across and grabs my chin. He looks – or pretends to look – angry. He moves my face to one side then the other. Then he turns to DC Hulk and bawls, 'Get out of my sight. Go on.'

The Hulk wipes a finger under his nose and goes out of the room without a word.

Dave shakes his head. 'Has he had a go?' he says to me.

'What does it look like?' I say. 'Perhaps I slipped while I was trying to sit in my chair.'

My lawyer snaps. 'That's enough.' DC Dave may be play-acting, but she isn't. Her eyeballs are popping and I can see tiny veins throbbing at her temple. 'Charge him or let him go.'

'I'm not going to charge you, Richie. I'm sorry that happened. He's Old School, Richie. That's how they used to do it. Look, boy, just give me something. Anything. Any tiny detail that will help me find her. You know where she is, Richie. Any tiny detail. Her mum and dad, Richie, they are going out of their mind. It would be better for them if they could find out what happened. You can see that, can't you? I mean, they are very fond of you Richie. They've been kind to you. Like a second mum and dad, right? You owe it to them. You can see that?'

'I don't know anything!'

'Just one detail, Richie. Help yourself. I beg you.'

And I start crying. I wish I could say that I didn't but I'm blubbing like a baby. It's not being smacked around, that's not it. Well it might have something to do with that, but mostly it's the thought of what might have happened to Tara.

'Is it true?' I manage to get out. 'Did Tara get rid of the baby?'

Dave nods at me, yes. He closes in across the table. My head is bent forward and he has a gentle but leathery hand on my neck. 'It's all right. Let it go, Richie. Let it all go. That's right. That's right. That's the way. It's all going to be all right. That's the way. Richie, did you hurt Tara?'

'Yes,' I sob, 'yes, yes, yes.'

'This is duress,' says my lawyer.

Dave nods. 'Richie, there's a stone. In the woods. A big stone and most of it is covered in orange lichen and moss. You know that stone, don't you?'

'Yes. Yes.'

'Around the stone we could see that all the ferns and the bluebells had been bashed down as if two people had been lying down there together.'

I sob out loud. There's a pain deep inside me.

'Is that where it happened, Richie? Is that where you did it?'

'Yes.'

He takes a deep breath, as if his work is done. He nods gently. 'How did you do it, Richie?'

I look up at him. 'Normal way.'

'What's the normal way, Richie?'

He's gazing deep into my eyes. I can't think why he wants to know that. 'Just ... normal ...' I say.

'You're going to have to tell me what's normal.'

I look at my lawyer. She's gazing down at me, her arms folded tight around her. Her brow is furrowed. 'How many ways are there?' I ask her.

She says, 'He's talking about *sex*, for goodness sake!'

DC Dave blinks and looks disappointed in me, like I've just let him down. 'So you had sex there?'

'Yes.'

'And after you had sex, that's when you did it?'

'What?' I turn to look at my lawyer. 'Did what?'

I look back at DC Dave and he is so focussed on me he has the expression of a man trying to pick a lock with a hairpin.

'Richie, there's the stone in the bluebell wood. And on that stone we found a ring.' He holds up something shiny for me to see. It's the ring I'd given Tara.

'Where did you get that?'

'It was on the stone. It had been placed there. Did you put it there after you'd done it?'

I'm like a drunk suddenly feeling sober after a gallon of coffee. 'Wait,' I says, 'wait. When I says to you I did it I mean that's where we first had sex. Nothing else. By that stone. A year ago. I haven't been there recently!' With a sense of panic I turn to my lawyer. 'Tell him that's what I meant!'

'Enough!' says my lawyer. 'That's enough. Charge

the lad or let him go. You can see he's under duress.'

Dave raises his eyebrows. 'You were so close, Richie. So close.'

'Can he go?' says my lawyer.

Dave indicates that the way to the door is clear. Julia Langley gathers her pen and notes from the desk and stands up. 'Come along, Richie.' I follow her. Dave doesn't even look at me. He just looks at the wall as if he's very tired. Very tired and very sad.

Outside in the corridor the fat fuck stands leering at me. The corridor is narrow so we have to squeeze by his bulky figure. 'See you *vewy* soon, *Wichie*,' he says in that high-pitched warble. 'See you *vewy* soon.'

12

'Fairy tales are about money, marriage and men. They are maps and manuals that are passed down from mothers and grandmothers to help them to survive.'

Marina Warner

That was the happiest time of my life. I sat on that pretty white horse, feeling his presence behind me, the breath of him on my neck and I felt a trickle inside me, like everything that had happened to me in the past was dissolving. I hadn't the slightest idea where he was taking me. I couldn't care less. I trusted him. I knew that if I was wrong, and that if he might harm me in any way, then I was no judge of character. I believe that I saw all the way through him to his every intention towards me, and I was content with what I saw.

We soon turned out of the bluebell woods and across a narrow road on to a bridle path giving way into a field. The field was lined with trees gone wild, drunk with the mayflower. There was a glistening stream where the horse stopped to drink and after that the horse moved on at a slow pace for what seemed like hours before we even spoke a single word to each other. Yet the sun barely moved in the sky. I felt dreamy, lazy, sleepy and yet safe on the back of the horse, with his strong, sun-tanned arm around me to balance me and my knees in the panniers.

'What's in these baskets?' I asked in a kind of slumber.

'Blossoms,' he said.

'Why do you want those?'

'We eat it.'

I gave a little laugh at his joke. Then I closed my eyes and gave in to the gentle swaying gait of the horse.

After a while, and just to remind myself that I could still speak, I murmured to him, 'How long before we get there?'

'We pass through with the twilight,' he said. 'Then we're there.'

I think of that often now, but never even questioned it at the time, so content was I. We'd been going for a while and I remembered that he knew my name but I didn't know his. 'Come on, tell me.'

'Ah names,' he said. 'Now where I come from there are people who say that once you can name a thing, you own it.'

'What a silly idea.'

'Is it silly? If you can name a thing you can put it in a box and close the lid on it. This box or that box. If you can't name it, it runs free. Isn't that true?'

'How did you know my name is Tara?'

'Well that was very strange. I saw you sitting by that golden rock in the bluebell woods and the name just popped into my head from nowhere. A little voice said, *Tara* and *a child of the sky*. What do you think of that?'

I tried to think of his name, to see if anything would pop into my head. I emptied my mind and waited for a whisper. I believed it would be given to me. But nothing came.

'And don't waste your time trying to do the same trick,' he laughed. 'Because I'm guarding it.'

'So why won't you just tell me your name?'

He became serious. 'I can give you a name. I could make up any name, and you wouldn't know the difference. But where I'm from, see, we all have a secret name. It's known only to the clan, sort of thing.'

'Clan?'

'Clan. Tribe. That's just a way of speaking. But anyway, this name, by keeping it a secret to the tribe, has power. And if you have it, they say – though I'm not sure I agree with them – well, it gives you power over that person.'

'This is mad. I'm riding away on a horse with a man who won't even tell me his damn name.'

'Oh, I am going to tell you. I am, for sure. But first I want you to hang on, because we're going to canter a bit now; otherwise we'll miss the crossing at twilight.'

I assumed he meant that we would be crossing a river, maybe the River Soar or the Trent into Derbyshire or Nottinghamshire. I had no idea where we were but if we were crossing either other than by bridge then it was going to be an exciting splash. I'd never wet-crossed either of the wide rivers on a horse, and I meant to ask him. But I didn't have a moment to put the question, because the horse flicked forward its ears and then went straight from walk to canter, and we were away, hard-riding across a field of emerald green.

Oh it was thrilling!

He was such a good horseman. I'd had riding lessons since I was a little girl, and for some years the use of a pony in return for leading the week-end treks. I could ride, and ride well, but with a saddle and stirrups; yet he was attuned to his horse in a single current that ran through the animal, through him, and through me too.

We took the field at a canter and then galloped up the incline of a hill. The wind streamed my hair behind me and the white mane of the horse flashed white gold in the rays of the dying sun. We jumped a fence, we took a stream, we leapt over a fallen log. The hooves pounding on the dry grass quickened my heart and I thought *this is terrible this is terrible I'm falling in love with this man and I don't know where I'm going.*

The horse started to slow as it reached the top of the hill, and then he pulled her up so that she went into an easy trot for the last few yards. The animal was breathing fiercely, for it had been a good long gallop. The dusk was settling around our shoulders now and the sky had gone an eerie blue black. When we got to the top of the hill we could see the last red streaks of the sun like the scrap of something torn on the mountains in the west, mountains I didn't recognise. We crested the hill and the horse picked its way through stones down towards a dark woods. Not like the bluebell woods we had left, but much more dense and shadowed, though the horse and her master both seemed so very sure of the path that I never questioned either for a moment.

'When do we reach the crossing?' I asked at last.

'The crossing? Oh we've done that.'

'We did? When? When did we do the crossing?'

'Back there a-ways.'

I didn't recall any crossing. I asked him about it again.

'Good God, woman, you do ask a lot of questions!'

It was only when we were coming out of the woods, with the sun completely gone and the moon coming up that I realised I wasn't going to be home that night. It's not that I wanted to turn around; but I suddenly felt uneasy about Mum and Dad and how they would be worried about me. I needed to get a message to them. I thought as soon as we pass a house in this remote place I'll knock on the door and give them the number and ask if they would please phone and tell them that I'm fine.

The moon went behind some clouds and we emerged from the wood to find not houses but a shadowy, sandy beach. The quartz in the sand twinkled in the half-light with an electrical intensity. I was astonished. I couldn't believe we had come so far east or west, but when I made some comment he said no it wasn't the sea, but a lake. I peered across the water trying to discern the farther side. In the morning, he said, in the morning I would be able to see all around the lake. And it was true: I could see tiny lights burning here and there out on the water, which I took to be the reflections of dwellings on the far side of the lake.

The water was deep calm, like a layer of oil, but with a sweet, honest odour of mud and weed. We trailed along the edge of the lake for perhaps half a mile and soon we came to a large, ramshackle house all in darkness.

'Look, I share this place with others, but there shouldn't be anyone here just now.'

The horse came to a stop. He jumped off and then he helped me down. Everything he did for me was like a little display of chivalry. At first I thought it was a performance, to charm the pants off me, but it was no act; it was his way. He smiled at me briefly and then led the mare into a small stable at the side of the house.

I followed. Once inside he whisked the blanket off the horse and threw it over a bar. Then he picked up a dandy-brush.

'Let me,' I said, taking the brush from him, and I began to brush down the horse.

He watched me carefully. 'You know about horses.'

'Yes.'

'A woman who knows about horses. Can I marry you?'

I laughed but when I looked back he wasn't smiling. I finished brushing and then I ran my hand down the mare's leg, squeezing the fetlock a little, and the animal easily showed me her hoof. 'But she's not shod,' I said.

'I don't ride on the road,' he said dismissively. 'And those farriers that you see around, well, they're like thieves. Come on, let's go inside.'

Well, it was a bit of a tip.

There was no electricity. 'Wouldn't have it in the house. Makes people grow crackers,' he said.

Sometimes I didn't know whether or not he was joking. 'It might make you crackers or it might not,' I countered, 'but at least you can see your way.'

'We have light.'

An old-fashioned brass oil lamp stood on the kitchen table. He lit the wick and rolled a brass wheel to bring up the flame, then lit a second which he took through to the living room; at least I thought it was a living room, but there were a couple of mattresses with coverlets dumped alongside the walls and with long thin pillows so they could be used as beds. The walls were covered with paintings and wood-carvings and musical instruments: unusual musical instruments, as if they'd been collected from exotic countries. I instantly thought about Richie, but just as quickly I let go of the thought.

But the cobwebs! Even in the shadows I could see the cobwebs stretching between some of the wall-mounted paintings and instruments. Anyway, I thought, there hasn't been a woman's hand turned here for a good while.

I looked round for the telephone. I had a cock and bull story in my head that I was going to tell Mum and Dad, about running into an old girlfriend whose parents had a caravan by the sea. I was going to tell them we'd gone there on the spur of the moment. I could carry it off, I was certain.

'What are you looking for?'

'Where's your phone?'

'Phone?'

'I've got to call my parents. They'll worry about me if I don't.'

'There is no phone.'

My heart stuttered. 'No phone! Who the hell doesn't have a phone?'

'I'm sorry. We rejected all that sort of stuff.'

'But isn't there one in the village? There has to be a phone!'

'Village? We're nowhere near a village. Look, is it important?'

'Of course! I have to let them know I'm fine.'

'Tara, how old are you, darling?'

'Fifteen, nearly sixteen.'

His face crashed. 'Fifteen! Fifteen! Yes, now I see the problem. Now I see it. Well. Oh dear, oh dear.' Suddenly this man who looked so vital and youthful in the bluebell wood looked fatigued and care-worn.

'I shouldn't have brought you here. It was a mistake. I was spirited away.'

Spirited away. Did he mean by me? But I was thinking practically. 'Isn't there a phone in one of the other houses? What about those across the lake.'

'No. None of them. I told you we reject all that.'

'But how do you pass messages? Across distances, I mean.'

'Letters. Word-of-mouth.'

'Oh God!'

'I'm going to have to take you back, aren't I?' he said sadly.

I thought about it. Riding back through the dark – if that were possible – and turning up at maybe four o'clock in the morning; or staying over and returning to face the music in the daylight. Either way it was going to be rough when I got home. 'Can you ride in the dark?' I asked.

'That's possible. Why do you ask?'

'Because maybe we should go back at once.'

'At once,' he cried. 'We can't go at once. We can't make the crossing tonight!'

'Well, when can we?'

He sighed and blinked at me as if he was only now seeing me for the first time. He shook his head sadly, then grabbed the oil lamp, carrying it across to a cupboard. The cupboard was crammed with old books and rolled charts, antique charts of the kind you might expect to find in the captain's cabin aboard a great sailing ship. He took one of these down and brought it to the table. I could see it was made not of paper but of a kind of beautiful creamy vellum. He unrolled it and placed the oil lamp on one side to hold it down. Securing the other end with his hand, he pored over the map.

All I could see were beautiful hand-drawn pictures of the phases of the moon. There were also exquisite half-tinted sketches at each corner of the chart, cherubic depictions of the four winds, their cheeks puffed, blowing gales. The chart itself looked complicated, with busy numerical columns inked in black. He ran his finger across a line of numbers. 'Here,' said. 'That's the earliest time we will be able to make the crossing.'

'When is that?' I asked.

'Six months' time,' he said.

So I stayed there with him until the six months were up. And at the first opportunity I came back. That was just before Christmas. And I found that for the rest of you twenty years had gone by.

13

'It was during the eighteenth century that William Shakespeare was reconceived as a child-like genius, an idiot savant, partly because he broke the rules of Tragedy, but also because he wrote his plays prior to any cultural consensus that informative obedience to ascertainable reality ultimately told us more about our human experience of the world we inhabited than any myth or fairy tale or fabulation could possibly do.'

John Clute

From the dining room Amber could see her father's battered pickup truck turning into the front yard. 'Dad's back,' she called.

'Has he got Tara with him?' Genevieve wanted to know.

'No. Wait. He looks pretty cross.'

'Really?' Genevieve hurried through to the dining room and peered out of the window. She'd spent half the day cooking and baking. Tara had been invited to have tea with them. It was supposed to have been a family evening where everyone could get to know Tara without Dell and Mary refereeing, commenting on or gate-keeping every remark and every response to every remark. Meanwhile the expression on Peter's face was as easy to read as the headline on a tabloid newspaper. 'Oh.'

She opened the door for him. He raised an eyebrow at her and squeezed into the hall.

'Did you see Aunt Tara?' said Amber.

'You bet I did.' Peter shucked off his coat. Then he kicked off his shoes and tried to embed them in the overflowing shoe-basket, but they fell to the floor. He sighed, tried again, failed.

'I like Aunty Tara,' Josie said, 'even if she does smell funny.'

'Good,' said Peter. 'And it's patchouli oil. Now, could you kids all go into the lounge while I have a chat with Mummy?'

'I want to hear,' said Josie.

'No you don't. It's boring.'

'No it isn't,' she shouted back. 'It's interesting. Isn't it, Amber? Isn't it interesting?'

'Get!'

Peter didn't say *get* very often, so when he did the kids knew it was time to *get*. He went into the kitchen and reached down a bottle of cognac from the cupboard, spinning the cap. He poured himself a careful measure. 'Want one?'

'No,' said Genevieve, closing the kitchen door and leaning her back against it. 'Where is she?'

'I whipped her back to Mum and Dad's.'

'Whipped her?'

Peter sat at the kitchen table and took a slug of his cognac. Then he put down his glass. 'Fuck-and-a-half.'

'Like that, eh?'

'I dragged her back to Mum and Dad's and I told Dad to ask her to repeat the same story she'd told me. Then I told Dad that if he wanted to strangle her, I'd cheerfully dig the shallow grave.'

'Whoooo!'

'You bet it's fucking *whooo*.'

Genevieve opened the door to check no one was listening on the other side. Then she closed the door again and joined Peter at the table. 'It was always going to be *whooo*, wasn't it?'

'Not this much *whooo*.'

Genevieve didn't ask him to expand. She propped an elbow on the table and rested her chin in her hand, patiently waiting until he was ready to tell her.

'The fairies took her.'

She blinked. It was a long blink. He nodded.

'The fairies, then.'

'Well, she took a couple of hours to tell me but it was as simple as that in the end.'

'And you said?'

'I said: "Oh, if that's all it was, don't worry, you're back now, safe and sound and this evening we're having lasagne." That's what I said.'

'I think I will have a drink. To celebrate the existence of the little people.'

'Oh, they are not little.'

'Really?'

'No. And they don't have wings. And you can mistake them for ordinary people. Apparently.'

'Do you know, I'm seriously worried about the gene pool I married into. How did you leave things?'

'At a certain point in the story I marched her back to the car, bundled her in and drove back to Mum and Dad's place. All the way in silence. That was some journey.'

The door burst open and Josie ran in. She had a wet finger in her mouth. 'I've got a wobbly tooth!' she shouted, fingering a little canine near the front of her mouth.

'Come here and let me see,' Genevieve said. 'When it comes out we'll put it under the pillow.'

'Oh yes,' Peter said. 'We'll tell your Aunt Tara to alert her friends.'

Josie put her mouth very close to Peter's face and wobbled her tooth. He poured himself another glass of cognac and ran a hand through his daughter's hair.

Richie answered the door to Peter in a long threadbare dressing gown. 'Second visit in a couple o' days. The neighbours will be talking.'

There was a bottle of milk on the doorstep. Peter picked it up and brought it inside. Richie closed the door after him.

'You look like shit,' Peter said. 'Make some coffee will you?'

'You do it. I don't feel too good.'

Richie slumped on his sofa and sparked up a cigarette. Peter put the milk in the fridge and noticed it was empty except for a jar of jam and another half-empty milk bottle. He filled the kettle, lit the gas stove and made a quick survey of the state of the kitchen. It all reminded him of the houses he used to share with other young men when he was at university. Richie didn't seem to have moved on in all that time.

'Sugar?'

'Lots,' Richie said. 'Three at least.'

Peter waited until the kettle boiled. Out of the corner of his eye he saw something dart under the fridge. He made two cups of instant coffee and winced at each spoonful of Richie's sugar. Then he took it through to the living room, where Richie sprawled displaying the cracked toenails of his bare feet by resting them on the arm of the leather sofa.

'Been on the piss?'

'No.'

'Really? You look like you've got a bad hangover.' He moved a guitar aside so he could lower himself into an armchair.

'I've been getting these terrible headaches. Can't sleep a wink.'

'Seen the quack?'

'No. It's only just come on these past couple of weeks.' He slurped the hot coffee and pulled a face.

'You're going to want to see Tara at some point. And even if you don't want to see her, she's threatening to come and see you. I thought I'd warn you about the state she's in. She's like a bag lady. I mean her head is all over the place.'

'It always was.'

'Not like this.' Peter gave him the story in short-hand. He suggested that Richie get the details from Tara herself.

Richie held his cigarette to his lips, thinking about it. 'Sort of runs in the family, then?'

'What?'

'Puck.'

Peter looked sheepish and scratched his head. Then he sat upright with a hand on each knee.

When the boys had their band they had a bass player called Gavin. He was a good bass player. At least he could keep constant time with Peter, which was more than any of the other seven bass players who passed through their band. The band was given an insignificant spot at Glastonbury festival on one of the minor stages at an unearthly hour; but at the time if felt like they had been admitted into the court of the king. While they were down in Glastonbury and after they had played their set and while they were all in a mood of soaring spirits, Gavin introduced a mysterious and attractive woman of indeterminate race into the company. The woman, who said her name was Layla, put an unidentified pill in Peter's mouth. With Peter holding his mouth open in readiness and proffering his tongue before washing the pill down with a swig of beer, he can hardly be said to have been tricked.

Four hours later Peter announced that he had changed his name to Puck and that he was off to Avalon. He very much wanted Layla, who had so kindly donated the pill, to join him on his quest. Gavin, who had his own designs on Layla, objected. Peter stood up and roared at Gavin. That is not to say he shouted. He *roared*, uncannily like a lion, in a roar that actually seemed to make the neighbouring tents tremble. Festival goers rushed out of their tents to look, with stoned eyes, upon whoever or whatever was making the noise, so Peter did it again. Gavin wisely retreated. Layla was so impressed by Peter's leonine and earth-trembling roar that she stood up and announced she was on the bus for Avalon, newly ticketed.

Peter and Layla walked off together hand in hand. It was a week before Peter turned up back in Anstey, flatly refusing to discuss where he'd been.

'We lost a good bass player,' Richie said, 'as I remember.'

'That was different,' Peter said. 'And she's not as coherent as I was.'

Richie cackled. A cancerous, throaty cackle. 'How does she look?'

'You know, in a certain light she doesn't look any different. And I mean no different at all. Then when you look at her in another light she looks kind of … cobwebby. Her brain is full of cobwebs, that's the thing. Hey, are you okay?'

Richie was wincing. 'I think this coffee is making my headaches worse.'

Peter told Richie that Tara, not knowing Richie was still at his parents' old house, had asked him for Richie's address but that he'd withheld it. He'd wanted to check that Richie was prepared to see her. Though he felt it was only a matter of time before she found out, and that if she was anything like the Tara of old nothing would have stopped her coming to say her piece.

They talked for a while about Richie's music. His chequered career. He dug out a CD. Peter could tell from the printed paper inside the jewel-case that it was pretty much a home-made project, and he wondered where all that talent had burned away. Though Peter had played too, he always knew he never had the flair that would lift him up into the stratosphere. Richie had it. It just never happened for him. Peter had maintained a hobby interest, but sometimes a whole year might pass without him picking up his drumsticks. Zoe strummed her guitar more often than he rattled his skins. His playing belonged to his teenage years; he had put all his ambitions away, as if they were a childish thing

But Richie was different. Back then, Richie was burning with it. Angry, headstrong, in-your-face like a lot of people, but all that rage resolved in clean composition and strong, simple lyrics. It should have worked out for him; he should have made it. But something happened that just deflected him a single degree or so from the trajectory or flight that nature had intended. His was a talent that had burned in the darkness and had gone out in the darkness.

Session work for the studios was good for several years, but that had dried up when Richie had failed to make a couple of bookings. It was okay for millionaire pop-stars to be belligerent arseholes and to fall over drunk, but for working musicians – real musicians – rock 'n' roll had very little to do with it. You put in the hours and you played for pay, and you had to count your coin at the end of the work like any office or factory jack. Richie admitted he was broke but, he pointed out, he was still writing songs after twenty years, and that counted for something.

'I am so fucking sorry we doubted you Richie. So sorry.'

Richie waved a hand through the air, but there was a tremble in its flight. 'It's an old hurt. I was angry, I admit.'

'It's unforgivable. What we did.'

'Look, anyone at that time would have suspected me. It was the only sensible explanation. There was even a time back then, you know, when the police were questioning me, when I had to ask myself if I really had killed her. They had me pretty close to a confession, you know. Did you know that?'

Peter just nodded. He was feeling deeply ashamed. His lack of faith had lost him a great friend in life and he knew this was a noisy, angry clock that could neither be put back nor muted.

'I will see Tara at some point,' Richie said. 'I will.

And there's another thing maybe you can help me with. I'd like to see your mum and dad. Just to look them in the eye, Pete. Not to say anything, not to be saying cruel words. I'm past that. But just to look them in the eye as to say: see, I told you I was telling the truth.'

'We abandoned you,' Peter said. 'We just abandoned you.'

'It was hard, I don't mind saying. Your mum and dad were closer to me and kinder to me than my own parents ever were. You know that. It was hard.'

'I'll see if I can do it. There will be a lot of tears.'

'I'm not afraid of tears,' Richie said. 'Not any more I'm not.'

Peter got up to go. 'You should see the quack about those headaches,' he said.

Richie held up his hand for a high-five. Peter grabbed it and gripped. He went to the door to let himself out. 'By the way,' he said, 'you've got mice in the kitchen.'

Peter got into his car and he drove for about a mile. Then he stopped the car in a leafy lay-by, switched off the engine and wept.

'Cleary said, "Throw it on her." Mary Kennedy, an old woman, mother of Mrs. Burke, brought the liquid. The liquid was dashed over Bridget Cleary several times. Her father, Patrick Boland, was present. William Ahearne, described as a delicate youth of sixteen, was holding a candle. Bridget Cleary was struggling, crying out, "Leave me alone." Simpson then saw her husband give her some liquid with a spoon; she was held down by force by the men for ten minutes afterwards, and one of the men kept his hand on her mouth. The men at each side of the bed kept her body swinging about the whole time, and shouting, "Away with you! Come back, Bridget Boland, in the name of God!". She screamed horribly.

Summary of trial transcript, (1895)

After being questioned by the police that day, when Richie got out of the police station he went not to his own home but to the Martins' household. There Mary answered the door.

'They think it's me,' Richie said, trembling on the threshold. 'The police think it's me.'

'What have you done to your face?' Mary said.

Dell came up behind her. 'Come inside, Richie, come inside.'

He limped over the threshold. His swollen ankle was hurting badly. They sat him down at the kitchen table and they made him drink tea; though his lip had swollen so fat by now he had trouble drinking it without dribbling the tea down his chin.

'Did they give you a pasting, Richie?' Dell said.

'What does it look like?' Mary said. 'They had no right to do that. No right.'

Dell wanted to know how things were left with the police, and Richie said that he thought he was still a suspect. Richie asked Dell if he would talk to the police, explain that they were making a mistake, and Dell said he would. It was absurd, he said. Absurd. When Richie asked where Peter was they said he was up at the Outwoods. The official searches had stopped but he wasn't prepared to give up on finding something.

'I should go up there and join him.'

Dell looked at Mary. 'Richie,' Dell said, furrowing his brow,' is there anything that you haven't told us? Anything at all. Any tiny thing that would give us a clue as to where she might be. Or a clue as to her state of mind.'

Richie shook his head.

There was of course one thing he could have said. He assumed that soon enough the police would tell the Martins that Tara had been pregnant and that she had aborted the foetus at a clinic. They would have to. He was on the edge of blurting it out himself, but he was prevented by a strong sense of self-preservation.

His reasons for not doing so were only partly selfish. He knew that the Martins would feel betrayed and that he would feel the lash of Dell's fury and Mary's contempt. But he felt it wasn't the right time to tell them.

Tara's disappearance had so diminished them. They had been transformed overnight from confident, poised parents in their prime to frail, powerless, elderly and lost individuals. The once noble architecture of their family lay in rubble. Worse than that, a hoar frost, it seemed to Richie, had settled on their shoulders.

They talked, and they combed every fine detail with him. He admitted that he and Tara had had a dispute, but when pressed he said that it was all about whether they were going out for the evening or staying in. Richie had wanted to go out; Tara had wanted to stay in.

It was a shocking lie, given the real reasons for the argument; but it was so simple and prosaic that it seemed to convince Tara's parents.

After a while he announced that he was going to drive back up to the Outwoods to help Peter with the search. He knew he should tell Peter about the pregnancy; knew he should break it to at least one member of the family before the police did.

'Right,' said Mary. 'And I'm going up to church. It's been a long time since I've been on my knees and the only thing I can think of doing right now is praying. Are you coming with me, Dell?'

'No, Mary. No.'

So Richie had left them divided about their appeal for divine help and he had gone home. It was his intention to go up to the Outwoods, to find Peter, to keep him company in the fruitless task of searching under scrub and checking out hollows and peering behind fallen logs: everything the organised police search had already done without result.

But he didn't. When he got home his father was

out. Probably up at the Coach and Horses soaking up glasses of foaming amber ale with his cronies. Richie inspected his fat lip in the mirror. There was still dried blood under his nose and his teeth were sore from where a huge set of knuckles had mashed his lip against his mouth. He took a shower, trying to scrub a way an impression of dirt picked up from the police station. He stood under the shower for a long time, leaning his bruised cheek against the cold of the ceramic tiles while the hot running water sluiced against his back.

He lost an hour or so that way.

He dressed again, went downstairs and slumped on to the sofa in a listless agony, the torn tendons in his foot pulsing with pain. There he fell into a fitful slumber, and when he woke up again it was way too late to entertain any idea of going back up to the Outwoods.

He watched television for a while, then went to bed, but lay awake thinking about Tara. He had to concede there was a pretty good chance that she was dead. He didn't think – like the police – that she was up there in the woods, buried under earth and leaves, her corpse already decomposing. The chances were that she had been dragged or persuaded into a car, driven off somewhere. That would have meant that she would have been raped; and if she had been raped then she would have either been dumped or killed, and if she'd been dumped they would have heard from her by now. The unthinkable alternative was that someone was keeping her as a prisoner.

The most hideous thing about it all was the inability to do anything. He knew he could wander through the woods like Peter, turning over every leaf and acorn. But his time would have been better spent asking people about cars seen in the area at the time of Tara's disappearance. He was furious with the police that they'd been questioning him when they might have been doing exactly that. He would tell them in the morning: he would march into the police station and tell them how to do their job.

Sometime after midnight he was woken by the sound of someone stumbling into the house through the front door. It was his father. He heard his father shout up the stairs. 'Richie! Richie!' But Richie chose not to answer. Then the house went quiet. When his father came swaying home from the pub he would just as likely fall asleep on the sofa as put himself to bed.

In the morning Richie got out of bed late. His dad had shuffled off to work and he had the house to himself. He sat around in his T-shirt and shorts, brain-dead. There was a quarter-ounce cache of cannabis belonging to him and Peter. He'd stashed it in a twist of silver foil hidden between the mattress and the base of his bed. Richie was always custodian of the dope because there was no chance of his father stumbling across it; whereas Mary was always cleaning and tidying Peter's room as an efficient form of inspection. She'd once found a little stash of LSD microdots and wanted to know what they were. Peter told her they were breath-fresheners. She wanted to know why he needed breath-fresheners. Peter had said to keep his breath fresh. Mary said, rather indignantly, that it was to be hoped he wasn't in the habit of kissing random girls. Peter had said no, he wasn't.

Richie pasted cigarette papers together and heated the cannabis before crumbling it on to a slim stick of tobacco. The he lit up, and grabbed his Gibson. It was a handsome guitar with a deep tone and glittering strings, something he had managed to buy only through great sacrifice. He strummed a few chords, trying to put into words his anguish about Tara, but it was all too raw, too immediate. At least the dope diminished the pain of his ankle. He stuck the roach-end of the burning joint between the strings at the head of his guitar, copying some famous musician he'd seen at a concert.

The morning rolled away on a cloud. He put together another joint. He was strumming a chord when he happened to look up to see a face at the window. The face glared in at him. It made him shiver. It should have been a friendly face.

It was Peter glowering at Richie through the glass.

Richie took the joint out of his guitar-head, got up and limped to the door.

Peter brushed past him and came inside.

When Richie followed him back into the lounge he said, 'Good morning to you, too.'

'Been smoking our dope?' Peter said.

Richie held out the joint in his hand. 'Want some?'

'Not in the mood. My sister's been abducted or killed and I'm not really in the mood to skin up and smoke dope, Richie.'

'Right.' Richie held the smoking joint in his hand, not knowing if the correct thing to do in the light of that remark was to put it out or to leave it to burn away to nothing. He took a drag and then left it smoking in an ashtray. 'You going to sit down?'

Peter relaxed. He sat down and picked up Richie's Gibson, thumbing the strings very lightly.

'I'm not stopping.'

'Okay.'

'Mum and Dad said you'd promised to come up to the Outwoods yesterday. Promised to come and help me keep on looking.'

'I was going to, Pete. I didn't make it.'

Pete was gripping the neck of the guitar very tightly. 'They said you'd promised.'

'I was planning to come.'

'There's only me up there now, Richie. Only me. No more police. No more volunteers. No you. Only me.'

'The police stamped on my foot. Seriously. It's hard for me to get around. I had to—'

'Gets lonely up there, Richie. On your own. Only the wind blowing. Lonely and cold.'

'I should have come. I can hardly move, mate.'

'But you're blowing dope and strumming the guitar.'

'What is it? You want to say something to me? You just like the fuzz, are you? Think I did it?'

'I don't know what to think.'

'Thanks a fuckin' bunch, mate. My best pal. Here, why don't you try to beat a confession out of me, just like they did yesterday. Want to stamp on my other foot?'

'Didn't get a confession though, did they?'

'Why would they?'

'They've told us. Tara was pregnant. You'd got Tara pregnant.'

Richie put his head in his hands. 'Bastards,' he said softly.

'She had an abortion. Know what she did? There was a school trip she was supposed to go on. Instead of going on the school trip she went to a clinic. The police found it all out.'

'I didn't even know that. I didn't know she'd done that.'

'Why didn't you tell us, Richie?'

'Not your business, was it? Even so, I was going to tell you. Honestly I was. I was waiting for the right time.'

'Makes all the difference. Thing like that. You could have told us. Now on top of one terrible shock, my mum has had another kick in the teeth.'

'They haven't told her, have they?'

Peter nodded grimly.

'I have to go round to talk to them.'

Gently thumbing another chord on the guitar, Peter said, 'No. You'd better stay away. They don't want to see you now.'

'You don't think I hurt Tara, do you? Tell me you don't think that.'

'Doesn't look good, does it? You got her pregnant. She had an abortion. You had an argument. You say you left her up there in the Outwoods. Even if you didn't hurt her, you are responsible for what's happened, aren't you?'

'I can't deny that.'

'You don't leave a girl on her own in the Outwoods.'

'She ran away from me, Peter! Ran away! And she didn't go missing that day anyway. You're not making sense!'

'Then you go and keep this thing a secret. Why would you do that, Richie? That's what the police were asking me. Why would he go and do that? Then I started thinking about the afternoon I spent up there searching on my own, after you'd promised my folks that you would come and join me. I thought about why you would stay away.'

'Shit, you really do think I did it! Why don't you just come out and say it?'

'Then I come here this morning. And what do I find? You're smoking a nice sweet little joint, playing the guitar. Chilling out. All relaxed. Doesn't look good, Richie.'

'Peter.'

Peter stood up. 'I'm going now,' he said. 'I'm going back up to the Outwoods.' He held the Gibson by the neck and offered it back to Richie.

But when Richie reached out for it, Peter took the neck of the Gibson with both hands and swung it against the wall. It cracked and splintered. Peter swung it again, this time dangerously near Richie's head, and smashed it a second time against the wall. Richie shrank back into his seat as Peter smashed the guitar over and over against the wall, until all he was holding was the neck of the thing and the broken strings.

'You're to blame, Richie! Whatever happened, you're to blame!' He bunched his fist in Richie's face. 'I should break your teeth like I broke that guitar! I could! I could break your fucking strings!'

Peter left Richie cowering and hurried outside. He must have left the front door open, because moments later, while Richie was staring down at the broken fragments of his treasured Gibson, another figure appeared. It was the fat DC who had beaten him at the police station.

The DC surveyed the smashed guitar. 'Gonna give us a *wittle* song wi' that, *Wichie*?' he squeaked in his high-pitched voice. 'Come along son, you're wanted back down at the station. Hang on a minute: what's that I can smell? I do believe you've been on the potty, *Wichie*.'

15

'These Siths or Fairies they call Sleagh Maith or the Good People ... are said to be of middle nature between Man and Angel, as were Daemons thought to be of old; of intelligent fluidous Spirits, and light changeable bodies (lyke those called Astral) somewhat of the nature of a condensed cloud, and best seen in twilight. These bodies be so pliable through the subtlety of Spirits that agitate them, that they can make them appear or disappear at pleasure.'

Reverend Robert Kirk, 1691

'It's to be hoped you've calmed down a bit.' This was Mary, answering the door to Peter. Mary frequently prefaced her wishes with *it's to be hoped*. It's to be hoped the trains will run on time. It's to be hoped there's enough food to go round. It's to be hoped that the sky doesn't fall. 'You've upset everyone.'

Peter kissed his mother and assured her that he had calmed down. Mostly he had. His visit to Richie's place had been cathartic, and because he was alone and with no one to see him he had allowed himself a good cry in the car. After a few minutes he'd pulled himself together and found a cigarette from the contraband pack in the glove compartment.

'Have you been smoking?' his mother asked. 'It's to

be hoped you haven't started that habit up again.'

He was almost forty and yet she still sometimes spoke to him as if he was fourteen. He wondered if it was ever possible for parents to see their offspring as independent adults. Zoe was fifteen going on twenty and he knew it was going to be difficult enough for him to release the arrow from the bow.

He chose not to reply. Dell was in the kitchen, fixing a fused plug on a lamp. Peter drew a chair from under the table and sat down, watching his father wield a screwdriver. They were making Tara's old room comfortable. Mary had been out buying new duvet covers and pillowcases and new curtains for the room. It seemed they were enormously busy with these tasks so that they could run away from the real job of asking Tara any questions.

'Where is she?'

'Upstairs having a nice bath,' Mary said. 'Don't make her cry again, Peter. Promise me you won't make her cry again.'

'I promise, Mum. It's all right. I'm not going to shout or raise my voice. Okay?'

After they had walked together through the Outwoods on New Year's Day, and after Tara had given Peter her explanation about what had happened to her, he had driven her straight back to their parents' house and had asked her to recount the same story to Dell and Mary.

He hadn't got the reaction he'd expected. Mary and Dell had listened patiently to the abbreviated version. Then, when Tara had finished, Mary had proposed that she make a pot of tea. Dell for his part had heartily agreed that, yes, what they all needed was a nice cup of tea. Peter had exploded. Things were said. Mary had asked him to leave.

'You all right?' Dell asked him, fiddling with a tiny screw.

'Yes I'm all right.'

'Good.'

'So everyone's all right, Dad. All right?'

'Has your Mum gone upstairs?'

Peter leaned back in his chair to look. 'Yes.'

'Shut the door then.'

Peter got up, shut the door, and sat down again.

Dell laid his screwdriver and the plug on the table. 'Now listen to me, you bloody silly bugger. I'm not happy with her fucking story any more than you are. Neither is your mum. But Tara is ill. You can see she's ill. And very likely she might get iller, especially with you raging and snorting and charging round like a bull at a gate. Now the last thing we want is to push her over the edge or to make her so confused that we drive her away again. So you just keep your opinions to yourself. All right?'

'You're just going to accept everything she says? No word about what really happened?'

'At the minute, yes. Exactly that. Sometimes in this life you have to understand that we don't *need* to know everything.'

Chastened, Peter looked away. 'I've just come from Richie's. Don't you think we owe him something? We made a big mistake over that. He even served a stretch for that bit o' dope they found at his house.'

'Whose fault was that?'

'Mine, partly.'

'We'll come to Richie when we're ready. In the

129

meantime you'll shut it and you'll treat her with kid gloves until she gets better.'

'Will I?'

'In this house you fucking well will. Now I don't want another word on the subject. How are the kids?'

The television was flickering in the corner without anyone paying it much attention. Tara came down swathed in a towel robe, still wearing her dark glasses, her hair wet, smelling of shampoo. She took a place on the sofa, drying the ends of her hair with a towel.

'Peter, I'm going to have to see Richie at some point,' she said. 'I wondered if you could arrange it.'

'There's no hurry for that,' Mary said.

'All in good time,' said Dell.

'No, it needs to be done. He'll know I'm back,' she said looking at Peter. 'I owe him the same explanation I've given you.'

'He'll be in no hurry,' said Dell. 'It was a long time ago.'

Tara stood up. 'Mum and Dad have done up my room,' she said. 'Come on Peter, I want to show it to you.'

'I'll come up with you,' Mary said.

But Tara gently pressed her back into her chair. 'No, Mum. I want to show him. You two stay here.'

Peter rose to follow Tara upstairs but not before Mary had shot him a warning look that seemed to carry a whiff of cordite. When they got up to the room, Tara closed the door and invited Peter to sit down on the bed.

'Do you remember what this room was like when I left?' she said.

130

'Pretty much.'

'No, exactly. Do you remember what it was like exactly?'

'More or less.'

She went over to the wall adjacent to the window. 'Remember what was here?'

'Poster?'

'Good try. It was a giant butterfly. Blue. There was a poster over here. What was it?'

'Joy Division.'

'You're guessing. I didn't like them. It was a poster from the film *The Lost Boys* with a pledge of undying devotion to the Kiefer Sutherland character. But I also had a poster of The Cure; and over here was a double-decker ghetto blaster and I kept a Walkman over there; thin floaty scarves draped here, stacks of cheap bangles on a pole. Hair irons, you know, straighteners and crimpers by the wall sockets; could have burned down the house. Doc Martens over there with fluorescent laces, I loved them. The knackered hi-fi you gave me. And lots of leather belts to be worn with white grand-dad shirts, and there was a trilby hat hanging behind the door and another hat, a fedora with a blue felt band that I got from Richie, and over there a corkboard with dried roses pinned to it and scraps of paper with snatches of poetry and I could tell you what was written on each scrap.'

'What's your point? That you can remember your own things better than I could?'

'The carpet which has now been replaced had a spot here where I spilled some India ink; the curtains were unpicked at the hem and stuck with pins because I hadn't finished the job of trying to make them longer.

I could go on effortlessly. My point is, all this stuff, all this stuff was my life, and to me it was here almost like yesterday.'

'So? You've got a good memory.'

'We'll go into your room next. We'll see who has the best memory of *your* stuff?'

'Thought about all this, haven't you?'

'You betcha!'

You betcha! was one of Tara's favourite expressions before she disappeared. She said it early and often.

She sat down on the bed next to Peter and took his hand. 'I want you to know a couple of things before you jump to conclusions. Firstly, I know that Mum and Dad think I'm mentally ill and that's why they are being gentle with me. I also know that you think I'm either mentally ill or I'm lying my head off. That's fine: I didn't expect you to respond in any other way, and I'm sure I would be the same if the roles were reversed.

'My God, I thought long and hard before telling you what I told you. I knew the risks. I knew you would be angry, or that you would think I was sick. I considered developing my travel-round-the-world story, but I also knew that although it would be more acceptable I would get caught out pretty quick because I haven't been anywhere in my life except one, single other place. So I decided to tell the truth whatever the consequences.

'Now it has also occurred to me that I might be lying to myself, for deep, dark psychological reasons. People do that, don't they?

'I want you to consider this. What have I got to gain by telling you this story? It would be simpler to say that I ran away. I would cause myself a lot less trouble if I said that. I could work through the anger and the abuse that would follow. But by telling you this I've put myself at great risk. I don't expect you to believe it, Peter. Do you understand? I neither expect you to, nor do I need you to. I have told you a story that I don't expect you or anyone else to believe for a single second.'

'Well,' Peter said. 'We're eye to eye on that.'

'Peter I'm in deep trouble. Deep trouble. What I do need is help. What I'm telling you here is the truth. I wish it wasn't. I've been away six months and I came back as soon as I could and when I got back everything had changed. It had all changed so incredibly I didn't even dare come home. I spied on this house and slept rough for three days. I didn't talk to anyone. I had no money. Look at this five-pound note with the Duke of Wellington on it. I'd had it in my pocket but you can't spend it anywhere cos it's not legal tender anymore. I was starving and I almost froze to death but I couldn't knock on the door because I was terrified. Terrified! Mum and Dad had grown old. But I quickly realised there were only three people in the world who could help me. My mum, my dad and my brother. I have nowhere else to go. Will you help me Peter? Will you?'

Peter stared at Tara. She was still the teenage girl. But he could see care-lines in her, too. She was holding the withdrawn bank note out for him to take, as if it might purchase his belief. It was almost possible to believe in what she was saying, and to see there a sixteen-year-old girl, with her slender half-starved frame; but then a blink would bring him back to his senses.

'I will help you. But you would have to do what I say.'

She nodded.

'Would you be prepared to see someone?'

She nodded again. 'I saw this coming. But yes.'

He took her hand. 'Okay. We'll go downstairs and we'll keep the peace. It's been very hard for those two.'

'I know.' Tara started to cry.

Peter hugged her tight. 'Welcome home, Tara. Welcome home.'

They went downstairs, and Mary in particular was happy to see them appear to be on good terms, though Dell raised his eyebrows at him. Mary asked Peter if he wanted something to eat.

'Not hungry, thanks Mum.'

'Have just a sandwich.'

'Not bothered.'

'I can cut you a nice ham sandwich. Ham and mustard.'

'No, really.'

'Cheese? There's some nice Cheddar.'

'Honestly no.'

'It's no trouble.'

'Oh for goodness sake! Okay! I give in! I'll have a bloody sandwich!'

'You don't have to have one,' Mary said, 'if you don't want one.'

'Some people feed you with love,' Tara said, 'and some people love you with food.'

Peter told Tara all about Richie; about what transpired with the police after her disappearance; about what had happened between them. She was distressed to hear that Peter and Richie had never spoken again after the incident with the smashed guitar, and that Richie had spent a short time in prison after being sentenced for dealing in cannabis. She told Peter that she desperately wanted to meet with Richie if it was going to be possible and he agreed to try to set up a meeting.

Tara also agreed that Peter could arrange for her to see a doctor. They decided, for the time being, not to tell Mary and Dell about this.

Peter left the house but not before kissing Tara and his mother. He also kissed Dell, something that would not have been done twenty years earlier.

When he got home, Peter saw an elderly neighbour out on the street and looking somewhat forlorn. It was Mrs Larwood, a frail and grey-haired figure who lived across the road. Peter had helped her once when she had slipped on some ice. She was a sweet lady who had baked him a cake in gratitude for the small things he had done to help her; though the girls were unkind and said she was a witch. Because she looked distressed he stopped his truck.

'Mrs Larwood. Everything okay?'

Mrs Larwood took a moment to focus on him. She had cloudy cataracts on her eyes and her sight was poor. She'd lost her cat. She hadn't seen it in a couple of days. It was a ginger, she reminded him, with a pretty red collar. She wondered if it had got trapped in someone's outbuildings. Peter promised to check his workshop and the attached buildings. She was grateful and turned back to her home.

Peter drove on and then had a second thought. He carefully reversed his truck and wound down his window a second time.

'Have you got a photo, Mrs Larwood? Of your cat?'

'Yes.'

'Let me have it and I'll get one of the kids to run off some leaflets from the computer. We can stick 'em on the lamp-posts in the neighbourhood then people will all check their buildings.'

'That would be so good! You're so kind to me!'

'It's nothing. Dig out the photo and I'll send one of the kids over to get it.'

'Thank you Peter! Thank you so much!'

'Goodnight, Mrs Larwood.'

16

Being a farrier was hard graft, but it was a very good
business for making social contacts. Peter shod the
horses of the local Justice of The Peace, the wife of the
constituency Member of Parliament, the daughter of
the CEO of the local council and a lot more people
connected with the great and the good. What's more,
he found that when these people discovered that he had
a university degree, their attitude towards him changed.
Their tone of voice softened; they relaxed; they didn't
grin quite so much.

Unknown to them Peter charged wildly different
prices, depending on whether he liked his customer, or
if they were members of the Hunt, or according to what
he thought they could afford. If anyone ever questioned
his fees, which they rarely did, he happily referred them
to another farrier who charged much lower rates. Then
if they asked why those rates were lower – which they
inevitably did – he simply raised his eyebrows and
made no comment, allowing the questioning party
to conclude that low rates meant shoddy work. This
technique lost him no customers at all in a dozen years.

But one man he never overcharged was his local GP, a man called Dr Bullock, a handsome and tall Londoner from the East End who practised without fear or favour and without air or grace. Bullock had two sweet daughters who wanted ponies, and knowing nothing about horses he'd not been too proud to ask Peter for help. Peter knew exactly where to get ponies and what to look out for and how much to pay; and for all this information the doctor was grateful. He in turn had made himself available at all anti-social hours for Peter and his family, especially when the children were very small. One time a shard of hot metal had bounced back from the anvil and lodged in the corner of Peter's eye. Still bleeding he'd driven not to the A&E but to Bullock's surgery, where the doctor abandoned a patient, took out the hot shard on the spot, patched Peter up and sent him home.

The two men got along fine and often went for a pint together at The Green Man. It was over a beer that Bullock told him it wasn't like finding a good horse. 'And you can't even look in their mouths,' Bullock said. 'It's a fucking minefield finding a good shrink.' Bullock said he could easily refer Tara to a psychiatrist but that they would have to wait for some time for an appointment on the NHS. Unless she'd just attacked someone with a chainsaw. If Peter wanted to pay privately, Bullock knew a good practitioner who lived locally. He was a bit cranky, Bullock warned, and semi-retired; but he had a very strong reputation as a no-nonsense shrink and one who wouldn't draw out the consultation in the interest of fees.

So two days later, Peter drove Tara to the house

of Vivian Underwood in the Leicestershire village of Thringstone.

'Thringstone's Fault,' said Tara.

The land lay on a massive geological fault to which the village had given its name. The coalfields ended and butted up against folded volcanic rock. The day they learned this in school was the day they learned to say that everything was Thringstone's fault.

Peter stopped the car outside a three-storey Victorian palisaded villa, half-covered in rampant ivy. The house boasted a massive gable. The front of the building faced north, untouched by the sun's rays.

'Looks a bit gloomy,' Tara said, showing no signs of wanting to get out of the car.

Peter sniffed. He looked the house up and down. It did have a Gothic aspect. 'It's fine.'

They had to climb ten whitewashed steps to get to the front door. Peter rang the bell and identified himself through an intercom. Eventually an elderly woman with a severe case of Dowager's Hump opened the door. Peter had to fight to avoid turning to look at Tara. The old woman said nothing in response to Peter's greeting, simply closing the door behind them and leading them up a flight of highly polished stairs, trailing her tiny hand along the stout wooden banister. There was a sizeable landing with small tables containing glass museum-style cases, each case exhibiting a curio. One case had a pair of eastern silk shoes with curled and tasselled toes; another contained a stuffed weasel; another contained a ceremonial knife.

'You're joking,' Tara whispered.

Peter ignored her as this silent acolyte of the mind's mysteries opened a door to a large room. It was a kind of library, but with one or two more glass museum cases. The floorboards of the room were polished to the same high standard as the stairs and a threadbare oriental rug lay across the middle. Vivian Underwood stood at the far end of the room by an ornate fireplace in which a cheap gas fire had been installed and was burning cheerfully, struggling to warm what was a very large room. Underwood had an impressive shock of white hair. He was dressed in a brocade smoking jacket and his leather slippers revealed bare, white, bony ankles. He was smoking a cheroot.

'You're the short notice,' he said, biting on his cheroot. He had a booming style of speaking. 'I wanted an afternoon nap but then I remembered I promised that Bullock I'd see you. He's a good sort and he said you were too. That goes a long way. I smoke. Got a problem with that?'

'No,' said Peter.

'Not really,' said Tara.

'Good because if you have got a problem with it I can't see you. Can't smoke, can't see. You can't smoke anywhere these days. That's why I gave up and organised my practice from home. You can drive a bloody car pell-mell with a high risk of slaughtering a thousand little children a year but you can't smoke in case they get a whiff of your tobacco. What sort of a country is that?' He looked at Peter, as if Peter was responsible for all this legislation. 'Who are you?'

'I'm Tara's brother.'

Underwood marched over to Peter and put an arm round his shoulder, turning him around and in one deft move propelling him back through the open door. 'Well Tara's brother, nice to meet you but you're surplus to requirements and you'll find a comfortable waiting room along the hall. Thank you.' He closed the door before Peter had time to recover.

Tara had to stifle a giggle.

'We don't want brothers listening to us, do we, Tara?'

'I suppose not.'

'Take a seat.'

Tara glanced round. There were several seats. 'Which one?'

'You decide, and I'll pretend I haven't already drawn some conclusions about you by the chair you choose.'

Tara looked around the room. There was a writing desk with an executive chair behind it and a hard-backed armchair opposite. The huge desk was clear but for three impressive objects: an opulent, marbled ornamental pen-and-inkwell set; a large antique hour-glass of beautiful blown glass and cinnamon-coloured sand in a heavy oak frame; and a big yellow bath-time plastic duck. Other choices of seats were a rather battered but comfortable looking leather sofa against the wall; two matching armchairs lodged by the fire; and two more upholstered hard chairs drawn up by the window and illuminated by streaming sunlight. She chose one of these.

Underwood picked out a legal notepad from his desk drawer and sat in the chair adjacent to Tara. He produced a beautiful onyx fountain pen from the folds of his smoking jacket and began writing. 'Full name.'

'Tara Lucy Martin.'

'Mrs, Miss or Ms?'

'Miss.'

'Date of birth.'

Tara told him. He stopped writing and looked up.

'That would make you thirty-six.'

'Correct.'

'I'd say you were in your late teens. Or early twenties. At the very most.'

Tara looked at Underwood and didn't blink. He shook his head, as if saying he wasn't prepared to speak. The silence endured until Tara said, 'I'm not yet seventeen.'

Underwood took a puff on his cheroot. 'You'd better tell me what this is all about.'

'I'm not crazy.'

'Who says you are?'

'You will. You will when you've heard what I've got to say.'

'Try me. I've heard some good ones in my time, kiddo.'

So she told him about the bluebell woods, and the man on the white horse, and the gallop through the twilight, and the return home. Underwood listened attentively without a single interruption, making notes occasionally, mostly peering at her with steely blue eyes; only occasionally drawing on his cheroot, and then pursing his lips to release miraculously thin streams of blue smoke.

When she'd finished he laid down his pad and his pen and said, 'That's an impressive one.'

'You can say I'm crazy now.'

'Okay, you're crazy. Consider it said. Now can we move on and do things my way? Right. I've only had two of these abduction cases in my long career and one of those was a UFO abduction. Neither of these went on for your rather spectacular twenty years.'

'Did you believe them?'

'Who?'

'The two people who had been abducted.'

'One yes, one no. In one egregious case the individual in question was just afraid to tell his wife where he'd been for three days. In the other case, which was many years ago, I believe it was genuine. Let me complicate that remark: that is to say, Tara, that I believed that the subject believed her own story.'

'And me?'

'My instincts are that you believe your own story, yes. But, just as a kind of exercise, could you let me outline a few logical possibles?'

'What does that mean?'

'It means I want to put a few explanations to you, just to see how you respond to an argument.'

'Is this a kind of game?'

'Maybe. But a serious game. Like chess. Will you humour me?'

Tara sighed. 'Go ahead.'

Underwood held up a hand, fingers splayed, and counted his *logical possibles* on his fingers.

'One, if we can deal with it first, is the obvious chance that you are lying for complicated reasons of your own.

'Two is that you are a partial amnesiac. You left home a long time ago and you have – for reasons unknown – blanked out twenty years of your life.

'Three, you have received a trauma of some kind and your damaged brain is now desperately trying to construct a story *for yourself* to logically explain what has happened to you.

'Four, there are family or psychological reasons why the truth of what happened is so unacceptable to you that your psyche cannot accommodate it and you are passionately lying *to yourself*.

'Five, you are, for want of a better word, schizoid, and therefore delusional in your apprehension of time and your experiences.'

He went back to the beginning of his counting fingers, tapping away as if he had one more, looking at Tara.

'Is there a number six?'

'Yes. Number six is that events took place exactly as you described.'

'Well,' Tara said. 'Thanks at least for number six.'

'There are many more scenarios, but will you continue to play with me for the moment?'

Tara shrugged.

'I want you to entertain the notion that all of these six possibles have equal value. That is, can you for the moment accept that any one of these six reasons might explain what happened? And that none of them is more or less likely than any of the others?'

Tara furrowed her brow. She thought for a moment. 'Yes, I can accept that idea.'

Underwood sat back. 'Your response there is rather bad news, young lady. Bad news because it indicates – to me at least, though not everyone would accept the validity of my test – that you are rather sane.'

'Rather sane? And that's bad news?'

'Yes. If you had indicated a pathological need to advance the value of your story above the others then I could have gone to work on you in a different way. But now I know I'm dealing with a rather sane person, my work is much more complicated.'

'I don't understand you, but I like you,' Tara said.

'Don't try to charm me. I'm like a bear in the woods,

uncharmable. Now then, I'm going to conduct a physical examination. Blood pressure and so on. You okay with that?'

'Yes,' Tara said, still smarting from his retort.

'Right, roll up your sleeve.'

He performed a basic health check on Tara. He measured her blood pressure, her weight and height, he examined her respiratory system and he asked if he could take a blood sample for a cholesterol test. He put his hand on her belly and he looked in her ears.

'All good,' he said. 'Can you go down to the lady who let you in, Mrs Hargreaves? Can you tell her to book you in to see me after my last appointment tomorrow afternoon? And can you tell her that I want a urine test? Then wait with Mrs Hargreaves, would you? One more thing: send your brother back in. He'll want to know what's going on.'

Tara went down to find Mrs Hargreaves and after a moment Peter reappeared.

'Come in and close the door,' Underwood said. He beckoned for Peter to sit on the sofa, but chose not to sit down with him. Instead he stood over Peter with arms folded. 'Anything I tell the brother is not to be repeated to the sister, understood?'

Peter had to resist the temptation to look around the room to see if Underwood were referring to someone else. Then he said, 'Sure.'

'Not at all. Nothing is discussed.'

'I hear you.'

'I wouldn't tell you anything; but you'll only feel cross and excluded. How old is your sister?'

'She's thirty-six. I know she doesn't look it, but she is. Thirty-six.'

'A question that might sound odd but I have to get it out of the way: you are absolutely certain this is your sister?'

'Absolutely.'

'It couldn't be an impostor, someone who looks like her?'

'There's not a chance of that.'

'Okay. I think you understand I had to ask you that. Just to get that possibility out of the way. Now from talking to her, from listening to her thought patterns and her words and observing her body language, there is not the first hint that there is anything at all wrong with her.'

'Except that she thinks she's been living with the fairies for twenty years.'

'Correction: she thinks she's been living with the fairies for *six months*.'

'What's the difference?'

'Huge difference. The point is at this early stage I can't diagnose. She's showing no sign of initial schizophrenic or paranoid or depressive behaviour. In fact she presents as very healthy, with no outward indicators of even a mild neurosis; though I would readily admit that some patients are very good at masking their symptoms. I am absolutely opposed to medication at this point in my assessment. Okay?'

'Fine.'

'Yet she has this delusion.'

'I'll say she does.'

'Yes, I want you to say she does. Are you religious? Do you believe in God?'

'No.'

'Me neither. I happen to think that all people who

146

believe in God are delusional. I just don't think it's a bad thing. Let's say that they are constructing a delusion in a positive and useful way, in a way that helps them in life. For the moment I want you to see what Tara is doing in the same way. She is constructing a useful delusion.'

'What's it got to do with me?'

'Would you waste your time being angry or arguing every minute of the day with someone who has chosen to believe in God? No. I want you to adopt the same behaviour with Tara as you would with such a person. I want you to tell your parents to do the same thing. For the time being.'

Underwood asked Peter if he would bring her to see him again the following evening, and Peter was about to say he would when the telephone rang. Underwood walked over to his desk and picked up the phone.

'Hello Mrs Hargreaves. Thank you. Yes.' He listened, and he fixed Peter with his gaze as he listened. 'Very good. Thank you once again, Mrs Hargreaves.'

He put the phone down and came back to stand over Peter. 'They're all done down there. She's ready to go. Bring her to me again tomorrow and we'll pop her back in the oven.'

17

'If you want your children to be intelligent, read them fairy tales. If you want them to be more intelligent, read them more fairy tales.'

Albert Einstein

'Why have I got to do it?' Jack was red in the face.

'You haven't *got* to do it,' Peter said. 'No one said that you've *got* to do it. You don't *have* to do anything.'

'Right. If I haven't got to do it, then I won't.'

'You haven't *got* to do it, but you are *going* to do it.'

'Why?'

'Why bloody why? Why has everything got to be why?' Peter had a good relationship with Jack. The boy had hit the teenage years and Peter had let him assert himself here and there: kids weren't like horse-shoes, you didn't shape them over an anvil. But he wasn't about to surrender all discipline and sometimes he felt he'd been too lax as a father. Genevieve had once said he'd been tougher on his daughters than he had on his son. He hoped that he hadn't stored up trouble for later; and he thought he needed to stay on top of things now.

'She's an old woman, living alone. She's got no one around to look out for her.'

'If you're so concerned about her why don't you do it?'

'Let's think about that shall we? Little think? Maybe my time is taken up with hammering iron to pull in a few quid so that you can have air-rifles and computers and X-boxes and iPhones and what the hell else?'

'Fine!'

'It's called being kind, Jack. Being kind. You just go over there, knock on the door, get a picture of her tabby and run off a few leaflets. What's the big deal?'

Jack's face changed from red to puce. His eyes became narrow slits. 'I said I'd do it!' he bellowed and rocketed out of the front door; and he would have slammed the door theatrically but the swollen wood stuck in the frame, denying him that most satisfying of sound effects.

Genevieve appeared behind him. 'Oh, you're back. When you're done with parenting that tantrum, Josie is also having a pretty big one in the living room. Something to do with who owns the TV. How did it go with the shrink?'

The shrink, Peter told Genevieve, had a funny way of making you feel like you were five years old. Neither Peter nor Genevieve had seen a real shrink before: not up close, anyway. But Peter was pretty certain they didn't look much like this one, in his braided smoking jacket, puffing on a cheroot. He was, Peter thought, like something from another era. Not twenty-first century anyway. Possibly not even twentieth century. He just hoped that Underwood's techniques were more up to date.

Genevieve wanted to know if Underwood was going to blame it all on the family: things Dell and Mary did wrong. Peter shrugged and said probably. He had no idea what kind of a shrink Underwood was. They agreed that the fact that he hadn't already taped up Tara with medication was a good sign. Maybe.

Peter told his wife she would have a chance to meet Vivian Underwood herself the following evening. He had to get back to work, bend a few horse-shoes, make some money. He had appointments to keep.

'Vivian? Isn't that a girl's name?' When Peter didn't reply Genevieve said she would take Tara, and that Zoe would be under instructions to look after the children.

'Speak of the devil,' Genevieve said as Zoe swung into the kitchen. 'I need you to look after the kids tomorrow afternoon.'

Zoe looked at the ceiling. 'God! Do I have to?'

'Yep,' Genevieve said with a sweet smile. 'You have to.'

'Who is it?'

'It's Jack. Jack from across the road.'

Jack waited. He heard the whisper of a bolt drawn back, and then a second bolt. Then he heard the tinkling of a loosened chain. A tiny face peered back at him, elderly but elfin, and topped off with a short helmet of gleaming silver hair. A pair of blue cataracted eyes blinked.

'My dad said I should come about the cat. Your cat.'

'Have you found him?'

'No. My dad said get a photo. He said you had a photo. Of your cat. So we can do some … leaflets.'

'Oh yes! He did! Come in!'

Jack would rather have waited outside but the old woman held the door for him so that he felt compelled to step into her narrow hallway. She closed the door and beckoned him to follow. Jack winced.

Her lounge was tidy but faded. The walls were papered with a flock design that might have been fashionable forty years ago. Heavy velour drapes and net curtains held the outside world at bay with a mesh of fabric and dust. To Jack it seemed like the house was infused with the smell of the old lady: not a bad smell, but an antique smell.

'Sit down,' she said. 'While I see what I can find.'

This was exactly what Jack didn't want. He'd hoped to stand at the door, grab a photo and make a speedy withdrawal. But here he was, perched on the very edge of an armchair with no possibility of the smart exit.

The old lady came back with a plate, on which was a slice of dubious-looking ginger cake. She offered the plate to him.

'It's all right,' said Jack.

'What's all right?'

'I'm okay. Thanks.'

'Oh, you go ahead. I know what boys like.' She thrust the cake at him. He had little choice but to take it. 'Cake. And lemonade. I have some lemonade some-where, if I can find it. I know what boys like.' And she went back to her kitchen in search of more of what boys like.

Jack looked at the cake. He wasn't at all sure he was prepared to risk it. He wasn't at all confident about what was in it. What if she knew? What if she knew all along what he had done to her cat? Maybe she was just pretending to be friendly. Faking it.

Mars Larwood returned with a glass of lemonade, and even before she handed it to him he could see it was flat. He guessed that the bottle had been in her cupboard untouched for three or four years. And now he was going to have to eat the suspect cake and drink the flat lemonade.

The old lady stood over him, smiling, stroking the backs of her hands, one over the other.

He bit into the ginger cake.

'I baked that,' she said.

'Cool,' said Jack. He allowed a few crumbs to fall into his mouth. He felt stupid saying cool. For one thing no one said cool any more. For another thing he knew that no one of Mrs Larwood's generation said cool either.

'Don't forget your lemonade,' she said.

It occurred to Jack that maybe Mrs Larwood was a tiny bit too interested in seeing him eat the cake and drink the lemonade. Standing over him like that. Making certain it all went down. His younger sisters talked about her as if she was a witch. Maybe she was. He wondered again what was in the cake. There was something sharp and unsavoury in that cake. It wasn't just ginger. Maybe she did know exactly what had happened with the cat and she'd been waiting for the opportunity to get him over here. Maybe the cake was poisoned in some way. Or maybe the lemonade was not lemonade at all: maybe it was a potion.

He lifted the lemonade to his lips, took a miraculously tiny sip. It tasted like lemonade, flat, but still like lemonade. He tried to make an exaggerated swallowing motion. His Adam's-apple felt like a stone in his throat.

Mrs Larwood smiled at him. 'I'll get that photo,' she said, turning and leaving him sitting alone in her parlour.

After a few moments she came back with a photo. Jack stood up rather quickly and took the photo from her outstretched hand. He didn't look at it; didn't want to look at it. 'Right. I'll do it,' he said, already inching towards the door.

'What will you do?' she wanted to know.

'Scan it. Print it out. Leaflets. On my computer.'

Mrs Larwood pressed her hands to her face, as if she'd just experienced a hot flush. 'I'll tell you a secret.'

Jack blinked. He looked at the door.

'I'm ninety-two years of age and I have a secret.'

Jack nodded and felt his Adam's-apple bob again in his throat as he swallowed.

'Come with me. Come on.'

Jack didn't want to follow, but he couldn't see how he could resist her command. He followed her through to her back room. There, under a gate-legged table, was a large cardboard box.

'Look in there,' Mrs Larwood said.

Jack hesitated.

'Go on!'

He reached down and lifted the lid of the cardboard box, very slowly, as if an animal – maybe a dead cat somehow resurrected, a zombie cat – might leap out of the box at him claws extended. But there was no zombie cat. There instead, still in its factory Styrofoam packaging, was a computer, a monitor and a printer.

He looked back at the old woman, confused.

'Yes. I'm ninety-two. And I'm going to go on to the internet. Yes, I am. I'm told it's like another world.'

Her 'secret' having been revealed, Jack relaxed slightly. 'How long has it been in its box?'

'Six months. I'm a little bit afraid to take it out. I

bought it and I don't really know what to do with it.'

'Oh.'

'I'm waiting for someone who knows what they're doing with these things. Is that an exciting secret?'

'Yes,' Jack said. 'I'd better take this photo and scan it before ... I'll do it. I'll go now.'

Jack turned and headed for the door. Mrs Larwood followed, smiling and making clucking noises of gratitude. She told Jack what a sweet, kind boy he was helping her in the business of finding her cat. Her cat, she assured him, was her best friend in the world.

She opened the door for him. He crossed the threshold, and against all his instincts, he heard himself say, 'The computer. I can set it up for you. One day. I can set it up. If you want.'

'Oh, I'd love that! I'd love you to set it up! There was a man coming to do it for me but he didn't come. He wanted fifty pounds to set it up. If you do it you can have the fifty pounds.'

'No,' Jack said. 'No. I'll just do it.'

Mrs Larwood's hands flew to her face again. 'Oh you're so kind – you and your father, both the same! So kind!'

Jack looked at her cataracted eyes. They were swimming with gratitude and it made him feel queasy. 'I have to go now.'

He turned and walked slowly down her driveway, holding the photo almost at arm's length. He was afraid to look back. He reached her gate, lifted the stiff latch, opened it and felt it swing behind him on its spring. He exhaled a huge sigh to be clear of the house.

Then he heard her calling him back.

He turned and she was advancing towards him down

the driveway. She had something wrapped in a tissue. 'Your cake,' she said. 'You forgot your cake!'

'Do I come in with you?'

Genevieve had driven Tara to her second appointment with Underwood. They'd talked about Peter's work, how he'd become a farrier after – or in spite of – going to university; they talked about Josie's temper-tantrums, and Amber's creativity, and Jack's recent moodiness and Zoe's boyfriend. All this they discussed while Genevieve just wanted to say, *'Oh for fuck's sake, Tara, where have you been for twenty years?'*

'You can come in if you want,' Tara said. 'There is a sort of waiting room. You could even sit in on my session as far as I'm concerned. I don't know whether he'd allow it.'

'But it's private,' Genevieve said.

'I don't want it to be private. I want everyone to hear it all. You all think I'm crazy so what difference does it make?'

'No, Tara, we don't think—'

'You're lying to be kind. Don't. I don't want that. Come on, let's go in. I'm going to demand that you be allowed to sit in.'

They got out of the car. Genevieve filed behind Tara up the stone steps thinking that she'd rather not be allowed to sit in, thank you. But she felt certain it wouldn't be permitted, so said no more.

Tara introduced Genevieve to Underwood, who wore the same smoking jacket and leather slippers. 'I'd like her here.'

'Not how it works,' said Underwood.

'It's what I want.'

'No.'

'I insist.'

Underwood bit his lip and smiled. He folded his arms. 'How well do you know each other?'

'Not at all,' said Tara. 'We met for the first time a couple of days ago. We've spent about an hour or two in each other's company. She's my sister-in-law but we're strangers.'

'So why would you want her in our session?'

'Because I feel like I've known Genevieve for twenty years. Somehow. Even though I don't know her at all I trust her implicitly and would tell her everything that was said here anyway.'

Underwood knitted his eyebrows and seemed to regard Genevieve in a new light.

'I really don't think I should,' Genevieve said.

'Hush!' Underwood snapped at her. 'I'm thinking.' He stroked his chin and regarded Genevieve steadily, squinting at her as he did so. Genevieve shuffled under his gaze. Tara smiled. 'It's unethical, unorthodox and unEnglish,' Underwood said. 'All right, you sit over there in that chair and you fade into the background and observe.'

Genevieve tried to protest. 'Really, I don't—'

'Over there and not a peep. Now, let's crack on.'

18

'I speke of many hundred yeres agoe,
But now can no man see non elves mo.
For now the grete Charite and Prayers
Of Limitours and other holy freres,
That serchen every lond and every streme,
As thick as motes in the sunne beme
This maketh that there ben no fairies,
For there as wont to walken as an elfe,
There walketh now the Limitour himself,
And as he goeth in his Limitacioune,
Wymen may now goe safely up and downe,
In every bush and under every tree,
There nis none other Incubus but he.'

Geoffrey Chaucer

The case of TM is one of the most interesting examples of confabulation I have encountered in my career so I am writing up my brief surgery notes with a view to retirement publishing. Confabulations, notoriously difficult to distinguish from delusions and chronic cases of lying, are rarely found not to have an organic foundation, though I don't rule it out in this case.

TM was brought to me by her brother when she had returned to the family fold after an unexplained absence of about twenty years. I was surprised when the brother, a burly alpha-male of middle years led in his sister, a slightly built thirty-six-year-old woman who looked pathologically young for her age. At first glance one would have taken her for a teenager or someone in her early twenties. I've learned not to jump to conclusions but I instantly suspected a hormonal disturbance, or anorexia nervosa, or both.

TM appeared wearing dark glasses, which she was always reluctant to remove, claiming to be extremely sensitive to light. I asked her if she had seen an optometrist and she had not. Her medical records showed no history of eye problems and an appointment I subsequently made for her with an optometrist reported no abnormalities. Her supposed light sensitivity was part of her elaborate confabulation.

Significantly, when offered a variety of seats in my study she chose the window chairs.

Outwardly confident, she maintains steady eye-contact and presents normally: no nervous fidgeting, no twitching nor tics and very little physical leakage apart from occasionally winding her finger in her hair. Tells her story with alarming candour. Eye movement to upper left suggests remembering, not inventing on the spot, but she could have told her story many times and therefore be 'remembering' previous inventions.

TM appears to be suffering from a profound amnesia spanning some twenty years, though she is neither retrograde nor anterograde in the sense that she has perfect – one might say advanced – recollection of all events before her disappearance and of all events since her return. The memory gap of twenty years however is complete. That in itself leads me to suspect that the cause of the amnesia was a trauma experienced twenty years ago, and possibly but not necessarily even a second releasing trauma more recently.

There is no doubt in my mind that the patient believes her narrative to be true and that her case conforms to Berlyne's definition of a 'falsification of memory occurring in clear consciousness'. Berlyne defined two types of confabulator, the provoked and the spontaneous. The provoked confabulator invents in response to probing, offering piecemeal, fleeting fantasies often combined with real-time memories. The spontaneous confabulator maintains a consistent though often bizarre outpouring maintained with fierce conviction. TM is certainly in the latter camp.

Recent discoveries about the nature of memory have changed our thinking. An outmoded view of the human brain is that it is like a computer, storing files that can be retrieved or sometimes lost. Now we know that memory is reconstructive, and that we remake our memories each time we visit them, more or less according to our values and experiences, which may of course have changed since the date of the events we memorise. But there exists beyond this reconfiguration an executive control of this function, presumably stopping us from too fanciful a reconstruction of every memory.

The confabulator is someone who has lost executive control.

The most common cause of this loss of executive control is a rupture in a tiny blood vessel in the brain, temporarily cutting off the flow of oxygenated blood to areas of the brain essential for the recall of memory.

Note to self: It is as well to remember that healthy people confabulate, too.

I have arranged for the patient to undergo CT

scanning in due course, to look for signs of trauma or arterial damage in the brain. In the meantime it is important to reassure the Martin family – a sceptical lot, in a healthy sense – that TM is not deliberately attempting to deceive them. I'm convinced she believes every word of what she says.

What is fascinating is that the confabulation posits no apparent threat to the integrity of her hold on current reality. Indeed it is presented as memory, past and completed. The ending has been written into the confabulation. Clearly the narrative has been constructed to make sense of some overwhelming experience – but at the moment we have no clues as to what that experience might have been. Until we are able to locate any organic foundation for the amnesia and confabulation we will proceed with a psychological investigation underpinned by an understanding of the needs of the confabulator.

Herstein said that 'confabulation is a knowledge problem'. That is to say, if the knowledge isn't there, the mind tells stories to fill in the gap. Our consciousness is interpreting reality, rather than driving it. Thus we might find the origin of the gap by looking at the story.

19

'The English word "fairy" comes to us via the Old French **faerie**, deriving from the Latin **fata**, meaning "fate" and **fatum**, meaning oracle or utterance.'

Etymological Dictionary

You see in some way that first night at his house, the house where I came to live for the next six months, was the most extraordinary evening of all of them. He had told me that you couldn't argue with the charts, that it would be six months before I could go back again; six months before I could see my mother and father, and my brother, and Richie, and anyone else.

And naturally I didn't believe it.

At first I became upset. But my distress was his distress. He came to me and he held me and he promised me that there was nothing to be done. Then he tried to explain the charts, the columns of figures and the positions of the moon and stars, but all I could see were beautiful illustrations and meaningless tables of numbers.

My instincts were that I should flee, just get away from that house, away from the lake that shone with an eerie blue light. But there was no question of finding my way back at night. My instincts for self-preservation were already telling me to play along with what I was being told, to feign acceptance, to pretend to give in to exhaustion. It occurred to me now that he had brought me there to be his prisoner. But I could see by the hurt in his eyes he harboured no ill intention towards me. No, I knew I could wait out the night and then slip away. I told myself that by first light I would get myself out of there; maybe steal his horse. I would just wait until the moment was ripe.

He asked me if I was hungry, but I couldn't even think about eating. He asked me – and I say *he* because at that time he still hadn't told me his name – if I was thirsty and I said yes, I would take a drink. He went away and came back with two tiny glasses. Absurdly tiny, of bubbled green glass and smaller than egg-cups, but in each of which was a spit of yellow liquid. I took the thimble-sized glass and almost laughed. But he touched glasses.

'By this drink I promise to return you, if you should want me to, at the earliest time; and I promise to keep you from all harm; and if I fail in either of these two promises may I lie down dead.' And then he tipped back the tiny liquid and looked at me blinking. Then he burped. 'Now you have to drink.'

I went to drink, but he stopped me.

'Wait! Where's your oath?' he almost shouted at me.

'Oath?'

'Of course. You don't drink this stuff without an oath.'

I didn't really know what an oath was, though I supposed he meant some kind of promise.

'I promise,' I said, 'to be more careful.'

He looked surprised at that, but I tipped back the liquid. It wasn't even an eyeful, but it was sweet like

162

honey and spicy like peppermint, and no sooner did it go down than I felt a mighty burp rip free of me. I felt stupid, but he seemed to think nothing of it. And instantly I felt calmed and refreshed, and even had he offered me more of this drink I had no need of any more.

I felt peaceful, and inside me I felt the calm of the lake and the moonlight pulsing on the water. The light was sinister and beautiful at the same time. It was how I imagined an Arctic midnight. But it was velvety and the night sky through the window was a comforting cloth of stars. It was a balm to the eyes. I stopped fretting, and I thought well, if I'm here for the night I may as well make the best of it because the evening out there seems beautiful.

'Can we go and sit by the water?' I asked him
'Nothing could be sweeter.'

So we went outside again and we walked on the sand. He took off his shoes and said I might do the same. He said he preferred to feel the earth sing through his feet, and that shoes stopped you from hearing the song of the earth; and I thought well, that's very poetic, so I took off my shoes and we walked on the fine grey night-sparkling sand that formed a beach around the lake. The sand was warm and gritty and yet soft at the same time and though I didn't hear the earth singing through my feet I did enjoy the feel of the sand between my toes, which was like the stroking of gentle fingers.

He looked at my toes and said what pretty toes I had, and that he would make a ring for my toe if I wanted. I looked at him, and with the moon rippling on the water like the presence of a ghost but sweet, and the whisper of the sand under our feet and the eerie evening light reflected in his eyes I knew with absolutely certainty that this man was falling in love with me.

Of course I am, he said.

'What?'

'I didn't speak,' he said. 'It's the murmur of the lake.'

We sat down. He was very careful not to crowd me. In fact I told him he could sit a little nearer. Then he explained that because I was still only fifteen and not yet of age that he couldn't touch me. He said that when he'd first spied me in the bluebell wood that he'd taken me for someone older. But it didn't matter he said, because he would happily wait for me.

'Wait for what?'

'Wait for you to say when you are ready and if you are ready. It's for you to say if the gate is open or closed.'

And I thought *what gate*? Occasionally he spoke in riddles like this; and at other times I didn't know if he had spoken or if I had just heard his voice inside my head; or if there had after all been something in that drink he'd given to me; or if as he said, it was just the murmur of the lake.

We talked at length and he asked if he could hold my hand, and because I trusted him not to press things further, I let him. He wanted to know everything about me. He wanted to know what music I liked and what books I'd read. I told him, and he listened. He said he knew the books I'd mentioned but was a bit out of touch with the latest songs and so would make a point of listening to the titles I'd reeled off for him.

I had no more fear by now. I felt at ease with him. In fact by now I wanted to get nearer to him; I wanted him to hold me, but I didn't dare to say this because I felt he might take it the wrong way when all I wanted was to be held. So instead I asked him his name again. And this time he told me.

I'm not about to tell you his name. That's between him and me, and there's a good reason for that. But because you're curious and I can't keep referring to him as he, I'm going to give you one of his lesser names, of which he had over a hundred. We'll call him *Hiero*, which he pronounced Yarrow.

He asked me if he could whisper me to sleep. I had no idea what he meant. But I blinked my eyes and the next thing I knew, he was holding me in his arms. In one blink he was holding my hand and in another blink I was lying in his arms, and he was whispering to me in a strange and beguiling language. I knew I was going under; going to sleep, that is, but I had no interest in stopping it. I no longer had any need to pretend I was exhausted because I wanted sleep to take over me. I recall his whispering in my ear and the whispering became the same sound as the murmuring of the lake.

Then a knocking awoke me; a sound like that of a large bird tapping its beak on a window. I looked round and I saw that I was lying on one of the scruffy mattresses placed against the floor in the living room of the house. There were no curtains at the window and the sun was coming up and streaming bright through the dusty glass, illuminating all the huge cobwebs of the house. Hiero was asleep almost beside me. I guessed he must have carried me back from the lake. He had pulled up another mattress beside mine and was deep asleep.

But the tapping continued. It had a certain noisy rhythm and it seemed like it was coming from the kitchen. I was still fully dressed. I ran a hand through my knotted and tangled hair and I sat up. I got to my feet and stepped over the deep-sleeping form of Hiero. The door to the kitchen stood ajar and I went across to see what was making the tapping sound.

When I got to the door I gasped.

Fully illuminated by the brilliant sunlight streaming through the window was, stretched across the wooden kitchen table, a naked man. He was lying on his back. Sitting astride him and with her back to me was a naked woman. Her golden skin shimmered with an oystershell-like sheen of perspiration. She had lustrous long hair, blonde hair streaked with nut-brown and platinum all part-braided and tied back, and her hair stuck to the glowing sweat of her back. She was riding the man beneath her, and the thrust of her pelvis was clacking the uneven table leg on the kitchen floor.

She somehow sensed my presence. Without breaking rhythm she turned and looked back at me across her shoulder. She didn't appear cross at being caught in this act, but she didn't look pleased either. She kept a steady gaze on me. 'Who are you?'

I said nothing. The smell of their sex was like smoke in the room. The man lifted his head from the table and looked at me from around her hip, and then he beckoned me to come nearer.

'You wait your turn,' the woman said to me, sharply, and then she twisted away, thrusting harder at the man.

I slammed the kitchen door, hard, and skipped back to where Hiero was sleeping. The banging of the door roused him. He lifted his head and blinked happily at me.

'Do you know there are two people *fucking*,' I said, '*fucking* on your kitchen table?'

'Oh.'

'In the next room! A man and a woman!'

'Well. Who is it?'

'Who is it? Who is it? I've no idea who it is!'

'It's probably Laila. Or one of the other women. Just leave them to it and they'll soon be gone.'

I stared at him. 'They'll soon be gone? What sort of place is this?'

'Well,' he said, scratching his head. 'I did warn you I shared the place with others.' He was casual about the whole thing. 'Do you want breakfast?'

'Not after what I've just seen on the kitchen table. I need a shower.'

'There isn't a shower. We wash in the lake. I'll come with you.'

'No, it's okay.'

I needed some time to myself. I was already planning to leave, but I wasn't about to announce it. It wasn't even that I thought Hiero would prevent me from leaving; but I just wanted to slip away quietly. I had an idea that I would take the horse and just retrace our steps.

But I had to go through the kitchen to get out. The couple who had been fucking on the table had stopped and were lying in each other's arms, sleepy in the afterglow, their sweat shimmering in the sunlight on their hips. I slipped past them, went outside and walked down to the lake.

It was a beautiful morning, but the sun was lancing off the water and it hurt my eyes; by which I mean my eyes felt grazed by the intensity of the light. I had to use my hand as a visor. It was as if there was a grittiness in the particles of light, a grittiness that left my eyes feeling sore. And yet everything I looked at seemed to be rinsed clean, or somehow new, in the way that everything appears new when you are a child.

At the lake's edge I stopped and threw some water on my face. It was crystal and cold and it took my breath away. The droplets of water on my hand, beaded with spectral light, looked both more simple and more complicated than they had at home. I squatted there for a while gazing at the water on my hands – I don't know whether like a simpleton or a philosopher.

The stable where the white horse was kept was just twenty or thirty yards from the house. I guessed Hiero might be watching me from indoors so I squatted there on the sand wondering whether to go right away to get the horse or to wait for a better moment when no one was around.

Then I heard a whisper in the sand and heard someone's gentle footsteps coming up behind me. I thought it was Hiero but I turned and saw the woman from the kitchen moving towards me.

She was still naked, and in that spectacular, iris-grazing light she was stunning. Her dark eyes were on me. She was tall and lithe, somehow like a racehorse; her skin tawny, very lightly freckled. Her cheekbones were so high you could have cut yourself on them. Her long many-coloured hair hung lower than the amber nipples of her breasts. I had to fight to stop myself looking at her pussy and her long, slender legs. She was easily the most beautiful woman I have ever seen, and though I have always thought of myself as pretty I felt by contrast a wizened little frump.

She said nothing as she walked by me and into the

water, but she trailed a hand through the air towards me, either as a gesture of recognition or dismissal, I couldn't tell. She stopped, turned and sluiced water over her shoulders, all the time keeping her eyes on me, and the water effervesced on her skin, foaming with milky light.

'Beautiful this morning,' she said. She spoke with a trace of an accent I couldn't place. 'Take off your clothes and come in.'

'Thanks. We like to keep our clothes on where I come from.'

'Don't be sullen. Come in. I know you want to lick my pussy.'

'Jesus Christ! What is this place? A camp for perverts?'

I was disgusted. I turned and walked back up the beach towards the house.

'My mistake, I'm sure!' Her shout bounced off me. But there was mockery, not apology in her voice.

As I approached the house I heard talk and laughter. I saw through the door that it was Hiero, sharing a joke with the other twisted pervert from the kitchen table. They were smoking hand-rolled cigarettes and talking loudly.

I turned on my heels and made straight for the stable. There the white mare snorted at me when I opened the stable door. I took the ancient blanket from its pole and flung it over the mare's back. The only tack on offer was the worn leather bridle and a crop. I looped it over the horse's head and trotted the animal out of the stable.

There was a track running through the trees behind the house. I decided to walk the horse out that way, because I would be seen if I crossed the beach – not least by the twisted goddess washing all the sweaty fuck off herself in the lake – and I calculated that I could make my way through the trees to the far-end of the lake. It wasn't difficult, though the path ascended through the woods before I found a trail back down again, and I soon joined up with the path by which we had arrived, marked by an avenue of trees. When I knew I was clear I mounted the horse and I set off at a trot.

The mare was beautiful. She responded well to me. She picked up my intentions almost without any aid from me. If I thought trot she made it happen. If I thought canter she took off. I rode for two hours without stopping: cantering, trotting or walking. I was confident of my path because I have a keen sense of direction and I recognised distinctive features – rock formations, glades, a hollow, a stream, a tree twisted and bent by the wind – all from the previous night. Plus I knew we had come roughly west and I could get my compass bearings from where the sun was still rising ahead of me in the sky.

Two hours later I stopped and let the mare drink from another stream. I got down and let her take some rest, while the sun stood still and boiling at its zenith.

After the mare was rested I got back on the horse and followed what I thought was a bridle path. All the time I was looking for the grassy incline – we'd cantered up it after galloping across that lush green field, so I was searching the landscape for a slope running down to the same field.

But I couldn't find it.

I wasn't afraid because I knew that all I had to do now was to keep the sun at my back and that eventually

I would wind up at some farm or village or small town and from there I could telephone Mum and Dad. They would be as angry as ferrets in a sack but they would come and fetch me in the car. But I trotted and walked the mare on for another hour or two without seeing a single sign of a dwelling house.

I turned the mare off the bridle path and took her up the side of a hill, and from its crest I was able to look all around me. All the time I was scanning the landscape for the glitter of the Trent or the Soar, or for anything that might show me through Derbyshire or Nottinghamshire or Leicestershire and back into Charnwood Forest, where all would be well. The countryside looked beautiful but unfamiliar; beautiful but foreboding. I was lost.

'No, you're not lost, because I've found you.' It was Hiero. He was speaking from behind me, standing on a crag in his white shirt sleeves.

'You've been following me.'

'I couldn't abandon you now could I?'

'I want to go home.'

'And so you shall. But you can't just yet.'

'Stop lying to me! Just point me the way and I'll go! Just put me on the path: that's all you have to do, put me on the path.'

'Your life has taken a different path now, Tara.'

I jumped down off my horse and ran to him and lashed at him with my riding crop. He flinched as it caught his jaw and the side of his neck, but he made no defence and no retaliation. I saw a weal appear immediately and a streak of blood on his neck where the crop had landed.

'I deserve it for bringing you here,' he said. 'I know I do.'

I started crying, because I didn't know what to do and I was frightened.

He pulled me towards him and he held me. 'Don't Tara, don't; because yours are the tears of heaven.'

'Just put me on the path! Please! Just put me on the path! I want to go home.'

He held me for a while. 'I could put you on the path, but it would still take you six months to get there. I'm going to take you back to the house again, and I'm going to tell you how it is with us folk here.'

20

'Nimmy Nimmy Not,
Your name is Tom Tit Tot.'

English version of Rumpelstiltskin

'You don't see many doctors smoking. In their surgeries.' It was the first thing that Genevieve had said since Tara had begun her story. Underwood was at his desk typing up notes directly on to a PC. Tara was taking a toilet break and Genevieve had to speak to him right across the room, a distance of a dozen paces.

He didn't look up. 'Quite motherly, aren't you?'

'Am I?'

He made a few more keystrokes. 'Do you know why she wanted you here? Against my wishes?'

'She trusts me?'

'Nothing to do with trust. It's to do with finding people to populate her Peter Pan world. You're her Wendy.'

'I am?'

'Oh yes. Wendy has to keep everyone safe. Keep everyone in order. Look after all. Be mother to the lost boys and girls.'

'Tara already has a mother.'

'One she ran away from, yes. But she needs a safe one. A surrogate mother. You're the perfect candidate.'

'Should I be worried?'

'I don't see much to worry about. You are Wendy because you've been trusted with the verbatim report. You're an acceptable conduit back to the family. You're an in-law, aren't you? That means you're inside and outside at the same time. She's clever, that Tara.'

'So, what is your diagnosis?'

'I don't discuss my cases with other than immediate family. Sorry.'

'Am I being told off about something here?'

'Only for banging on about my smoking habit, I'd say.'

'You know what? You're plain rude.'

Underwood glanced up from his keyboard. He looked pleased. 'Look at those framed certificates on the wall. I worked hard for the right to be rude. I'm a licensed fool.' He puffed happily on his cheroot. 'Do you want one of these? They make a lovely stink.'

'God he's weird,' Genevieve said to Peter, back at The Old Forge. They were enjoying a glass of wine and a few rare moments together, with all the children either in bed or upstairs and abducted by the internet.

'I quite like him,' Peter said. 'Did you tell him you have a Masters degree in Psychology?'

'Christ, no. Anyway psychiatrists are suspicious of psychologists. I'd rather let him stereotype me and see what he has to say. Fucking Wendy. He was trying to provoke me. For some reason.'

'So what will he say? Bottom line.'

'He's refreshingly jargon-free, but I'd guess he'll tell us Tara is a Pathological Narcissist, and that her story is an elaborate compensation for an inability to face up to adult chores and functions. He'll suggest that the explosive shock of discovering herself to be pregnant age fifteen – and the hasty abortion coupled with the fear of family disapproval – caused a crisis and a state of arrested development. Rather than face up to it all, she ran away.

'He'll tell us that typically these people – Pathological Narcissists, not shrinks – have no steady job, never get married, raise no family, put down no roots, have no real friendships or long-term relationships. She's been bumming around for twenty years, basically.

'He might even go so far as to say that she is suffering from a form of Psycho-social short stature, which is what some chronically abused kids suffer from and their growth gets stunted. She might have partially switched off the ageing hormones and that could account for why she looks so young.'

'Jesus. I'm glad I only bend horse-shoes for a living.'

'She's not the only bent person in the world, Peter.'

'I know that. It just sounds so very fucked up.'

'Come on. Everyone is fucked up.'

'Why do you think she's chosen to come back now?'

'I've been thinking about that. See how sweet she is with our kids? I think she wants kids of her own and time is running out. So she's regrouping by coming back. You have to go where the wagons are circled. I admit not all women seem to want to pump out kids like I do; but even women who hate the idea of having kids have unconscious drives.'

Peter and Genevieve had wanted more children but it wasn't possible any more.

'I feel so sad for her,' Peter said.

'I know you do. Come here. Have a hug. Speaking of sad teenagers, do you think Jack is okay?'

'Why?'

'I don't know. He's looking a bit shifty lately.'

'Oh, he's pissed off with me 'cos I told him to help out the old lady across the road. He's okay. By the way, you know what you were saying about narcissistic whatsits?'

'Yes?'

'No steady job, never got married, raised no family, put down no roots, no real friendships. Reminds me of someone else.'

Richie concluded his guitar set at The Phantom Coach with a big barnstorming blues finish, milking the applause. He hosted a weekly music night in the large function room at the back of the Coach and it always attracted a good crowd. The event was called *Indie* night. Richie always said he hadn't a clue what *Indie* meant as a category since he couldn't see how anything anyone did was independent of everything else, but it always attracted a much bigger audience than if he labelled the evening Folk, Rock, World, Blues or Pickled Pig Music. The plain fact was that Richie was highly accomplished in all of these genres – even the last one – and could, if he wanted, blow any of the guest artists or bands right off the stage.

But he was modest and he never stole the light. He was always expected to offer a guitar spot, either solo or accompanied by a couple of grizzled and fossilised old hippie musos he'd known for years; and even though his playing was way too superior to most of the guests he always made sure a visiting act concluded the evening's performance. Unless they were awful, and that night the guest band, three kids called The Dogs, were atrocious. Richie salvaged the evening first by appearing to approve of the boys by joining them on stage, and then rounding off with a glittering smoky blues and folk medley in which he found himself showboating.

Showboating because his headaches were getting worse and he thought that if he could lose himself in his music, then the pain might recede. Meanwhile he was self-medicating with chasers of beer and whisky. It didn't matter: stone cold sober or in his cups he could always put an audience in a spell.

These live performances somehow never quite carried over into his recordings. And there had been recordings over the years. He'd knocked out three vinyl albums with major record labels. The first two albums had bombed, despite healthy reviews in the national press, so 'the difficult third' was to fly or die. It died. He came back a few years later, by which time almost all recorded music had migrated from vinyl discs to CDs, with a couple of releases on a smaller but respectable label. He mixed genres. His stuff was a moody and eclectic blend of blues and rock that he'd translated into the synth-rock world but with growly vocals. He was always missing the wave.

Between all this he was often in demand for sessional studio work and more than once he added memorable licks or riffs to this or that pop-diva's limited ideas. He spent a lot of time doing what he called 'polishing turds' only to see the polished turd rocket into the stratosphere, trailing silver, gold and celebrity stardust. His only acknowledgment might be a modest kill-fee. Session artists didn't get royalties.

One time he polished a turd so lovingly it spent twenty weeks at the top of the singles charts. He'd added a catchy intro and a complete bridge to a lame three-chord trick brought dead-on-arrival into the studio by a well-known egomaniac with an orange tan and a huge floppy fringe. The song got picked up by a major movie and sold in the millions all over the world. Richie got none of it.

He'd had enough. He got the support of the Musician's Union and gathered together enough money to mount a court case to claim some royalties from all this success. The floppy fringe lied shamelessly in court and so did the record label. Richie lost, and even though everyone knew that the real work was his, the failed action left Richie busted and broke.

Thereafter a decline of ambition set in. You can be an ageing rock star; but you can't be an ageing wannabe rock star. All that was left for him to do was to focus on being a damn good musician.

Apart from the flashes of migraine, the evening had gone well after The Dogs had been ignored-off-the-stage. Richie and his accomplished fossils had pulled the audience back into line with a sparkling and versatile set mixing standards and classics and some of Richie's own compositions on a theme of lost love, all of which, though none but Richie knew, were about Tara and the losing of Tara.

There was just a single fly thrashing in the ointment. All night, one member of the audience had been giving him the evil eye.

When he was a young musician Richie had learned to blank out the audience, or at least to see it as an homogenous creature, a multiple-eyed many-tentacled lumbering beast there to be tamed and charmed. But now, with his musicianship being so expert and so relaxed that it seemed effortless, he had plenty of time to look around, to note nuances in the audience response and to check out individuals. It became an interesting hobby: watching people watch him.

And there was this one scruffy weather-beaten dude who had spent the entire evening squinting with malevolence at him from the side of the hall. The man sat alone at a table nursing a single pint of ale for the duration, exuding disdain. Richie knew professional cool when he saw it: A&R men from record companies who refused to be impressed by anything, watching sullen and unsmiling and unmoved. This was not professional cool on display. This was something else.

The man was expressionless but somehow hostile. He wasn't interested in the music. He wasn't attracted there by the drink, or by the company of the audience. He just seemed to fix his neutral but chilling gaze on Richie.

Even for the pro that Richie was, it was unnerving.

When Richie finished his shimmering big blues finish at the end of the evening he earned rapturous applause from the hundred and fifty people in the hall; but from this sullen, staring man, nothing. Not a flicker of interest. Just a baleful gaze.

Richie set his guitar down on its stand and stepped offstage. Behind the stage was a shabby hallway that passed for a backstage green-room. It did no more than give the performers a place to appear from and retreat to, and the audience the illusion of a dressing-room area.

There Richie found a towel and the glum consortium

of The Dogs, three lads with stubbled chins and tousled hair. It seemed to Richie that the dress code of the kids was exactly the same as it was when he was starting out.

'That was something special,' one of the boys said.

Richie nodded and wiped his face of the sweat induced by the stage lights and the overcrowded atmosphere of the pub. 'Thanks. Praise from another musician is the best kind.'

'We were shite and you know it,' said one of the other boys.

'You weren't shite; some of what you did was good. You just lost the audience, and once you've lost them it's very tough to get 'em back.'

'Got any advice for a young band?' said the first.

'Don't look at me, 'cos I've fucked up everything I've touched. Here's good advice: do what I don't do.' He picked up a sports bag stuffed with CDs. 'Now I'm going out front and if I can flog a handful of these I might eat this week.'

Richie went out again and set up the CDs on a table near the stage. He could usually sell ten or a dozen copies at a good knock and that helped bulk out his slender income. He always mentioned the CDs two or three times during the evening, so there were a few people waiting by the stage with ready cash.

Someone wanted his CD signed and Richie was happy to snatch off the cellophane packaging and sign the cover; otherwise he would pocket the flat ten pounds he charged for each copy, offer a handshake and look to the next person in the line. He sold a few copies and then turned to a young woman in dark glasses and a leather jacket who had already picked up a CD from the table.

'Of course, I want it signed,' the young woman said. 'Fuckin' hell,' he said, 'fuckin' hell.'

He just hadn't expected her to turn up at one of his gigs. That was not how he'd imagined it after Peter had said that Tara would want to see him. His hands trembled. He needed a glass of something.

She didn't take off her dark glasses. Even though the venue was dark, he could see her looking shyly but evenly from behind the tinted glass. Her lips were slightly parted. 'Well?'

'Okay,' Richie said. 'Look, go through to the lounge bar. It's quieter. I'll finish up here and come through.'

She looked at him again, quietly placed the CD back down on the table, turned and went.

Someone else wanted a copy. 'Nice set, Richie,' a disembodied voice said. Money changed hands. He signed a couple more copies. More money changed hands. He hardly knew what he was doing. He nodded and smiled but his heart thumped and his migraine was splitting his skull.

Then there was just one more person wanting a copy. It was the man who had been giving him the evil eye all evening. 'Sign one for me,' said the man.

Richie looked into the stranger's eyes. There was no recognition. As far as he could tell the man was a complete outsider. 'What's your name?' Richie asked.

'Just sign it.'

Richie signed the copy and accepted the ten-pound note that was pressed into his hand, and the man slipped away through the noisy crowd of drinkers.

'He looked like a wrong 'un,' said one of the boys from The Dogs.

Richie blew out his cheeks, shook his head and

gathered up his bag of CDs. He planned to come back for his gear later. Squeezing through the drinkers he accepted a few pats on the back as he went. 'Nice one, Richie.' 'You ain't lost it, son.' 'Lovely stuff, Richie mate.'

Then he went out of the room in search of Tara.

21

*'In a utilitarian age, of all other times, it is a matter of
grave importance that fairy tales should be respected.'*
Charles Dickens

The lounge bar of The Phantom Coach was the oldest
part of the pub. It had a low ceiling with exposed oak
beams, and horse-brasses on the exposed-brick walls.
The room winked with reflected light on copper and
brass. Richie found Tara sitting at a table in the corner,
a delicate ivory hand resting on the empty table. She
was still wearing her dark glasses.

He asked her what she was drinking, and she asked
for a snakebite, a cider and bitter mix with a shot of
blackcurrant, a ridiculous concoction they used to drink
when they were kids. Drinks at The Phantom Coach
were on the house for Richie. He ordered himself a
more sensible pint of bitter and whisky chaser.

Setting the drinks on the table, he sank down beside
her. He tried to look into her eyes behind the dark
glasses. He thought she blinked. She picked up her
cloudy glass of snakebite and took a sip before carefully replacing it on the table.

'I'd like you to take those glasses off.'

'The light hurts my eyes.'

'Could you take 'em off anyway?'

'Why?'

'So we can talk.'

'Talk with your mouth. Not your eyes.'

Richie didn't answer.

Tara sighed and took off the dark glasses, folding them and placing them on the table beside her glass. Her eyelashes fluttered. She squinted at him.

Christ he thought, Genevieve was right. She did look incredibly young. 'What's a-matter with your eyes then?'

'I'm sensitive to light.'

'Seen a doctor? Optician?'

'No.'

'You should. Get it sorted.' He took a sip of beer and the foam left a trace moustache on his upper lip.

'Maybe I should.'

'Don't leave it. That's when things go wrong.'

Richie tipped back his whisky and he winced, not because of the taste of the scotch, but because of a flash of migraine. He tapped his whisky tumbler on the table and looked at an elderly couple almost canoodling near the door. He and Tara had been thrown out of this very pub twenty years ago for a bout of over-exuberant kissing.

'You don't seem to have much to say,' he said.

'No. I don't.'

Without knowing it Richie instantly fell back into the rapid dialect he might have spoken with Tara twenty years earlier. 'I mean Peter tole me, like, he tole me all abart this fuckin' story you giv' 'im. Christ that's precious, that is, precious. Comin 'ome wi' that on yer back. Teks some trunk, Tara, it teks some trunk and I always knew you 'ad a beautiful imagination, burra

184

would nerra guessed that you'd think anyone else would cop a story lark that. It's soo bad it's good. It's soo far aht it's … what can ah dream up that is sooooooooo off the wall they'll atta believe it, double-bluff, kind o'thing, shit or bust.'

'Right.'

He came out of dialect again. 'Twenty fucking years Tara. Twenty. And I almost got banged up in a prison cell for doing you in, but you know what? I have been in a prison cell. I have.' He tapped the side of his head. 'In here. Twenty years, hard, breakin' rocks.'

The elderly couple by the door looked up as Richie raised his voice.

Tara reached across the table to stroke Richie's hand but he snatched it away.

They sat in impossible silence for a while.

'Your playing is incredible now,' she said.

'Yeah?'

'Really. I can't believe how different it is.'

'Well, you'd hope for a little improvement after twenty years, wouldn't you?'

'But, it's like you reached your goal. You're as good as you wanted to be. Better.'

'Where you been, Tara?'

'I don't know.'

'Yeah? You don't know?'

'No, I don't know. I'm not pretending. I just don't know. I can account for six months and then there's a gap of nineteen and a half years that's missing. I'm seeing a shrink. He's going to help me find the missing years. And before you say anything I don't expect you to believe me. I don't expect anything except hurt, anger, contempt and puzzlement. Now can I put these glasses back on because this light is really hurting my eyes.'

Richie looked hard at her. Her face didn't seem a day older than when he'd last seen her. She had a pleasing tan now that she'd never had; a tawny or golden hue that suited her. When he looked into her eyes he saw hurt, but he also saw youth, the crystal fountain. He thought there were tiny, silvery laughter lines around her eyes that hadn't been there before. There was something in her demeanour, however, that had never been there before, something that sat on her shoulders. It might have been wisdom, but whatever it was, it was new.

Richie nodded and she slipped her dark glasses back on. It occurred to him that she might simply be hiding behind the shades, using them so that her face couldn't be read properly. Sore eyes were a convenient cover for people who didn't want to be seen. 'You really don't know where you've been? What are you, like an amnesiac?'

'Apparently. Except for six months. Which are very clear to me.'

Richie glanced away from her again, in exasperation, but as he did so he spotted someone glowering at him through a small glass panel in the door to the lounge. It was the man who had been staring at him throughout his performance that evening.

He mouthed back at the figure: 'Want my arse do ya?'

Tara had to turn to look over her shoulder in order to see who Richie was scowling at, but she was too late and he'd gone. 'What is it?'

'Some bloke giving me the dead-eye.'

'Who?'

'No idea but if he doesn't fuck off I'm going to slam my fist in his face.'

She smiled, but it was a painful smile. 'You haven't changed in that regard.'

She reached out to touch him again, and this time he let her stroke the back of his hand. He shook his head. 'How are you getting home tonight?'

'I'll walk.'

'It's nearly two miles.'

'We used to think nothing of walking two miles. Or ten. We'd walk ten miles back from some concert with a crap band.'

'I'll drive you home.'

'No thanks. I watched what you put away on stage all night. Sink a battleship.'

'Then, I'll walk you home.'

'No need.'

'Yes, I will. You never know who's out there.'

'All right.'

'Drink up. Let's go.'

'It's not eleven o'clock. The landlord hasn't called last orders yet.'

'That's all changed. They don't do that any more,' he said. 'That's all gone.'

Richie collected his guitar and amplifier and the rest of his gear and dumped it in the boot of his estate car in the pub car park. He planned to walk Tara home and then walk the further mile to his own house; he would collect his car in the morning.

Before locking his car he handed Tara one of his CDs. 'Here. Might as well have one o' these,' he said.

'CD right?'

'Duh.'

'I've never actually played one. I remember how you used to go on about vinyl records giving way to tapes. And now tapes have given way to CDs.'

'Are you winding me up?'

'No. I saw some at Mum and Dad's house. It's just a disc, right?'

'Come on, let's get walking.'

They set off along the footpath and after a few hundred metres they came to a stile giving way to a field. 'Go the Badger Track?'

'Of course.'

A track ran across a field and then alongside a thin copse; and from there lay a climb up a country lane to the top of hill before a minor road snaked its way to the Martins' house. They had walked it in the darkness or under moonlight many times together, years ago, sometimes with Peter; more often hand-in-hand. No one else called it the Badger Track. They did because one night on their way back from the Coach they'd encountered a huge black and white striped creature in the middle of the path; it had stopped dead and looked at them almost in astonishment before scuttling away.

More than one spring evening before Tara disappeared they had lain down in the grass after a night at The Phantom Coach and had sex; and that was where Tara had fallen pregnant.

'Can I tell you about a dream I had last night?' Tara asked him as they took the track across the field. There was still a dusting of snow caught in the grass. A waxing moon shone down on the snow and the earth underfoot was crusty and hard. 'I keep hoping that my dreams will unlock what's going on. I wanted to tell it to the shrink but he wasn't interested. I always thought shrinks were supposed to be interested in dreams.'

'Tell it to me.'

'I was walking up here and I was looking for you. At first it was a trick, you know, a joke, and you were supposed to be hiding. I got anxious. I looked all round here. Then I found a big pile of leaves and I scraped a few off the top and there you were, sleeping. I said, "what are you doing?" You woke up and yawned and you said, "Hibernating." Then I woke up. What do you think that means?'

You're the one, he said, you're the one who has been hibernating, if that's what it was. Not in my dream, Richie; in my dream it was you. That don't change anything. Yes it does. I don't know how it does but it does and aren't you cold? A bit, I was expecting to drive home. You're pissed so why would you drive and anyway do you want to take my arm?

That's a good 'un. Twenty years not a peep and now you want to snuggle up. Pardon me if I don't go along with that one.

You don't want to take my arm but you do want to walk me home through the snow in that thin jumper. I'm having a smoke want one no? Is it true you can't smoke in pubs any more? Stop taking the piss. I'm not I really am not hey there's a fox.

With Richie about to light the cigarette in his mouth, they watched a fox slink through the slender birch trees, its russet coat and tail painted silver by the moonlight. It stepped into moonshadow and was gone.

Do you remember the badger? Course I remember the badger. Do you remember what you said to me that night? To hell with all that, where you been, Tara, where you been?

She took off her dark glasses and looked at him straight. Her pupils were hugely dilated, spinning with moonlight, like someone who had been taking drugs. She looked right into him and for a moment he felt dizzy and scared.

Think back on that promise. If I left you it doesn't cancel it out. You're my one hope, Richie. My one horse in the race. Mum and Dad are just too shocked and bewildered by my coming home; Pete is in a rage with me; his wife looks at me like I'm a specimen of piss in jar; and then there's the shrink who just stares at me like he wants to pull my pants down and spank me. And then there's you, Richie. You, the man I've hurt most but the only one who can give me half a chance to work all this out.

Give us a break, Tara.

See that spot over there? We fucked over there didn't we? Well as true as that is true, what I'm telling you is all true. All I ask is that for one second you open up your mind, for one second, and allow the possibility for that one second that I might be telling you that something extraordinary happened. Really happened. Then after that one second you can go back to thinking I'm a liar or I'm insane or whatever you want. But I demand it, I demand one second.

Nope, can't do that.

You have no idea, Richie. None of you. There is a veil to this world, thin as smoke, and it draws back occasionally and when it does we can see incredible things. Incredible things, Richie.

What things?

Don't make me prove it, because I can put things in your mind if I want to. Really I could.

You've already put some murderous thoughts in my mind, Tara.

One second. One second in which you entertain the idea that the world is not exactly as you think it is; that everything unusual can't be reasoned away.

No.

Just one second. The time it takes to say your name. Because if I get that from you then I have a fissure in the wall and I can make the fissure into a crevice and I can scratch the crevice into a hole and then the wind will blow through and the wall will start to disappear.

What are you on, crack cocaine?

Don't need it where I've been.

Come on, that's your house down there with the light on: haven't been in a long time.

One second, Richie: give me one second of your life.

'You want to come in?' Tara asked him, with Richie hesitating at the gate. 'Mum and Dad need to see you.'

'I'm not sure I can.'

'Really? They feel the need to ... you know ... put things right.'

'Another time, eh?'

'Okay. If you think so.

'I do.'

'Well. Good night then.'

'Good night, Tara.'

They waited at the gate, looking at each other.

'Thanks for walking me home.'

'I enjoyed it. I think.'

'Oh, do you want me to get you a coat? Dad could easily lend you one of his.'

'No. I'd have to come in, and all that.'

'And all that.'

'Well, good night. Again.'

'Okay.'

Richie swung away and retraced his steps. He glanced over his shoulder to see Tara stepping into the house. A security light had switched on above her head. He turned up his shirt collar. The pavement was gleaming with a rime of frost and the bright moon lit his way. At least his headaches had passed.

One second she had asked for. One second, whereas if she only knew it she'd had twenty years. He'd deny it if she asked but of course he had entertained the idea that she might be telling the truth; or at least the truth as far as she understood it. The thing that had made him fall in love with Tara all those years ago was her integrity. She was so scrupulously honest as a teenager that she often put the adults around her to shame. Neither was it the kind of honesty that doesn't care about trampling on another person's feelings. She had empathy in spades. She just wouldn't compromise what she said to advantage herself or take the easy way out of a situation. It was an unusual trait in anyone.

Richie decided that Tara believed what she said. That, of course, was not the same thing as it being true.

What shocked Richie more than Tara's clinging to her story was how he felt about her. Nothing had changed. A lot of waters had flown through him since the day she disappeared. Drink. Drugs. Women. But he felt as passionate about her as he did all those years ago. The intervening time might not have happened.

As he walked through the frost, under that brilliant moon, he was flooded by memories of making that same walk after escorting Tara home so many times before. The landscape had hardly changed. Maybe a farmer's fence here or there might have been different, but nothing else. As he reached the crest of the hill bordered by the woods, he had a frightening thought. He wondered – just for a second – if the last twenty years had been a strange hallucination, and that really he was still in his late teens with his entire life before him. Maybe one of the psychedelic drugs they used to take back in those days could do that. Maybe he would wake up in the morning to find that the years had rolled back.

It could have been a comforting thought; but it wasn't. It made his stomach squeeze.

He stopped alongside the copse to light a cigarette. He flicked his lighter, inhaled and turned to look back down the valley, towards Tara's house. Then a figure came rushing out of the woods to push a brick into the side of his face, and Richie blacked out.

22

'Tush, tush. Their walking spirits are mere imaginary fables.'

Tourneur, The Atheist's Tragedy *iv, iii*

TM made a big fuss about bluebells at the start of her account. I'm not sure of the significance though I do think it represents permission. In the same way that alcohol or drugs offers permission or partially excuses a determination to violate some social code or other. It's as if she wants to blame the bluebells themselves for her transgressions.

Of course the use of alcohol or drugs represents a wilful determination to keep an appointment with some persuasive force or need in the unconscious mind. Rationally speaking, blaming one's behaviour on alcohol or drugs is like blaming the ladder by which you descended into a pit, or the staircase that took you down to a cellar, for what you found there.

She describes the bluebells as intoxicating and she also describes her path through the pool of bluebells as transgressive. She wants to be drugged by the bluebells, so that she can have access to her alternative world. Her life has already been turned upside down before her seducer comes along. The sky is in the earth, she says, and the earth is in the sky. There is incidentally a certain kind of logic in her thinking. Bluebells are associated with the spirits of the earth – I am consciously avoiding the word fairies, since I take the principles of animism and *genius loci* rather more seriously. Further, all parts of the flower, bulb, leaf and sap, do secrete a poison: they contain glycosides similar to digitalis and so are as dangerous as foxgloves.

This all may be an indication that she was intoxicated by drink or drugs at the time of her disappearance or abduction; or that she was in a state of mind parallel to inebriation. Either way we may assume that TM finds relief at the standard excuse of intoxication by the fragrance of the flower.

The site of her seduction is highly significant. There is a rock, the location where she says she lost her virginity to her boyfriend Richie. She removes the ring he gave her and places it on the rock. I take this to be highly significant. The rock is a kind of island in the sea of bluebells, a place of stability, rationality. When she takes off her ring and places it there she has already cast herself adrift. There seems to be no going back from this point.

It is here that fable and well-known narrative takes over the account. A mysterious male appears on a white horse. If we seem to know him, that is because his archetype is well established in literature, and it is at this point that TM's personal story confabulates with that of literary convention. The antecedents are manifold and presumably TM has heard all of these stories right from the cradle. She even signals to us that she was going into a certain kind of story-telling mode when she describes placing the ring on an 'emerald cushion of moss'.

Her story from this point seems to be drawn from books, a confection of half-grasped tales. There is of course a well-known literary tradition of famous abductees. Thomas the Rhymer kissed or slept with the Queen of Elfland and rode with her to her kingdom. When he returned, seven years had passed. Similarly, there is the ballad of a fellow by the name of Tam Lin, half fairy and half mortal, who collected the virginity of any maiden who passed through the forest of Carterhaugh. Tam Lin, it should be noted, rode a white horse. And on it goes: stories of abduction by fairies or by elves (the species interchangeable, one from the Latin root, one from the Teutonic root) are as numerous as the stars, and even though these two famous fellows are male abductees, the more common form of the story is that of women abducted. These are the clearly identifiable sources of TM's outlandish tale.

She hasn't exactly copied the stories; but what she has copied is the poetic conceit, that is to say a poetic summation of her experiences. She has enclosed the kingdom of her twenty years inside an acorn cup. She's made it her own life. To understand it all, we have to approach her tale in the same way that we would approach a dream, looking for clues that add up to a pattern that will inform us about the present state of her wounded psyche.

The dreamlike quality of the world she has moved into is intimated when she tells us she 'might have fallen asleep'. Whether she did or not is immaterial. The next thing that happens is the appearance of her suitor, if that's what he is, or in a darker sense her abductor and possibly her attacker.

He appears on a white horse. I have already alluded

to the traditions regarding such an animal, but it has more significance. The horse stands in for many unconscious passions, and the apparition of a black horse may be associated with war and death but commonly the female libido. In the case of white horses however, the symbol is universally positive, often an emblem of the irresistible life-force and is linked to the Celtic goddess Rhiannon and her Roman incarnation Epona, a goddess of fertility. To declare it a sexual image would be to understate the case, because travel by a white horse moreover often indicates a spiritual journey of some kind, perhaps to the underworld, perhaps to a supernatural place. The arrival of the seducer on his horse is complicated. In this case the maiden wants to be seduced and transported to a new level of consciousness. She lets her hair down from the tower of her longing.

What follows is a fairly prosaic account of ritual teasing, a preliminary to cosying up that might be experienced by any boy or girl. They lie with their heads together against a moss-covered stone. That moss-covered stone may be an altar at a wedding ceremony, or it may prove to be a tombstone. But what is important is that bluebells scent the air like incense and there is the irresistible excitement of courtship ritual. She is very willing.

She *was* very willing. And that is why she took off her ring.

23

'Some time afterwards she was lifted out of the bed by the men, and carried to the kitchen fire by John Dunne, Patrick, William, and James Kennedy. Simpson saw red marks on her forehead, and someone present said they had to "use the red poker on her to make her take the medicine". The four men named held poor Bridget Cleary, in her night-dress, over the fire; and Simpson "could see her body resting on the bars of the grate where the fire was burning." Fire, particularly applied to iron, is a traditional method of warding off a fairy, or frightening a changeling into leaving so that the real person can return. The "certain liquid" was urine, traditionally believed to force the changeling to flee; Bridget was repeatedly doused with human urine.'

Summary of trial transcript, (1895)

'Where are you?' Peter was just finishing up shoeing a mare that wouldn't stand still, a nervous grey with a wall-eye that had tried to bite him and then kick him. He'd insisted its owner – the wife of an estate-agent – take the reins and hold the creature while he did the job, and it had bitten her on the back of the hand instead of him.

Being kicked, bitten and burned came with the far-rier's job, like having a strained back. But when the horses bit or kicked their owners he couldn't help feeling an unnecessary fizz of satisfaction.

'I'm at the hospital. I called your house and Gen gave me your mobile number.'

Peter looked at his watch. 'I've got another appointment over that way. I'll pick you up and you'll have to sit in the car while I do the job, or I'll be late.'

'Appreciate it, Peter. There was no one else I could ask.'

Peter put away his mobile phone. 'Friend of mine,' he explained to the estate-agent's wife as she nursed her bitten hand. 'He got mugged on the way home from the pub last night.'

He ran his hand down the leg of the mare so that he could gently lift its hoof, and the creature tried to kick him again.

Richie was waiting at the hospital with a black eye and a bandaged head. He climbed into the cab of the truck and Peter drove off. Richie told Peter that he'd woken up freezing on the Badger Track. He'd staggered to the road and tried to hail passing cars but seeing his bloodied condition no one wanted to help. Then a minibus full of nuns had stopped and had driven him the hospital.

'Nuns?'

'Yeah, nuns. Six of 'em.'

'Really, nuns?'

'Yeh, nuns. No one else would stop.'

Peter wanted to know what Richie had been doing up on the Badger Track at that time of night, and Richie told him he'd walked Tara home from the pub. Peter had blinked at that but kept his eyes on the road.

He didn't even know Tara had been out. They talked about the assailant. It hadn't been a mugger, Richie explained, because when he came to check his pockets he still had his wallet with his credit cards and cash, and his mobile phone.

When Peter asked him if he'd got any enemies, Richie laughed and said only the Martin family, who for twenty years thought that he'd done Tara in. Peter bit his lip. Then Richie said no, he didn't have any enemies, even in the music biz where hatred and loathing of other artists was compulsory. Then he remembered the man who had been staring at him all night in The Phantom Coach.

'You've no idea who that was?'

'Not a clue.'

'You say he looked like a gippo?'

'Not exactly. Not a pikey anyhow. More like a roadie who fell out of a tour van. Staring me down in the pub.'

'Did you get a look at the guy who attacked you?'

Richie had already been through this with the police. They had interviewed him at the hospital about the attack. Richie was able to tell Peter that the police officer who interviewed him was the same local PC who had been in the station when he was being grilled after Tara's disappearance. He hadn't recognised Richie, but because the man was still in his uniform, Richie recognised him instantly, even though the elderly policeman had lost most of his hair and had put on a few stones in weight. Asked by Richie if he remembered the case the policeman said he did; he also said that he'd heard that the 'girl' had turned up again after all this time. When Richie asked him if he remembered the CID man beating the crap out of him the officer said he didn't remember that; but he followed his answer with an old-fashioned look.

'Funny,' Richie said to Peter, 'I had my jaw near broken just after Tara left, and then the same again just after she came back. Funny.'

Peter turned the truck into a stable yard where he was scheduled to shoe three more horses. 'You can help me,' he said. 'But stay out of sight because with your face like that you'll frighten the horses.'

Richie proved to be useful and wasn't above lugging Peter's portable furnace around, or holding a bridle while nails were hammered into horse-shoes. In return Peter bought him lunch at a pub. Peter had a pint of beer; Richie had a pint and a whisky chaser. Then they had another round and this time Peter had a chaser, too. Richie wanted to go a third but Peter pointed out that he was driving and he had an errand to run.

'In fact I can take you straight home or I can show you something interesting,' Peter said.

'I've got nothing at home,' Richie said.

So Peter drove him to see Tara's shrink. Underwood had asked Peter to drop by at a time when Tara wouldn't be present. Why, exactly, Peter didn't know, but Underwood had suggested that he kept mid-afternoons free if possible, and that if Peter was out that way he should call in.

'You've got to see this bloke,' Peter said. 'Never mind Tara, he looks like he's the one who's been living with the fairies.'

So they went in and were greeted solemnly by the ancient Mrs Hargreaves, who whispered that Vivian was having his afternoon nap, but it was never longer than fifteen minutes if they wouldn't mind waiting. She looked pointedly at the bandage looped around the crown of Richie's head. Then she led them upstairs to the landing and the waiting room before shuffling away.

'Vivian,' said Richie, after she'd gone.

They both had a look in the museum cases at the silk shoes and then they sat down next to each other on hard chairs in the waiting room. Peter folded his arms and Richie did too. 'It's quiet,' Richie said.

'Mmm,' Peter replied.

Richie crossed his ankles in front of him. He unfolded his arms and then folded them again. Then he snorted briefly. Peter looked at him to see what he was laughing at. 'Vivian,' Richie said. Then Peter made a kind of grunt. The grunt seemed to pass back to Richie because he snorted louder. Peter tried not to get pulled in but, in bracing himself, somehow a tiny pellet of snot shot down his nose and landed on his knee. Richie's snort turned in to an asthmatic wheeze. In less than a second the two men sat upright on their hard chairs, their bodies quaking and shuddering mercilessly, like two schoolboys convulsed with the giggles in morning assembly. They both squeezed their ribs, gripped by panic and hysteria. Holding back their hilarity was like trying to nail down the lid on a barrel of eels. Richie gulped in some air. Tiny little high-pitched squeals, like trapped gas from a balloon, pushed out from between Peter's clamped cheeks.

It was too much for Richie. He had to get up and make a dash for it. In the process he shouldered aside the white-haired man who had arrived at the door of the waiting room. Vivian Underwood was attired, as before, in brocade smoking jacket and leather slippers.

The psychiatrist turned to watch Richie, who was now howling his head off, dash past him and make his way down the stairs.

Underwood said nothing about the spectacle of a man in a prominent head bandage roaring down the staircase, and instead invited Peter into his consulting room. Struggling to contain himself, Peter followed Underwood into the study, where he was offered a choice of chairs. The mood of the room sobered him a little. Peter opted for one of the chairs drawn up by the fireplace.

'Thank you for coming in,' Underwood said. 'It would help me enormously to hear your views on one or two things.'

'Sure.'

'We could start, quite simply, by you telling me – in your view – what you think is going on with your sister.'

'Okay. My view is not very deep, I'm afraid. I think she got pregnant, had an abortion and did a bunk because she couldn't face us. Why she's come back now with this cock and bull story is beyond me.'

'Nothing more complicated, in your view, to be found?'

'That's why I'm paying you.'

'Fair enough. When she did a bunk, as you say, do you think she felt in physical danger?'

'Oh no. My dad had never lifted a hand to her. There would been a lot of wailing and gnashing of teeth but no one would have hurt her. Physically.'

'Physically, as you say. But that's as far as your own guesswork goes?'

'I told you it was simple. I could say that maybe she's a Pathological Narcissist, and that her story is an elaborate compensation for an inability to face up to adult chores and functions. But I don't know what that all means.'

'Who the hell have you been talking to? Is this your wife speaking?'

'Yes. How did you know that?'

'Relax. We can smell it on each other. Anyway I'm not one for labels: they change every couple of years like the hemlines on women's skirts. And in any event I'd disagree. The Narcissistic personality is character-ised by self-importance and lack of empathy. That's not your sister.

'The problem I have with your sister is that while her story is outrageous she exhibits none of the usual indicators of disorder associated with delusions. Your wife may be right in that there is a grandiosity in her tale, but I'd expect certain things to come with that. As a pathology, delusion is different from what we might call dogma or plain stupidity. Her belief in her story isn't any different to the belief in certain faiths. If she's mentally ill, then so is half the population. We have to leave that and look elsewhere.'

'Elsewhere?'

'It's not the six months she's telling us about that I'm concerned with. It's the nineteen and a half years she's holding back. Somewhere in there I think we'll find a trauma, and that trauma will have started the clock ticking on this fantasy she is so vividly reporting. The reason I've got you here is so that you and Tara's parents can listen out for tiny fragments of that near-twenty years of existence. Anything to build on. And by the way, I really don't think she is consciously lying or hiding information from you: I believe there is a huge gap in her memory. You're going to have to get used to that.'

'She seems willing to co-operate, at least,' Peter said. 'I wondered if there were any tests we could do, so that we could present her with evidence of her age. At least confront her with the science of it. Do you know of any tests that prove conclusively how old a person is?'

'Oh there is one. But the person has to be dead.'

'That's going a bit far.'

'Indeed. It's not as easy as you would think. You could remove a tooth from her mouth and have that analysed, but that also seems rather extreme. On the other hand, X-rays of her teeth would conclusively reveal her age plus or minus a couple of years. Do you happen to know a sympathetic dentist?'

'I do. I'm shoeing his daughter's pony on Friday.'

'Are you a blacksmith?'

'Farrier.'

'Of course. The other thing about a dental check is that it would prove conclusively that she is who she says she is.'

'Oh there's no doubt of that.'

'You sure of that?'

'I'm almost one-hundred per cent certain.'

'Almost. So there is a tiny margin of doubt?'

'Well.'

'Okay. Thank you for coming in.' Underwood got to his feet and Peter did too. The psychiatrist escorted him to the door. 'Mrs Hargreaves will see you out. By the way. Who was that laughing lunatic with the bandaged head?'

24

'Think what you would have been now, if instead of being fed with tales and old wives' fables in childhood, you had been crammed with geography and natural history!'

Charles Lamb to Samuel Taylor Coleridge

Jack thought maybe he would just deposit the pile of freshly printed leaflets on the old lady's step and make a quick getaway. A breeze chased dead leaves across the yard as he approached her door and he had an idea that the leaflets would just get blown off the step. He looked around for a stone or a brick with which to weight the leaflets but he couldn't see anything to hand. Instead, he rang the bell.

Mrs Larwood came to the door and after the usual and interminable drawing of bolts and chains, there she was. Jack offered her the leaflets without a word. She looked at them with her cataracted eyes. She didn't seem to want to take them from him.

'You're so kind it makes me want to cry,' she said.

'They came up well,' Jack said. 'I mean it's a clear picture. I mean you can see the ... you can see it's your cat.'

'I'm losing hope for him, I'm afraid.'

'Well, you shouldn't do that. You shouldn't give up.

You should never give up. Someone might … look, these need to be put on lamp-posts. I asked people to check their sheds and outhouses. I didn't know your telephone number so I put your address. Here it is. They need attaching to lamp-posts. All of these.'

'How will we do that?'

'Just some tape. Tape them on.'

'I'm not sure I have any tape.'

'I have some at the house. Some tape. Okay I'll do them. I'll tape them on.'

'Come in and have some lemonade.'

Jack took a deep breath. 'No, I'll go and do these. They need doing. The quicker I put these up the more chance there is. Of someone finding the cat. In a shed. Maybe.'

She wagged a finger at him. 'All right. But after you've done it come straight back here. I insist. I'll have some cake and some lemonade for you.'

I'm thirteen, Jack thought, *I don't fucking well want cake and lemonade*. 'Okay,' he said. 'Sounds good.'

Jack hurried away clutching his sheaf of printed leaflets, feeling the old lady's clouded gaze watching him go. That was it; that was his day screwed up. His dad had told him it was just this one job, but one job leads to another. Now he was going to have to tape up the leaflets, all of them, all round the neighbourhood, and then after that go back over there and drink flat lemonade and eat shit cake. When there were a thousand things he'd rather do. These were the last days of the school holiday, and this was how he was spending them.

He crossed the road and returned to his own house, where his mother asked how he'd got on with taking the leaflets to Mrs Larwood. He ignored her and stomped rapidly upstairs. In his bedroom he found some electrician's tape and then he stomped downstairs again. He marched past his mother without a salute and went outside again.

He stopped at the lamp-post directly outside Mrs Larwood's house. She was watching him from the window. He avoided eye-contact with her as he taped up the first of the leaflets. The electrician's tape didn't stick too well to the concrete post and he made a pig's ear of the first leaflet. But he found it would work well enough if he bound it tight, top and bottom, and overlapped the tape.

Jack had printed fifteen leaflets. At first he'd knocked out just half a dozen. Then he'd thought that if he was doing the job, it ought to be done properly, so he'd printed another six. What with his preview copy that made thirteen, which he thought was an unlucky number, so he'd rolled off an extra couple more. After that it occurred to him that it was senseless putting up a leaflet on every single lamp-post in the neighbourhood. They should only be posted at serious intervals. With fifteen leaflets to post that would take him well outside of the immediate neighbourhood.

He didn't know exactly how far a cat might stray in ordinary circumstances. He tried to be scientific about it. He calculated that a cat might easily stray up to a mile away but that the chances of it wandering that far would diminish proportionately the further you got away from Mrs Larwood's house. For the leaflets to be effective, (or at least for the campaign to look effective) he thought that maybe they should be concentrated in the streets within a quarter-mile radius, with one or two extra leaflets at a greater distance.

He went back to get his bike. The idea that this was going to take him all morning enraged him. It was when he was taping a poster to his seventh lamp-post that he was struck by an idea. He looked hard at the picture of the ginger cat that he'd killed and buried. The only thing to truly distinguish it from other ginger cats, he thought, was its bright red collar.

He didn't know too much about cats. He was more about dogs. If anyone tried to substitute a dog it was unlikely you could get away with it. Unless that is, it was a very close match indeed, and it had an identifiable collar, with a familiar tag clearly stating its name and revealing the address of its owner. Of course it would have to be a really good match.

And cats were even less distinctive than dogs. Heck, if someone put seven ginger cats in a room and asked you to pick out yours, you'd be hard pressed. Especially if you were very short sighted, as Mrs Larwood was. It was wild but it might work. Dig up the dead cat. Get the collar off it. Go to the Ginger Cat Rescue Centre or whatever it was they had. Put the old collar on the new cat.

One happy old lady.

Jack knew it was a long shot; but then heck, a cat is just a cat.

He spent the rest of the morning posting the leaflets, mulling the idea.

'Do you know what?' Peter said to Richie after they drove away from Vivian Underwood's consulting rooms. 'That's the first time in twenty years that I've laughed so hard that the snot shot down my nose.'

'Me too, Pete. Me too.'

'We used to laugh like that all the time, we did.'

'All the time,' Richie said.

'I've missed you, mate. I have.'

'Oh Jesus.'

'Tell you what. I've got no more appointments for the rest of the day. You remember this one?'

Peter indicated to pull off into a roadside ale-house called The Three Horseshoes.

'Oh Christ!' said Richie. 'Didn't we get banned from here?'

'That was twenty years ago, mate. But they can't turn me away. Three horseshoes is the sign of the Worshipful Company of Farriers.'

'Is it now?' said Richie.

They were indeed banned from The Three Horseshoes twenty years ago. Back then it was a rough-house watering hole oozing nicotine and run by a bald-headed bruiser called Amos McNamara, who kept a cricket bat signed by the England team behind the bar, and it was for breaking heads rather than for admiring. The place had had more than a lick of paint since then. Now it was a gastro-pub, welcoming families and coach parties.

They sauntered into the bar and enquired about the health of Mr McNamara and the resting place of his cricket bat, but the new owner, though interested, couldn't help with any information about either. He thought the old boy was dead, but couldn't say for sure. They found a corner and touched glasses of foaming ale. There was a good-natured dispute about why they'd been banned. Richie said it was because Peter had ended up on all fours one evening with Richie riding him round the bar, like a farmer riding a pig to market, slopping ale everywhere. Peter said he was getting that confused with the time they were banned from The Gate Hangs Well. Richie bought another round of drinks, with chasers, and said no, they were banned from The Gate Hangs Well for complaining about the quality of the beer after they'd spent four hours drinking it.

Richie asked about the life of a farrier and Peter said it was a living, and he in turn asked about the life of a musician, and Richie said it wasn't a living; and Peter bought another round, with chasers. The drink was going down well so he said he'd leave the truck where it was and they could get a taxi. Richie pointed out that it was only a couple of miles driving distance.

'I don't care if it's a couple of yards. I don't agree with drink driving.'

'You wouldn't have said that twenty years ago,' Richie said.

'No, and maybe that's the good thing about growing up,' Peter said a little sharply.

'All right. I was only saying.'

'Only saying? Maybe if you had small kids you'd have a different attitude. The way people drive around here. Fuck.'

'All right! Don't get bent out of shape!'

'If I had my way I'd lock up anyone who got behind a wheel after drinking.'

For a moment it could have gone wrong right there. Their diverging attitudes on a point of law might have represented a huge gulf between them. But after the third pint they relaxed again and got on to the subject of Tara. Richie asked Peter what he made of it all.

'Well, the shrink says—'

'*Vivian*,' said Richie.

'Yes *Vivian*. Vivian says—'

And they started laughing again, for no reason that they could think of.

When this unreasonable laughter subsided, Peter tried again. 'Vivian says that she's probably had a knock on the head and that it's made her on the one hand forget everything that's happened in the last twenty years, and on the other hand make her go back to her teens, which is why she's come home.'

'So you don't think she's … making it all up, like?'

'No Richie. I did at first. But no. What about you?'

'No, she ain't making it up. She really believes it. I can tell.'

The two men supped from their glasses in silence.

At last Richie said, 'You don't suppose—'

'Don't even go there,' Peter growled.

'You don't know what I was going to say!'

'Yes, I do.'

'Do you fuck as like! You've no idea what I was going to say!'

'You were going to say: do I suppose that at some weird level there might be something in it.'

'Like hell I was.'

'No? You've spent one evening with her, walking her home, and she's already started to pull you into it. One evening. That's what she's like. Always was. She'd have you believing anything.'

'Give over! What do you think I am?'

'You know what she's like. Better than I do. She could always do that.'

'Dah!'

'All right. Be honest. Go on now: tell me exactly what you were going to say. Be honest for once in your big hairy life.'

Richie looked him in the eye. 'I was going to say: *do you suppose that at some weird level there might be something in it.* I'll get another round of drinks.'

And to make it square Peter got another round and Richie said that since they were going to the trouble of calling a taxi after drinking so much they might as well have another chaser in that case; and in that case Peter said they might as well chase the chaser. And the rounds chased the chasers and the chasers chased the rounds and pretty soon they were shouting and laughing and banging the table and the new landlord, just like the old landlord, said they were upsetting other customers and if they didn't keep it down then he would ask them to leave.

'You can't ban us,' Richie said. 'We're already banned. It's a contradiction in terms.'

'In fact we've got a life membership ban from this place. Oi, Richie, I've just remembered why we were banned! You were showing everyone your arse.'

'*You* were, you mean. *Your* arse, you mean.'

'That's enough,' said the landlord.

'You can't throw him out!' Richie protested genially. 'He's a worshipful shipmaster of the high-farrier order. What is it? High company. What is it?'

'Right, let's have you out,' said the landlord. He put his hand on the back of Peter's chair.

'We're going, we're gone,' Peter said, standing up, eying the landlord beadily, offering a handshake that the landlord pretended not to notice. 'No shakey? No shakester? That's one thing about Amos McNamara, he would always shake your hand. This place has gone badly uphill, my friend. Badly uphill.'

Then they were outside in the car park, feeling the cold.

'Did we just get thrown out?' Peter said.

'For nothing. For nothing at all. That's how it is these days. You can't smoke; and you can get thrown out for any good reason you can think of. '

'Gimme a cig.'

They stood in the car park, smoking exuberantly. After a histrionic performance of stamping on the stub of his cigarette Richie took out his phone and called a cab company. The first was busy so he called another. A cab was available but it would be twenty minutes. They looked back at the pub and thought about going back inside to wait, but then remembered they'd just been barred from the premises. Then Peter said fuck it, he wasn't going to spend half an hour freezing his nuts off waiting for a cab and that they should get in the truck. Richie protested, but feebly. Peter pointed out that it was only a few miles away.

Ten minutes later Peter looked in his rear-view mirror and saw a police car. 'Oh.'

'Drive steady,' said Richie.

'If he gives me a breath test I'm fucked with my job.'

'Don't panic. Drive steady.'

The police car tailed them, but after another mile the blue lights flashed on. 'That's it. I'm going to have to pull over.'

Richie was already unwinding the bandage from his head.

'What you doing?' Peter asked.

'Shut up. Pull over. Then tie this round your head. We'll switch seats and I'll say I was driving.'

'You can't do that.'

'You've got mouths to feed. I don't need my licence.'

'No, Richie.'

'Just do what I say, right? It'll be fine.'

Peter carefully pulled over and switched off the ignition. The patrol car also pulled in, at a short distance. Richie was already scrambling across into the driver's seat. Peter tried to squirm from under Richie but got the gear stick up his arse and he trapped his foot round the handbrake. There were a few seconds of unpleasant closeness and porcine grunting before they managed to extricate themselves from each other. Peter looked in the wing mirror. The police officer was just getting out of his car. Peter grabbed the bandage and swathed it round his head, though he didn't manage to tie it. It hung rather loose.

Richie composed himself in the driver's seat. He wound down the window.

'I admit it officer,' Richie said. 'I've had a cigarette in a public place. Line up the firing squad.'

'Don't I know you?' said the officer.

It was the same officer who had both detained him after Tara had disappeared and who had interviewed him at the hospital that very morning. 'Oh Christ, yes,' Richie said. 'We're dear old pals.'

25

'O see ye not yon narrow road,
So thick beset with thorns and briers?
That is the path of righteousness,
Tho after it but few enquires.
'And see not ye that braid braid road,
That lies across that lily leven?
That is the path of wickedness,
Tho some call it the road to heaven.
'And see not ye that bonny road,
That winds about the fernie brae?
That is the road to fair Elfland,
Where thou and I this night maun gae.'

Thomas Rhymer, trad.

Hiero put me on the horse and fetched me back to the house all over again. This time he led me most of the way, and we went in silence. He walked in front of the mare, and I could see the vicious weal I had laid on him with the riding crop.

It wasn't the last time I tried to ride out of there. Over the next few weeks I tried to find my way out many times, either on the back of that white mare or just by walking away. In the early days Hiero would simply follow me. Or he would catch up with me and let me know he was following me, and he would tell me to let him know when I was tired so that he could lead me back. Then he wearied of the game and he stopped following me, and off I would go, sometimes sleeping out in the fields and waking with the cold dew on my face. Then if I got tired I would mount the mare and because she knew the way I would just let her take me back.

Hiero promised me he wasn't lying. I would find my way back after six months he said, but not before. He told me that these things had to be done according to strict rules of physics, rules I didn't understand, rules pertaining to the time of the year and the time of the day and the position of what he called the celestial machinery, which I took to mean the moon and the stars, but which he said was something else altogether.

After that first time I tried to leave he took me back to the lake and to his house. The sex-crazed woman and her lover were eating at the table when we returned. She got up from the table and, seeing his wound, went straight to him.

'She did this to you?' When Hiero didn't reply she said, 'I can't believe you allowed her to do this. It shouldn't go unpunished.'

'My business,' was all Hiero said. 'My business, my portion.'

I said I wanted to go out, that I wanted to talk, so we left the woman and her lover and we went to the edge of the lake, where we sat down on the glittering, quartz-rich grey sand.

'I don't like that woman. Can't you get rid of her?'

'Look, I told you, it's not my house.'

'Is it her house?'

'No. We don't own things. Around here, everything belongs to everyone.'

'So if I take the horse again tomorrow,' I snapped back at him, 'no one is going to stop me?'

'No one is going to stop you.'

'So you're like communists or something?'

He had to suppress a smile because he knew it would enrage me for him to look amused. 'Not exactly.'

'Is it a commune?' I'd heard of a place near Quorn, not far from the Outwoods, where the people ate only macrobiotic food and slept freely with each other and smoked dope until they pissed their pants.

'Of a kind.'

I looked across the lake. Everything was so vivid that it still seemed to graze my eyes, as if something was gently scraping my retina. It occurred to me that the lake had changed colour since the day before. Where it had been a blue black it was now much more of an aquamarine, as if the light itself had changed. But it also seemed to me that the shape of the lake had changed, and that where I had previously looked at an elliptical body of water it was now like a long cylinder. There was something unsettled and unsettling about the earth and the landscape in that place. As if it was remoulding itself all the time.

But I had other things to think about.

I was still demanding to know why I couldn't go home and all he would say was that there was no road, no way, no possibility. The crossing opened again in six months and even then you could only slip by at the precise hinge. When I complained I didn't understand anything he said he told me that there were four hinges to the day: dawn, mid-day, dusk and mid-night. These he said opened up the crossing, but only at certain times of the calendar. 'Tara, the world is more complicated and beautiful than you people have ever understood,' he said.

'*You people?*'

'I'm sorry,' he said, taking my hand. 'I didn't mean it to come out like that. But you can't fight it. The thing to do is to make the best of it while you're here. Learn things. See things with different eyes. I'll make sure that you come to no harm and that no one touches you.'

I didn't much like the sound of that.

He looked into my eyes. 'My dearest hope,' he said to me, 'is that you get to like it here, and I'm sure you will if you can only stop pining for your old life. Things are different here. But if after six months you're not happy then I'll make sure you go back safe and sound. That's a promise.'

But I still couldn't accept any of it, and then while we were talking I felt a slight tremor in the earth. Hiero's eyes bulged.

'Did you feel that?'

'Yes,' I said.

He leapt to his feet. 'Quick, into the water,' he said. I watched him as he stripped off his clothes. 'Get naked,' he said.

I didn't see why I should. I sensed some kind of emergency but I didn't see how taking off my clothes would help. Then shag-woman and her lover both came running pell-mell from the house, and they were both shrieking. They were trying to tear off their clothes as they ran, stumbling, running, still screaming.

The pair were joined by others who emerged from houses and cottages further along the bank of the lake.

Strange looking creatures all of them, lithe figures running in a state of half undress, trying to rid themselves of their clothes as they ran towards us.

'Into the water Tara!' Hiero shouted. 'Into the water!

I felt frightened. By now we had been joined by maybe fifteen or twenty other people, all of whom were either stripping off their clothes on the sand or who were splashing into the water as they did so. They shrieked and screamed and I could hardly hear Hiero above the noise.

He was still shouting and beckoning me on and I felt a wave of terror, until I saw that he was smiling, and though all these other folk were shrieking they were also laughing. Bewildered, I waded out to him and he grabbed my hand, and just as our hands touched I felt the water fizz and foam and crackle, and a current pass through the water to our bodies, and then there came an almighty thump that flung us over in the water.

Unable to resist the shockwave, everyone went over together, and I felt the foam of the water pass through me, tingling and vibrating and it seemed to pass inside my veins, making my blood buzz and vibrate. The shock of deep pleasure made me laugh out loud, and for a minute I was helpless with laughter, involuntary laughter, just like all the other people who had been turned over by the shockwave.

They were all laughing like hyenas or chattering monkeys, and I was too.

I got to my feet and now everyone was holding hands. Somebody grabbed my hand – not Hiero, for I'd lost him in the water. Another hand enclosed my free hand on the other side and everyone stretched out in a long, linked line just before a second shock wave tipped us over. This time the pulse was stronger and I felt the communion of all those bodies as the power surged through the line. The laughter reached a scary pitch, a hysteria moderated only by a feeling of health and wellbeing, as if my blood had been emptied out and replaced by a transfusion of silk. I looked at the water and it had become an iridescent pool, sparkling and roiling with colour. The light overwhelmed me and made me want to laugh and cry at the same time.

Hiero, laughing his bloody head off, came staggering towards me through the water.

'What's happening?' I shouted as he grabbed my hand.

'Hahaha tee heeh hee nanana it's an ejaculation is what it is Tara! Hahaha hahhheee—'

'A what?'

'Tee heee hee *ejaculation*!'

And then another throb of energy struck us and we were thumped sideways. I felt both the benign energy of the water and the shock of power from Hiero's hand flutter through me, and I knew in that moment how he loved and adored me, and the detection of unselfish love passing from him to me transmitted in a wave to the stranger holding my hand on the other side. And I was laughing again even though there were tears of sadness running down my face, a mixed-up folly of mirth and sorrow.

I think the jolts – the ejaculations – came seven or eight more times, and then stopped suddenly, and at last the laughter and shrieking died down, though everyone remained hand-in-hand in a long line for a good while afterwards, catching their breath, hoping for another jolt, not knowing if the earth would deliver more.

But it was over and the moment had passed and eventually the folk moved out of the water, returning to wherever they had come from. Only a few diehards remained in the water, desperately hoping for another shockwave.

We lay on the sand, Hiero and I, recovering from the hysteria; I in my soaking clothes, because I was the only person who hadn't taken them off, and for which modesty I now felt a bit foolish. I asked Hiero what had triggered these seismic movements and he looked at me blankly.

'It's the gift of the lake,' he said.

'What?'

'It's what lakes do.'

'Not where I'm from they don't. I've never seen that.'

'Oh yes, you have. But your people don't know how to notice it. It's what the lake does when it's pleased.'

'Oh come off it,' I said, laughing at him.

He looked at me seriously. 'Really.'

'I mean,' I said, 'it's not like the lake is a living thing.'

This was perhaps the worst thing I could have said. He looked suddenly alarmed. He put a hand, sticky as it was with grey sand, over my mouth. 'Hush, darlin' girl! Hush! The lake hears your every word and knows your every thought.'

I made to answer this nonsense, but I saw further alarm in his eyes and he pushed his hand further on to my mouth, forcing grit on to my lips. Only when he felt I wouldn't say any more on the subject did he take his hand from my mouth.

'The lake listens,' he said quietly. 'The lake watches. The lake knows everything.'

I didn't know what the hell he was talking about.

I had no chance to reply because one of the diehards who had been standing in the water long after most of the others had gone came striding out of the shallows, his muscles running with glistening droplets of water and light, and he spotted me.

'Yum yum!' He was strong and handsome, with very tanned skin and hunter's eyes, grey and green. He had his long hair tied at the side and the water was still dripping off his hair and sluicing down his body. He smiled at me, showing a row of strong white teeth, with one missing at the corner of his mouth.

He leaned down quickly and through my wet blouse he gently squeezed a nipple between a thumb and forefinger. Hiero grabbed his wrist and twisted it away. 'Not for you, Silkie,' he said firmly. 'This one's not for you.'

The man called Silkie stepped back. 'Possessiveness? I would have thought that decision was up to her.'

'It is up to me,' I snarled, 'and I don't want you touching me again.'

The man looked nonplussed, as if no one had ever spoken to him like that before. 'You've bought a ghost into the camp, Hiero.' Then he looked at me. 'Your loss,' he said. He turned and walked back up the beach towards the further houses.

'A what into the camp?'

Hiero grunted. 'You might find that the men here aren't used to being rejected. And the women never so.'

'He was a creep.'

'It takes some getting used to.'

'I don't plan to get used to that, thanks.'

'No. You don't have to.'

Something I was soon to discover about the commune

was its rampant sexual permissiveness. The people who lived there fucked openly, frequently and – it seemed to me – indiscriminately. The boys fucked the girls and the girls fucked the boys and the girls were the most persistent initiators. Plus the girls fucked the girls and the boys fucked the boys, and often they all did it to each other in a daisy-chain.

Maybe you find that erotic. I didn't. I don't. In fact quite the opposite happened, and I soon realised that I was the only person there who wasn't sexually active, with the exception of one person. That was Hiero. He was saving himself, it appeared, for me, if ever I decided I wanted him. Most of the women in that place expressed astonishment. They regarded him with concern and pity, in the same way you might have sympathy for someone with a broken leg. They brought him fruit and made conscious efforts to 'cheer him up' when he protested he didn't need cheering up.

It was all the fault of the *ghost* he had brought into the community. A *ghost*, I later discovered, was to these people someone who had died a virgin.

I didn't try to tell anyone that I wasn't a virgin. Meanwhile there was no shortage of offers from those who wanted to relieve me of the burden of virginity.

And that, in the end, was what led to Hiero being killed.

26

'Nevertheless – and here is a great key to the under-standing of myth and symbol – the two kingdoms are actually one. The realm of the gods is a forgotten dimension of the world we know.'

Joseph Campbell

She talks of making a crossing. We can be sure there is no crossing, at least not in the material world. There is no border, no gateway nor checkpoint. There is not even a river to ford. The 'crossing' she has made is from the safe place of what she feels is her domestic incarceration to a place of open possibility. Her psyche has opened up like a flower to her own unconscious longings. She has 'crossed' from the restricted, rationalised world of the local, the world of her safe childhood, to the open, creative and chaotic world of the universal, to the more dangerous realm of the adult.

Yes, she has met someone. But still we don't know who or what he is, and we don't know anything about her intentions.

What can we say of the place at which she arrives? We are told there is a sandy beach, though it appears to be more lake than sea. We can safely say that it is a version of the land of Tir Na Nog or some other fabled land beyond the reaches of any map; a place that can only be reached either by arduous voyage or through an invitation by one of its fairy residents. It exists, in a very precise way in a plane of the mind, and although this is true for TM's story, we can be sure that this place has some kind of parallel in the material world, and it is here we get some insight into where she went, at least initially.

There are descriptions of what appears to be a commune of some kind. Certainly it is a gathering of folk with what might be called anti-establishment values. The house she describes as cobwebbed and rather filthy by the bourgeois standards to which she is accustomed at the Martin household. But there appears to be high value placed on the Arts and on Music, because we hear details of musical instruments and descriptions of books and beautiful illustrated charts. Scholarship, at least, seems to be prized in this commune to which she has been brought.

The house is shared, we know that. There is no electricity and there are no phones available. The electricity may have been turned off because no one has paid the bills, but the rejection of telephone communications seems radical and indicates an ideologically-based group of people perhaps living an 'experimental' lifestyle, possibly anarchistic in character. There appears to be no property ownership, no rigid social structure and no obvious leadership or hierarchy, and this might point to an early eco-group or green-living project; alternatively we might be looking at a religious troop or fringe spiritual cult, though TM's report offers no clues in the way of religious dogma. Even though these events happened twenty years ago it might be possible to make enquiries to see if there were any such communes either in the immediate locality or say within a thirty mile radius.

Yet even though there are no telephones available to her, we can assume that there was nothing stopping her from simply walking out and finding her way home. There is nothing at all to suggest that she was being held against her will, and we are surely not to take seriously the idea that she couldn't find her way back. Again we must reassert that TM was perfectly happy to be there until some process of disillusion had set in, by which time she might have felt that she had disgraced herself to her family and couldn't face returning. And I think we have the answer to why that might have been.

TM makes much of a ritual drink she takes with her seducer. The drink comes in a ridiculously tiny glass and two things are happening here. Once again TM is falling back on traditional fairy lore. The food and drink of the fairy folk is dangerous. Tradition has it that their hospitality should be resisted, because those who do partake of the offered food and drink can never leave this enchanted place. And so with TM. The drink, along with her oath, 'traps' her in this place, at least in her own head. But there is a more mundane level to all of this. After the drink TM reports that she 'feels calm' and finds the night 'velvety'. She is drunk and is trying to excuse her behaviour by minimalising the quantity of the drink. How many people lie about how much alcohol they have consumed and claim to be surprised by how they came to be in such a state? This is a young girl's post-debauch lament that she had no idea how much she was drinking or that 'someone put something in her drink'.

And although it is not reported, this debauch probably led to sex. This conclusion is guaranteed not by any admission, but by the force of her outrage against the sexual act itself. She is in an overly energetic state of denial.

Her revulsion of the open sexuality she describes is a projected revulsion of her own behaviour around the time of her disappearance. She has sublimated her distaste for what happened to her and blamed it on 'the other', which in this case is the community in which she had been living. The sex she sees happening openly in the commune is always described in orgiastic rather than sensual terms; the sex is mechanical rather than loving. TM expends a great deal of energy distancing herself from these sexual activities. Rather too much energy.

A word or two here about the family context, such as it is, though the patient has been distanced from her own parents for some twenty years. The patient's brother has stepped into the father's role in bringing her here and arranging for her wellbeing. I've also been able to meet the brother's wife, a psychologist by academic training. I put it to her that we have here a complete Darling family, with TM as one of the lost children seduced away by Peter Pan. She was less than amused, though confirmed her own role in that she continues to want to take hold of the story by advancing a few theories through her affable husband, who raised the question of *pathological narcissism,* a phrase his wife had surely equipped him with. These people really do have an almost superstitious belief in the power of words, as if by naming Rumpelstiltskin they suddenly have power over him. Similarly, they desperately want to name the condition. This is the academic way, and I have to say that it's less than helpful.

TM's account does have the pervasive pattern of grandiosity that is an indicator of narcissistic personality disorder, but the trait's two other most common indicators, the need to be admired and the lack of empathy, are absent. In every single case of NPD that has come before me the patient has gone to great lengths to seek my express approval (and why wouldn't they want the approval of someone who is on the face of things fascinated by them?), whereas TM couldn't care less whether I like her or not. On the other hand she never exhibits irritation, boredom or distraction and her co-operation with my line of questioning is fully empathetic to my own needs. I am happy to dismiss the narcissistic diagnosis or any variant forms of NPD.

I do, however, suspect an inability to face up to adult functions. The nature of TM's revulsion of sexuality may confirm this. The question remains as to whether this was caused by trauma resulting in amnesia, or by chronic fear of family disapproval.

The most puzzling thing muddying any potential diagnosis is the complication of TM's extraordinarily juvenile appearance. I have encountered examples of psycho-social short stature in which growth hormones freeze, but TM's physiognomy doesn't correspond at all. In most cases of psycho-social short stature we see a thickening of limb growth, whereas TM's appearance corresponds more roughly with anorexia nervosa.

But only roughly. TM is, I think, grown to her full height as a woman, and although she exhibits the slender physiognomy that would be unsurprising in a teenage girl, she is extremely slender for a woman in her mid-thirties. I looked instantly for Russels sign, the scarring or knuckle markings often caused by ramming the fingers down the throat, and found none; no lanugo or soft hairs growing on the face; no enlargement of the cheeks. She indicated to me that her periods were regular. Finally, the other telltale signs of an anorexic, such as wearing baggy clothes to conceal the disorder, or complaints about a cold room (I keep my surgery at an ambient 19 degrees, often prompting complaints even from non-anorexics) are absent, and she seems not to be sad, lethargic or depressed.

Just remarkably thin for a woman her age. I haven't ruled out anorexia nervosa, but nothing I have yet seen has encouraged me to rule it in. Her fresh, juvenile appearance is a real puzzle.

I'm not certain whether TM is reporting a story – her confabulation – that she has already laid out in completion, or whether she is changing it subtly as she reports it to me. Neuro-linguistic leakage appears to suggest she is reporting from memory (of a previously told tale, that is) but as she tells her story and stares into the middle-distance it always seems to me that she is in the saddle of inspiration.

Though I sense a crack in the egg. No longer is she drawing on traditions of English fairy literature. Having led us into fairyland by the traditional and antecedent routes, she is now having to create a geography for it; and that geography is no longer being drawn from the well of tradition. Instead it is being constructed from the pressing concerns of her own psyche, and this is where she will reveal herself.

Her sublimation of sexuality is clear from her portrait of the living lake. The lake itself is, of course, a mighty symbol of the unconscious in general, and of the condition and temperature of her own troubled psyche in particular. Here we see a community experiencing a communal orgasm of sorts, a shared ejaculation. We have a simultaneous rendition of the sexual act away from which she still wants to run; but it is embraced by communal participation and approval. I take this to be a sign that she has a deep desire for re-integration with her family and acceptance by the community which she left behind.

We are also now given names – those closely guarded codes which were originally designated as secrets. The seducer is named at last and he is called Hiero. I'll risk a guess and say that she has at some point in the last twenty years spent time in France. *Hier* is the French word for yesterday, and she has drawn a clear line between her life now and her life in the past. There is the world of yesterday and the world of today.

The name is also compounded with the designation *Hero*, which is exactly what she wanted him to be. This man is prepared to fight for her – to the death. She projects her girlish fantasies on to the idea of a protective male who would prevent a repetition of the assault or attack that caused the crisis in the first place. A devoted, non-sexual male. A father figure. It does seem significant that the man who at first appears to be a Lothario figure, a seducer, is the man who promises celibate protection.

Hieros is also an ancient Greek word for sacred. This man is almost a religious projection (and I understand from TM's brother that her parents, particularly her mother, are religious people).

In this fantasy of the martial protector, TM can

maintain the status of the little girl. She can repress the unpleasant events that perhaps took place in the Outwoods and she can refuse to grow up to be a mature woman with a sexual nature. So strong is her impulse to do this that she has arrested the production of growth hormones through some process of *hypopituitarism*. The pituitary gland at the base of the brain only has to decrease the secretion of one or more of the eight hormones it releases to make this happen. She compounds this apparent anti-ageing process by wearing teenage or youthful clothes. Her diet keeps her skinny as a whippet.

Hiero, no longer the seducer, switches role from Id to Super-ego in that he now has to fight off the dazzling, handsome and virile Silkie. In Scottish folklore a silkie or a selkie is a shapeshifting creature, a kind of seal who can take off his or her pelt and become human. TM knows her folklore very well, at least on an unconscious level, for the tale of the silkie is so often the tale of the footloose woman, the unfaithful wife, the faithless lover trapped by her domestic ties. It is an image, projected into the male silkie, of TM's very own frustrations.

And in another sense Hiero and Silkie are shapeshifting variants of the same projected and idealised male. They both operate as shadow figures to TM's juvenile female: the one a wise and spiritual protector, the other a virile and handsome but rapacious young man. What woman has never been caught between these disparate desires? Take one and you end up yearning for the other. This, in a dark place in her own psyche, TM understands very well.

And so they fight, to the death it seems, while

those dark forces ringed about the combatants cheer; meanwhile the rational side of TM safely objects and is properly appalled. The competing forces within the human consciousness are, when the mind is out of joint, aggressive and determined to restore equilibrium. TM is rehearsing in her tale the violent battles being conducted inside her own psyche.

27

'Any man can lose his hat in a fairy wind.'

Irish saying

Tara was a willing volunteer for any kind of tests: dental, psychological or medical. Peter had once saved one of his customers a lot of veterinary fees when he had diagnosed black mould on the hoof and offered a simple peroxide solution. The customer's father was a dentist, Iqbal Suida, a Muslim with an impressive long black beard. Peter decided to call in his favour and the dentist was very happy to oblige.

Though the dentist had agreed to make an examination of Tara's teeth, there was a problem in getting hold of her dental records. The dentist Tara had seen as a child had retired many years ago. Iqbal told Peter that the files would be available somewhere but that they had to be tracked down. It might take a long time.

Meanwhile it had come as a surprise to Peter that modern science had no way of offering an exact test for a person's age, unless they were dead. Passport, political asylum and criminal justice authorities still faced the same problem many times over. Crystalline proteins in the eye's lens make it possible for radiocarbon dating; but only when the eye has been removed. Radiocarbon dating was also good for dating a tooth within a couple of years, but again the tooth would need to be removed. Meanwhile Iqbal said that X-ray evidence could be accurate plus or minus a couple of years. He agreed to make X-rays of Tara's teeth and to have the plates sent off for analysis.

Peter dropped Tara off at the dentist's surgery. After that he called in at the police station to deliver his motor insurance and ownership documents. As far as the police were concerned, Richie had been the one drink-driving, but as owner of the vehicle Peter still had to provide his documents for inspection. He was still in the dog-house with Genevieve about that episode with Richie. At least Richie had insisted on persisting with the charade that he had been driving rather than Peter. The police officer had wanted to know why it was that Peter was wearing the bandage when only that morning he had interviewed Richie in hospital. Peter had said it was all fun; that they were always doing things like that. They suspected that the old copper knew the truth: and they thought he knew that they knew. Regardless, Richie had been the one taken to the station, where he duly and unsurprisingly tested positive for alcohol. The officer had at first wanted to take Peter along too, but Richie had talked him out of it.

Since the keys to his truck had been confiscated, Peter had walked home, sobering a little as he went. He'd walked at least half a mile before he remembered that he still had Richie's bandage trailing loosely round his head, and for no reason.

Jack had heard his dad come home, and he heard his mum asking *where was the truck*? His dad had an unfocused gaze and he was holding a long length of white bandage. When he heard his mum ask his dad if he were drunk, he wanted to stay and see how the interesting conversation might develop, but he was also quick to spot an opportunity.

He hurried to the outbuildings, took out the stainless-steel spade and sprinted to the top of the garden. There he dragged away the dead bush covering the disturbed soil and immediately began to dig. He worked quickly and after a few spades of soil he was already sweating. Pretty soon he struck the corpse of the cat.

It was a distasteful job, but he was relieved to find that the corpse was still in pretty good order. He loosened all the soil around the neck of the creature and found a silver buckle on the red collar. He gagged. There was no odour rising from the dead creature, but he gagged anyway. The buckle was tight and it resisted his fingers. It required both hands to work it loose. Finally he got the buckle open and was able to drag the collar free.

He piled all the loosened soil back over the dead cat and carefully covered the disturbed ground with twigs and sticks before dragging the withered bush back into place. He cleaned the steel spade by wiping it on the grass, returned it to the outhouse, and went back inside.

'Where's Dad?' he asked his mother.

'He's gone upstairs to lie down for a while.'

'Is he okay?'

'Ha!'

'Is he drunk?'

'Ask him.'

Jack kicked off his shoes and went up to his bedroom. He decided to hide the red collar between his mattress and the base of his bed. Then some thought made him wince. Instead he took the collar to the bathroom and rinsed it under the cold water tap for a good few minutes. He patted the collar dry with a bath towel before going back to his bedroom and hiding it behind some football annuals on his bookcase.

After that he went downstairs, slipped his shoes on again and marched brightly across the road to Mrs Larwood's house. He rang the bell and within a few moments there came the usual drawing of bolts and the unlatching of chains.

'Oh,' said Mrs Larwood. 'Has he been found?'

'No,' he said. 'I've come to do your computer.'

'Come in.'

Jack dipped his shoulder to squeeze past Mrs Larwood without making eye contact. Before Mrs Larwood had closed the door and joined him in her living room he already had the monitor out of its packaging.

'Goodness! I'll put the kettle on, shall I? Or you'd probably prefer lemonade wouldn't you?'

'No! No need. I mean I'll have tea. Although I don't want anything.'

Jack unpacked the PC and began assembling it at super speed on her dining table. He attached the monitor to the PC and jacked in the keyboard and the mouse.

'So many parts.' Mrs Larwood said, watching him.

'Where's your power socket?'

Jack had it assembled, plugged in and switched on in under five minutes. He steered the computer through its set-up. 'Do you want a password?'

'What?'

'I'll leave it open. Do you want a screensaver?'

'What?'

'You can have any picture you want on the screen.'

'Can I?'

'Yes. Anything.'

'What sort of picture?'

'Well, you can have a picture of the sea or the mountains or the Outwoods or anything you like.'

'The Outwoods? I wouldn't go there if you paid me a million pounds!'

'Why?' Jack asked reasonably.

'Can I have a picture of my cat? The one I gave you?'

Jack blinked. Something itched at the back of his knee and he scratched the place hard. 'Yes.'

'Put that on then.'

'I'll have to, you know, scan it and download it.'

'Will you?'

'Yes.'

'How will you do that?'

Jack had come to plant in the old woman's mind the idea that there had been a sighting of her cat, in order to prepare the ground for the moment when he could turn up with a new ginger tom in the red collar. But now that he was in the same room as the woman he couldn't bring himself to raise the subject.

The PC drive whirred and bleeped. 'What's it doing now?'

'It's still setting up.'

'Am I on the internet now?'

'No. Have you got a server?'

'What?'

'You have to, you know, pay.'

Jack explained to Mrs Larwood that she could get an internet connection through her telephone company. Then it occurred to him that the wireless signal from The Old Forge might be strong enough to hook up Mrs Larwood's computer. After all, he knew the security passwords and key-codes. Peter set up the passwords and key-codes to maintain parental control for internet access, but kept forgetting his own codes and regularly had to ask Jack for them. Jack made a fist of explaining it all to Mrs Larwood in minute detail but he could tell that by now she was only pretending to understand what he was talking about. In the end he said he would try to piggy-back off his home system across the road while she waited for a connection to be installed by her phone company.

'You're going to give me a piggy-back?'

'Yes.'

She seemed satisfied with that and went off to make tea. Jack found that a connection to The Old Forge was readily available, and that the signal strength was adequate. By the time the cup of tea that he didn't want had arrived, he had already set up Mrs Larwood with an email account and an internet identity.

'I've given you a piggy-back on our system,' he said gravely.

'Have you? Here's your tea and I've brought you some cake.'

'I've given you an email address. You can send people emails. You are Larchwood21.'

'Larchwood? Couldn't I be Larwood?'

'No. There were too many other Larwoods. Is Larchwood21 okay?'

'I'm sure it is.'

'You're ready to send emails.'

'How exciting? Who shall I send one to?'

'Well,' Jack scratched the back of his knee again. 'Who do you know who has an email address?'

'No one really.'

She looked a little crestfallen so Jack volunteered his own address. He said Mrs Larwood could send him an email if she wanted. Mrs Larwood wanted to know if that was really necessary, since he was right there, in the room, right now, and she could tell him anything she wanted to. They could, if they wanted, she said, just sit here and have a good natter instead. Jack didn't know he was being teased. He wrote down his address. Mrs Larwood saw that it was *jackgiantkiller* so she asked what her name was; and Jack said that Larchwood21 was her account name but she could have other accounts in different names.

'Why would I do that?'

'You can pretend to be other people. Make out you're younger or older or whatever.'

'Is that honest?'

'Okay, you could have one for friends, and one for ordering things so you don't get spam.'

He explained to her about spam. And about emails from Nigeria.

Mrs Larwood eventually said that she didn't want anything dull and she wanted a name like his. She suggested *madoldbitch*.

Jack blinked. 'A bit strong.'

'You think so? I thought it sounded fun.'

'Okay. I'll set it up.'

'Yes, change it to *madoldbitch*.'

Jack supped his tea. 'Why did you say that?'

'Say what?'

'About the Outwoods.'

'Been up there, have you?'

'Yes.'

'I wouldn't.'

'Why not?'

'Not saying. Otherwise you would think I was a *madoldbitch*.' Mrs Larwood made a kind of snorting noise, as if she had choked back a laugh.

'No I wouldn't.'

'All I'm saying is that you wouldn't get me to walk up there. No. Wouldn't go near the place. There are powers.'

'Powers?'

'You've seen how Nature made that place. The rocks? This way and that. That place lies on a fault. Geology. Do they teach you that at school? You don't think Nature has accidents do you? You'd be a fool if you did. You might know a thing or two about that computer and emails from Nigeria. But if you don't know that you don't know nothing. How old are you?'

'Thirteen. My Aunt Tara was walking up there when she was fifteen. She disappeared. Now she's back.'

'Who?'

'My Aunt Tara. They thought she was dead. Everyone did. But she came back on Christmas Day.'

Mrs Larwood put down her tea cup. 'What, this Christmas?'

'Yes.'

'When was this? I mean when did she disappear?'

'Twenty years ago. She was walking up there. Now she's back.'

Mrs Larwood took Jack's cup off him, even though he hadn't finished his tea. Her brows were knitted. She also confiscated his untouched cake. 'That's enough chatter now. Quite enough. You be on your way.'

Jack was baffled. He knew he had been given his marching orders but he didn't know why. He hauled himself to his feet. 'Do you want me to shut this down?'

'You leave it. Come on, let's be having you.'

Jack remembered that his mission was to suggest progress in the hunt for the ginger tom. But he knew that now was not a good time to mention it. He was on the step when the door was closed behind him. He heard chains rattled into place and bolts shooting home.

Madoldbitch, he thought.

Peter had spent the day at work, sweating out his hangover. In the afternoon, still sticky with perspiration and lugging his portable gas furnace on to the back of his truck he heard the ringing tone of his mobile phone. He heaved the furnace on to the truck.

It was the dentist, Iqbal Suida. 'Peter, how are you?'

'I'm fine. Did you get a chance to look at Tara?'

'I did. She is a charming lady. We had a good chat. I took some X-rays and a few other samples.'

'I appreciate it.'

'No problem. I'm happy to return a favour. But I have to say things are a bit complicated.'

'What does that mean?'

'Well, I'd prefer to see you in person.'

'It's okay, you can tell me now. Is it about Tara?'

'How old is your sister?'

'She's thirty-six.'

'That's what I thought you said. Well look, I'll come straight out with it. The lady who came to see me today, she's not your sister.'

'What?'

'Peter, I've done the X-rays and I'll send them off for analysis just as I promised. But I'm telling you this as a friend: I don't need any scientific analysis. I'm an experienced dentist and I've looked in a lot of mouths. Even at a glance I can tell you that the person who came to see me today isn't any older than eighteen or so.'

'I don't get it.'

'I'm sorry to be telling you this. I know what I'm looking at. Charming as she is, Peter, there is no way that person can be your sister.'

28

'Di gav henne drikke av raude gullhorn,
Dei slepte der nedi tri villarkorn.'

('They gave her drink from a red-gold horn
They put therein three seeds of bewildering-corn.')
(Liti Kjersti, trad. Norwegian folk song)

I said to him, 'Is that all you do here? Fuck each other
and play in the water? Is that all you people do?'

It didn't matter how insulting I made it sound, he
would just smile at me and wait until I'd finished speaking. He never once interrupted me nor did his words
ever cross over mine.

'We do lots of things.'

'Like what?'

He thought for a moment. 'Well. We take time off its
hook for one thing.'

'Lovely. How do you do that on a Sunday?'

'Well, it's easy enough. You just have to spin time
backwards and forwards in the same moment.'

'Oh! Simple.'

His features twisted between a smile tugging him one
way and a frown pulling the other. 'Oh I see: you're
mocking me. Very good. Good straight face. I like it. I
like it when you mock me. I need mocking.'

'Well, you were mocking me.'

'No, I wasn't. That's what we do. Stop time and start it up again. Kind of. I mean you don't want to stop time altogether now do you? That would be living in the past, wouldn't it? And the excitement of life is what the future will bring, good and bad, isn't it? And anyway the past is only there inasmuch as it delivers the right now, isn't it? And the present is only here inasmuch as it delivers the future, you see that? And the future of course isn't here at all.'

'Shut up! Shut up!'

'I'm serious. I mean you wouldn't want to be frozen in time, like a fly in amber, now would you? I mean however sticky sweet it was. Back then. Back whenever. So you have to run time backwards and forwards in the same moment, don't you?'

'And how do you do that? Exactly?'

'You want to try?'

I couldn't understand any of it, so I gave him a long, hard look. But I had a strange feeling that it was a look that knew it had been there before; and would be there again. 'I think so.'

He got to his feet. 'I'll be back in a beetle's heartbeat. Meanwhile, think of a moment in your life you would like to live again.'

I thought hard. It wasn't so easy. I didn't want to be a child again, for sure; no schooldays, certainly not; holidays were fun but no; and there were sweet moments with Richie, but that all seemed done with now. Then, as Hiero returned holding something in his hand I remembered something much more recent. 'It was when we were on your horse. Shortly after we'd met and I'd climbed up behind you and—'

'I know it.'

'—and we were cantering up that green meadow. There was a moment when you leapt the horse over a stream.'

'I know it. We've been there together many times.'

'We were in the air. What do you mean by that? We were mid-flight in that moment before touching down on the other side of the stream. The air was sweet. I didn't know what was ahead. I want that again; that moment again.'

'You shall have it.' He opened his fist, and in the palm of his hand I saw a single blood-red berry.

And I was there.

And the horse was in the air, not frozen exactly but not moving either, with the horse's wild mane floating like an anemone in the sea and the leap not completed; and the air was sparking, charged with that ozone before a storm and blue light and the moment was full of possibility; and we were not frozen in time because I could dismount and run around the horse, which I did, and yet I could still see myself behind him, still mounted on the beautiful creature, and I was bent forward into its giant leap, the sweat of the horse in my nostrils, the gleam of it on the animal's flanks, my fingertips digging into his hip-flesh, and the both of us on the horse making the leap, still moving but not so fast as I was circling about it all, because I could fly, swoop and fly; and he was at my side laughing and yet and yet and yet he was still on the horse's back with me hanging on behind him, it was insane and the air was smoky with ozone and I felt a tearing as if the sky might rip.

'Can't stay here too long,' I recall him saying.

And I remember nodding because I knew in my guts

that was true, and we went back and suddenly I was drinking something from a tiny glass – no, some fluid sucked itself right out of my mouth – and filled a tiny glass that was in my hand, and I handed the glass back to him – no he took it back from me – and the fluid in the glass streamed upwards against gravity and back into a pulpy red mess between his fingers before re-fixing itself into a shiny red berry and I said *yes I'm sure* and then he spoke and smiled and though the words were unintelligible I knew he'd said, *Sure you want to do this? There's no going back.* My head nodded itself. *Sure? Yes, Sure? Yes* and him holding out the berry in the palm of his hand.

I had to shake my head, hard, shake it all off me like a dog flicks water from its back, and I came to with my legs crossed on the grass beneath me, in exactly the same position I'd been in earlier, all as if nothing had passed.

I was shocked. 'What just happened?'

'Well. We sent time in two directions.'

'Did you drug me?'

'It was the berry. Now you know how to do it yourself.'

'What berry is that?'

'It doesn't grow in your world. Though there is something you should know. If you do that again and again you'll forget.'

'Forget what?'

'Goodness me!' He smiled that infuriating smile of his. 'I don't know. I can't remember!'

29

'When I examine myself and my methods of thought, I come to the conclusion that the gift of fantasy has meant more to me than any talent for abstract, positive thinking.'

Albert Einstein

Peter called Underwood and told him what the dentist had said. He had also anticipated the psychologist's response: it was inconceivable, he told Underwood, that the woman could be anyone other than Tara. As soon as the dentist had reported to him his extraordinary conclusions, Peter had gone to see Tara. Futile as he knew the enterprise to be, he had quizzed her on minute details of experiences they had shared in childhood. He also tossed in a few lies, designed to trap an impostor, but she correctly called him on it each time.

There were sequences of events that Tara knew in fine detail. She even turned the tables on him, and proved to his satisfaction that her memory of their shared childhood was better than his. The impostor theory made no sense: their parents had no serious money she could expect to inherit and there would be no financial motive for such an extraordinary charade. In any event, Tara had a large mole near her underarm, and another smaller mole on her throat, plus other minute features that Peter knew intimately.

All this he reported to Underwood, so that there wouldn't be a ghost of doubt about it.

Underwood listened. He told Peter he had been thinking about the case. But more than that he wasn't prepared to say. For one thing it would be unethical. So Peter asked if he might offer a theory or two.

'These would be your wife's theories?'

'Well yes. We've been checking out the internet together.'

Underwood clasped his hands to his head and pretended to look depressed. 'Go on. Try me.'

There is a condition, Peter said, called *hypopituitarism,* a defect, in which the secretion of some of the hormones associated with the pituitary gland is blocked. It could be a disease, he said, or it could be caused by a trauma to the brain, but it often resulted in an arrest of the growth hormones. It could be, he went on to suggest, that if Tara did suffer from a trauma when she disappeared or was abducted, then the brain might have gone into a shock, choked off the hormone supply and permanently frozen her physical development. How common is that? Peter wanted to know.

'Not common,' Underwood said. 'But not unheard of. And I'm already considering it.'

Peter also suggested that if Tara had been raped and injured, she might be closing off her memory of the event; an event she might associate with adulthood and therefore unconsciously choosing to remain a child.

'There's something misaligned in this theory,' Underwood said. 'She doesn't talk like a child. Nor does she sound like a child.'

'No. It's all a shot in the dark.'

'So where would you want me to take it from there?'

'Well, I was wondering if there are tests we could have done.'

'Tests for *hypopituitarism*.'

'Yes.'

'You're bending the shoe to fit the hoof, aren't you?'

Peter ignored that. 'If only to rule it out. *Hypopituitarism*, I mean. Meanwhile we continue to see if you can get to the bottom of what happened that day in the Outwoods. That is, if you're prepared to keep seeing her.'

'Can I remind you, Mr Martin, that *you* are paying *me*?'

Underwood had despatched Peter, with his theories, to the waiting room while he and Tara sat at her preferred seats by the window. 'Can I ask you, Tara?' It was early evening; dusk was gathering outside and the street lamps were flickering on. 'Now that you've been home for a few days and you've had a chance to settle in, can I ask you: what do you think happened?'

'I haven't got an alternative story for you, if that's what you mean.'

'So you believe you went to live with the fairies for a while?'

'That's your word for them, not mine. I've never used that word. Neither is it a word they would be happy with.'

'But they were what we commonly call the fairies?'

'They certainly never used that word for themselves, nor would they recognise it. And anyway it conjures up something they most certainly are not. You, Peter and several others have used that word and I haven't corrected it because I don't see the point arguing.'

'But these were people living in another dimension?'

'What's that? What's another dimension? Sounds like science-fiction.'

'Another place, then.'

'Oh most certainly in another place, yes.'

'Could you take me to that other place?'

'No.'

'Why not?'

'There are only certain times of the year you can get there, so far as I understand it. And only certain times of the day on those specific dates. Like now. It's dusk. They call this the hinge of the day.'

'Can you tell me those dates?'

'Some of them yes. I don't claim to understand it all. They have scholars who know it all because it's complicated. But I remember being told that the equinox and the solstice were possible dates, but that the moon had to be right, and all that stuff.'

'All that stuff?'

'Like I say, I didn't entirely follow it. But in order to come and go you have to be precise.'

'But if we went together at dusk on the spring solstice, you could take me there?'

'I think so. That is to say, I believe it would be possible. I'm not hundred per cent sure of the way but having been once I think that maybe I could. But I wouldn't do it, because I wouldn't want to get trapped there for another six months. Or twenty years as it turned out. Once a lifetime is more than enough for anyone.'

'Quite. This place. You've already described it to me, the lake and so on. But when you returned here, did you bring anything back with you, any token, any memento, any object of any kind?'

'No.'

'Nothing at all.'

'I tried to steal one of their charts, to bring back with me. The illustrations, the artwork, is incredible. Stunning. They put a high value on art and music. But I was caught, and I had to leave it.'

'That's a pity.'

'It is. You would have taken one look at a single example of their illustrated charts and you would have believed me instantly. There are colours you haven't seen.'

'Really.'

'You're a clever man and you think you know a lot. But you're a baby compared to what they know. I'm a baby; you're a baby. Their charts, their maps: they have the whole world mapped in fine detail and you can spread it out in front of you, calfskin and it's only the size of a newspaper and you have like magnifying glasses, optics that you move over them and it has everything, this street, this house, my house, all in coloured detail, hand-drawn it blows your mind and it's not just maps! They have globes of the world and you use optics in the same way and they are suspended in mid-air and you think surely there must be some fine wires holding them in the air, but oh no, they just float it's their knowledge of physics it's phenomenal and not just globes they have models of the planets orbiting and the course of the stars you walk into this chamber and you walk between these glowing orbs and it's the universe all suspended there you can pass your hand over and around you find what's keeping it aloft it's like some gravity-defying perpetual-motion apparatus, an orrery, one that looks like it's made of brass and mechanical levers but really it's an orb made of spiders' webbing but pulsing with light and things like that they tried explaining it but it was all so far above my head it's just mind blowing, mind blowing, the maps they have, it's not like geography in school, they map the edges of unknown places, old ruins, ancient forests, new lands but also at the borders of being born, sexual awakening, death, it would blow your mind.'

'Would you like a glass of water Tara?'

'I'm fine.'

Underwood nodded. He waited a moment for Tara to recover steady breathing. 'So nothing came back from that world with you. Nothing we can examine.'

'Unfortunately there is. I doubt you'll be able to examine it, though.'

'Why do you say that?'

Tara looked out of the window. 'Without making any sudden moves, do you think you could look down there? Behind that tree across the road. Do you see a man loitering there?'

Underwood turned his head. 'Yes, I see him. In the shadows.'

'I was followed back here by that man. I'm doing my best to ignore him. If you were to speak to him he would verify my story. He would be my proof. But you'll never catch him.'

'That's one of them? These people?' asked Underwood.

'Yes.'

'What's he doing here?'

'I told you, he followed me. He's stalking me.'

'Have you told the police?'

'Ha!'

'And what does he want?'

'He wants me.'

'Tara, let's just suppose that I went down to talk to that man. Let's just suppose I asked him what he's doing. I think he would tell me that he's waiting for a bus. You see, there's a bus stop just a few yards away from where he's standing right now. Let's suppose he told me that he was waiting for a bus. And if I said your name, and asked him, and he said he didn't know you, would you accept that you are deluded, and that you don't know him at all?'

'Go ahead.'

'That wasn't a yes.'

'Yes. Go ahead.'

'I'm not for one minute going out there, Tara.'

'No, you wouldn't. You couldn't.'

30

'No one loves a fairy when she's forty.'

Music hall song

It was almost midnight when Zoe got back from The White Horse. She'd broken the *eleven sharp* deal. Peter had made it explicit. She was to be back in the house by eleven; and that didn't mean leaving The White Horse at eleven; nor on her way by eleven, but back home with a foot across the threshold by the stroke of eleven; and according to the clock on the living room mantelpiece, not someone else's clock, wristwatch, phone, hourglass, sundial or any other timepiece, chronometer or instrument of time measurement here or in the known universe of any description.

And here she was, almost fifty minutes late.

Richie had told Genevieve, who had told Peter, that The White Horse was a skanky drug den. But Zoe had explained that it had been closed down and had re-opened under new management, and that the venue had been running alcohol-free teenage nights, strictly monitored by trained security staff.

Peter was sceptical. If there were no drugs and no alcohol to be found on the premises, then why would any self-respecting teenagers want to congregate there? They might as well go to church, he pointed out.

'Music,' Zoe had argued. 'For the music.'

'A likely story,' Peter had said. A raised eyebrow from Genevieve had stopped him chasing that theme any further; and anyway he didn't need a reminder that you didn't go to church in the hunt for merry tunes.

In the end Peter had pressed Zoe's boyfriend into service. 'Michael, a word,' he'd said, tapping the boy's breastbone. 'You get her back by eleven sharp. You. If *you* don't get her back here by eleven, *you're* to blame and *you'll* be the one I'm coming after. And I'm a big bloke. And *you* won't see her again. Got me?'

The boy blushed right through his acne. He coughed. 'Right.'

Peter held out a huge hand that wanted shaking. Michael had looked at the proffered paw before laying his own tiny, white, uncalloused hand deep inside it.

'You look a man in the eye when you make a deal with him, Michael. In his eye.'

'Right,' Michael said, glancing at Peter's eyes, then looking away quickly, then recovering quickly to look back again.

'Give him a break!' Genevieve had almost shouted.

'Dad!' shouted Zoe.

'Never mind all that. Me and Michael have struck a deal, haven't we, Michael?'

'Right.'

And Peter had been confident that the struck deal would stick. But here he was at ten minutes before midnight, and it hadn't. Peter and Gen had waited up, discussing what they might say, how they might handle it. Peter admitted he was pretty cross, but he didn't know whether to be cross with Zoe or with Michael. Gen didn't want him to make too much of a deal of it. It was every father's problem. He himself had spent most of his teenage years in reckless pursuit of pretty girls and he didn't need anyone to point out what was on the mind of the average adolescent male; on the other hand he didn't want to make a fool of himself by draping his daughter in a chador or a veil.

Zoe was a slim, raven-haired doe-eyed beauty and he was relieved that she didn't feel the need, like a lot of her contemporaries, to dress like a Hollywood hooker. He was persuaded that by the time she was sixteen the levee would burst anyway. He just felt a moral duty to sandbag right up until that moment. He and Gen had shared a bottle of red wine as they waited up, and when Zoe's key hit the lock of the front door he felt it necessary to put his spade into the sand.

He stood up.

'Steady on,' Gen said.

'I'm not going to get mad,' Peter said.

Someone came bowling through the front door. It was Michael, hands held up high in military surrender. Peter looked over his shoulder and saw that Zoe was just behind him.

The boy looked wide-eyed. 'Let me explain—' he began.

'Stop right there,' Peter said.

'No but I want to—'

Peter advertised a huge palm in the air, like a traffic policeman. 'Stop.'

'The thing is—'

'Enough. I don't want the dog ate my homework excuses. I don't want the traffic was heavy. I don't want anything. I want eleven o'clock.'

'The dog ate my homework?' Michael said, scratching his dreadlocks.

'Give him a chance,' Gen said.

'Dad!' Zoe said.

'Never mind all that. I'll come to you in a minute, Zoe. But first you, Michael. A deal is a deal, right?'

'Dad, listen to him and stop making a fool of yourself!'

'Careful!'

'It was Aunt Tara!'

'What?'

'Aunt Tara. She was down at The White Horse. She was off her face, Dad!'

'What?'

'That's what Michael is trying to tell you. We would have been home. If it wasn't for Aunt Tara.'

Peter looked at Michael.

'It's true,' Michael said.

It all spilled out. Half way through the evening Zoe had noticed that her Aunt Tara was in the mosh pit, dancing like someone on the wrong end of a high-voltage cable, throwing herself about, clearly drunk.

'But you said it was teenage night!' Peter said.

'Yeah, it was,' Michael put in.

'She was completely pissed, Dad.'

'But you said there was no alcohol!'

'She had like a plastic bottle of water that was like full of vodka. That's how they bring it in.'

'They?'

'Anyone who wants to get sloshed. Don't look at me I can't stand the stuff.'

'Me neither,' Michael put in helpfully. 'Well not much anyway.'

'I saw her and I thought, right, you're going a bit, Aunt Tara,' Zoe said, 'and I kept my eye on her, and she was snogging every boy she could find there, you know, tongue down the throat like one of those lizards after a juicy fly and I says to Michael shit that's my Aunt Tara and she was out of it, doing this weird dance wasn't she, Michael, like jumping up and down—'

'Pogo,' Michael said.

'Right, pogo, shit dancing, but like someone's put a firework up her arse and she's giving it all this honestly Dad and swigging from whatever is in the plastic bottle and all these stupid boys around her have got the hots for her and I thought there's gonna be trouble. I nearly phoned you.'

'Why didn't you?'

'Well I didn't. Anyway after a while she starts flashing her tits and all this—'

'Stop stop stop,' Peter said. 'Is this true?'

Michael nodded. 'And it's like ten-thirty and I says come on we *gorra go* 'cos of your dad – 'cos of what you said – and then a fight breaks out around her and the bouncers pile in and while the bouncers are dealing with these lads that are kicking off there are three other lads, like on her—'

'On her?' said Genevieve.

'Yeah,' said Zoe, 'like all over her and I thought they were trying to pull her clothes off so I says to Michael—'

'She says to me we've got to help her and I thought no thanks I'm gonna get my head kicked in if I get into that, but then Zoe's marching in on them. Giving it some, so I have to follow her,' Michael turned to Peter, 'to protect her like, and Zoe does her judo thing, yeah, her judo thing and she puts one guy on his back and had another in a lock and the third one's going to take a swing at Zoe and so I jump on him and the next thing one of the bouncers has got me by my fucking hair sorry Mrs Martin by my hair and all Tara is doing is going *what the hell's the matter can't a girl have a good time* like that and I don't even think she recognises Zoe she's so off her face and so we missed the bus.'

'Right,' said Peter.

'Right,' said Zoe.

'But I like made sure we got the next one. Which was a bit late coming as it happened. Sorry.'

'Right,' said Peter.

'So is that okay?' said Michael.

'Yes. It is. Well. Well.'

Genevieve dived in. 'Thank you for bringing Zoe back safely, Michael. Do you need a lift home?'

'No my parents don't get over-excited if I'm a bit late.'

'Right,' said Genevieve.

'I'm not saying you're over-excited,' said Michael. 'I'm not saying anyone is.'

'Okay,' said Peter.

'What are you going to do about Aunt Tara?' Zoe wanted to know.

'Never you mind that,' Peter said.

Well,' Genevieve said, standing up and clapping her hands. 'Did you both have a nice time?'

'Go to sleep,' Genevieve said.

'I can't.'

'I can hear your brain rattling.'

'I can't stop that, can I?'

Genevieve sat up and switched on the shaded bedside

lamp. The soft amber light filtered through her hair. She put her hand on his chest. 'So what's to do?'

'What the hell was she doing there?'

'She obviously thinks she's a teenager.'

'How many teenage girls neck vodka and flash their tits?'

'Well. Maybe one or two.'

'Do you ever wish you were that young again?'

'What and do all that stuff?' said Genevieve.

'Yes.'

'No. I didn't do all that shit when I was young and I don't have fantasies about doing it now, if that's what you mean. What about you?'

He thought about it. 'The only good thing about being sixteen was the erections you got.'

'Are you going to talk to her about it?'

'I don't know. I'm paying that basket-case of a shrink to do that. Or I thought I was. I mean what happens with that? He just has conversations with her at an hourly rate. How long is a conversation? An hour. When does he say there has been enough conversation?'

'When Tara makes the breakthrough, I guess.'

'Breakthrough. From where into where?'

'I'm turning out the light. Go to sleep.'

She reached out a hand and clicked off the lamp. 'Tara Tara Tara,' Peter said. 'Where in hell are you?'

At that moment Tara was letting herself in at her old home. She stumbled in the shadows, dropping the key she was never given when she lived there twenty years earlier. As she bent to pick it up she caught her head on the door, already ajar, and stepped back against the cabinet at the foot of the stairs. The glass pieces and best china jingled in the cabinet. Tara steadied herself, and tried to steady the vibrating cabinet.

She took a moment to breathe in the darkness. It was around one a.m. and she was anxious not to wake her parents. But there was a soft light coming from the kitchen.

'It's all right, I'm awake.' It was her mother's voice.

Tara swayed slightly, rubbed a hand across her face and stepped through from the hall to the kitchen. She went straight to the sink and filled a glass with water, which she drank quickly. Then she slumped down into a seat at the kitchen table.

'Though if you were trying to be quiet,' Mary said, 'you made a poor job of it.'

'Sorry.'

'I thought I'd wait up for you.'

'No need for you to do that.' Tara released a tiny burp.

'You're drunk.'

'I had a little weeny weeny weeny drink. It's true enough.'

Mary stood up. A plate, covered by a second inverted plate, rested on the worktop. She removed the top plate. 'Here I've made you a sandwich.'

Tara took it gratefully.

'I can't get used to the idea of going to sleep before you come in. Your father says I must leave you to do what you want. Though he wouldn't be happy to see you in this state.'

Tara munched on the sandwich. 'I'm not a child any more, Mother.'

'Aren't you?' Mary said sharply. 'What are you then?'

Tara stopped munching. She put her half-eaten

sandwich back on the plate. Then she stood up, swaying slightly. 'I'm going to bed. Goodnight.'

Mary watched her daughter weave along the hall and heard her ascend the stairs. It was another hour before she followed her.

31

'Deeper meaning resides in the fairy tales told me in my childhood than in any truth that is taught in life.'

Johann Schiller

Richie woke to the sound of his doorbell ringing and a hefty banging on the door. He instantly thought it was the police. Then he remembered he wasn't in any trouble with the police, unless of course you counted the recent case of drink-driving. Though as far as he recalled the police didn't come in the early hours over a traffic offence.

Early hours for Richie meant before eleven a.m.

The banging persisted. He swung his legs over the side of the bed and rubbed his eyes before reaching first for a cigarette, then his lighter, and after that for his spectacles. Only then did he pull on a pair of boxer shorts and pad over to the window. He looked down and saw Tara. She was holding on to a bicycle and was hammering on the door with her free hand. Some instinct made her look up. The weak morning sunlight glinted on her dark glasses.

Richie opened the window. 'Wait.'

He shuffled back across his bedroom, stuck his fag in his mouth and rifled the pockets of his jeans until he found a set of keys. He went back to the window and flung the keys down to Tara. They landed beside her on the concrete flagstone. 'Get the kettle on. I'll be down.'

By the time Richie had showered, dressed and hauled himself downstairs, Tara had made tea for both of them. When she heard him coming she poured them both a cup.

'Where's my mug?' he said. 'That's not my mug.'

'What?'

'I want my favourite mug.'

'For fuck's sake Richie, when did you turn into such an old man? *I want my favourite mug.*'

'When? When you were away is the answer to that. I am an old man.'

'No you're not.'

'Yes I am.'

'No you're not.'

'Yes I am.'

'You're not.'

'This is fun. We could do this for hours.'

Tara made a moue.

'Just give me the tea. What time is it?'

'Half ten. Richie, I'm struggling. I'm struggling.'

'What?' Richie lit another snout.

'I'm telling the truth. I'm telling the truth and no one believes me. Not my own mother or father. Not Pete. Not you. Not that freak I have to see.'

Richie snorted. 'Vivian.'

'Yes, Vivian. You think it's funny?'

'Well yes. Just his name, like. It always makes me laugh. I don't know why. I really don't. I know another Vivian and his name doesn't make me laugh in the same way. Funny that. Smoke?'

'No. I'm glad you find it amusing. Anyway that guy

is trying to persuade me that I've had a giant hallucination, and I'm giving him a chance. Really I am. Perhaps that's what happened. The thing is, when everyone is trying to persuade you that a thing you know to be true isn't actually true, you start to believe them: not because it is true, but because it's easier. It's just the easy way out.'

'Right.'

'Oh yeah, right. You have no idea what I'm talking about.'

Richie thought about the day he was taken to the police station and asked to confess to the killing of Tara. 'I do have an idea. I do.'

Tara took off her sunglasses and looked hard at him. Then she put them back on again.

'Do you have to wear those. Even indoors?'

'Since I came back the light plays tricks on my eyes. I get a kind of grit in my eyes if I don't wear them.'

'Sleep? We used to call that sleep. Like the sandy stuff that washes out of your eyes when you are sleeping.'

'He used to say that.'

'Huh?'

'Oh this guy. The one who led me away. He said we – meaning us, here, in this place – we were all sleeping.'

'You mean your fairy fellah?'

'They're not like what you think, Richie.'

'What do I think?'

'I don't know. Little people with lacy wings and hats made out of acorn cups. They're not like that at all, Richie. They are fucking dangerous.'

'Right.'

'You would never mess with them. Not if you knew. Never.'

'Right.'

'You say right one more time and I will kill you. Do you want anything to eat?'

Richie told her to get something from the breadbin. She set about toasting the bread and poaching eggs, and she put the kettle on again to make more tea. She gave a sudden start. 'Richie, you've got mice in your kitchen.'

'I know that. They have a nest behind the fridge.'

'This place is a tip. It's unhygienic.'

'What do you care?'

'I want to move in with you.'

Richie shook his head, quickly. It wasn't a negative response. It was an involuntary twitch, the kind of response he might have made if a gnat had flown into his ear. Now it was his turn to take off his spectacles. He polished them on the hem of his T-shirt, replaced them on the bridge of his nose and stared hard back at Tara.

'You're not against the idea, then?'

'What's brought this on?'

'I can't stay at Mum and Dad's much longer. It's driving me crazy. They watch everything I do with bated breath. They watch me clean my teeth. They watch me brush my hair. They watch me eat. I suspect they even come into my room at night and watch me sleep. They don't say much. They just watch. I feel like a bomb is going to go off. Plus Pete is going to call you.'

'Why's that?'

'He's going to tell you stories about me being out on the town.'

Richie's mobile phone chirruped at that exact moment. Richie picked it up. The screen told him that it was Pete calling. 'You're psychic, you are.'

'Don't tell him I'm here.'

Richie clicked to answer and put the phone to his ear. He turned around and looked out of the window. 'All right Pete? Yeah? She's here right now. Yeah.'

Richie listened. He interjected occasionally with a few grunts. Then he clicked off and put his phone in his pocket. He looked at Tara.

'I went down to The White Horse.'

'Right. Teenyboppers' pub. Sounds like you had a good time.'

'I just wanted to be with people of my own age, Richie.'

'Your own age?'

'Yes!'

'So why do you want to move in with me? I'm an old fuck.'

'No you're not.'

'Yes I am! I don't want to go down The White Horse drinkin' snake-bite till I vomit! I don't wanna dance in the mosh pit with my nose trapped in someone's funky armpit. And I don't wanna spend the evening telling someone what a shit they are 'cos they don't like the same music as me and nearly getting into a fight over it. Do you know what? I don't want to be young. I actually fuckin' like getting older. I do! I'd rather stick my dick in a high-speed kitchen blender than go back to being a teenager. If that's what you wanna do, Tara, if you want to get off your face down The White Horse you got the wrong guy coming back 'ere. I got my whisky, I got my bit o' puff, I got my mug for my tea and I got my carpet slippers. End of.'

'I have to get out of that house, Richie.'

'It ain't gonna work darlin'.'

Richie collapsed on to the sofa and lit another snout. They sat in silence for a while.

'You said I used to roll sweet joints for you.'

'You'll find even that's changed, if you haven't already. Most of the smoke you get nowadays is called skunk. It's rubbish, and it's so strong all you can do is sit with your mouth open, drooling at the world, like you've had a lobotomy.'

'I still do a good back rub.'

Richie sighed. 'You'd have to take me as you find me.'

'I'll clean up the place.'

'That's up to you. Don't expect me to weigh in.'

'The mice would have to go.'

'I'll set some traps.'

'You don't have to do that!' Tara was on her feet. The argument had been settled. She was moving in with Richie and they both knew it. 'What time is it? Okay. You got any incense?'

'Incense?'

'Joss sticks.'

'Maybe in that drawer over there.'

Tara rummaged through the drawer indicated. She found some old broken sticks of sandalwood and busied herself arranging them in the kitchen in a half circle, poking them into any available crevice. Richie stood in the doorway, watching, bemused.

'Fuck is this?'

'Shhh. We need to wait till the stroke of mid-day. When I start, don't say anything. Open the front door and the back door and leave them open. And you'll need your guitar.'

'What? I ain't singing to no mice.'

'Acoustic. I need an E note when I ask you for one.'

'You're fucked up.'

She stuck her tongue out at him. 'We know that already. Get your guitar.'

'I've got ten fucking guitars.'

'Ten? Who needs ten? Get an acoustic with a nice deep E note.'

Richie went away muttering but did as he was told. He came back with his Taylor 914CE, wanting to show it off to Tara, something he could never have afforded when they were together. He tried to make his face suggest that he was only playing along with this nonsense; in truth he was intrigued. By the time he'd returned, Tara was lighting sticks of incense and some of them were already streaming smoke.

She told him again to open the front and back door and then briefed him to settle on the sofa and shut his mouth. She said that on a signal she wanted him to sound a lower E note and to pluck it once every four beats.

'That's not gonna sell, is it?'

'Shut up and do it.'

Tara watched the clock and on the stroke of twelve she pointed at him and he plucked the low E string. Tara squatted, putting her mouth near to the foot of the fridge, and started to chant. It was a low, barely discernible chant, repeating phrases he couldn't make out; but he nevertheless did as instructed and kept time and plucked the string.

After a few minutes Tara got up and, swaying in time to her own chanting, walked slowly around the kitchen. She made a motion that Richie should pluck harder, and he did.

A slight breeze blew through the house, stirring the streams of incense. Tara walked towards the back door, beckoning to Richie that he should follow and that he should continue to pluck his string. He did as he was told and followed Tara out of the house. She led him to the front of the house, still chanting. Richie did a quick take to see if any of the neighbours could see them. He hoped he'd got away with it, and when Tara led him back into the house through the back door he followed. She closed the door behind him and motioned for him to return to the sofa. She continued to chant, swaying into the kitchen, occasionally squatting and putting her mouth near to the foot of the fridge. After fifteen minutes her chanting became softer and softer until he couldn't hear her any more.

She straightened her back and smiled at him. 'That's it. You can stop. They won't come back.'

Richie looked at her quizzically. Then he laughed and his laughter completely seized him. 'Haha! That's what I loved about you! You were always doing things like that. You were always full of shit like that!'

She wasn't smiling. 'Say what you want. They won't come back.'

'Right.'

'You don't know everything, Richie.'

'I dare say I don't.'

'You haven't been everywhere. I've learned things you don't know about.'

'Right.'

'Have it your way. We'll see.'

'Right,' Richie said. 'We'll see.'

32

'They live on cherries, they run wild—
I'd love to be a Fairy's child.'

Robert Graves

You have no idea. You can't begin to see. You have eyes and yet you walk in the shadows. You have ears and they are stuffed with noise. You can't take a caress without flinching. You have food and spices from all continents and nothing surprises your palate any more. Your lips don't even know how to speak. You shout, you mumble, you strangle your words. Right, you say to me. Right.

I am sixteen years old and in only six months I have lived more than people five times my age. If you stay at home and plug your mouth with booze and your eyes with TV have you seen anything? Stay at home. Drink. Eat fat and sugar. Mow the lawn. What do I care?

You don't know everything. I've learned things while I was away. See that trick with the mice? It's called Charming. Anyone can do it. A fool. All you have to do is make the mice unwelcome and they go. You don't have to mince them in traps or bait them with poison.

Those people, you know they don't hate us. They pity us. They say we are clumsy, brutal and dominating. I learned a new way to ride a horse while I was away. You don't need a saddle, or a bitted bridle. You don't have to shred its sensitive mouth to get a horse to take you where you want to go.

As for playing with Time, Richie, not even in your dreams have you been where I've been. And believe me, if you go there, if you have your eyes burned open, only love can bring to you back, and I came back for you.

Here are some things I learned. (Look at your eyes! I know you don't believe any of this. But it doesn't matter.) I can levitate, if only for a few seconds. I'll prove it when I'm ready and not before. I can make myself almost invisible. I can find great strength; the strength of an elephant. There are other things I didn't have time to learn. I saw some of those people pass through walls. It's true! Other things I did learn, frivolous things: I can bring a man to the point of orgasm just by looking at him if I want. Remember the woman on the kitchen table I told you about? Shag-woman? Her name was Ekko. She showed me how to do that. It's easy. Ridiculously easy.

But there are far more significant things. How to see for the first time. There are forces, Richie. You can train yourself to see them. There are sounds just beyond the range of normal hearing, and you can train yourself to hear them. But here you blunt all your capacities with greed and booze and dope.

No it won't stop. And once you begin to hear and see you can't stop it. That's what I was doing at The White Horse, if you want to know. I was doing what we used to do when we went there together. I wanted to blast myself with drink and noise to see if I could stop it. But that only works for a little while. You wake up. You blink. It's all still there.

Sometimes I think we are the dream; that this is the dream. When we sleep we get a chance to see what life is really like. That's it. Our daily lives are just a brief dream of what it means to be fully conscious. And I don't say I like it.

Hiero couldn't be with me always. He had work to do. They grow their own food. They are fruitarians. They eat only fruit, nuts and seeds and won't have anything to do with cooked food. And when Hiero was away, Silkie, the handsome man from the lake, came creeping around.

He was quite sweet. In fact it was him who taught me the mouse charming trick. But I just kept him at arm's length. At first Hiero didn't seem bothered about Silkie hanging round: Hiero said if I wanted to do anything with Silkie then that was my decision, no one else's. He assured me that neither Silkie nor anyone there would force themselves on me. That wasn't their way with women.

But then one day Ekko, the woman who was fucking on the kitchen table, shag-woman, came to me and said that Silkie was pining for me and becoming ill. She asked me to fuck him, as a favour to her.

'Please,' she said. 'It's beginning to get on everyone's nerves.'

'What?' I told her. 'You want me to fuck him just because he's got a long face?'

She was quite put out. 'Look at how thin he is! You can see it's making him unwell! He hardly eats, pining for you. Just lie down on the sand with him for half an hour, what on earth is the problem with your lot?'

I told her that '"my lot"' were not in the habit of lying down on the sand with every Tom Dick and Silkie who wants it. I told her that 'my lot' had a habit of saving it for people we care about a great deal.

'I've heard of that,' she snapped back at me, 'and it's just preposterous. Preposterous and ridiculous. It's completely against nature and it's not surprising to see what a desperate mess your lot have made of everything.' Then she started shouting at me. 'It affects us too, you know! We have to share this place! It isn't yours to do what you want with!'

I told her I didn't care what she said I wasn't going to make a slut of myself just because it suited her. She stormed off, and I thought that would be the end of it. But it wasn't.

I tried to keep myself to myself when Hiero wasn't around. There were wonderful things to discover. I would walk in the woods or by the lake, marvelling over some of the plant life I had never seen before. There were coloured fungi growing amid the roots of trees; I mean blue toadstools and red mushrooms; and there were other miraculous plants.

There was a flower of stunning beauty; large, the size of a football, and it was pink and yellow, made of tiny flower heads, and it seemed illuminated from within. I sat gazing at it. I was so absorbed I never heard anyone coming up behind me. Then I realised that Silkie had quietly settled down beside me.

'You like this one?' he asked me.

'Oh yes.'

'We call it *charnas*, something like "*group mind*" in your language. Watch.'

He leaned across to the flower and gently pushed his finger into it. Immediately I realised that it wasn't a flower at all, but a thousand bugs that flew up, disturbed. Each bug was like a tiny glittering fleck of pink or yellow light. They flew up in a cloud. I gasped.

'Watch,' he said.

After a few moments of frantic fluttering the cloud of bugs started to re-settle together in the same place. Within a few minutes they had composed exactly the same 'flower', all over again.

'They are communing with each other,' Silkie said. 'They draw strength from the hive-mind.'

'But are they bugs or are they a flower?'

'They are both!'

'It's beautiful. I've never seen anything like it.'

'Yes. It's what we do when we all have group sex. It's the same thing.'

'Oh for God's sake!' I shouted at him. I stood up. 'How to kill a wonderful moment!' He looked hurt, regarding me with confusion etched into his handsome features. I marched away, angry, not even looking back to see if he was following me.

Things came to a head the next day when Silkie approached me and said that he wanted to tell me his real name. I didn't know what this meant, but later I learned that this offer had shocked the entire community to its core. When I told Hiero that Silkie had said this, he turned quite pale. He asked me if it was something I wanted. I asked if Silkie wanted to tell me his real name, what difference could it make?

You see their real names are not names at all. They are sounds, secret sounds that when spoken set up an eternal vibration between two people. Disclosing your secret name is like giving someone a gold ring. To speak your name is to offer a binding promise.

'The difference is,' Hiero said, 'is that I now have to fight him.'

I was shocked but I had no say in the matter. Nothing I said made any difference at this point. Hiero went off and issued a formal challenge to Silkie and the challenge was formally accepted. Naturally I was appalled, but Hiero didn't seem unduly anxious. In fact he seemed to look forward to the whole thing. I pleaded with him not to let this go ahead, but to no avail. I went to Silkie and told him that it should be stopped, but he just smiled sadly at me. Even Ekko was of no help. She told me I'd started it just by being there, and the men would finish it. I told her to tell the pair of them that they were acting like fools, and that I wanted neither of them and that as soon as I could get out of that place I would be gone.

She laughed in my face. 'Tell them yourself,' she said.

There was great excitement in the community. People I'd never seen before poured out of their dwellings around the lake and came down to the sandy beach, bringing food and drink and blankets on which to sit, all as if it were a gala day. They chattered and made bets on the outcome as a fighting ring of hemp ropes was constructed near the water's edge. I was told that the fight would take place at dusk.

I refused to watch. I went back up to the house. But I could hear the laughter and the excited chatter. I looked out of the window and they had brought flaming brands to stick in the sand at the water's edge. I closed my eyes and covered my ears, but it was too much. I went back down, determined to stop it somehow. But the sky had changed. It had gone the colour of burgundy, and the lake was the dark blue of a damson. The flames danced off the still surface of the water, and as I walked down I passed a couple who were openly fucking against a tree. The woman was hugging the tree while the man had her from behind. Another couple were shagging in the long grass. There was no shame. These perverts were fucking openly, obviously wound up by what was going to happen.

The place reeked of fuck and blood-scent.

When I got down to the sand I could barely break through to see what was going on. Hiero and Silkie were standing naked, hands on hips, staring at each other. Silkie, baring his teeth was the taller of the two, but Hiero had a much stronger build and smiled confidently. I thought they were going to fist fight, but another man entered the ring with two cruel blades, like machetes, and he stuck them both in the sand in the middle of the circle. Before I knew what was happening I heard a blast on a horn and a great cheer went up from the crowd, and the two men ran full pelt towards the blades, arriving at the blades almost at the same time.

Hiero, being a split second behind, went in sliding, kicking up earth and sweeping Silkie to the sand. Hiero was on his feet first, and he swept his heel up into the air before bringing it down like an axe on Silkie's face. I heard a sickening crunch and already Silkie's nose was mashed and bloody. A huge cheer went up from the crowd.

Hiero reached for a blade and brought it down where Silkie was lying, but the younger man rolled clear, backflipping with miraculous skill, like a lithe animal, so that he landed crouched and set, waiting for the attack. Hiero now stood between him and the second blade. Silkie lunged, but it was a feint and Hiero made the mistake of trying to finish his opponent with a sweeping blow from the machete. All he sliced was air and it left him off balance. A backfist punch to the ear sent him staggering, and another cheer went up, this time in Silkie's favour, and in that moment Silkie picked up the second blade.

I saw Ekko in the crowd. Her eyes were gleaming, yellow, like a cat's. She was sweating with excitement and the light from the flames ran across her skin like amber beads. I begged her to stop it.

'Stop it?' she said, baring her teeth at me in a terrifying smile. 'You can't stop it. One of them has to die.'

'Die?'

She waved me away, eager to watch the combat in the ring. Again the firelight shone in her yellow eyes as she shouted encouragement to the fighting men. She was avid for it, a beautiful woman made ugly with blood lust.

Silkie kicked high and caught Hiero on the side of the head, but Hiero countered with a swipe of his blade. Silkie folded his body expertly and the blade missed opening his guts by a quarter of an inch; but it gave him the advantage and he grabbed Hiero by the wrist, twisting him round. Hiero fought back by spinning hard into Silkie's embrace and striking a stunning blow from his elbow into the other man's bloodied jaw, but miraculously the younger man maintained his wristlock. They were bonded in a lethal embrace now, each with a free knife-hand but no room to make it count. Without warning, Silkie dropped to the floor and in that moment I saw Hiero's undoing.

Silkie collapsed all his weight into a squat, and,

suddenly released, was able to spring back upright, dragging his blade upwards in a single gutting action. Hiero felt his belly spring open, and he swayed, already knowing it was over. Their eyes met as they stood off each other for a moment. Then Silkie hacked his knife at Hiero's throat, and Hiero crumpled.

There was no cheer. The crowd watched in silence. I was screaming at them to let me through but I had to beat against a wall of backs. By the time I fought through to Hiero, two men were already dragging him away by the legs. His blood soaked the sand. I could see the wide open wound in his belly. I cried at them to let me go to him, tears scalding my cheeks, but I was bundled away. They wouldn't let me go to him. No one else seemed to give a damn. It was vile, vile and evil and no one seemed to care.

But then Ekko pulled me away. 'Let them do what they have to do,' she shouted at me, pulling me away. 'You don't understand our ways. It's over.'

'No, I don't understand,' I wailed at her. 'How could you let this happen? It's like it's all sport to you. You're all twisted. Twisted and perverted.'

'And you're very young,' she said. 'And you're now under Silkie's care.'

I ran back up to the house. I would have left immediately but I knew there was nowhere to go. At the house I flung myself on the bed, weeping and trembling with the shock of everything I'd witnessed. After a while I recovered enough to look out of the window. Down by the lake they had lit a huge funeral pyre and I could see they were hoisting a body on to the pyre. I let out a wail so loud I saw people turning and looking back towards the house. After a while someone came in. But through my tears I couldn't even tell who it was. It didn't even seem like a complete shape, more like fragments of a wispy garment coming towards me, and then I realised it was Ekko and she was speaking to me, chanting words I didn't understand, and she reached out with two bony fingers and closed my eyes and all I know is I fell into a swoon.

I woke up in the morning to birdsong, with the sunshine streaming through the dusty windows, illuminating cobwebs in tender beams of light spilled across the room. I knew I had to get out of that place. I knew I had to try again.

I wanted an end to the madness. I wanted home. I wanted you, Richie. I wanted Mum and Dad.

I went out. There were snoring, naked bodies lying on the sand near the house. It looked like the aftermath of a carnival or an orgy instead of a ritual killing. I went to the stable and I took the white mare again and threw a blanket across her back. I didn't care how long it took me. There had to be a way home and this time I wouldn't give up.

But the landscape had changed. The paths I remembered were no longer there. The hills and valleys almost seemed to have been reordered. And even though my heart was sick and I was unable to shake off the ugly images of the slaying of Hiero the light was unbearable and beautiful.

The sun was up and I want to say that it was golden, but it wasn't golden it was the colour of treacle. I want to say the grass was green, but it wasn't, it was turquoise, the colour of a quarry pool. The rocks were lion-coloured and glimmered with quartz, and the sky I wanted to call blue was in reality lilac. And the colours were moist. It was as much as I could do to prevent myself from getting off the horse and putting my hands into these colours, to see if they would come off on my fingers.

It was like the world had been re-made, and, though I resisted the thought, it felt as if something to do with the killing of Hiero had remade it. I wandered on my horse through hollows in the land and across hills. I had no idea where to look to find my way back home. I just knew that I would wander until I found it, even if it would take me twenty years.

I stopped only to let the white mare drink or graze. And then on I went. At night I slept under a bush, or another night I spent sleeping in a crevice between granite boulders. When I woke in the morning I had a fat tear on my cheek. A little lizard crawled from the crevice and hopped on to my chest. I gasped but I wasn't at all repelled by it. It climbed up on to my face and it drank the teardrop on my cheek and I knew it was trying to comfort me. I don't know why I knew. Then it left off drinking my tear and pattered across my eyebrow and pushed its tiny damp snout against my forehead in a spot right between my eyes. It tickled, but in a nice way, and I felt the tickling go right to the seat of my brain and I heard the lizard say *Don't worry*. Then it hopped off my face and disappeared into the crack it had come from.

The world started opening up for me. I knew exactly where to go for food. I found pools to drink from, mushrooms as big as my fist and apple-sized berries. I only had to look.

One afternoon I'd stopped to let the horse drink and I sat with my back to a rock and a bumblebee came by, buzzing round my head. I reached out and carefully took its wing between my thumb and forefinger. The bee didn't mind. It grew in size until I was able to climb on its back. We went flying, quite low to the land. I let the bee know what I was looking for, the crossing, the path home. But we couldn't find it and after several hours on the bee's back I dismounted and the bee became small again and flew off.

You'll say I dreamed it; of course you will. I'm not so sure.

Then on the third evening I saw the moon coming up and I made my camp on a hill top, on a flat slate table of rock that was like a mysterious altar covered in a bed of sparkling green moss, and there in the sky, slightly east and west of me the sun and the moon met, just briefly, and I sensed everything would be well.

I covered myself in the blanket from the mare and I slept, and in my sleep the lizard led me to a clear pool and there were stones in the pool. The lizard told me each stone was a dream and if I picked up a stone I would have that dream, so I picked up a stone and the dream was you Richie, you! But you were older, as you are now. And in the dream I taught you some new chords for your guitar, imagine that. Then I picked up more stones and had more dreams and when I woke up, someone was sitting beside my mossy bed.

'Are you ready to come back now?'

I blinked. The figure was in shadow with the rising sun at his back.

'Hiero! It's you!'

I leapt from my bed and embraced him.

'Of course it's me! Who d'ye think it was.'

'But you were dead!'

'Dead? No, no, it would take more than that to kill one of us. But I've got a nice souvenir to show for it.' He lifted his shirt and showed me a wicked scar across his midriff. But it was healed. 'That's the first time I've let young Silkie best me in a fight, I'll tell you. I must be getting old.'

'But I saw them burning your body on a pyre!' I hugged him again.

'No, gracious, that wasn't me that was a *form*. Did you know you smell like that old mare?'

I didn't understand, but I didn't care. Hiero was alive. I was so pleased to see him that I wept.

'So you do care about me then?' he said.

'Of course I do!'

'So why did you run away?'

'I thought you were dead! I just want to go home.'

He looked at me sadly. 'I know that. It's taken me a long time to find you, Tara.'

'But I've only been gone three days!'

He shook his head. 'No no. You've been gone a few months. Your time to go back to your people is near.'

He told me that I only had seven days in total, before the crossing opened again and I could go home. I became excited and he looked more than a little sad. He warned me that things wouldn't be easy when I returned home, that things would not be the same. Of course I didn't heed his warnings; I had no idea what he meant. How could I? And then he told me flat out that he loved me and that he wanted to know if there was any hope for him. I let him down gently, and he asked me if there would be any hope if he were to come with me back home. I told me couldn't see that happening.

He turned and squinted into the sun and he seemed to accept it.

I let him lead me back to the lake and to his house where I passed the next seven days in anticipation of coming home. In order to make the time pass more quickly I learned as many things as I could while I was there. Oddly there seemed to be no more animosity between Silkie and him, and Silkie left me well alone, seeming to blush and walk away whenever I came near.

On the day before I was due to leave, Hiero begged me on his knees to stay with him. He cried and hung on to my legs. Then when he realised that I wasn't going to change my mind he seemed to become angry. He demanded to know what I had that was so important to go back to. I told him I had you, Richie.

'Blast him,' he said to me. 'I will blast him.'

Richie, I think you know now who it was who attacked you the other night.

But nothing he said was going to stop me from leaving. Everyone was cool with me for leaving; Ekko and one or two of the others I had come to know better, but none of them tried to stop me or to talk me out of it. And finally, when the day came, Hiero was true to his promise, and he delivered me to the crossing and he faithfully brought me back to all of you.

33

'To light a candle is to cast a shadow.'

Ursula Le Guin

I am now even more convinced that TM is constructing on the hoof, as it were, rather than 'remembering' a previously constructed confabulation. The indicators are there. Today in the surgery she looked out of the window and saw a man waiting near a bus-stop. She seamlessly wove the presence of this random figure into her narrative.

TM is certainly prone to nervous excitement. Her report of maps and globes was wildly speculative and she seemed to be building in a Cassandra complex quite wilfully, wanting to be disbelieved. I led her – as gently as I could – back to reality in asking if she owned any physical object or token smuggled back from her alternative world. For the first time since our initial session she introduced into her confabulation material from the present context by looking out of the window and challenging me to confront the poor man at the bus-stop. This depressing development has changed my view of what I at first saw as a case of contained confabulation. It now seems to be spilling into a more conventional case of paranoia.

I say depressing because the paranoia will deflect

any attempt by me to affirm a narrative which I had hoped was already completed. My job is to interpret the problem-saturated story that I have been given and to find a preferred alternative version of events satisfactory to the patient. If the condition is indeed paranoid the story will invent new problems for me to defeat any alternative, positive version of events. There will be no 'end' to the story.

Beyond that I can be confident that there is a strong force of sexual denial at large in TM's tale. We now have a name for the beautiful sexually-incontinent female who earned TM's disgust. It is Ekko (as TM spelled it out to me) which is of course Echo, and an echo of TM herself. That is to say, that the woman copulating so casually, promiscuously and without discrimination over the matter of gender, whether on the kitchen table or at the lakeside, is clearly TM herself.

Ekko is orgiastic in her appetites and clearly enjoys the sexual attentions of other people in the commune. By objectifying her own appetites in this way, TM can trigger her moral censure of the behaviour that led her to leave her home in the first place, thus avoiding responsibility. Likewise, Ekko seems excited by the idea of combat: excited to the point of lust. TM's search for a man who would fight for her and protect her reaches in Ekko its logical expression, but here again TM in condemning the behaviour of Ekko manages to dodge all moral blame.

Meanwhile the external data betrays this assumed moral position. TM's fierce maintenance of an image of eternal youth may indeed be a protected or deflected (but still excessive) interest in personal appearance. It is a form of passive exhibitionism, provocative and attention seeking in itself. TM's brother has reported to me that she has been seen 'out on the town', behaving seductively and inappropriately. She is in turn, he reports, excessively sensitive to criticism or disapproval. This may of course all point to a formal Histrionic Personality Disorder, but complicated by the need to subsume sexuality under a need for approval within the moral strictures.

Note to self: this business with the dental records needs to be cleared up. At the moment all we have is the unsupported and subjective observations of a dentist.

34

*'No doubt we shall have to sit there all bloody evening
listening to some awful drivel about fairies.'*

William Heaney

Jack logged on to his computer and found an email
from Mrs Larwood. It was written like a piece of
English composition.

> *Dear Jack,*
>
> *Thank you for your great kindness in helping
> me with my computer equipment. As you can
> imagine, it is all quite taxing for an elderly person,
> but with your help I seem to have got there. There
> is a reason that I am writing to you, and it isn't
> just because you are the only person in my email
> address book. It concerns your Aunt Tara. I would
> very much like to invite her to have a cup of tea
> at my house. Of course, she may be too busy to
> come and chat with a dusty old so-and-so like me,
> but I do hope you will forward this invitation to
> her. Meanwhile I hope you are keeping well and
> managing to get out from time to time. At least, it
> does seem to be a little warmer and I hope you are
> taking advantage of the better weather.*
>
> *Yours sincerely, Helen Larwood.*

Jack read the email a second time. He was going to have to show Mrs Larwood how to write an email.

He typed a reply.

Hi, Jack here. No problem I'll tell her. Oh by the way we keep emails short. You don't need to go on about the weather unless you're having an actual real chat about the weather. We also chop stuff. I would write prob but I've written problem out in full because you're new at this. You could say, hi can you ask Tara to come by for tea. That would do it. I'm not stopping you from writing long emails if that's what you want but you probably don't.

Then he pressed send, and wrinkled his nose.

He opened his desk drawer and took out the leaflet with a picture of Mrs Larwood's cat. He still hadn't made any plans to find a replacement. He put down the leaflet and made an internet search for local cat rescue centres.

Richie had been getting serious migraines. They'd been getting worse since he'd been attacked. He went to see his GP, who was concerned enough to get him an early appointment at the hospital for a CT scan.

He went along to the hospital, where he was asked to change into a gown. He was given a sedative and was also injected with iodine-based contrast material to help the doctors analyse what they could see from the scan. The injection made him feel flushed and left a metallic taste in his mouth.

He was asked to lie flat on a sliding table that could

glide into the white doughnut-shaped CT machine.

'Science fiction,' said Richie.

The radiographer smiled thinly and asked him to hold his breath at intervals while the X-ray images were taken. Each rotation of the scanner took only about a second as it photographed a thin slice of his brain.

When he was interviewed he told the consultant that the migraines had started just a couple of days before Christmas. No, he'd had no history of migraines before that date. Yes, the pains came every day, sometimes several times in the day.

He was told that he would have the results in a few days and he was asked if he had someone to drive him home. He said no, he didn't. It was recommended to him that he didn't drive home because of the sedative.

'Right-o,' Richie said. 'I hear you.'

He left the CT unit and walked back to the hospital car park, got into his car and drove home. On his way he had to pass by the Martins' house and he decided to call in.

'Look at the state of you,' Mary said when she greeted him at the door. 'Come in.'

'Is Tara home?'

'I'll make a pot of tea. Have you been in a fight?'

Neither Mary nor Dell had been told about either the attack on Richie, nor about Peter's run-in with the law over drink-driving. There was a conspiracy not to pass on bad news to people of their age, as if, like children under the age of sixteen, they wouldn't be able to handle it well. And with Mary fussing about tea, the twenty years of silence between them may have been as nothing.

'Do you want a sandwich?'

'No thanks Mrs Martin. Is Tara home?'

'She's in the bath. Dell is out playing bowls. He'll be sorry he missed you. Now, you always had three sugars in your tea.'

'Still do, Mrs Martin, still do.'

'I can easily make you a cheese sandwich.'

Richie knew from twenty years ago that Mary wouldn't let up. 'Go on then.'

He sat in the lounge on the tan leather sofa, looking at the velour curtains and the ornate wall lamps, trying to remember what had changed and what hadn't. He'd spent a lot of time at this house in his teens, waiting for Tara, watching TV, eating meals with the Martins, sometimes sleeping over on a bed made up on the couch that had been replaced by this tan sofa. It had been his second home. He heard Mary call up the stairs to let Tara know that Richie was there.

When Mary came back with the sandwich and the tea, the china cup shivered on its saucer. Mary had developed a tremor over the years. 'Where's the old radiogram? You got rid of it?'

They'd had a furniture-piece cabinet-sized record player on which he and Tara used to spin his vinyl albums. It was already outmoded, with sliding doors that concealed the equipment and a glass-fronted radio tuner that dialled into frequencies with exotic names like Hilversum, Helvetia, Luxembourg and Telefunken.

'Years ago.'

'I would have 'ad that. Collector's piece now.'

'You could have had it. Dell chopped it up.' She nodded at the dark bruises on his face. 'What's this then?'

'Someone attacked me the other night. Jumped from behind a tree.'

'Who did?'

'No idea.'

'They steal anything?'

'No.'

Mary fixed her eyes on him. 'It's getting so you don't want to go out of the house. I don't know what the world's coming to.'

Richie slurped his tea.

'Did she say anything to you?' Mary said.

'What?'

'When the two of you were out the other night. I'm wondering if she said anything to you. Anything other than this load of old rubbish she's told us.'

'What has she told you, like?'

'I'm not even going to repeat it. It's just a load of old rubbish.' Mary got up and closed the door, then sat down again. 'I don't mind telling you Richie, I'm starting to get sick of her around the house and she's only been back a few days. She spends hours in the bath. She came back drunk as a lord the other night. And the only explanation we've been given is this load of old rubbish. I'm ready to slap her face and tell her to pack her bags, but Dell won't hear of it. We have to tiptoe round her. It's not fair.' Mary swiped at her eyes to get rid of a resented tear. 'It's not fair, Richie.'

'Don't get upset.'

'And look at you.'

'What about me?'

'Coming here. The way we treated you.'

'Never mind that.'

'I lost you as well as her, didn't I?'

'Don't go getting upset, Mary.'

They sat in silence until Mary recovered. She said, 'Well what do you make of it all?'

Richie put his cup and saucer down on the carpet, and leaned forward. 'I think she's fragile.'

'Fragile!'

The door opened, and there stood Tara, fragile, pink, scrubbed, squinting and smiling at Richie. She raised her eyebrows at him and he knew right then that if she asked him to follow her over a hill, or swim across a river, or to leap off a cliff with her, he would do it.

'Richie,' she said, 'would you drive me over to Peter's place?'

'Sure.'

'But you haven't had any breakfast!' Mary protested.

'Not bothered.'

'She only eats fruit,' Mary said to Richie, in a kind of disgust. 'Fruit and nuts. Where's that going to get you?'

'I don't know, Mrs Martin.'

'I'll get my coat,' said Tara.

Mary offered Richie a thunderous look. Richie picked up his cup and saucer but Mary took it from him and whisked it off to the kitchen, giving Richie a chance to go out to the hall and ask Tara if she'd told her parents that she was moving in.

'Not yet.'

'What's that?' Mary said, overhearing.

'Oh well,' Tara said, 'I was going to wait until Dad was here before telling you. But I'm going to move in with Richie.'

'Oh,' said Mary, stunned.

'Just for a few days. See how it works out. Right, Richie?'

'Sure.'

'What am I to tell your Dad?'

'Let me tell him, will you?'

'Whatever you say. Nothing surprises me these days. Nothing at all.'

'Look Mum, I'm not going away. I'm just going to give you and Dad a bit of space. I can see I'm crowding you here.'

Mary turned her back. 'You do what you want, my girl. You always have.'

Tara had the front door open and was beckoning Richie to beat a hasty escape.

'I'll be seeing you then, Mrs Martin,' Richie said.

'Yes,' Mary shouted back with a wavering voice. Then she thought better of her manners and darted back to reach up to Richie and to give him a kiss on his cheek. Richie looked back at her. Mary was trying to smile, but her eyes were black storm-holes of terror and grief.

'I feel sorry for your mum,' Richie said as they drove away.

They drove directly towards a pallid, rising sun, and Tara put on her dark glasses. 'When I was fifteen I couldn't wait to get away, and I can't now. It's not my mum's fault. Nature doesn't want two women under the same roof.'

'But it's up to you if you want to leave.'

'Of course it's up to me.

'I mean it's not like you're sixteen, is it?'

She turned to him. He glanced up from his driving and he could see she was scrutinising him, trying to look to the bottom of his remark.

'I didn't mean anything by that.' He changed the subject quickly. 'Why do you need to go to Pete's?'

'I got some garbled message from Jack. Something about a neighbour.'

Peter was out working when Richie and Tara pulled up at The Old Forge. Genevieve and the kids were all there. Zoe opened the door to them. She looked strangely at her Aunt Tara, who smiled sweetly back.

'Is Jack in?' Tara asked, without ceremony.

Genevieve was sitting on the bottom step of the stairs, de-fleaing one of the lurchers with a plastic comb. She didn't look up from her task. 'He's up on his computer.'

Tara stepped round Genevieve and hurried up the stairs. Genevieve, startled from her task, turned to watch Tara go. Jack's bedroom door was heard to open and close firmly. Genevieve gave Richie a quizzical look. Standing beside her was Zoe, and behind her, Amber, and beside her, Josie. All looking to Richie for an account of why Aunt Tara was unorthodox, inexplicable and in Jack's bedroom.

'Where's that guitar o' yours?' he asked Zoe.

She went to fetch it for him.

He stepped into the living room, sat down on the sofa and patted the seat beside him. Zoe followed and lowered herself on to the sofa. Richie played a chord on the guitar, and then a second chord. Amber and Josie trailed into the room after their sister, but remained standing, watching Richie intently, as if an act of conjuring was about to happen. Josie was wide-eyed. 'Talk about fairies, Genevieve,' Richie said, 'your girls all look like they just fell out of an acorn cup.'

'They're hobgoblins,' Genevieve shouted from the stairs.

'Our dog's got fleas,' said Josie.

'Is that a request?' Richie said.

35

*'**Pouk-ledden** was the Midlands term for being led astray.'*

Katherine Briggs, A Dictionary Of Fairies

Mrs Larwood heard an almost timid knock on the door. She drew back her bolts and chains and knew instantly who Tara was. She beckoned her in with a smile and led her through to the back of the house, offering her a seat at the table. The new computer rested proudly on the table, its monitor swirling with light and colour from a screen saver.

'You're very switched on,' Tara said.

'It's that Jack. He's got it all sorted for me. You can take off your coat.'

'He's a nice boy.'

'He is. Tea?'

'No thank you.'

Mrs Larwood filled a kettle and set it on the gas flame, almost as if she hadn't heard. From the kitchen she said, 'Do you find you need to wear those dark glasses all the time?'

'I damaged my eyes,' Tara said.

After a short while Mrs Larwood returned with tea and cake, all laid out neatly on a tray, with a tiny milk jug and a bowl of sugar cubes and a set of silver sugar-cube tongs. It seemed to Tara that Mrs Larwood was a lady from another era; as was she.

'Mrs Larwood, Jack said you wanted to see me about something.'

'Oh yes. I'm very grateful to you for coming over to see me.'

'That's okay.'

'I heard you had been away and I wanted to welcome you home.'

'Thank you.' Tara had the strange sense that Mrs Larwood was circling, testing her, trying to get her measure.

'Jack said that you went up to the Outwoods on the day you went away.'

'That's right.'

'I don't like the place.'

'Really? I'm quite fond of it myself.'

'After what happened to you there?'

Tara put down her tea cup and looked hard at Mrs Larwood. 'But you don't know what happened to me there.'

'Quite correct. I don't. I was hoping that you would tell me.'

'It's a very long story and I really can't face the idea of telling it again. I've told the story to a number of people by now and I don't know if I can face the idea of repeating it all over again.'

'I can understand that.'

'Have you ever told a story over and over so many times that it gets worn smooth and some of the truth gets knocked off the edges? After a while you start to even doubt it yourself because you've told it too often.'

'Yes, I understand that. Will you have some cake? It's Jack's favourite.'

After Tara had left for Mrs Larwood's house Jack thought he'd better do something to move along his plan. Tara had burst into his bedroom, asking him to explain why he'd phoned his grandparents telling them that Mrs Larwood had wanted to meet her. He'd un-packed all that he knew – which wasn't much – but had blushed when he'd made mention of Mrs Larwood's cat and how he'd come to print out leaflets for her. Something in the way Tara had looked at him made him suspect that Tara could see right through his story. He couldn't say how or why he thought she knew. It was just the way she had removed her dark glasses to look at him and then had crossed her legs.

A tingle, nothing else.

His Aunt Tara was spooky.

There was another thing that bothered him greatly. It was that when Tara had come into his bedroom, her proximity had given him an erection. Not that erections were new to him; in fact they seemed to have become an almost permanent condition. But she was after all his aunt, and no one's aunt was ever that hot. It was unnatural.

After she'd gone he'd been unable to prevent himself from releasing a vast sigh of relief. He turned his at-tention back to his computer and made another search of local cat welfare and rescue centres. He was already noting down an address when the door to his bedroom swung open. He immediately logged off.

It was Josie. 'What are you doing?'

She hung on to his door handle, turning on a single

foot, smiling at him. At least Jack assumed that she was trying to smile. Sometimes Josie's smiles looked more like a gash in a Halloween pumpkin.

'You don't come into my room,' Jake shouted, 'without knocking. You understand that?'

'You mustn't shout at me. I'm telling.'

Jack got up and looked out of the window. He'd been in trouble with his dad for bellowing at his sisters, and by looking out of the window he was really only biding time as he tried to think up some other form of punishment or retribution he could inflict on his baby sister. But he spotted something at the bottom of the garden.

At first he thought it was a rag, caught in the mesh fence at the far end of the garden. It swayed slightly in the wind. It was rust coloured and too far away to properly make out. But Jack had a bad feeling about it.

'What is it?' Josie said, coming into the room to stand beside him at the window.

'Nothing.'

'What did you see? Can I see?'

He pushed her away from the window. 'It's nothing.'

'Why can't I see?'

Jack grabbed her arm and looked her in the eye. 'Do you want a Chinese burn?'

Josie's eyes grew large. 'No.'

'Well just remember how lucky you are, having a brother who gives you NO CHINESE BURNS, Josie. None. That's very lucky, isn't it?'

'Yes.'

'Yes. No Chinese burns. What a lucky sister you are, having such a great brother.'

'Yes.'

'Right. Now I'm going to let you play with my microscope kit.'

'You already gave me that.'

'Just shut up and play with it. Or else Chinese burns. And things very much like that.'

He sighed and left Josie in his room looking baffled, shut the door on her and hurried down the stairs.

'Where you going?' Genevieve said.

'Outside.'

This question and answer was a catch-ball mother and son tossed at each other so many times no one actually heard the words any more, but the exercise seemed to satisfy both parties. Jack slipped on his shoes and, trying not to look like a teenager in a hurry, marched up the garden path, shooting nervous glances over his shoulder.

The ginger flag swayed on the fence at the top of the garden. As he approached, his worst fears were confirmed.

'Fuckfuckfuckfuckfuckfuckfuck.'

The rust-red flag on the garden fence was not a cloth at all; it was the desiccated, mangled corpse of a ginger cat and it was somehow lodged in the mesh of the fence itself. It had been dragged half way through the fence but no further. The wire mesh had been torn away at the top. Some of the bones of the cat poked through its ragged and frayed fur.

Jack knew exactly what had happened. A fox – the very fox at which he'd thought to take a pot-shot right at the beginning of all his troubles – had dug up the corpse of the cat and had tried to drag it away as a prize of carrion. It had succeeded in getting the corpse as far as the broken fence but had somehow impaled it

302

on the twisted and broken wires. After failing to drag it through it had abandoned the thing to nature. And for everyone to see.

'Fuckfuckfuckfuckfuckfuckfuck,' went Jack, his teeth chattering.

He moved in closer to free the corpse but was repelled by the condition of the thing. It stank and its skull was visible through the dried fur. Its eyes looked eaten away. Jack gagged.

He ran back down to the shed in the outbuildings and found a pair of his father's gardening gloves. Returning to the impaled corpse he attempted, at arm's length and protected by the gloves, to free it. He didn't even want to look at the thing and tried to keep his eyes averted as he grabbed the dead cat by the scruff of the neck. A tuft of ginger hair came away in the fingers of his gardening gloves. He opened his hand and the tuft of fur was carried away on a breeze.

Teeth gritted, trying to stop his gorge from rising, Jack steeled himself and grabbed the corpse with both hands. It didn't want to come free. He tugged again. At last he tore it off the fence. There was a ripping sound and he was left with a generous portion of the dead cat in his hands. The rest of it was still lodged in the fence. He went back in and freed the remaining scraps of cat.

He was sweating. He wanted to vomit. He left the portions of cat on the ground and went back to the shed, returning with a Sainsbury's supermarket plastic carrier-bag. He put the bits of cat in the bag, gathered up any loose or strayed tufts of fur, and tied the handles of the bag together to seal everything inside. Too much air had been trapped inside the bag along with the corpse and it had inflated like a balloon.

'What are you doing?'

It was Josie. She had followed him outside. He had no idea how long she'd been watching him.

'Nothing.'

'What's in that bag?'

'Nothing.'

'Well, why isn't it empty?'

'What?'

'If there was nothing in it, it would be an empty bag. But that's a full bag.'

'No it's not.'

'Yes it is.'

'It's a rat that I shot with my air-gun.'

'No it's not. Can I see it?'

Jack brushed her aside and marched down the path with his inflated bag, determined to smuggle it past the kitchen window. He heard the obligatory little piglet's squeal of protest, *I'm telling!* but he blanked it.

His mother was in the kitchen and he saw her glance up as he hurried past, holding the bag low and averting his eyes. He made it past the kitchen window and beyond the door. The tall back gate was bolted, but he felt he'd got by unchallenged.

'Jack!'

It was his mother calling him back.

He stopped in his tracks. 'What?'

'Where are you off to, Jack?'

'Just out.'

Genevieve popped her head out of the back door and smiled at him. 'Hold your horses. I've got a letter I want you to post for me.'

Jack said nothing.

Genevieve looked at him, then she looked hard at

the inflated bag he was carrying. 'I'll just go and get it. One second.'

His mother disappeared back indoors and Jack took the opportunity to sling the bag over the tall gate. He heard it land with a dull thud on the other side.

Genevieve came back with her letter and gave it to him. 'You okay, Jack?'

'I'm fine.'

'Hmmmmmm,' said Genevieve.

'I've got to go.'

'Right.'

Jack inched open the gate so that his mother might not see the corpse-bag on the other side. He squeezed through the gate, closing it carefully behind him. There, on the other side of the gate and looking at the bag on the floor of the driveway were Tara and Mrs Larwood.

36

'It is Christmas Day, the werewolves' birthday, the door of the solstice still wide enough open to let them all slink through.'

Angela Carter

'Tell me what happened,' Vivian Underwood asked Tara, 'tell me what happened when you came back.'

They sat in the favoured chairs drawn up by the window. It was late afternoon and though the diffuse winter sunlight was dipping behind the ancient spreading cedars of a neighbouring property, it touched Tara's delicate features, illuminating otherwise invisible tiny blonde hairs on her cheek. She squinted to summon the memory, and even behind the dark glasses Underwood could see the crinkled traces of laughter lines around her eyes.

'Hiero was desperately upset at my leaving. He seemed to be so insulted. He demanded to know what I had at home that he couldn't give me. He said I should make a list. He couldn't understand why anyone would want to trade a space of light and beauty and knowledge for what he called a grubby site of shadows. Meaning here. I admit, sometimes when I look around I don't know either.

'When I pointed out that I had a family, he said that

his entire community was a family; when I said I looked forward to an education he challenged me to say what I might study that had more value than the things I had learned in the short time I'd been with him; when I told him I had a boyfriend waiting for me, he darkened.

'He wanted to know my boyfriend's name. I told him about Richie. I told him that I'd treated Richie badly and that I regretted it, and that I missed him. He asked if I loved Richie and I said I thought I did. He said, "I will blast this Richie. I will blast him. I will blast his brain with cobweb and fog; with vapours from stagnant pools and from the filthy fens; with thorns of ice and leeches of fire; with darts of rank air and black dreams of scorpions; with soot from chimneys and lime from the kilns." All these words were like creatures pouring from his mouth. I was shocked. I made him stop speaking like that.

'But his manner towards me had changed. He became sullen, surly, barely talking to me. He was chained to his promise to return me here but now he hated me for it. We rode together on the white mare, him seated behind me, but this time I didn't feel his arm around me.

'We cantered a little way, and I knew we had made it over the crossing because the light changed. Where I had slowly become used to the brilliance of the light where I had been, now everything had a jagged, smudged quality. And where the light had grazed my eyes, now it seemed to rake and sting. And it was cold! The wind hacked at me like a knife. But the landscape became familiar, and I knew I was in Charnwood again, dear Charnwood, somewhere where the three rivers meet, and rising in the distance I could see the Outwoods.

'Though the season had changed. Winter had come. I asked him to let me get down but he insisted that he would set me down where he found me, and even though I didn't want to be in the Outwoods and wanted to be at home, he wouldn't listen to me. He barely spoke. I was shivering, and as we trotted on, small flakes of snow began to fall.

'It was up in the Outwoods that he delivered me, at that very rock where the bluebells had been growing in such thick, perfumed colonies. But now there were no bluebells and no songbirds. The bracken was dead, the trees were bare and the track was muddy. I got down from the horse and turned to speak to him, but he steered the mare away from me.

'"Why?" I said to him. "You have to answer one thing! Why did you choose me?"

'He shook his head as if he didn't believe that I didn't know the answer to my question. "Tara, because you were the Queen of the May." And with that he kicked at the mare's flanks to canter her away. I was left alone, exactly as I was found.

'My first instinct was to run, and I did, I ran. I pelted down to the road, stumbling, slithering in the black leaf mould, running to get home.

'In the short time I'd been away someone had built a car park, with public toilets and notice-boards offering information about the place. I resented these things. They gave me a bad feeling in my stomach. There were two cars parked there, and I didn't like the shape of them. They didn't seem to be quite right. Sculptures near the entrance – wooden figures – made me feel queasy. All the time I was squinting into the jagged light, and my senses were tingling and I knew things had changed, but it was too soon for me to see how much. I mean even the cars were different. The designs of the cars. I knew something had happened.

'The snow was falling and I was shivering. I spotted a man with a dog walking back to his car. I stepped out of the trees and asked him if he would give me a lift. He flat out ignored me and got into his car and drove away. I actually wondered if he even saw me. It was like I was a ghost trying to communicate with people on another plane. I was shocked by his rudeness. I felt cold and weary and overwhelmed and I know I started crying.

'After a while a married couple came by. They looked like they'd been hiking. She had a patch over one eye, like a pirate's patch. She paused and asked me if I was all right. I said no I'd been dumped there and I needed to get back home. The couple exchanged looks, and then the woman offered me a ride. I saw myself reflected in the passenger window and suddenly appreciated what I must have looked like. I wasn't very clean and my clothes hadn't been laundered in the six months I'd been away.

'Once I was in the car the woman tried to break the tension by talking to me. She asked me if I was all ready for Christmas. I said that I was, but I couldn't work out how it might have been Christmas, since I'd been away exactly six months and that would make it October. When she asked me where I wanted to go I gave her my home address. But when we passed through Anstey I knew everything was out of joint. The cars were all different, the buses were different. There were electronic signs that I'd never seen before. The roads had changed. The shops had changed and some old decorative store fronts had been replaced by plate glass windows. Even the public telephones had changed – where were the old red phone boxes, so comforting and reassuring? It was all detail, just fine detail, but important detail to me on this homecoming day and it all felt wrong.

'I was beginning to panic. I think I was hyperventilating. The lady in the passenger seat turned her head to look at me with her one good eye. She asked me if I was all right. Even this seemed sinister to me, as if she were in on some joke.

'When the car approached the end of my street I got them to let me out of the car before we reached my house. I was nervous about going in. For one thing I anticipated a dreadful reception; but quite apart from that I couldn't process all the changes that had taken place. A petrol station had closed down and only its broken canopy remained, defaced by graffiti, a sheet of newsprint blowing across its forecourt. A newsagent had become a charity shop. A housing development had sprung up like mushrooms after a night of rain, and a video camera, like a surveillance device, was angled down at street level.

'Even the door to our house had changed. Someone had built a PVC-and-glass porch to mask off our old blue door. And, as I looked, an elderly man came out of the porch door. He was a bald-headed man, with a tuft of white hair behind each of his ears. He looked beaten down by life as he opened his car door and climbed inside. And I realised it was Dad. It was my dad, and he was old.

'I know that I cried out. I bit into my knuckles. I couldn't help it.

'As he reversed the car out of the drive – a new car I

didn't recognise, I turned and ran. I ran blindly, feeling like I should hide, hide my face. I had tears in my eyes and nowhere to go. I ran until I came to the crossroads, where the pub that used to be known as The Old Bell Inn had a new sign and had been rechristened The Snooty Fox. But I had no money to go inside, so I walked on and I came to the public library and I went inside just to get warm and to gather my thoughts.

'But even that place had changed. It had automatic doors! Inside there were rows of TV screens and people were hunched over the screens. I had no idea what this all meant. I thought the people must all be watching television. The age of the internet had arrived while I had been away.

'And then I laughed, because I knew what was happening. I was in a dream. I was still dreaming that I was on the back of a giant bee. All I had to do was wake up, but in order to wake up I first had to fall asleep, and then this strange dream would all be over, and I would wake up at home, a foolish schoolgirl who after falling asleep amongst the bluebells had had the strangest dream. I was exhausted enough to fall asleep there and then. There was a lounge area in the library with newspapers and magazines, and I sat there, holding on to a newspaper and pretending to read it while I dozed.

'And I did doze. But when I woke it was not to find myself at home. A librarian, a kindly lady with soft brown eyes was shaking me awake. She apologised to me and smiled and said that I couldn't sleep there and that they were closing the library for the Christmas holidays. She gave me a leaflet stating when the library would be open after the break. It had the dates and it had the year, all clearly printed for me to read.

'Of course I didn't believe it. I had to ask the librarian what year it was. She didn't answer me. Instead she asked me if I had somewhere to go. When I repeated my question she went away and came back with a piece of paper. It had an address written on it; the address of a hostel, she said, where people could get food and shelter over Christmas. She smiled at me again. "It's going to be a cold Christmas," she said.

'She thought I was homeless! But I wasn't homeless; I had a home to go to, a family, loving parents, and a boyfriend. I walked back home again and I decided that whatever the consequences and whatever the circumstances at home, I had to declare myself. I didn't have a key to the house but we always kept a spare key under a small boulder near the front door. I decided I would let myself in.

'But the boulder was gone. There was no key, and even if there was a boulder and a key the door had been changed, and with it the lock! I rang the bell and I knocked at the door, and no one was home. I decided to wait in the garage next to the house, to keep warm. Even the garage was piled high with unfamiliar junk, but I waited, and eventually my father returned in his car. I watched from the garage, spying on my father as he got out, and as an elderly woman struggled to climb out of the passenger seat. The elderly woman was my mother. Her hair had turned silver. Can you imagine how I felt when I saw my poor mum and dad, turned almost overnight into frail, silver-haired old people?

'I couldn't breathe. I wanted to run to them, hug them, but I couldn't. I was too overwhelmed by the change, the hideous ageing that had taken place in them.

Instead I waited, hiding in the garage as they shuffled inside. I couldn't face the idea of presenting myself to them. I didn't want them to look in my eyes or see my expression twisted with horror at the lines engraved on their faces and their snowy heads, so I skulked in the garage, paralysed, bewildered.

'Darkness fell and I crept away. I walked the five miles into Leicester, in a kind of blindness, tears stinging my eyes. I found the address, given to me by the librarian, of the hostel. They took me in without asking questions. Most of the inmates were in a wretched condition – bag ladies, and drug addicts or feeble-minded women with their senses battered out of them by life. It was a grim place to be. I shared a stinking room with three other women. One of them talked constantly about a dead child; another curled in the corner, calling out in her sleep; a third ranted about how they wouldn't allow any drink in the place. But it was warm. You could get a hot shower and something to eat. Eventually I slept.

'The next day was Christmas Eve. We were told to leave the hostel between eleven a.m. and three p.m. No one there seemed to have any idea of what they were supposed to do in those hours. I was given an old coat. I spent the time walking around the town, trying to take in all the incredible but minute changes. I went to the central library to get warm and someone there showed me how to read back through newspapers on a screen, and this I did, trying to get a sense of all the things that had happened since I'd been away.

'Twenty years. I'd lost twenty years. In my head I could no longer deny what had happened, but in my heart I was never able to accept it. I still can't.

'And I knew that Hiero was following me. As I

walked through the town I could sense him behind me. Sometimes he made an effort to remain unseen, and at other times he didn't even care if I spotted him or not. He wanted me to know he was there. In the central library he sat up in the balcony, gazing at me through a gap between the shelves.

'After a while he approached me. "You see?" he said. "You see how it is? You see how you can't come back here?"

'I shut out his words and I focused on the newspaper archives, as if by an effort of will I could make him unreal, as if I could make all of this unreal. Eventually, a male librarian came along and said, "Is this man bothering you?" Hiero sneered at the man, but left without fuss.

'You see, I was in a state of shock. I had to process what had happened to me, and I couldn't. I went out into the streets again and drifted by all the shops, all the plate glass imported into the High Street, all decorated for Christmas and boasting unfamiliar glittering merchandise.

'I went back to the hostel, not because I felt comfortable there but because I couldn't face the truth, and I couldn't face my parents. I ate a meal there and in the evening a choir came, a local choir from a school, made up of adults and children. They sang carols for us, and they sang so beautifully and with such feeling that I cried and cried and cried until no more tears would come, just hot salt stinging the backs of my eyes.

'I lay awake that night trying to work out what to do. When I did fall asleep I had bad dreams, and I was woken up when the woman with the drink problem tried to get into bed with me. I screamed so loudly at her that someone came and led her away to another room.

'In the morning, Christmas morning, I decided that I would have to go home, whatever the cost, whatever the agony. I told one of the volunteers that I had a family after all, and that I should be with them. He was very kind. He drove me back to my house and waited while I knocked on the door. It had started to snow again, tiny flakes of snow, and I remembered how my dad would always bet on a white Christmas, and I wondered if he still did.

'When Dad answered the door, he didn't recognise me. Then Mum came to the door, and on seeing me she fainted.'

37

'On Friday March 15th, sometime in the morning Michael Clary fetched the priest. The priest performed a mass in Bridget's bedroom, while Bridget was lying in bed. That evening, according to Johanna Burke's testimony, Bridget was dressed, and brought through to the kitchen. Johanna testified: Her father, my brother and myself, and deceased and her husband sat at the fire. They were talking about the fairies, and Mrs. Cleary said to her husband, "Your mother used to go with the fairies, and that is why you think I am going with them." He asked her, "Did my mother tell you that?" She said, "She did; that she gave two nights with them."'

Summary of trial transcript (1895)

Tara weighed in at the general hospital undergoing a CT scan, paid for privately this time and yet without knowing it she found herself lying on the very same NHS flatbed and passing through the same doughnut-shaped scanner that Richie had stretched out on some days earlier; her scan was also supervised by the same radiographer who had photographed Richie. Tara was there at Underwood's insistence. He wanted to see if there were any signs of trauma to the brain – recent or old – that might explain an amnesia spanning twenty years. Underwood conceded that even if a trauma were exposed by the scan, it would be difficult to explain why her memory before her departure and since her return seemed to be in perfect working order; but then, he said, the workings of the human brain were often unfathomable, particularly in the process of the recovery.

The brain he said could hide twenty years of experience, but that didn't mean those experiences weren't there.

Knowing that Richie was waiting for her in the hospital car-park Tara lay still as the radiographer stepped out of the room to trigger the scanner. She was deeply worried about Richie. On the way to the hospital he'd had to stop the car, so severe was his latest attack of migraine. He had parked up, closed his eyes and held his fingertips to his temples while she sat helpless in the passenger seat. After about ten minutes the attack had subsided and he had carried on driving her to the hospital. Tara had wanted him to come inside, into the waiting room, but Richie had said he preferred to tip back his seat so that he could try to rest quietly in his car. Plus of course, you couldn't smoke in the hospital.

As the X-ray flickered over her, re-set and flickered again, she had three things on her mind. One was Richie, one was Mrs Larwood, and one was the *charnas* flower made up by bugs.

Tara's visit to the elderly lady living across the street from The Old Forge had been a strange one. Jack had somehow managed to communicate – or her parents had after relaying Jack's message – that the old lady's request to see her was somehow urgent. But when it came to it Mrs Larwood wasn't offering anything more pressing than tea and biscuits. Tara concluded that the old woman was simply being nosey. Perhaps she had been around the neighbourhood when Tara had disappeared and now just wanted to satisfy her curiosity.

But all the time she'd been in her house, Tara had felt the old lady was circling her, gazing with her cataracted eyes, probing, looking for confirmation of something unexpressed. When Tara came to the conclusion that her visit had no real purpose she had excused herself, but the old lady had got up and escorted her across the street back to The Old Forge. Only the appearance of Jack throwing bags over the gate and behaving in a furtive manner had given her the opportunity to get free.

Tara knew perfectly well that she herself was the peculiar one, the one with the outrageous story, the one seeing a shrink; but she often thought that everyone around her had a very breakable shell, too. Meanwhile the effort of maintaining a singular belief in the face of overwhelming opposition was exhausting. Tara could see how easy it would be simply to give way, to accept that she was deluded, to let the memory become a ghost and to then let the ghost fade.

The most extraordinary thing about it all was how simple it was just to carry on. There were meals to be prepared and eaten, dishes to be washed, clothes to be laundered, ironed and put on and taken off, beds to be slept in and made and unmade. The prosaic needs of day-to-day living blunted all impact of the miraculous; it demanded that the glorious be relegated. And she knew that even if she were able to convince everyone involved that she had witnessed something remarkable, had undergone a transcendental and miraculous experience, reached and returned from another world, it almost seemed like it would not ever and could not ever truly matter.

As she lay inside the doughnut of the CT scanner, with the photoflash triggering, resetting and triggering again she thought of the *charnas* flower. She saw it all over again and she knew she was one bug in the group flower. Scattered by the wind of what happened, however astonishing it was, she really hadn't travelled that far from the community to which she belonged. As the X-ray machine whirred and made another photograph of her brain she knew she had to return and take her place in the assembly of the flower. There was no other place to be.

Out in the hospital car park Richie felt that his migraine had subsided. He was experiencing coloured lights flickering behind his retina, tiny iridescent worms of radiance, but the pain had gone away. The attacks were irregular and unpredictable but they were getting worse. He thought maybe he was going to have to go in for a lifestyle change. No alcohol. No smoke. No sense of humour. Life unplugged.

If that was going to be the case, he decided, he might as well smoke while he still could. He opened his car door, stepped out, flicked his lighter and torched up a cigarette. As he inhaled the tobacco he thought he saw a small shadow flit at the periphery of his vision, like that of a mouse running beneath a fridge. He peered hard between the cars parked in rows but saw nothing. His driver door was still open a fraction. He opened it wide and leaned back against the sill of his car, luxuriating in his smoking.

He was scheduled to see his Consultant the following

day to get the results of his own CT scan. He'd spent the morning reassuring Tara that it was nothing, routine; and so it was nothing. That is, the scan itself was nothing. The seeded anxiety about what might be found was, however, not nothing.

Being with Tara again had made him review his life. The last twenty years had gone in a flicker. It compressed in the memory. Much of it had been lost to drinking or to being stoned, both of which were experiences that largely produced at best only smoky reminiscences. If the experiences had been good at the time – and he supposed they were – it would be nice to have strong recollection. But that didn't seem to be the way it worked.

The music – the making of music and the performing of music – produced memories, many good, some bad, some difficult. But he knew for sure that he'd spent too much of that time living not in the present moment of creating or playing music, but in the expectation or hope of some reward, some success. He had always been waiting for his life to start when that happened, when the recognition came. It had taken him twenty years to realise how utterly wrong-headed that was.

It was as if the twenty years didn't amount to much; that he hadn't actually been *present* for so much of his life. He wondered if he might be able to fix that now that Tara had come back. She had the gift of bringing him back to the present. He had played his guitar for her the previous evening and she had sat erect on his sofa and had been so focussed on him, he knew that she was the audience he had wanted all along. Plus he had a huge repertoire of songs – other people's songs and his own songs – that he could play for her, and play well.

And then while he was playing she had taken his breath away when she showed him how to re-tune his guitar a different way.

'That won't work,' he'd said.

'It will. Now play your normal chords, but one step up.'

He was astonished. She had been right. There were new sounds in the world. Sounds that – crusty old muso that he was – he'd never heard before.

'Where did you learn that?'

He shouldn't have asked. He knew the answer.

'I told you. I learned lots of things.'

Being with Tara again lit up the present. He had been playing for so long in the anticipation of success that he never saw the moment come up on him when he had realised it was not going to be. There was a time of anticipation and a time of regret, with nothing in between; and the regret was informed by the understanding that by hanging on to his music he had been trying to hang on to his youth. After that there was nothing to do but to commit to the present, and that meant being the best he possibly could, with his chosen instrument, for the people who wanted to listen. That's how clear Tara made things for him.

Richie smoked his cigarette, thinking about some songs he wanted to re-arrange in this extraordinary new style when he heard the rush of footsteps. But even though he was distracted by thoughts of Tara and of musical chords, he was ready.

He'd been ready from the moment he'd been discharged from hospital after the first assault, because he knew in his bones that a second attack was always imminent. Even though he now preferred the quiet life, Richie was a street-fighter. Both his instincts and his experience informed him that a second assault would follow, as sure as counting for the thunder that follows lightning, and that it would happen in an open space at a time when he was alone. And so he'd always been ready.

The sound he heard behind him was a light-footed skitter on the tarmac. He dropped the butt of his cigarette and stepped out and away from his car. There was a rush of a shadow and an astonishing high kick that whistled an inch past his jaw, but Richie grabbed his attacker, and, instead of blocking, he pulled the man further into the line of his own attack, so that his assailant went crashing into the gap left by the open car door. Richie moved quickly, stepping around to slam the car door into the figure crumpled against the driver's wheel. He slammed the door again, and again.

The dazed attacker tried to shield his head with a raised forearm, but Richie slammed the door a fourth time, catching the raised arm between the door and the roof of the car in a sickening crunch. There was a howl of agony from the shadowy figure trapped by the car door.

Richie knew now for sure that his attacker was the same man who had eyeballed him while he was on stage that night. He opened the door again and the man slumped to the floor. Richie put the boot in, hard.

'Who the fuck are you?' Richie roared. He could smell the man, smell his pain and his hurting breath and body odour mingled. 'Who the fuck are you?'

The man squatted, leaning against the bottom sill of

the car, nursing his injured arm, a rich stream of blood leaking from his nose. He was still trapped between the car and Richie, who was ready with the door, threatening to slam it on him again.

The man spoke in an eerie whisper. 'She's not for you.'

'Fuck are you TALKING about?' Richie roared back.

But he got no answer. From his squat position the man made a sudden spring, an impossible upright leap that took him over the open car door to land nimbly on the tarmac behind. Still nursing his injured arm, he ran.

'That's right, run, you fucker! Run!'

The man stopped and turned to call to Richie. 'Give her up. She's not for you. She's not for any of you.' And then he trotted away, disappearing behind a row of parked vehicles.

Richie was suddenly calm. He was pumped with adrenaline but now it changed and flowed through him like a sedative. He felt his body spasm. He lit another cigarette and stared at the space where the man had disappeared.

After a while Tara emerged, smiling broadly at him. Then her expression changed. 'What happened?'

They went to The Phantom Coach to get a drink. Richie had a pint and a scotch chaser. Tara had asked for snakebite, and he shuddered. Richie told her everything about the attack. Tara took her dark glasses off and pinched the bridge of her nose. She sighed and told Richie all she knew about Hiero, about how he had followed her everywhere, how he was still stalking her.

'That means,' Richie said evenly, 'that I've just had a fight with a fucking fairy.'

'They're dangerous,' she said.

'Think I don't know that?'

'And you shouldn't call them that. They don't like it. Are you starting to believe me?'

'No,' said Richie. 'Yes. Not really. Partly.'

'Are you okay?'

Richie was wincing. 'It's these migraines I get. They're like attacks of coloured light, but they burn like acid.'

'Can I get you anything?'

'Another scotch and another beer. Throw medicine at it. I'll be all right.'

'You don't look all right.'

'Tara, I'm all right. You've come back to me. That's all I need. That's all the medicine and the dope I need.'

'Richie!'

'Let me tell you something. You've been away for twenty years. But I have, too. I went into hibernation when you left me. All I've done in twenty years is write songs about you. I haven't really grown up, have I? Look at Peter and Genevieve. They've grown up but I've been stuck where I was when you left me.'

'Oh my God, Richie.'

'But that's changed. Time started again. A new clock started ticking. You've come back to me, haven't you, Tara?'

'Yes, Richie.'

'You have come back, haven't you?'

'Yes, Richie.'

38

'Creating simplicity often makes the heart leap; order has been restored, the crooked made straight. But order is understanding that things cannot be made simple, that complexity reigns and must be accepted.'

Marina Warner

Jack managed to scoop up the bag with the cat's corpse and to step around Tara and Mrs Larwood without overmuch conversation. Mrs Larwood seemed to want him to stay while she heaped praise upon his shoulders, telling Tara how he had helped her with her computer and what a fine boy he was. Jack had muttered some remark about being in a bit of a hurry; whereupon Tara had said something teasing. Both she and Mrs Larwood had giggled at him.

But as he walked away he felt both pairs of eyes boring into his back. He wondered if the plastic bag was transparent enough for them to be able to determine the shape of a cat's corpse. He was tempted to look down at the bag to gauge the opacity of the plastic; but he was certain that one downward glance would draw attention to what was inside it and almost certainly betray him, so he kept his eyes directed ahead of him and marched on with agonising and robotic purpose.

After walking for half a mile in this mode he came

across a builder's skip in the road, outside a house in the process of renovation. The skip had been filled with discarded bricks and old plaster and lath, plus bathroom fittings torn from the old house. Jack checked that no one was watching, and dumped the cat's corpse in the skip, hiding it under some broken lath for good measure.

From there he took a bus into town and went directly to Catline, the rescue centre he had researched on the internet. He had identified a specific cat from a gallery of photographs; it looked exactly like Mrs Larwood's cat, down to the detail. At least, he thought guiltily, it looked like Mrs Larwood's cat before it had been shot, buried, had decomposed and was dug up again. The favoured cat had the piss-poor name of Frosty; but that hadn't seemed an insurmountable problem because cats, as far as he knew, were not like dogs in answering to their names. There was little prospect of someone randomly shouting its name and the cat responding. All it needed was Mrs Larwood's distinctive collar; or rather Mrs Larwood's cat's distinctive collar. Jack felt he had a good chance of pulling this off.

At the reception desk he blushed when he told a heavily pregnant woman behind the reception desk that he'd had some email exchanges with a lady called Joanna. *Why the fuck am I blushing?* he thought angrily. *There's no need to blush.* While he fought back the pink, the said Joanna was summoned from the bowels of the cattery.

Joanna had dark hair that tumbled over her eyes and she wore tight-fitting but dirty blue jeans. She had lazy eyelids, and Jack thought she was hot for such an old chick; though he guessed she was well over twenty-one, and therefore well past it. But when she eyed him from behind her fringe of dark hair he found he was fighting another blush. Even from where he stood she smelled of what he suspected was cat fur. Or something like that. It set him on edge.

'Oh I didn't realise I was emailing such a good-looking young man,' she said airily.

The blush broke like a tsunami. That is, all his blood drained from his face for a second, leaving him pale, but it was only gathering strength to come back in force. The blush flooded from deep in his scalp and from low across the back of his neck, swelling like a foaming red tide across his cheeks, and crashing like a breaker around his ears. His ears were the worst. They flamed. He knew his ears would be flamingo pink and he hated himself with a vicious passion. Right at that moment he hated his own guts, for blushing so profoundly.

Joanne waited for him to speak. He couldn't. His tongue froze in his mouth.

She cocked her head to one side. Then she cocked her head to the other side, in an exaggerated and mocking gesture, waiting patiently for him to speak. Finally, she pressed her fingertips together, making a steeple that she held under her chin. Her eyes laughed at him.

'Frosty,' Jack managed.

'Just a bit.'

'Cat.'

'This is a cattery. You do know that, don't you?'

Joanna shifted her weight from one hip to the other, and Jack found himself with the biggest and most un-wanted erection he'd ever experienced in his young life. Now the woman behind the reception was looking at him oddly, too. Jack thought that both women could tell he had a huge erection. He hated his erection and he hated his blushing and he hated the young woman Joanna and her mocking eyes. What right had she got to give him an erection? He didn't even like the way she smelled.

Joanna glanced at the woman behind the desk. 'You want to come and have a look at him?'

It was with some relief that Jack realised Joanna was addressing him, not inviting the woman behind the desk to study his no doubt observable erection. He nodded. She beckoned him to follow her to the cattery, which he did. He'd been holding his breath and was relieved to find that he could ultimately take in air again. The young woman's buttocks swung in front of him and he had to quickly avert his eyes. He made the mistake of blowing out noisily – a completely involuntary act – and she glanced back over her shoulder at him.

Someone from the winding depths of the cattery called to Joanna and she abandoned him for a moment to speak with her colleague; for which release he was mightily grateful. When she returned he found he had almost recovered the faculty of speech.

'I emailed you,' he said.

'You did.'

'Saying what I was looking for.'

'You did.'

'And you said Frosty.'

'I did. And here he is.'

She had led him to a wire cage on a shelf, just one in a row of identical cages. The cat behind the wire was perfect. Jack had in his possession a picture of Mrs Larwood's cat – printed on a leaflet – but he didn't even need to get the picture out of his pocket to know that Frosty was a precise match. It was uncanny, so close was it in markings to that dead cat. It was even white-mitted on all four feet.

'You want to hold him?'

Jack didn't. He wasn't at all attracted to cats. He didn't want to pet the thing, coo at the thing or talk to the thing. In fact he despised the way that people would adopt a falsetto voice or any other kind of voice in order to address a cat. He just wanted to stow the creature in a box, get that red collar round its neck and drop it off at Mrs Larwood's place at the double, job done. But it occurred to him he'd better look like he was thrilled to see the creature so he made some poor efforts at emulating cat-lover noises.

She swung open the cage, made a gentle grab for Frosty and handed him over to Jack. Luckily for him, Frosty seemed happy enough, purring and nestling into the crook of his arm, blinking up at him.

Everything was going pretty well between them until Joanna mentioned a home visit.

'Home visit?'

'We don't just dump them on anyone.'

'Oh?'

'We check out that you're suitable for the cat and the cat is suitable for you.'

'Right. Is that really necessary?'

'You wouldn't believe what we see in people's homes. One family had a huge pet snake. Imagine.'

'Right. That must have been ... Right.'

Joanna puckered the corner of her lips and blew her dark fringe out of her eye. 'When do you want us to come?'

'I'll need to get back to you on that,' Jack said.

'Need to check your busy schedule do you?'

'Something like that.'

'See if you can find us a window in your calendar?'

Jack blew out his cheeks again. 'Yep.'

'No rush. Take your time. Whenever you're ready.'

'I mean, you'll probably want my parents to be there, won't you?'

She nodded slowly. She seemed way over-focussed on him. 'Plus there's the donation to think about.'

'We're okay with the donation,' Jack said rather too quickly.

'That's great.'

'How much is the donation?'

'Well we cover all bases: vet's fees, micro-chipping, inoculations, tick and worm treatment. It actually comes to around a hundred-and-fifty pounds.'

'What?'

'But we suggest a minimum donation of fifty.'

'Right. Right.'

'That going to be a problem?'

'No. No. I'll go now.'

'In a hurry now are we?' She put her hands on her hips. Those fractionally swinging hips, in her tight, dirty blue denim jeans. Her long forefingers slipped into the belt loops at the waistband of her jeans. And as she locked her gaze on his she swung those hips to the side, rocking slightly.

Jack turned and he knew he was colouring again. He felt the rush. He retraced his steps, knowing that Joanna was watching him leave. He crossed the reception, and the pregnant lady at the desk bid him goodbye.

'Yes,' Jack said by way of reply.

He walked to the end of the street, turned the corner

and found a brick wall; and he gave that brick wall a bloody good kicking.

Jack had a stroke of luck that afternoon when his mother asked him if he might stay in after school the next day and take care of Amber. Zoe would be out with her boyfriend and Genevieve wanted to take Josie to the opticians to find out if she needed spectacles. It would be a big help to her, Genevieve said, if Jack would hold the fort. Jack quickly calculated that his dad would be working and that he had a useful window of opportunity in which he could invite the visit from the cattery. He could make out that his parents had been called out unexpectedly. The visitors would check out the house, see that it was fine and release the cat.

'Sure.'

Genevieve was slightly taken aback. 'What, no protest? No demand for financial reward? No moaning?'

'Do you want me to do it or not?'

With that settled, Jack stepped outside with his phone and called the cattery to schedule a home visit for four p.m. the following day. When he came back he found Amber in the sitting room. 'If you're good tomorrow,' he told her, 'I might let you play on my computer.'

'Really?'

'Yes. If you're good.'

'Jack, I love you!'

'Shut up with that or I won't let you.'

The following afternoon, with Jack in full command of the house, the doorbell rang at about ten minutes before four. 'They're early,' Jack said out loud, though he hadn't intended to.

'Who?' Amber wanted to know.

'Go and play on my computer,' Jack said.

'Who is at the door?'

'Now! You have to go now! You go and play on my computer now, right now, or you don't get to play on it at all, and you know what that means?'

'What does it mean?' Amber asked reasonably.

'Get on my computer this minute!'

But Amber instead ran to the dining room at the front of the house and looked out of the window. Jack chased after her. 'It's Richie,' she said casually.

Jack's hopes crashed. He answered the door, holding it open just a crack.

Richie had a guitar-shaped carrying-case in his hand. 'Jack,' he said.

'Hello.'

'Dad in?'

'No.'

'Mum in?'

'No.'

'You in?'

Jack didn't answer.

'I've brought this guitar for your sister. It's a damn sight better than that thing she's got.'

'Right.'

'Jack, you're gonna have to open the door just a tiny bit wider.'

'Why?'

'See this guitar I've brought over for your sister? I'll never get this guitar through that little crack without damaging it. If I'm to bring it in at all, that is.'

Jack opened the door and extended an arm, generously offering to relieve Richie of the burden of the guitar. Richie didn't tender the guitar however. He looked as though he planned on keeping it for a while longer. Instead he asked where Genevieve was, and Jack told him. Jack shot a glance at the clock in the hall. It was now eight minutes before the scheduled visit.

'Everything all right, Jack?'

'Everything is fine.'

'Tell you what, let me in and I'll leave a note for your sister about the guitar.'

Jack hovered in the doorway, hearing his spinning plates crashing around him. He looked up the street. He looked down the street. There was no sign of the cat people. Then he stepped aside and let Richie in.

Richie swaggered through to the kitchen as if he owned the place. There he leaned the guitar, in its case, gently against the wall. 'It needs careful handling, that one. Keep it away from radiators, tell her. And out of the direct sunlight. Right?'

'Radiators. Sunlight. Check.'

'You been suckin' a lemon, Jack?'

'No. I haven't.'

'Has he been suckin' a lemon?' Richie asked Amber.

'Can I go on your computer now Jack?' Amber asked.

Jack nodded mournfully, and Amber skipped upstairs and out of sight.

'Tell you what. Get the kettle on. Make your Uncle Richie a cup of tea. Nice and strong. I'll stick around 'till your mum gets back.'

Jack knew he was doomed. He saw no way out. With a mournful but resigned face he filled the electric kettle and took out a mug and a box of tea bags. Richie watched him carefully; studying him.

'Quiet type, aincha, Jack?'

'Yeah.'

'Yeah. Nothing wrong with that. Too many people saying too many foolish things, isn't it, Jack?'

'Yeah.'

'Yeah.' Richie rubbed his chin. 'I'd agree with that. Why do you keep looking at the door?'

'I'm not.'

'Yes you are. You keep looking at the door as if you're expecting someone to come through it.'

'No I'm not.'

'Ask me how many sugars I take in my tea, then.'

'How many.'

'Three. And no milk.'

Jack opened the cupboard door, and, so shielded from Richie's suspicious gaze, he screwed his eyes tightly shut. Then he opened them again, closed the cupboard door, and though he fought against it mightily some demon inside him made him glance again at the door. This time there was someone there: he could see a figure approaching through the frosted glass. The doorbell rang. Jack stared at the kettle.

'Gonna get that?' Richie asked.

'Yeah.' He didn't move.

'Like, now, or maybe an hour after they've gone?'

Jack blew out his cheeks.

'What's going on?'

'Would you,' Jack said, 'that is would you just make out like you're my dad for a couple of minutes?'

'What?'

'It's just these cat people. Bringing a cat. It's nothing. It's just a cat. They need to see the house is okay. You could do that. You can tell 'em the house is okay. You could do that easily.'

'You want me to pretend to be your old man?'

'Just for a minute.'

'I can't do that.'

'Why not?'

'Immoral.'

The kettle billowed steam. Jack blew his cheeks out a second time. The door bell rang out a second time.

'You get the kettle,' Richie said. 'I'll get the door.'

Jack held his head in his hands as the kettle switched itself off and Richie answered the door. Richie was seen to step outside and Jack heard muffled conversation. Then Richie came in again, with a short, stocky man in a tan leather jacket. The man had a tic; he blinked too frequently.

'I'll show you round the house,' Richie was saying. 'As you can see we have the dogs but they're highly trained not to catch and skin squirrels. The kids are less well trained – this is Jack whom I think you've met – but we will civilise 'em one day. The kids that is. Though it's a losing battle, isn't it? Got kids of your own? No? Lucky you. You know which side your bread's buttered. These kids are good with animals; they know the dog's names and everything, come and have a look at the garden where we'll guarantee a steady supply of live rats to keep that cat entertained ...' Richie led the visitor outside, keeping up a steady brow-beating monologue.

Jack watched the two men walk out into the garden. Richie was spreading his arms wide, making the visitor laugh. They both stood facing each other. When Richie put his hands in his pockets, the man did the same. They stood square on. Richie was still doing all the talking.

After a few minutes they came back into the kitchen. By now they had somehow got on to the subject of music. Richie was smoking the air with the names of blues musicians, and invoking the titles of obscure albums, all the while leading the visitor through the house and back out through the front door.

Several minutes later, Richie appeared carrying a cardboard box with air-holes. He looked at Jack without blinking and handed him the box. 'I just had to give that bloke fifty notes.'

'I'll get it for you,' Jack said.

'You bet you will.'

'I've got it in my bedroom.'

Jack lit up the stairs and returned instantly with the cash: five ten-pound notes that for some reason Jack had rolled into straws. Richie took the notes, unrolled them, counted them pointedly and slipped them into his back pocket. 'Where's my tea?'

'Coming up.'

'Listen, you're not using the pelts are you?'

'What?'

'The pelts. Not making gloves out of them or whatever it is you teenagers do. I've read about this sort of thing.'

'It's nothing like that. Honestly.'

'Jesus, lighten up will you Jack? It's a joke!'

'Right,' Jack said. 'Hahaha. Right.'

When Genevieve arrived back from the trip to the opticians with Josie, she seemed pleased to find Richie there. Jack took advantage of the moment of greeting to slip out unnoticed with his box full of cat. He already had the red collar in his pocket. All he had to do was slip it round the neck of the new cat and deliver the creature to Mrs Larwood.

He opened the box and the cat, formerly known as Frosty, blinked at him, sneezed at the light and purred. Jack fixed the red collar around its neck.

It occurred to him that he could just release the cat in Mrs Larwood's back yard. He believed it might be better if she thought the cat had simply returned. But he suspected there was a danger of the cat wandering before short-sighted Mrs Larwood 'discovered' him, and so he chose instead to ring her doorbell and present her with the box.

The bolts and chains drew back. Jack held his breath. Mrs Larwood stood at the door blinking at him, not unlike like the cat.

'Someone found him,' he said, proffering the box.

Mrs Larwood gasped, took the box, turned and set it on the stairs. She opened the flaps with trembling fingers. 'Oh oh oh,' she said. The cat purred at her and leapt into her arms, curling its tail around her wrist and settling into the crook of her arm as if it had never been away. 'Look at you!' she said. 'Look at you.' Then she looked at Jack from behind the damp cataracts of her eyes and said, 'Where?'

'Someone saw one of my leaflets.'

'Are you hungry?' she said to the cat. 'I'll bet you are. I'll bet you are. Let me give you some milk. Come in, Jack, come in.'

Jack ventured just inside the door. Mrs Larwood disappeared into the kitchen. He heard the fridge door open. After a moment she returned to the hallway.

'He's lapping that up, Jack! Lapping it up!'

'Good.'

'Would you like some tea. And some cake?'

No.' Jack said too hurriedly. 'No thanks. I have to shoot off.'

Mrs Larwood stepped past him and closed the door. 'No, don't shoot off. Come and look at the way this milk is being lapped up! You wouldn't believe it!'

Jack pawed at his own face before following Mrs Larwood into the kitchen. Sure enough the cat lapped and lapped at the milk. The pair of them stared down at the creature in silence. It seemed like it didn't want to stop.

'Look at that!' Mrs Larwood said. 'Just look at that.'

'I have to go,' Jack said.

Mrs Larwood seemed not to hear him at first. Then she went out of the kitchen and came back with the cat-carrying box. She stooped and gently lifted the cat, putting him back in the box and closing the flaps.

'He's lovely,' she said, offering the box back to Jack. 'But he's not my cat. Of course you knew that, didn't you, Jack?'

'Mrs Larwood—'

'It's very sweet of you. You must have gone to a lot of trouble to find one that looks quite similar. Now I know I'm old; I'm also half-blind; but I'm not completely stupid. I'd be a very foolish old woman if I didn't know my own cat.'

'I didn't—'

'The collar, though, did belong to my cat. Which means that my cat is dead somewhere, and it also means that you know that, but didn't want to tell me.'

Jack first coloured and then found hot, stinging tears of shame springing from his eyes. 'I'm sorry, I'm sorry, I'm sorry.'

'How old are you Jack? Thirteen is it?'

He nodded, wiping his eyes.

'I'm going to tell you something. You didn't want me to know that my cat was dead. You were trying to protect me. Your instincts were good. But it would have been better if you'd told me then I would have been able to put it behind me. Pets die. People die. I know enough about life to know that when something like that happens, you can't put the clocks back. Do you understand me, Jack?'

He nodded.

'You're a good lad. Now take this box. And say to me, Mrs Larwood, your cat died but I've found you a lovely new cat.'

Jack could barely speak. He had a stone in his throat. 'Mrs Larwood,' he croaked 'your cat died but I've found you a lovely new cat.'

'He's a beauty,' Mrs Larwood said, taking the box from Jack all over again.

'Mrs Larwood, Mrs Larwood, do you want to know how your cat died?'

'No, Jack. I'll do my best to look after this one just as well as the other one. Now run along, and we'll say no more about this.'

Peter's day was done. He had just parked his van in the driveway at The Old Forge when his phone rang. It was Iqbal, the dentist. He had some information that he thought might interest Peter. He told Peter that a brand-new technique had just been developed by scientists at the University of California in the United States. DNA analysis of methylation patterns could accurately read a person's age to within five years. The reading

339

could be done by taking saliva samples.

Iqbal had no idea what Peter would have to do, beyond getting Tara to give up a saliva sample. But the science was now in place, he enthused. The mystery – or part of the mystery – could be solved.

Peter thanked Iqbal. He rang off and, still sitting in his van, he called his sister.

'We need some of your spit, Tara.'

'My spit.'

'Yes, your spit. Science has caught up with you.' He told her all about the wonderful scientific breakthrough. 'Would you be okay with that? If we found a way to get it tested, I mean.'

There was a pause before Tara said she wouldn't mind. 'My spit,' she said again. Her voice was inscrutable.

Peter sat in his car thinking about it for a while after he'd ended the call. Then he got out of the car, locked it and went inside, where he found Genevieve and Richie sitting in the living room. They were talking very quietly.

Jack crossed the street, relief and shame tearing at him in equal measure. He noticed that his dad's truck was parked in the driveway and when he got inside he found Richie and his mum and dad speaking in hushed voices in the living room. There was an atmosphere; some kind of adult drama, the character of which he couldn't grasp. He left them to it. He checked himself in the mirror and thought his eyes looked red, so he washed his face, dried himself hurriedly and came back down again.

He slipped quietly into the living room where the

adults were talking. His dad looked up at him, blinked heavily, then with eyebrows raised looked back at Richie.

'It's all right,' Richie said.

Jack quickly realised that Richie was giving permission for Jack to stay while they talked. Jack settled on the end of the sofa.

'How long has it been there?' Genevieve asked, in a slightly croaky voice.

'I didn't notice it until just before Christmas,' Richie said. 'But the scan suggested it has been growing there a long time. That's what the quack said, anyway. He says it's big. Says I shouldn't be here by rights.'

'And it's definitely malignant?' Peter said. Jack looked at his father. He thought his dad's face looked ashen.

'So they say. It's a malignant tumour all right. Still growing. Just bad luck, isn't it?'

'So, so, so how long have they given you?' Peter stammered.

'Six months, tops.'

'Can't they operate?' Genevieve said, shaking her head.

'Apparently not. They grade your tumours. I got a high grade. Which is more than I ever did at school.' Richie looked at Jack and winked. 'Here, I wrote it on a bit of paper. I can't even pronounce what I've got. Something about getting a medal.' He fiddled in his pocket and withdrew a scrap of notepaper. 'Here. Medulloblastoma. Of the cerebellum. More common in kids than adults. Now they want to drill a hole in my head and take some tissue samples. I don't fancy that much.'

'It's a biopsy,' Genevieve said. 'They have to.'

'There's even a complication with that. I can't remember the details.'

'Jesus,' Peter said. 'Have you told Tara?'

'No. We've only just got back together and things have been going great. And I don't know what I'm gonna tell her.'

And they all sat for some minutes in silence. Jack didn't move a muscle. He felt he shouldn't even blink.

Then Richie said, 'Funny thing is I was going to give up smoking. You know, health thing. Not much point of that now, is there?'

39

'I'm so glad you came,' Mrs Larwood said. 'I didn't
think you would, after I'd wasted your time on the last
visit.'

Tara came into the house and Mrs Larwood closed
the door behind her. 'It's understandable,' Tara said.
'Though I was starting to guess.'

'Will you sit down?'

'Only if you promise not to give me tea and cake.
I've agreed with Jack that your cake must be the worst
cake going.'

Mrs Larwood laughed and promised she would make
tea but wouldn't offer any cake. 'Can I say something
about the dark glasses, my dear? You'll find you don't
need them and after a while it all returns to normal.
Your sight, that is. You can stop squinting after a
while. And that terrible feeling of grit in your eyes, that
goes away too.'

Tara took off her sunglasses and thumbed her eyes.
She let the glasses rest on the table.

'Though I can't give you any assurances that there
isn't any long lasting damage. I've got cataracts. I've

343

had operations on them that have failed to help. I'll never know if that's just from old age or if it's because I damaged my eyes. And sometimes I think I'd like to see it again. That special light.'

Tara pressed the palms of her hands to her face. 'You don't know what a relief it is to find someone who has been there. Someone who doesn't think that I'm either lying or insane.'

'I certainly do know what a relief it is. You're the first person I've been able to talk to about it, too.'

'Really?'

Mrs Larwood sat down and peered at Tara through the gluey cataracts of her oyster-grey eyes. They were cataracts that had on them a shimmer, almost mother-of-pearl. 'Yes, really. I very quickly learned to shut my mouth about what had happened. They locked me up for a year.'

'No!'

Mrs Larwood nodded. 'Oh yes. Do you know that place they call the Pastures? Up on Forest Lane? It was 1952, and when I came back I tried to stop being honest but it was too late. I was put in that place with a lot of lunatics. It's a wonder I didn't actually go insane just from staying there – I could tell you some stories. Anyway, I calculated that I'd better tell them I'd run off with a chap who later abandoned me. They were much happier with that. They gave me electric shock therapy, to cure me of running away with chaps ever again. I lost great chunks of my memory. But I never forgot what happened in the Outwoods, or where I went, or who was there.'

'In the Outwoods? Is that where it happened with you?'

'Yes. As soon as Jack told me about you and the Outwoods, I guessed what had happened. As for the Outwoods,' she said. 'I told Jack I wouldn't go there in a month of Sundays. And I meant it.'

'I'm not afraid of it,' Tara said.

'I am. Very much.'

'I've been back up only recently. There's nothing to harm you.'

'Oh you don't understand. I'm not afraid of what's up at the Outwoods. I'm afraid of myself. I'm afraid of wanting to go back. Wanting to go back *there*.'

The kettle whistled and she got up to make the tea. She returned with a teapot, and china cups, and a little milk jug and a sugar bowl, and, despite her promises, a slice of the same ginger cake she had offered Jack and Tara before, dreamily setting them down on the table. 'I'm old and I've had my time. But if the opportunity presented itself I know I'd go back in a shot.'

'I can understand that. It's still an open temptation for me, too.'

'Then perhaps it's a temptation you should give in to.'

'I can't, Mrs Larwood. I've made a kind of promise.'

Mrs Larwood shook her head. The two women stared into their empty china cups as if seeing inside them tumultuous visions and apparitions. Mrs Larwood brought them both out of the reverie by slapping the table with the palm of her hand. 'And such sluts the women were there! Sluts!'

'Well, yes. The men, too.'

'You can't blame the men if the women have their legs open all the time. What do you expect? Sluts and slatterns. When I was there the houses were filthy, no

345

one did a hand's stir and the men never got anything done either. They had no electricity or gas or anything like that, and this is what it comes to if the women have their legs open noon and night.'

'Well. I kept myself to myself while I was there.'

'Did you?' Mrs Larwood said. 'Oh, I joined in.'

'Really?'

'Oh yes,' she giggled, 'I mean, how could you resist?'

'Somehow I did.'

'Perhaps you're stronger minded than I was. Though I must say I missed all that after I came back. The men here were pretty useless in that regard.'

Tara was more than a little surprised by the frail figure before her. 'But,' she said, 'why us? Why so few people? Why do you think it was us?'

'I've never figured that out, but I do think I was marked from the beginning,' Mrs Larwood said. 'The man who led me away from the Outwoods: I'd seen him before.'

'How?'

'It was the spring of 1951. The war was over and we were still on austerity measures in this country. Everyone was still on rations, you know, butter, meat, all that. You couldn't even get the cloth to make a pretty dress. But it was a lovely spring that year and the blossom came early. We had a vigorous cherry blossom tree that made a canopy over our gate, in the front yard. It was the year of the Festival of Britain, but somehow I always thought that the Festival of Britain was in the tree with all its sparkling flowers.

'While my parents were out one afternoon a man came to the door. He was handsome but he looked like he'd spent too long in the sun, and also like he could do with a good wash, but he twinkled his eyes at me. Could he, he asked me, cut some of the blossom from our tree? I saw that he had a horse-drawn cart waiting in the road. There were panniers on the cart, baskets, lots of them. Well, the tree was so laden with blossom I didn't see what harm it could be, so I said yes and before I knew it he was scrambling up in the tree, lithe and agile as anything, snipping off branches of the blossom and dropping them into one of the panniers from the back of his cart.

'I couldn't think what he wanted it for. I mean, it doesn't last, does it? You can't sell it. But there he was, in the tree, busying himself, snip, snip, snip. I watched him from the bedroom of our house, and I remember feeling a little alarmed that he was taking too much of the blossom.

'Then my father returned unexpectedly. I watched my father stroll half-way up the path and do a double-take on this man in the tree. He stopped dead and asked him what he was doing up there. I couldn't hear exactly what was said, but a fierce argument broke out. The air was smoked blue for a while and in the end the man got on his cart and he trotted his horse away.

'Daddy came in. Helen, did you tell that man he could take our blossom, he wanted to know. I told him that I'd given the man permission to take a few posies. But my father seemed to think he'd been cutting down half the tree. Anyway, that was that, and I thought it was the end of the matter.

'But then a couple of weeks later I went walking up at the Outwoods. I'd gone on a picnic with some girlfriends. We often went up there together, especially at bluebell time, when the bluebells make you want to faint with pleasure. Anyway, I got tired of all the silly chatter of my friends and I felt a kind of storm brewing in my head, so I walked a little way off. I sat down by a rock, and there he was, smiling at me, a straw in his mouth. And though we never discussed the argument he had had with my father I knew it was the very same man: the same man who had been in our tree, the blossom thief.'

'And you went with him,' Tara said.

'And I went with him.'

'And the light.'

'And the light.'

'I admit it was hard to adjust when I came back. Seven years had passed. Things had hardly changed.'

'Only seven? You were lucky.'

'I didn't think I was lucky when I was locked up and given electric shocks. You wouldn't wish it on anyone. I'd been in a kind of heaven. But the year in the asylum was hell. And one year there was like seven elsewhere. So you see, it was balanced out. I had to pay in the end. There is always a terrible and peculiar kind of accounting. I want you to be warned of that.'

'I've been seeing a psychiatrist. So far he hasn't given me any electric shocks. I think he'd like to. He's annoyed that I keep co-operating with him.'

'If I were you, I'd invent a lover and say that you ran away with him and you're very sorry and that you won't do it again. Then they'll leave you alone.'

'I would do that. But it's more complicated. You see the man who led me away? He followed me back here.'

Mrs Larwood blinked at her. 'Are you sure?'

'Yes. He's stalking me all the time.'

'My God! You've got to get him to go back!'

'I've tried. He's sick. He's pining and ill. I look out of my bedroom at night and he's in the garden, skulking in the shadows. If I go anywhere he follows me.'

'Oh dear. That's very bad news. We're going to have to do something about that,' said Mrs Larwood.

'It's worse. He attacked one of my friends.'

Mrs Larwood looked shocked. 'Now, and for your friend's sake,' she said, 'you have to be very careful indeed.'

Mrs Larwood said that on returning to find that seven years had gone by, she had met a man who had stuck by her even while she was in the asylum receiving electric shock therapy. He was she said the only man who didn't try to persuade her that she was insane, even though he found it impossible to believe what she was saying. He had accepted her. They married. But he in turn soon developed a debilitating, wasting illness. The doctors were unable to diagnose his problem. He couldn't eat. He never became well again. He wasted and died.

Mrs Larwood said she knew how it was done. She too had been followed home. She said they had used the technique of *blasting*.

'Don't say that,' Tara said.

'I see you know something of this.'

'I wish you hadn't told me that.'

'I'm sorry. But what I wanted to tell you was that I think I made a mistake, all those years ago, in coming back. I don't think I should have done. There is no place for us here, and our presence can become a harm to those we love.'

Mrs Larwood's new cat came rubbing up against Tara's legs, and so she went on to tell Tara about Jack and his antics with the cat. 'I wasn't going to tell you these things until Jack tried to fool me with this cat. Yes, I had ruined my own life, but I thought it wasn't my place to interfere in yours. Then when Jack did this I knew that I should talk to you, tell you what I know, and then at least you can make up your own mind. You see, I ruined my life by pretending I was the same person when I came home. But I wasn't. We can't be. I was no more the same person than was this cat my old cat. It took a thirteen-year-old boy to make me certain of that. Tara, you are not the girl who left here.'

'No,' Tara said. 'I'm not.'

'I'm sorry.'

'I understand. Thank you for talking to me. It was brave of you.'

'Brave? I don't know. I'm so afraid of hurting people just by speaking up. You know when my young husband was dying I was still receiving treatment as an outpatient, and a psychiatrist managed to put it into my head that somehow I was the one who was killing him. There you are. On one side you are blasted by curses and on the other side they blast you with drugs and electric shocks. One is a knave and one is a fool. One wants to steal the blossom; one wants to steal the light. Where are we left, you and I?'

Tara shook her head. 'The one I'm seeing seems mad as a hatter to me. Smokes like a chimney.'

'Smokes like a chimney? His name isn't Underwood, is it?'

'Vivian Underwood. You don't know him do you?'

'Do I know him? Oh yes. He was once a great proponent of electric shock therapy. I'll say I know Vivian Underwood.'

40

*'The fey wonders of the world only exist while there
are those with the sight to see them.'*

Charles De Lint

The client has commissioned me to do no more than
make an early report, about whether TM might need
medication or counselling or both; and whether she is
actually a danger to herself or to others. My report will
suggest doing nothing, at least for the present. Deluded
though TM is, I see no indication that she is likely to
harm herself or those around her. She has a good support network; she is not using drugs as far as I can
determine; she drinks only moderately; and her conversation when she's not referring to this wild episode is
rational and coherent.

She has lost a huge chunk of her memory. But the
scan I arranged for her showed no sign of trauma to the
head, or any kind of aberration whatsoever. I suspect
she hasn't lost her memory at all. Rather, she doesn't
yet want to find it. But many things about TM's story
are leaving me confident that she is busy – at least on
an unconscious level – working out the solution to her
problem.

I suspect something unpleasant probably happened
twenty years ago, in the Outwoods; or around the

time she was either abducted or led astray. Some deep sense of shame made it impossible for her to go back to the family hearth; a loving protective family that she felt she'd disgraced. Her repair time will, inevitably, be slow. But she is the principal engine of her own re-integration; not me or some other counsellor; not drugs.

It will take time but the confabulation is already beginning to shed its layers. In one layer we are in the timeless world of Tir Na Nog, a place of eternal youth. Significantly there are no children mentioned in TM's account. Not one. If this were a real piece of geography one would suspect that all this casual coitus would normally produce one or two babies. The reason for this is clear: TM is the only child in this world. Hence her distaste for the sexuality that probably led to her abduction, or possibly the experience of being raped all those years ago. Her confabulation is the wilful act of someone determined to remain a child, pre-sexual and almost prelapsarian.

Traditionally the fairies stand in for some violation of the sexual mores of a society. They are the wild force that whispers to us. It's not just the abducted individual who buys into this: as recently as a hundred years ago, there was even a legal case in Ireland in which a woman was murdered by her husband, who believed she'd been taken by the fairies. She returned, in disgrace of course. Neither she nor her husband could face up to what had happened. The family, and perhaps the community, found it easier to lay the moral blame on the unseen folk rather than face up to the shame and dishonour of what is all too human. In this case there was no need for supernatural agency, but the husband and his family preferred the fiction, or at least tried to hide behind the fiction.

In another layer we do seem to have a bona fide commune in which TM settled for a while, but I suspect we will never hear more of that until she chooses to tell us more. Maybe it was even a religious or spiritual commune. The evidence is there in the radical fruitarian discipline and some of the way-out ideas. This talk of levitation and mental powers is common amongst eastern cults. When we talk about the brain-washing of young people, all we mean is persuasion; young people are always well primed to be brain-washed and tend to be enthusiastic volunteers. Perhaps we fail them when we neglect to equip our young people with the tools of a healthy scepticism. But I digress.

My optimism comes from the details to be found in her story. The narrative method of psychology is a flawed and treacherous means unless the authentic details are supplied by the patient rather than by the counsellor. Even though she occasionally introduces new material into her story – the man at the bus stop – she has had twenty years to let her tale crystallise in her mind, without even knowing it. Every detail there has significance and can be revisited, reconditioned and offered back to her in a new and positive light. Every detail is a stone in the mosaic pattern of the thing that – deep down – she is screaming to communicate.

The detail that makes me most happy is the apparently insignificant portrait of the bug, or rather the bugs, that settle in the forest to make an individual flower. The forest with its winding pathways is the subconscious mind trying to make itself conscious. The image of the bug-flower is what Jung called a *mandala*, a circular motif of perfect integration. The bugs breaking up are an emblem of her fractured psyche; the action of the bugs reconfiguring themselves into a perfect flower or *mandala* is TM's wish fulfilment, a forward projection of her deep desire for the full integration of her disturbed psyche. Her family, and the re-integration inside the bosom of the family, is an expression of the very same compulsion to repair, but on a physical level. The bug-flower is a picture of her mind.

Amnesiacs and elective amnesiacs are, according to Freud, always unconsciously trying to repeat the cause of their amnesia. It is quite possible that she succeeded. From that moment the process of repair and reconstruction would have begun. The most significant act was for her to come back home. She reported to me that the first thing she wanted to do when she was reunited with her family was to walk in the Outwoods with her brother. She was ready to revisit the 'scene of the crime' as it were. This was a huge step on the path to full recovery.

TM thinks that I don't take her story seriously. On the contrary, I take it very seriously indeed. I approach her story rather like a dream she might have had; only it's a constructed dream, made of smoke and mirrors she can hide behind so that she doesn't have to face up to her personal history. This fairyland is a place she goes to hide from herself. I think she will recover the information of where she's been these twenty years when she's good and ready. We could use psychiatric methods to tempt it back but it's like pulling on a dried rosebud to try to make it into a rose. I prefer the method of interpreting her dream in a way that she can use to rebuild a new narrative of what has happened to

354

her. Her story, to be sure, but with my ending.

I have one last meeting with TM. I'm not confident that she will tell me anything that will yield up more information about where she has been. But I can insert into her story information and signposts about where she is going. I intend to try something that will at least prepare the soil for me to build in a competing end to the narrative-under-construction.

'Michael Cleary her husband; Patrick Boland the deceased's father; three Kennedy cousins and an aunt, and four local men including sanachie *(Irish storyteller) John Dunne, were all charged with wilful murder. During the murder trials conducted in the Clonmel courthouse, all charges of murder were reduced to manslaughter. Three defendants were discharged without penalty. Patrick Boland received six months' imprisonment, as did Michael Kennedy but with hard labour. James Kennedy got a year and a half imprisonment, while his brother Patrick Kennedy got five years for his part in the burial. Michael Cleary was sentenced to twenty years' penal servitude for manslaughter. After only fifteen years in jail he was released from Maryborough Prison on the 28 April 1910, with a gratuity of £17. 13s. 4d. He emigrated to Montreal, Canada, there to live out the rest of his life. Throughout his time in prison, Michael Cleary steadfastly maintained he had not killed his wife, he still believed right up to the end, that the fairies had taken her and left in her place a changeling.'*
Summary of findings of Regina v. Michael Cleary 1895

When Tara breezed into his study for what was to be their final session, Vivian Underwood was interested to notice a change in her manner of dress. Gone were the black jeans and the loose T-shirt, and the baseball boots, and the sparkling arms-length of bangles; gone too were the dark glasses. Tara wore a dark pencil-skirt, flat shoes and opaque black tights. Her tight burgundy sweater plunged at the front in a V neck, and the wild tumbling curls of her hair, which she had tied restrained in a neat pony-tail for the previous sessions, spilled around her shoulders, lustrous and nut-brown. Her fingernails were painted scarlet red. There was a marked sheen in her eye. She wore a little make-up, and her lips were painted with a delicate shade of pink and a provocative smile.

She was celebrating her release from counselling, Underwood noted with grim pleasure. But he was pleased to see this change in her attire. He knew that it signalled an advance. Attire, Underwood knew well enough, chattered when the personality remained silent; clothes spoke freely of secrets, hidden desires and wounded feelings when the subject wearing them was struck dumb. He also knew that sometimes they were just clothes.

'This is your last session with me, Tara,' said Underwood. 'We've had some fascinating conversations, you and I, but we have arrived at the end of the usefulness of those talks.'

'I've learned a lot from just talking to you,' Tara said, plucking a speck of lint from her sweater. 'I feel like it's my last day at school.'

'Quite. And just as before, you get to choose where we sit.'

'Let me see: writing desk with armchair opposite, that would indicate a businesslike defensiveness; the sofa, looking for intimacy perhaps; the armchairs by the fire, an interest in pretending we're all equals ... no, let's stick with those chairs drawn up by the window, open to the light, ready for new ideas.'

'Not bad,' Underwood said. *This hostility is new*, he thought.

'I've been watching you watching me.' Tara squinted at him, perhaps in parody of his scrutiny.

'And what did you see me seeing?'

'Oh, you've got it all mapped out. You know that everything I say means something else. I'm sure it all fits into some big picture in your mind.'

Underwood nodded at the seat and she took her place by the window. He lit a cigarette and fetched himself a heavy glass ashtray before sitting down. There was a small octagonal table next to one of the chairs and on this he placed the ashtray. 'You've been talking to your brother. Or to his wife, the lovely domestic-goddess-psychologist.'

'Not at all. Pete has refused to discuss anything you've said about me. I admit I badgered him about it. But he kept it buttoned. And as for Genevieve, she's the smartest one, and smart enough to know she doesn't know much. Anyway it doesn't matter.'

'Why doesn't it matter, Tara?'

'Because you've got your theory, no doubt. You don't believe a single word I've told you. And your word is more important than mine, isn't it?'

'Is it?'

'Oh yes. Look at all these impressive certificates on the wall. Neatly framed. You are old and wise and clever, and you know everything, whereas, well, me, ...' here Tara made a steeple of her hands and laid her cheek upon them, 'I'm just a young girl.' She fluttered her eyelashes for him.

'You're angry today.'

'A bit.'

'But you're not a young girl, are you Tara? Not sixteen, are you?'

'No I'm not. I'm much older than that. I don't know what happened. I was away for six months, but I gathered twenty years of experience in that time. My body didn't age, but my mind did. It matured, anyway. Maybe I gathered more than twenty years of experience in that six months. The difficulty is that some of the people I left behind didn't grow at all. And sometimes I find them infuriatingly simple. Like my mum and dad. Oh, I love them. Would die for them. But they watch junk television and read junk newspapers and repeat the phrases they got from their junk television and junk newspapers. Do you realise what a nightmare that is to witness?'

'I think I do.'

'I hoped to find them at home,' Tara said bitterly. 'But all that I found were shells of what they were. Husks. They'd allowed age to diminish them instead of mature them. And then there's my brother. Peter. He was like a beautiful animal when he was young. He burned with a flame. Now he's just a tired dad, hammering horse-shoes every day, bent over an anvil. Where did he go, my brother? And his lovely wife, up to her elbows in cooking and cleaning for her family.'

'It's called love, Tara,' Underwood said. 'It's what they do because they love their children. As your parents loved you.'

'But do they have to give up their souls? Do they have to?'

'They have to share out their souls, yes, they do. They are none of them in the same place where you left them.'

'Except for Richie. There is still a glimmer of light in Richie. He hasn't compromised. But he's dying.'

'Yes. Richie. Peter told me something about that. It's a bad lot.' Underwood got up and went to his desk. He came back proffering a tissue.

Tara took the tissue and wiped her eye. 'Richie, Peter. They were the blossom. They were the blossom on the tree.'

'As were you.'

'As I still am,' she corrected fiercely.

They sat in silence for some minutes. Underwood wanted Tara to feel her anger and hostility and to let it subside before he proposed what he wanted to do. Right then she was over-stimulated. So, with a neutral expression, he gazed out of the window.

A cloud passed in front of the afternoon sun. The light fell. Something creaked in his study. Almost to prevent himself from drifting to sleep, Underwood spoke. 'I have an idea of trying something, with your consent. One last effort to see if we can both get some more information about where you have been all these years. But only with your consent and co-operation.'

'Not going to give me electric shock therapy are you?'

'Good lord no. I'm ashamed to say I was too taken with that in the old days.' His face darkened. 'Why would you suggest that?'

Tara dealt him a thin smile. 'Just trying to guess what cards you have up your sleeve.'

'Nothing so brutal, I promise you. These days I try to tiptoe into the unconscious mind rather than bludgeon my way in.'

'Tiptoe. Really, I'm prepared to do anything. I'm game for anything.'

Underwood got up and went his desk, picking up the heavy, oak-framed old style hour-glass, and setting it on the windowsill. With his back turned he didn't see a flash of red as Tara touched her tongue with her finger, and even had he seen he would have thought it only a scarlet-painted fingernail. 'In a moment I'm going to set this running. I want you to keep your eyes on it. I'm going to use some relaxation techniques and I'll ask you some questions. Okay with that?'

'Yes.'

'You feel safe with me?'

'Yes.'

'Here we go then. Just keep your eyes on the sand.'

He inverted the hour-glass and the fine grains of cinnamon-coloured sand started streaming in the curve of the lower glass, billowing slightly like a skirt in a breeze, a tiny light spectrum refracting behind the rivulet of sand as it ran. Tara kept her gaze on the delicate stream, with almost a smile on her lips and a peculiar avidity in her wide-open brown eyes.

Underwood watched her watching.

'In a moment,' he said, 'I'm going to ask you to think of a key word but before that I just want you to stay with the sand. There, doesn't that feel good? By the way, you achieved this relaxation all by yourself. You're a natural for this. But in a moment I want you to select a key word. It will be your own word and I don't want you to tell it to me yet.

'Here you go. You can hear my voice. Here you go. That feels nice, again you just let the tension out of your arms, I saw it go, and that's good because it means you are happy and you feel good and you feel relaxed and you are changing. And now that your arm is relaxed, your shoulder can relax too, and so can that tense area around your neck, it can all go. That's good. I saw that happen, but again you did that all by yourself.

'Those sounds outside are becoming distant. Those sounds outside are fading away. You might notice that every time you blink that it's harder and harder to keep your eyes open.

'The sand is taking you where you want to be, isn't it? It's all right. You can let yourself go there. You can let go of that bad time. We don't need it, we can let that go. It feels very good to let it go, doesn't it? Of course it does. I wonder how deeply you can fall into a trance right now.

'I wonder how deeply. I wonder. I wonder what will happen when you let go of that bad time. I wonder. I wonder what will happen.'

Tara now had her eyes closed and her head had slumped forward. Her breathing was shallow. Her arms hung heavily at her sides.

'I wonder what will happen when you let go of that bad time. I wonder.'

Tara moved her head slightly and shaped her mouth to speak. She slurred. 'It is likely he will come?'

'Who will come?' Underwood said. 'Likely who will come?'

Tara moved her lips, like someone parched. 'It is likely,' she slurred again, very slowly, 'he will come.'

Don't press it, Underwood thought. *Back off.*

'I don't know whether you have completely relaxed, yet,' he said gently. 'Let's see if we can go further. Further.'

'Yes. Further.'

'So let's go further.'

'Further.'

'So let's go further.'

'Further.'

'So let's go further.'

Then something happened that wasn't supposed to happen. Underwood felt his own eyelids close. He battled back, opened his eyes and looked at the slumped form of Tara, uncertain now how many times he had repeated himself. His head was in a foggy place and he could still hear his own words, echoing back at him, but in a slow unfolding wave; elongated, as if the words were elastic and stretching slowly over his tongue; and that sensation was accompanied by a darkness, a fuzzy shadow that had fallen over his study. His eyelids were drooping again. He had to fight the impossible weight of his own eyelids.

At last he forced his eyes open only to see Tara sitting erect now in her chair, her own beautiful, large brown eyes wide open and gazing back at him. She was staring at him, unblinking, but her head was cocked and she was guarded, as if uncertain of some outcome. He knew he was going under again and he couldn't stop it. He was helpless, unable to resist, as if his own techniques of hypnotism had flashed back at him. His consciousness was eclipsing; or perhaps he felt a sooty inundation pouring over him like dim waves on the sand of a dark beach. He knew his head had slumped, impossibly weighted, and with Tara staring down at him all he could think was how utterly beautiful were her eyes; and there in the corner of her eyes the liquid sheen of them reflected the light spectrum from the hour-glass. He was going under and he couldn't stop it. His eyelids closed and he surrendered.

When he blinked himself awake he had no idea of how much time had passed. But Tara had gone from the seat next to him. In her place, gazing steadily back at him was a man. Underwood instinctively but slowly moved his head to steal a glance at the hour-glass. The sand was still running.

With great effort Underwood rolled his head again to look back at the figure in the chair. Now the man was glowering. He had a dark aspect, a tanned, weathered complexion. He was in need of a shave and his hair was a mass of dark curls worn down to his collar, a single gold ear-ring glinting in there somewhere. He wore a white shirt without a collar, and a black waistcoat; his baggy black trousers were gathered at the knee and stuffed into riding boots. He exuded an odour of menace: male sweat and gunmetal.

Underwood felt a flush of primal fear. He felt a thrill of cold.

The man leaned forward and the leather of his chair creaked slightly under him. He opened his mouth. 'I tried to tell you once before,' he said to Underwood in a quiet but angry voice. It was a voice that dragged in the throat, and the voice was out of sync with the sensuous lips. 'But you wouldn't listen to me.'

Underwood made to get up from his seat, trying to rise against a great weight. 'Where is Tara?'

But the man was faster to his feet. 'I tried to tell you before,' he said again, and he reached forward to

Underwood with his left hand, first and second fingers splayed out wide in a V. Underwood raised a hand up to protect himself but he was too slow: the stranger touched the psychiatrist's eyelids with his outstretched fingers. Underwood felt a jolt, a voltage, and he sank back into his chair, paralysed, as everything faded to black.

Moments later he came back to consciousness, and this time the frightening stranger was standing over him, holding aloft the heavy hour-glass, already in the act of bringing it down on Underwood's head. But the man was motionless, frozen in a menacing instant of tableau. The air was smoky with a smell like ozone and the light was flickering a dangerous nightfall blue.

Underwood tried to grip his chair, looking for purchase that would help him to leap from his seat but he was powerless to move. Then came a ripping sound, like canvas tearing, and the image before him broke up into a thousand tiny fluttering points of coloured light, like bugs suddenly disturbed and reflected in a beam of sunlight. The fragments of light quickly resettled back into a new image, and now Tara was standing before him, one arm aloft and gripping the assailant by the wrist. Neither Tara nor the man were looking at Underwood. Their eyes were locked on each other. It was as if they were in another place, indifferent to the presence of Underwood. There came another horrible rending sound, and this new tableau also fragmented, again into a flurry of brilliant bugs taking to the air; and again after a moment it settled into a new form. There was a brand new tableau in which Tara held the man's face in her small and elegant white hands, imploring him. The man was weeping. His tears were blue in the polar light. The hour-glass, no longer a weapon, had rolled on the floor.

In a final fracturing and resettling of the tableau, Tara was bending over Underwood, her first and second fingers splayed and stroking his eyelids shut.

Underwood came to again. Tara sat in the adjacent chair, gazing steadily back at him, her intimidating brown eyes still unblinking. He looked for the hour-glass. It had gone from the windowsill where he had set it running. He glanced down and there it was: it had fallen unbroken to the floor and had come to a stop half-way across his carpeted study.

The psychiatrist scrambled to his feet, like a man suddenly unshackled. He looked around and behind him. Of the dangerous intruder there was now no sign.

'Lost someone?' Tara said.

'Where is that man?'

Tara blinked. A long, supercilious, steady blink.

Underwood stepped over to his desk and looked behind it, as if the intruder might be hiding there. He looked again at Tara. He looked at the hour-glass. Spread out on his desk were a number of papers. They were his report on Tara. Some of the psychological phrases he had used about her had been circled or ringed about with the antique pen from the desk-stand. One page was blotted violently.

Underwood marched to the study door, grabbed the door handle and yanked it open. He peered up and down the landing and corridor. Then, abandoning Tara, he closed the door behind him and hurried downstairs.

His elderly secretary was in the act of polishing her desk. She was almost bent double, aerosol spray can in one hand and a cloth in the other. 'Mrs Hargreaves, Mrs Hargreaves, did you just see a man go out?'

She looked up. 'No, Mr Underwood.'

'You didn't see anyone come in?'

'No. I would have told you. As you know.'

'Or go out? You saw no one go out.'

'I keep the door locked at all times, Mr Underwood. As you well know.'

'Indeed, Mrs Hargreaves. Indeed.'

'Is everything all right, Mr Underwood?'

He stroked his chin and without framing a reply, turned on his heels and hurried back up the stairs to his office. When he got there, Tara was still in her seat by the window. Though she'd picked up the hour-glass, and now she held it steady, provocatively, between her thighs.

Underwood stood over her, his hands on his hips, breathing hard. She met his gaze evenly. Then he found his cigarettes and lit one, inhaling deeply, scrutinising her. 'You counter-hypnotised me,' he said at last.

'You fool, Mr Underwood.'

'Yes. I know you did it.'

Tara got to her feet. 'It's time for me to go.' She placed the hour-glass back on his desk with a delicate click and turned to the psychiatrist, offering a handshake. Underwood looked at her hand as if it might contain an adder, a razor, some device of evil conjuring. At last he took his cigarette from his mouth, stubbed it out in an ashtray and shook her hand, all the time watching her carefully.

'Not easy is it?' said Tara.

Underwood didn't let go of her hand. 'I would like to conduct some further sessions. Without charge.'

Tara shook her head. 'I don't have the time. But thanks for the offer.'

He released her hand. She was changed somehow. When he'd first been introduced to her he thought he was meeting a child. But now he saw in her a mature woman, wise in ways at which he could only guess.

'Really, Mr Underwood. *Histrionic personality disorder*. They don't like being called *fairies* in the same way that I don't like being called *histrionic*. Or other similar words. Which reminds me,' Tara said. 'Mrs Larwood sends her regards.'

Underwood shook his head. The name meant nothing.

'Never mind. Goodbye.'

'Goodbye, Tara.'

He watched her walk across the study and slip out of the door. He remained in the middle of his study, lighting another cigarette, smoking it down to its butt. After he'd stubbed it out in the ashtray he picked up the hour-glass and looked at the report sheets spread across his desk. He scanned the room again, as if still suspecting someone of hiding there somewhere, behind a chair, behind the drape curtains, under his desk.

He set the hour-glass back on his desk and returned downstairs in search of Mrs Hargreaves.

'I take it that was the last session with Miss Martin,' said Mrs Hargreaves.

'That's right. Mrs Hargreaves. Tell me, did we ever have a client called Mrs Larwood?'

'That's going back a bit, Mr Underwood, but I do think we did. Yes.'

'Do you think you could dig her file out of the archives for me?'

'I can do that. Are we finished for the day, Mr Underwood?'

Underwood sighed. 'You know something Mrs Hargreaves? I do believe I might be ready to finish for good. I actually fell asleep on my client this afternoon.'

'Well,' said Mrs Hargreaves, 'if you do finish, it will not be before time. Let me see if I can find that file for you.'

42

'*From the low white walls and the church's steeple,*
From our little fields under grass or grain,
I'm gone away to the fairy people
I shall not come to the town again.
You may see a girl with my face and tresses,
You may see one come to my mother's door
Who may speak my words and may wear my dresses.
She will not be I, for I come no more.'

Lord Dunsany

Genevieve had made lunch for the family. It was a mild chilli with salad and a huge loaf of bread still warm from the oven. Josie was helping her to lay the table, when she dropped a knife on the tiled floor.

'Sowwy,' Josie said.

'That's all right,' Genevieve said, stooping to pick it up. 'It means a visitor is coming.'

'Who says?' Josie wanted to know.

'That's what they say. If you drop a knife a man is coming; and if you drop a fork a lady visitor is coming.'

'Who says?'

'It's just what people say.'

'Which people?'

'Lots of people.'

'Is it true?'

Genevieve pushed her bottom lip out. 'Come on, slowcoach. Finish laying the table.'

Jack came into the kitchen. 'I'm starving.' He twisted a hunk of bread off the loaf.

'Stop it!' Josie shouted. 'We're having a visitor.'

'What visitor?' Jack asked his mother.

'Wash your hands will you?' Genevieve answered. 'How many times do I have to tell you that? Wash your hands before dinner.'

'I have washed my hands.'

'Liar! You've probably been poking rats' innards.' Jack was about to answer when the doorbell rang. 'Oh God, who the hell is that?' Genevieve said.

'It's the visitor!' Josie shouted.

'What visitor?' Jack wanted to know.

'It's a man!' Josie shouted, charging out of the kitchen.

'Don't let her answer the door,' Genevieve said to Jack.

'Why not?'

'Go and answer the bloody door will you!' Genevieve shouted. Too often it was a salesman in a suit or a hawker in a hoodie or the Jehovah's Witnesses in black serge. She finished the job of laying out the cutlery with half an ear to the exchange at the door. After a moment she looked up and saw Richie standing in the kitchen doorway in a T-shirt and jeans.

'Richie! We're just about to eat,' she said, swinging her pot of chilli on to the table. 'Shall I set another place?'

Richie didn't answer. Genevieve took a second look at him. He was shivering and his face was ashen. He looked ill. His eyes were red-rimmed and his pupils had shrunk to tiny bullets of dismay.

'You all right, Richie?'

He shook his head.

Josie came into the kitchen, squeezed past him and took Richie's hand. 'We knew you were coming,' Josie said.

Peter was in his workshop, sorting horse-shoes and nails into sizes and lengths. The fluorescent tube of his overhead light was flickering because of a failed starter unit. Whenever he was reminded that life was a losing battle to entropy, what with light-tubes flickering and horse-shoes and nails shuffling out of neat order the moment he turned his back, he was also reminded that humour and a cheerful disposition were the only known antidotes. It was just that he had neither humour nor cheer in good store.

Genevieve appeared in the doorway. 'You'd better come in.'

'What now?'

'It's not the kids. It's Richie.'

With the malfunctioning lamp illuminating then shadowing his face he blinked at her. 'What about him?'

'He's here right now. You'd better come.'

Genevieve turned and walked back to the house and Peter followed her indoors, with a steel one-seventy shoe in his hand.

There in the kitchen, pale faced, shivering and seated at the kitchen table, he found Richie. Peter closed the door behind him.

Richie didn't look up. 'She's gone,' he said.

'What?' Peter said.

'She's gone.'

'Who's gone?'

'Tara. Who do you think? She's just gone.'

'What do you mean she's just gone?'

'What I say.'

'Where's she gone?'

'No idea.'

'Fuck,' Peter said.

'Daddy swore,' Josie said. Genevieve turned and shepherded her away and into the lounge. Josie protested all the way. She wanted to stay with the visitor; she'd dropped the knife so it was her visitor. Voices were raised. Then the lounge door slammed shut and Genevieve slipped back into the kitchen, silent as a shadow.

Peter sat down next to Richie. 'Did she say anything?'

'No. She left a note.' Richie stuck a hand in his back pocket and brought out a scrap of paper. He slung it across the table. Peter read it carefully and put it back on the table. Genevieve snatched it up, read it quickly and also put it back on the table.

'I don't believe it,' Peter said.

'Do you want a cup of tea?' Genevieve said.

'Somebody once tell you you can mend everything with tea, Gen?' Richie said.

'Give him a bloody brandy,' Peter said.

'You give him a bloody brandy,' said Gen.

'I don't want a bloody brandy. I want Tara. All I ever wanted was Tara. Tara Tara Tara.'

'Has she taken her things?' Genevieve wanted to know.

'She didn't have much. But what she had is gone.'

Peter picked up the note again and studied it closely, as if a more revealing message might have magically appeared on the paper in the intervening moments. It offered no more than it had before:

Richie I'm saving you. I'm saving you from myself. Tara.

Peter put the note down again and laid his horseshoe across it, as if to stop it from blowing away in a wind. He picked up the phone and called his parents. He spoke with Mary and quickly established that Tara had been there to see them and had said her goodbyes. After a brief conversation he rang off. He reported to the others that she'd been collected by a taxi cab.

'Not a fuckin' white horse this time then,' Richie said.

'Apparently not.'

'Why did she have to come back in the first place?' Richie protested. 'I was perfectly all right as I was.' No one said anything. Then Richie said quietly, 'No I wasn't.'

'Let me at least give you something to eat,' Genevieve said, her maternal instincts working overtime. 'I have to say you look awful.'

'I'm not hungry, Gen. I couldn't eat a thing. Honest.'

Then Genevieve remembered Richie's hospital appointment. 'Don't you have to have another scan today? Before the biopsy? Wasn't it today?'

'To hell with that.'

'Not a chance,' Genevive said. 'Whatever has happened with Tara, you're going down that hospital if I have to drag you there. Peter will take you.'

'Yes I'll take you down there tomorrow,' Peter said. 'I'll wait with you.'

Richie was about to argue when the kitchen door opened. It was Zoe, pretty and vivacious and bright-eyed, streaming the perfume of shampoo from the shower, utterly oblivious of the conversation that had taken place in the kitchen. 'Hey Richie!' she said with a huge smile for him. 'I didn't know you were here!'

'Hi darlin'.'

'Know those chords you taught me? I've been practising them. Over and over. I've got it down really good. Well, not bad. And I love that guitar!'

'That's great darlin'.'

'Can I show you? Can I get the guitar and show you?'

'It's not the time, Zoe,' said Genevieve.

'It's okay,' Richie said. 'I want to hear.'

'Now is really not the time,' Peter said firmly, looking hard at Zoe.

Richie stood up. 'Never mind that. Get your guitar, Zoe. I wanna hear what you've got.'

Zoe looked at Peter and then at her mother, now realising she'd gate-crashed a crisis. But Richie insisted and at last Genevieve nodded briefly at her. Zoe went upstairs to get her guitar and Richie, without invitation, made his way through to the lounge. The children were all in there: Amber, Jack and Josie. Richie slumped on the sofa and told the kids to turn off the TV because Zoe was going to play. Sensing an unfamiliar mood, Jack complied and snapped off the TV with the remote control.

Zoe returned with her instrument, took a seat and self-consciously twiddled with the tuning on the guitar. Peter and Genevieve stood near the door. Zoe blushed. Then she started to strum a sequence of chords.

What she played wasn't complicated, but it was

exactly as Richie had taught her, accurate and in good time. She repeated the sequence, becoming more confident, and Richie let out a little laugh of pleasure. Zoe felt encouraged to strum louder. Then Richie's shoulders were shaking and he was sobbing quietly. Zoe, engrossed in her performance, continued to play. Then, in the middle of her strumming she glanced up to see all the children's eyes not on her but on Richie. Richie had collapsed forward, one hand squeezing his eyes shut, his shoulders quivering until at last he sobbed aloud.

Zoe stopped playing.

Genevieve stepped forward and put her hand on Richie's shoulder.

'God,' Zoe said. 'Was it really that bad?'

Peter sat glumly in the waiting room of the X-ray department of the Leicester Royal Infirmary. There were a few other people in the waiting room, either patients waiting for scans or the relatives of patients who were waiting for scans. Everyone seemed to be dazed, half-asleep. Richie had been in with the radiologist for a long time – too much time, Peter thought. In that period an elderly person had come and gone on a trolley pushed by a tattooed porter; and two policemen had turned up escorting a shirtless man with his arm in a sling. Both the elderly patient and the police prisoner had been processed through the system in the time that Richie had been with the radiologist. Peter hoped this didn't mean something very bad.

Peter had also used his waiting time to phone his parents again. He'd stepped outside to call them. Mary was philosophical; he recognised that she had slowly been hardening against Tara, and he wasn't surprised.

He detected something in her voice akin to relief. Peter also spoke to his father; Dell on the other hand was distraught all over again but was putting on a cheery manner. Dell suggested that Tara would be back again when she was ready.

Somehow, deep down, Peter knew otherwise.

He also called Genevieve. They hadn't had much time to discuss Tara's departure out of Richie's earshot. Peter said what a bitch she was. Genevieve told him not to be too hard because there might have been things about Richie and Tara's relationship about which they knew nothing, and about which Tara might have been reminded all too keenly.

Peter returned to the waiting room. Richie still hadn't been released. He closed his eyes. More time passed. He wasn't sure whether he'd drifted asleep when he became aware of someone standing over him.

It was Richie. 'There's a problem,' he said.

Peter blinked himself awake. 'What kind of problem?'

Richie sniffed and wrinkled his nose. 'Well. It's gone.'

'Gone?'

'Yeah, it's gone.'

'What's gone?'

'The thing. Tumour.'

Peter thought he might still be sleeping. He rubbed a broad hand across his face. 'What do you mean, *it's gone*?'

'I can't explain it. Neither can *they*. They want to do me all over again.'

'*Do you again?*'

'Scan.'

Peter stood up. 'Talk sense Richie. Please.'

The senior consultant came out, an intense man

with a close-cropped beard and a haircut almost like a monk's tonsure. 'Are you ready?' he asked Richie.

'What's going on?' Peter asked.

'Can he come?' Richie asked the consultant. 'It's a bit hard to take in.'

The consultant turned the full beam of his gaze on to Peter. He stroked his short beard. 'I don't see why not.'

There was an office adjacent to the radiography studio. The consultant led them to a computer monitor. He had two images on the screen. He pointed to the image on the right. 'There's your friend's scan from a few days ago. Here's the tumour: size of a bloody grape.' Then he pointed at the left-hand image. 'Here's today's image. No tumour.'

'A mistake,' Peter said.

'Exactly what I thought,' said the consultant. 'We don't normally collate the images at once but we do check to make sure the equipment has been running properly and the radiographer picked it up at once before calling me. At first I thought – as she did – that the images must be from two different people. But look here, and here, and here. There is no question. These scans are taken from the same brain.'

'Well, where's it gone?' Peter said. 'Where's the tumour gone?'

The consultant bunched a hand in front of his mouth and looked hard at Peter. He didn't have an answer.

'It can't just go!' Peter said.

'I want to check it all again,' said the consultant.

'It can't just disappear!'

'I've never seen it in all my career,' said the consultant, 'but sometimes it happens and it's called spontaneous remission.' He turned to Richie. 'Do you believe in God?'

'Nope,' Richie said flatly. 'And I ain't about to start.'

'Me neither,' said the consultant. 'Thing is, if you don't believe in miracles you're left only with the beautiful and unsolvable mystery.'

'I'll take that,' Richie said, 'if it means the tumour might have gone.'

The consultant appeared to smile and frown at the same time. 'Shall we get on with repeating the scan?'

'I'm ready,' Richie said. 'You all right waiting for me, Peter?'

'I'm right outside the door, brother,' Peter said. 'I'm right outside.'

43

'Come live by the great moon
That rules the strong tide
Climb up on my horse love
And be my sweet bride.'

Kate Rusby lyrics 'Sweet Bride'

A couple of weeks or so after Tara's second disappearance the family took a winter's afternoon walk in the
Outwoods. Peter and Genevieve were there with Amber
and Josie. Jack was there, too, even though Peter had
said no, don't be so bloody silly you can't take your
air-rifle. Richie was there, having become a regular face
at The Old Forge. He carried Josie on his shoulders
through the woods. Perhaps more extraordinary was
that Zoe wanted to be there too, and she'd dragged her
dreadlocked boyfriend along. Dreadlocked boyfriend
was very happy to be there because he thought Richie
was cool. He'd seen Richie play a set at The White
Horse.

Word had got around amongst those-in-the-know
that the *old muso* had come good and was playing fresh
material for the first time in a decade. It was standing
room only at The Phantom Coach. Everyone in the
local music world nodded sagely like old lags and said,
Richie, *yeah that Richie, he knows his way around a*

guitar; yeah that Richie that's a class act, that is. For some reason everyone claimed to be familiar with his music of old; and for some reason everyone wanted to know him.

As for Richie himself, he was still hurting badly over Tara; but he was working on a song to express the sentiment that the second hurt never wounded like the first. There were lines about a scar covering up an old scar. The song wasn't ready yet, but he was working on it. More miraculous than songs, however, was the disappearance of his tumour, and with it the headaches. The awful blinding migraines that had arrived with Tara had vanished along with her. There was an extraordinary co-incidence to it all, and one that Richie didn't like to spend too long thinking about; but for some reason it was a thought that wouldn't leave him alone.

His subsequent brain scans had revealed nothing. It all seemed like a bad dream. There was no evidence to show that there ever had been a tumour of any kind. The sum total of medical science, expert opinion and extensive doctoral experience had nothing to say about what had happened, other than, 'Be thankful.'

He was thankful; as thankful as it was possible to be without actually being on his knees. Beyond his emotional hurt he saw the world with rinsed eyes. A new light poured into his life and it made time slow. What's more Richie had found himself a complete family, and he'd been adopted into it. He'd supped at The Old Forge frequently since Tara had left, and he liked being around. When the incessant chatter and knockabout behaviour and bickering got too much for him he just left without a word, only to appear another evening after Peter had finished work.

'Has Richie gone?' Genevieve might say.

Someone in the house might answer.

No one seemed to mind or to find his intermittent presence an intrusion on the family. Genevieve cooked a little more food or packaged up leftovers for him to take home, an arrangement he was very happy with. She was on a mission to fatten him up and get him to eat healthily. If she found him skulking outside smoking a cigarette she took the ciggie out of his mouth and crushed it under her foot.

'No smoking anywhere on the property,' she said.

'Fuck! It's like a prison regime round here.'

'No it's not. You can smoke in prison. Are you hungry? Let me get you something.'

Peter was very happy to have him around. He was fun. He tried to teach the kids how to charm rats and mice away from the property. He said Tara had taught him and since the day Tara had exercised her powers in his kitchen, he'd never seen a mouse. Everyone was sceptical.

But he and Peter had twenty years of conversation and experiences to catch up on, and Peter had as many years of guilt to exorcise. He'd already committed himself to becoming Richie's gig-driver: after all, Richie had a drink-driving charge coming up and was about to lose his driving licence for a while. Peter also hired Richie to give regular guitar lessons to Zoe. They had an argument about it.

'I ain't taking your money. If I'd asked for cash for guitar lessons twenty years ago you'd never let me hear the end of it.'

'It isn't twenty years ago.'

'You'd have called me a capitalist hyena or somethin' o' that order.'

'Well you better take it and look happy.'

'A running dog of the merchant classes. Λ lackey.'

'We'll do you a proper hourly rate.'

'You can fuck off with that. If I want to teach Zoe it's up to me. An imperialist dog.'

'I'm not having that. If you're not paid then you can always make an excuse and slink off, can't you? Not doing it this week, sorry. Bit busy. Got something on. I know what you're like.'

'Do you?'

'Yes, I do. I want her to have proper structured lessons, paid for and accounted for.'

'What do you mean accounted for? I've never done accounts in my life and I'm not starting now.'

It took Genevieve to shame them into stopping. 'Are you two still arguing about that? For God's sake!' In truth they weren't arguing about the teaching of music at all; and she knew it.

They walked through the Outwoods, Josie still perched on Richie's shoulders, the two lurchers bounding and criss-crossing the tracks ahead of them. There were no bluebells; only the rust-coloured ghosts of dried bracken and brambles, plus a primal odour of wet leaves and mud underfoot. They arrived at the ancient protruding crags of green and grey rock, speckled with lichen turned the colour of marmalade by the winter temperatures.

'That's where she said she sat,' Peter said, and they all stopped and looked at the small and mysterious outcrop of stones.

There was a moment of communal silence, as if they

half expected the stones to begin to hum, or to pulsate, or to advertise their presence in some way. But there was only the penetrating stillness of the damp woods, until it was disturbed by the shrill call of a crow.

Genevieve shivered. She looked around her. 'Where's Jack?' she said.

He was missing from the pack. Everyone looked around for Jack. He wasn't there.

'Jack!' Genevieve called.

The woods breathed a hollowness back at them.

Genevieve felt a thrill of alarm. 'Did anyone see him?'

'No,' said Amber.

'No,' said Josie.

'I think he drifted off that way,' Zoe's boyfriend said. 'He followed the dogs.'

Peter looked nervously at Richie. Genevieve was already striding in the direction indicated. She called again. 'Jack!'

There he was, standing on a slight rise, partially obscured by a second outcrop of rock. He was gazing out across the woods, where the trees and the bushes grew thickest. The trees were mostly bare but the dense bramble offered plenty of cover. The two dogs were alert too, and motionless, gazing at the same spot; as if waiting for some tiny movement there that would release them into the thicket

His mother ran to him and hugged him from behind.

'What?' Jack said. 'What's the matter?'

'Nothing,' his mother said, feeling both foolish and relieved. 'Stupid. I thought I'd lost you for a moment.'

'I'm thirteen!' Jack protested.

'Yes.' His mother was embarrassed now. 'What were you looking at?'

'Don't know. I thought I saw someone looking at me. From the tree. Over there.'

Genevieve looked across into the tangle of dead bracken and dripping bushes. She could see nothing.

'I thought someone was watching us,' Jack said.

Genevieve kissed him. 'Come on. Let's join the others.'

They walked back to the family group, who were gathered around the stones waiting for them. The Outwoods, that in an instant could seem so singular and menacing, became familiar and comforting again.

Jack had spotted something in the woods, as had the dogs. Someone had been watching him. But to reveal who had been watching him would be to reveal who has been telling you this story all along. And, as you were advised earlier, everything depends on that detail.

Tara went away, and this time she went away for good. She didn't leave any further information. She had already tried to tell them everything she understood about what had happened to her, but they had either not wanted to hear or had found her report too unsettling, too risky, and therefore impossible. Perhaps she was speaking in a kind of code; or perhaps she was speaking the literal truth of what happened to her.

Twenty years is, after all, a long time. We are not the same people we were. Old friends, lovers, even family members: they are strangers who happen to wear a familiar face. We have no right to claim to know anyone after such a distance, and for Tara it was just too hard. That much I can say with certainty. And so she made her escape for a second time, in a canter through the woods, over crystal streams and across the broad fields to a bohemian land of light and fire, to a place where the sun and the moon meet on the hill.

Epilogue

'Our lives are our mythic journeys, and our happy endings are still to be won.'

Terri Windling

May Day, four months after Tara's second disappearance. It was spectacular bluebell time all over again. The weather was sunny and bright and the sky cloudless. The blossom around The Old Forge was high; the ornamental cherry at the front of the house was in full flush; the apple raced along abreast of the cherry; and the lilac and the sweet chestnut at the rear of the house were aching to follow. Spring was roaring in, and the air was heavy with pollen.

Peter had loaded up his truck to go out on a shoeing job. He'd ducked back into his workshop to pick up a laminitis treatment and another rack of shoes. As he emerged from his dark workshop, blinking into the sunlight, he spotted Zoe talking to someone at the front gate.

A giant ornamental cherry tree formed a spectacular gorgeous shell-pink canopy at the gateway to the front drive, and she was standing beneath it. She wore a pretty, short floral dress and flip-flops, exposing her coltish bare legs to the warm spring sunshine. She ran a hand through her long silky hair, and as she did so the sunlight shimmered along its dark waves like a quiet flame. She lifted her hair behind her ears and the light in it flared and then quieted again.

Peter looked at the man she was talking to, sizing him up. He was a handsome figure, rather older than Zoe. His complexion was weather-beaten, that of someone who lived or worked out of doors, and within a head of dark hair there was the glint of a gold ring at his ear. He was smiling and teasing, his white teeth flashing, and he was pointing at the upper branches of the cherry tree.

Peter decided to go and see what it was all about. Still clutching a box of steel horse-shoes under his arm he made his way up the yard. But the man looked up, and when he saw Peter coming, the expression on his face changed. He held up a hand in farewell to Zoe, and, rather too quickly, he walked away.

By the time Peter drew abreast of Zoe the man had made it several yards down the street and was already climbing into a white van. Peter and Zoe watched him drive away.

'Who was that?' Peter asked.

'No idea.'

'What did he want?'

'I just stepped outside to make a phone call. I'm standing here and he asks if he can have some of the blossom. He says he's taken a fancy to some of the cherry blossom. He asks me if he can get his ladder out and go up and cut some of the branches, so I says well how much do you want? And he laughs and says oh just a little bit. And I'm just about to say I didn't see why not; I mean there's plenty of it, right?'

'Right.'

'Then he looked up and saw you. You scared him away, Dad.'

'Didn't I just.'

The pair stood together under the laden cherry, gazing down the road, even though the white van had long gone.

'Zoe.'

'Yes, Dad?'

'If he comes round again ...'

'Tell him he can't have the blossom.'

'Right.'

Zoe grabbed her father and planted a spontaneous kiss on his cheek. But she glanced again back down the road before going back inside.

AUTHOR'S NOTE AND ACKNOWLEDGEMENTS

All writing is an aggregate construction. This story has numerous antecedents, but the slippery nature of its truth is testified by the number of times it can mutate. Meanwhile my intention in prefacing the chapters with quotations is not to lay claim to parity of any kind but to hint at just some of those writers – living and dead – whose work champions the fusion of Realism and the Fantastic.

A number of astonishing and accomplished writers and musicians gave me personal permission to preface chapters with their wonderful words: Antonia S. Byatt pointed the way for me in inspirational work that erases the line between fantasy and a psyche in distress; John Clute, whose remarks about Shakespeare I quote, is a literary critic whose work is like food for the starving; writer and musician Charles De Lint has an encyclo-paedic knowledge of folklore and uses it so elegantly to blend classical fantasy literature and mainstream fiction; Ursula Le Guin, possibly the wisest woman on the planet writes fantasy which leaves you in no doubt that you are reading about 'this' world; Kate Rusby 'the Barnsley Nightingale' allowed me to quote her lyrics from the song *Sweet Bride*, itself a beautiful new rendering of an old tale; I am very grateful to Siri Randem's extensive knowledge of Nordic folk-music and folk-tale and for her translation from the Norwegian of *Liti Kjerst;* Marina Warner, the presiding genius in any discussion of the cultural significance of folk-tales and fairy-tales, is plain magnificent; and Teri Windling whose extensive and heroic work with *The Journal Of Mythic Arts* and The Endicott Studio has done so much to honour mythic artists past and present. I stand in awe before all of these thinkers and writers. I recommend anything written by them and I thank them for their generous permission to quote. A fuller reference to the work and influence of these inspirational creators can be found on my website www.grahamjoyce.net

Angela Carter is another mighty influence and the quote from *The Bloody Chamber* is reproduced by permission of the Estate of Angela Carter c/o Rogers, Coleridge & White Ltd. Even if he ultimately surfaced as one of Chaucer's *Limitours* Bruno Bettelheim's *The Uses Of Enchantment* laid a trail in thinking about fairy tales and I'm grateful to Thames & Hudson for permission to quote. Likewise from Carcanet to quote from Robert Graves' poem *I'd Love To Be A Fairy's Child*. WH Auden from *Afterword To The Golden Key* permission from Curtis Brown Ltd. The Joseph Campbell quote from *The Hero With A Thousand Faces* comes by permission of The Joseph Campbell Foundation.

I didn't quote but would also like to acknowledge the fine work of folklorist Anna Franklin and the splendid insights of critic and academic Gary K. Wolfe. All other permissions have been applied for.

Unstinting personal and professional support comes from both my agent Luigi Bonomi and my editor Simon Spanton at Gollancz, and I'm very, very glad to have it. Finally my love and gratitude to my wife Suzanne, who is also my first-reader and full-time *consiglierie*, and to my children Ella and Joe who put me in my place.